ALAMEIN

Iain Gale has strong Scottish and military roots. He is editor of the magazine for the National Trust for Scotland. He lives in Edinburgh with his family.

D0062378

By the same author

Four Days in June
Man of Honour
Rules of War
Brothers in Arms

IAIN GALE

Alamein

The Turning Point of World War Two

HARPER

Harper
An imprint of HarperCollins*Publishers*
77–85 Fulham Palace Road,
Hammersmith, London W6 8JB

www.harpercollins.co.uk

Published by HarperCollins*Publishers* 2010
1

A catalogue record for this book
is available from the British Library

ISBN: 978 0 00 727868 8

Set in Sabon by Palimpsest Book Production Limited,
Falkirk, Stirlingshire

Printed and bound in Great Britain by
Clays Ltd, St Ives plc

Mixed Sources

Product group from well-managed
forests and other controlled sources
www.fsc.org Cert no. SW-COC-001806
© 1996 Forest Stewardship Council

FSC is a non-profit international organisation established
to promote the responsible management of the world's forests.
Products carrying the FSC label are independently certified
to assure consumers that they come from forests that are managed
to meet the social, economic and ecological needs
of present and future generations.

Find out more about HarperCollins and the environment at
www.harpercollins.co.uk/green

To my mother, who heard the church bells ring
and to Captain Philip Harris, Royal Sussex
Regiment who was there

CONTENTS

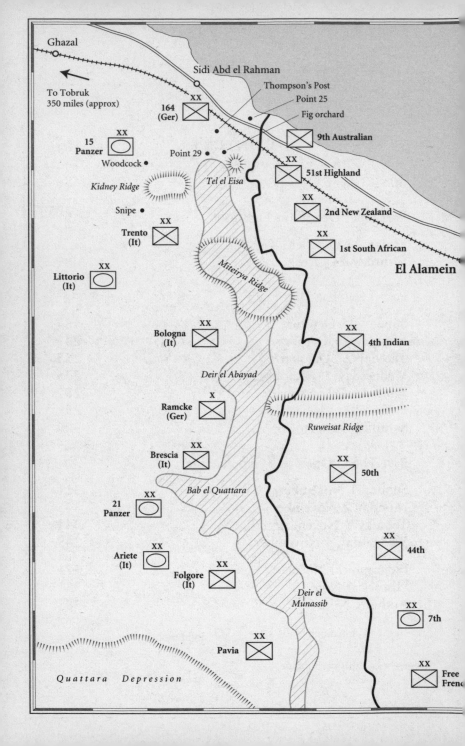

Mediterranean Sea

Coast road

Railway

To Alexandria
65 miles (approx.)

To Cairo
100 miles (approx.)

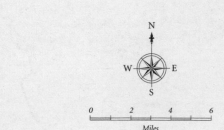

XX
1st

XX
10th

N

W — E

S

0   2   4   6
Miles

El Alamein, 23rd October

 High ground

 German minefield

—— British Front Line
23rd October

 Infantry Division

 Infantry Brigade

 Armoured Division

PART ONE

Operation Lightfoot

Friday 23 October

ONE

9.00 a.m.
Forward HQ, Eighth Army
Burgh-el-Arab, El Alamein
Freddie de Guingand

The stage was set. The players were waiting in the wings. They had rehearsed to the last detail and Montgomery, he knew, was now fully satisfied that they were ready. Yesterday the General had addressed the men, or their officers at least. Everyone down to lieutenant-colonel, from all three corps had been there. De Guingand had never heard his commander talk with more confidence. It would be, Montgomery had told them all, a 'killing match', a 'dog-fight' that would last for as many as ten days, or even twelve.

De Guingand had been surprised by the vehemence of the rhetoric. They must all, Montgomery had said, be imbued with a burning desire 'to kill Germans'.

'The German' he had told them, 'is a good soldier and the only way to beat him is to kill him in battle.' Even the padres, Monty had joked, should kill Germans: 'one per weekday and two on Sundays!'

That of course had provoked a real roar of laughter from the officers. And that de Guingand knew was all part of the commander's aim. Morale was of the essence:

'Morale is the big thing in war, gentlemen. We must raise the morale of our soldiery to the highest pitch; they must enter this battle with their tails high in the air and with the will to win. And win we shall, my friends. Of that I am in no doubt.'

De Guingand looked at the map spread out before him on the table. Surveyed for one last time the positions of the Divisions, the Brigades. Hoped to God they had got it right. For all their sakes. He moved his eyes across to the right of the map, to where on the table lay the piece of paper containing the typewritten message which had been circulated that morning to all troops serving with Eighth Army. De Guingand glanced at it once again and a paragraph caught his eye:

'The battle which is now about to begin will be one of the decisive battles of history. It will be the turning point of the war. The eyes of the whole world will be on us, watching anxiously which way the battle will swing.

We can give them their answer at once, "It will swing our way."'

His eye travelled down the page:

'Let us all pray that "the Lord mighty in battle" will give us the victory.'

De Guingand peered out of the tent at the endless desert, filled as it was with men and machines frantically going about the business of war. Well, he thought, this was it then. The die was cast and there was nothing that he or anyone else could do about it now. He felt a sudden realization of the responsibility that rested on his shoulders. Montgomery might be the commander, but he knew that it was only through him that those commands must be channelled and that should he make but one mistake; misinterpret one order . . .

5

Monty's penultimate words echoed in his mind:

'Let no man surrender so long as he is unwounded and can fight.'

It was hardly Shakespeare. But something in those words gave him real comfort and he hoped that the men would share in that. The general had ended with a simple message: the sooner they won, the sooner they could all go back home to their families. But de Guingand knew only too well, as he knew did Montgomery, that no matter how hard any man might fight, no matter how many Germans he might kill, there was nothing any of them could do that would guarantee that they would make it back home and not end their days in the dust of the desert. And he wondered how many of them would have to die before the lord of battles granted them their victory.

TWO

2.00 p.m.
Just behind the Allied front line
Captain Hugh Samwell

He had been lying in this position for almost eight hours now and one thing was abundantly clear. Soon, no matter what happened, he was going to have to take a piss. The hated order had come through the previous evening and issuing it to the men had been an onerous task: Strictly no movement after dawn'. It had produced a predictable collective groan. Even more predictably some wag had yelled, 'Lucky Dawn'. The CSM had cautioned him, but there were no charges on the eve of battle. And anyway, thought Samwell, that sort of thing was good for morale. Besides, sending up army-speak was a field sport. But for all the levity, Samwell and every man in his platoon knew that when the army said 'strictly' it meant it. No movement. He wondered whether their people at home would ever hear about that, would ever really understand what it actually meant.

He shifted again and eased the cramp in his leg. His bladder felt like a football about to burst. Looking around the slit trench for the tenth, perhaps the twentieth time he saw nothing that might act as a makeshift urinal. Then, suddenly it came to him; the water bottles. Samwell dug gingerly around in his pack which lay between his legs and after a while his hand alighted on a familiar glass shape. It was an old whisky bottle; one of two he had retrieved at the mess and filled with water. Reluctantly he opened it. His dry mouth ached for a drink but he realized that even the movement of raising the reflective bottle to his lips might attract the attention of an enemy observer. He reverted to his first thought and taking care not to make any conspicuous movement managed to get it on its side and gently let the contents run out. The noise brought fresh torment to his aching bladder. He urged the water out: *Come on, come on, empty you bugger.* Finally, when he thought that enough had gone, he managed to manoeuvre the bottle towards his trousers and, unbuttoning his fly, carefully moved until he was just in the right position in the neck. The relief was palpable. A feeling without parallel in his memory.

For a moment, as he buttoned-up and stowed the full bottle deep in the sand of the trench, Samwell was conscious of the absurdity of it all. Here he was, a grown man, an officer in a proud Highland regiment, lying on his back in a hole in the desert with his dick inserted into a bottle. He almost laughed out loud but managed to stifle it. War was like that, he thought. So unnatural that it was bound to create situations which even an artist or poet would find hard to imagine. Much of it was farcical. And thank God for that. They had all learned to laugh in the face of death.

He took out the book he had just received in the post: *They Die with their Boots Clean.* It was a novel about the Coldstream Guards. Its title hardly seemed to make it appropriate reading for the circumstances, but his wife knew only too well what he liked to read and he thought of her kindness in sending it to him. He reached inside his battledress and took out the precious photograph that

8

had come with the book, of his wife and their two small children. Allan was three now and little Inge only two. He looked closely at his wife, his darling Klara. Took care to take in the lines of her face and her eyes. Those deep blue eyes. Oh my darling Klara. He murmured silently: 'Why did your countrymen have to make this war on us?' His wife came from Cologne. He had met her there before the war and they had married quickly, two young people hopelessly in love. They had thought that at first they might settle in her home town. His German was passable and there were opportunities for talented engineers in the new Germany. Hitler's Germany. But Klara had seen what was coming and wanted no part in it. So they had settled in Scotland, in a modest house at Dalmorglen Park in Stirling, a quiet residential cul-de-sac of new homes.

Samwell had had a good job before the army took him. Not bad at thirty-one to be a managing director. His company, Scottish Radio Industries in Denny, was a relatively new business producing wireless sets, but it was expanding and seemed to have a bright future. And the workers were a good bunch. Solid, dependable types with a keen work ethic. But then the war had come and in an instant their dreams, along with those of millions of others like them, had been fractured into a thousand fragments.

Samwell of course had been one of the first to get into it, as Klara had known he would be. He was already a soldier in the Territorials. Commissioned second lieutenant in January 1938, his army number was 73830. To answer the call and go permanent into the regulars had seemed only natural. They had been mobilized in August '39.

Of course he'd been teased about his age at Aldershot. Even before he'd been old for an officer cadet. The younger men had called him 'uncle' as they did any of the older intake. He didn't mind. They were good lads for the most part and his eight or ten years' seniority won him a respect which they did not have for each other. He had revelled in the mess nights when the rooms seemed to sparkle with the light reflected from the regimental silver and they might have been fighting Victoria's wars rather than this struggle against an inhuman enemy.

Soldiering came naturally to Samwell. He had been a good officer cadet at school at Glenalmond, and had been under an Argyll sergeant then. He himself wasn't a Scot, of course. Born in Cheshire, in fact, just before the last war. Now though he found himself a lieutenant, acting captain now, in one of the proudest regiments of the British army, Princess Louise's Argyll and Sutherland Highlanders. A Scottish regiment. A highland regiment. Perhaps, he thought, the coming battle would confirm his rank. He intended to make something of himself in the army. Well, once you were in you were in. Might as well give it everything you could, like anything in life. Even if afterwards he returned to the business in Denny, it would look good on the records, maybe even help his career in Civvy Street.

Samwell thought like a soldier now. His mind had entered into the army framework wholeheartedly and without restraint and the army had moulded him into an effective officer, a leader of men. Much of his job was however keeping records. Acres of paperwork. And all the everyday duties of the company officer: siting latrines, foot inspections, arranging sentry duty, pay parades, making sure there was sufficient ammo and rations, censoring letters and organizing games to keep the men occupied. At times he felt a little like a cross between a kindly schoolmaster and a local council official. And then there were the endless route marches, the fatigue, the sleepless nights. The desert brought its own problems: the great skin-searing *khamsin* sandstorms that ruined rations and ripped tents to shreds; skin sores, dysentery, jaundice and the ubiquitous flies. No sooner had you opened your mouth to take a bit of bread and jam or a fried egg, than it was covered with flies.

He tried to read some of the book, which strangely was written by a man with a German-sounding name, Gerald Kersh, who had apparently served as a guardsman himself. For the second time he wondered why they were fighting the Germans and how it all made sense. The book wasn't so bad. A look at the men in one platoon of the Guards in our own times. A passage caught his eye: 'We had discussed the retreat from Dunkirk. The Cockney, Bob Barker said: "But it was a bit of luck the sea was smooth anyway." Hodge, opening one of his blue eyes, said: "Why, don't ee' see? The Lord God starched out his hand over that water. He said: 'Now you hold still and let my children come away'."'

He wondered whether God would be with them in the coming fight. God had always been with him. He thought of home. Of his father, Edward, the rector of a small church in Falkirk and his mother at work in their modest house, keeping up appearances even though the war had meant cuts in all directions. They had been so proud when he had been commissioned into the Argylls. They were the local regiment of course, with their HQ at Stirling Castle. How many hours had he spent in the regimental museum poring over the battle honours and the relics of past campaigns?

He loved the regiment. Klara often teased him about it: 'Oh Hugh, I think that you must love your soldiers more than me. Men in skirts . . .' Then he would laugh and feign anger and chase her around the ktichen, at last catching her and kissing her, checking all the time that the children were not near. God how he loved her. If only

11

this could all be over and he could be back with her. With her in his arms. He tried to put her face from his thoughts. But once bidden, like a genie from the bottle, it would not go back. Not at least until his lovesick heart had had its fill.

He tried hard to concentrate on the matter in hand. But nothing lay around him save sand and rock and the men, silent and motionless. Somewhere he heard a tank engine turning over, and overhead in the distance the distinctive hum of planes. Allied planes, he thought with a feeling of comfort. His mind drifted back to Stirling, to the museum. He tried to replace Klara's divine image with that of some regimental relic. The colours carried at the Battle of New Orleans when the regiment had been all but wiped out by the American army; the bagpipes played at the relief of Lucknow as the Argylls had marched into the city; the drum carried in the Boer War with its bullethole; the watch that had saved the life of Private Watson in Salonika in 1918.

He wondered if there would be any similar trophies and relics from the coming battle. For a moment Samwell felt a weird sensation of abject fear mixed with pride and elation. He felt almost euphoric. He was about to take part in a battle that would surely go down in history as one of the greatest. He knew in the same instant that this too might be the defining moment of his own life. He was suddenly aware of hard breathing close by and turned to see who was with him in the trench. But he was alone and realized that the breathing was his own. He tried to calm himself. To take part in such a battle was nothing new to the regiment. Hadn't it fought through Spain with Wellington? It was the Argylls too who had been the original 'thin red line' at Balaclava under Sir Colin Campbell. And they had come home with seven VCs from the Indian Mutiny.

A fly landed on his right leg and he recoiled at its bite before flicking it off. It flew back and he swatted it hard, killing it. He looked down at the turned-up shorts, the rolled-over socks and the non-regulation desert boots that so many of his fellow officers had also adopted, including the general himself. It was an uninspiring uniform. Khaki and beige bleached to nothing by the desert sun. They were hardly the stuff of the thin red line, he and his men, certainly by their appearance. No ostrich-feather bonnets and tartan sashes for us, he thought. We are modern warriors. We fight in the colours of the desert. We are creatures of the sand and rock. Like rats, scorpions, lizards we burrow, scuttle and hide while around us the iron dinosaurs roam. It was a primeval contest, this desert war, fought on the most unforgiving terrain known to man. Yet perfect for tanks. Like a great ocean, but of rock and sand. For a few minutes his trick worked. He was in the museum again, touching the relics, the RSM telling him their history. But all too soon Klara came back to him again. Klara. Oh God. Her sweet face filled his every thought. Desperately trying to lose her, he went over again the drill they had learnt for the coming attack. They had been told to walk forward. Slowly, taking their time. It was precisely the same drill that his father had been ordered to follow commanding a platoon of the Cheshires on the Somme in 1916 and not for the first time it occurred to Samwell that it might have the same catastrophic consequences. Wasn't Montgomery, for all his famous reforming zeal, nothing more than a veteran commander of that terrible war? Had he not learnt from its mistakes? They had been told that the barrage that was to precede them would be the greatest in all history. Rumours were that a thousand guns would open fire at once. He prayed that they would be effective.

Then there were the mines; thousands of them apparently,

laid by the Germans and Italians across the front. He knew that the sappers would be out there before them in their two-man teams, were out there now for all he knew with their new Polish mine detectors. They would mark the cleared paths with white tape. All the infantry would have to do was follow the tape. But what, he wondered, if the sappers got lost or if the tape was blown away by shellfire, or if they missed their way? Better not to think.

There was one good thing though about their walk forward. They had been told that the pipers could play. Just as they had in 1916, he thought, and in India in 1857 and in the Crimea and at Salamanca. The news had given him a tremendous kick. Just like in the old days, he thought. Pipers at the head. No colours now of course waving in the breeze above the bonnets, but kilted pipers all the same, even in this age of mechanized war.

He scanned the desert once again, but saw nothing. Looked at his watch. It was five minutes past four, 16.05 hours. He sighed. They had been told that the attack would go in that evening; 21.40 hours had been given as 'H' Hour. He reached into his sack and once again pulled out the over-printed map which showed all the known enemy positions as noted by the air reconnaissance. Any fear had subsided now and once again he felt the sensation of being present at a great event, though as an observer rather than a participant. He imagined himself as he would be in five hours' time, advancing at the head of the platoon to the skirl of the pipes. To go into battle with the pipes – it was more than he could have hoped for.

It must have been after seven when he awoke and realized to his horror that he had been asleep. He wondered for how long and looked about him at the other trenches

14

and foxholes, but the men, or what he could see of them, appeared not to have noticed him, or at least not his misdemeanour. Samwell shook his head to clear it and rubbed at his eyes. He couldn't, he reasoned, have been asleep for too long as he did not have that telltale layer of sand on his body that came when you dozed off in the desert. Nor could he feel any fresh fly bites. At the most five minutes, probably less. It was getting dark now and he began to become aware of activity about him. At last. He saw a shape, a man scurrying towards him, his silhouette marked by the distinctive Balmoral bonnet unique to highlanders; his batman, Baynes, an affable Glaswegian.

'Mister Samwell, sir. There's some hot food coming up and the CO's doing his rounds with a sitrep, sir. Just thought you'd like to know.' He peered at Samwell's face and red eyes: 'Crikey, sir, you look like you're all in. Fit to drop off. You all right, sir?'

'Of course I am, Baynes. Sand in my eyes, that's all. Thank you for that. Better get back or you'll miss your own scoff.'

'Nothing much to miss there, sir. Desert chicken again I'll bet.'

'Ah yes. What would the British army be without its bully beef?'

'Better off I reckon, sir. But I'd better not miss it. See you later sir.'

As Baynes disappeared back to his trench, Samwell again went over the drill for the attack and then Baynes reappeared at his side. 'Stew, sir? It's really not that bad.'

'Thank you, Baynes.' Samwell took the mess tin and began to eat, hungrily, washing the food down with a mug of black tea. 'No milk again?'

'Sorry, sir. It's that problem again with the purifying tablets in the water. They've made the milk curdle. Stinks something rotten, sir.'

15

Samwell was just drinking down the last of the gravy when he was aware of a man standing above him outside the trench. He looked up.

'Don't hurry, Hugh. Finish your dinner.'

Samwell stood up and, putting down the mess tin, climbed out of the trench and saluted his commanding officer, Colonel Anderson.

'Sorry, sir.'

'Well, Hugh. Ready for the off?'

'Quite ready, sir. Can't wait.'

'Good. The men seem to be raring to go. Let's keep them that way till H Hour, shall we?'

'Sir. Is it true that we're going to have pipers?'

'They've been authorized by Division. Good idea if you ask me. Remains to be seen whether it'll actually happen, but I'm inclined to think it might. D'you think it would help the men?'

'Most certainly, sir. And it would put the fear of God into the Jerries.'

Anderson laughed: 'Yes, Hugh, I daresay it would. Well, we'll see, shan't we. Good luck. Remember to follow the tape. And walk slowly, Hugh. We don't want to run into our own barrage do we? The Jerries won't know what's hit them. Just walk forward and don't forget to collect the prisoners.'

THREE

4.00 p.m.
Between Haret-el-Himeimat and
Deir-el-Munassib
Colonel Marescotti Ruspoli

'Luigi. Tell me again. Why is it that you wear a spanner around your neck?'

Lieutenant-Colonel Marescotti Ruspoli had lost count of how many times he had asked the same question in the past few weeks. Of course he knew the answer. That was not the point. He looked at the six young men who stood before him, their uniforms as clean and fresh as their smiles. They smelt of Italy, of home and he envied them the fact that they had seen that blessed place such a short time ago.

The question was a ritual.

Ruspoli sat in his 'office': an unstable folding chair behind a table made from ammunition boxes in the command trench that lay a few metres behind the front line of his unit's position. The Raggruppamento Ruspoli, made up from the VII/186th and the VIII Battalion of paratroops and several artillery batteries. Just under one and a half thousand men in all. Not that there were 186 regiments of paras of course. In fact there were just two.

But they were the elite fighters of the Italian army and jealously proud of the fact.

As he prepared to listen to the familiar reply Ruspoli munched at what was left of a hunk of dried salami that the cook had been keeping for him specially. Having handed out a few slices to his battalion officers, he was now savouring every last mouthful. Ruspoli was a fine-featured man of fifty, younger-looking than his years, with a thin moustache as dark as his black hair and small yet kindly brown eyes.

His orderly, Luigi Santini, laughed and replied: 'Well you know, Colonel, how long we've been waiting for those anti-tank guns?' He held up the spanner: 'I reckon that this is the only way we're going to be able to fight the enemy tanks when the attack comes. We take them to bits bolt by bloody bolt.'

The young men laughed. Ruspoli too, although he had heard the joke more times than he could remember. The fact was that the men sitting around him now were mostly a new intake, there to replace the dead and wounded from the last attack. It was a habit of his, to invite them to meet him face to face when they joined the unit. He liked to think of them all as a family.

You could easily tell the new boys from the veterans, and boys they were, barely out of school. For one thing their uniforms were still the original colour and had not been faded by the sun. He cast his eye around the newcomers, and smiled as he saw that they still wore their tunics buttoned. Most of the old lags had their shirts forever undone to reveal their thin, sun-browned torsos. Their fatigue caps had long since lost any semblance of shape; most too had discarded the distinctive tropical topees. Helmets were more practical and the only effective defence against the redhot shards of shrapnel that at some point during the day were sure to make an appearance in the

18

trench. These were not of course the usual low-sided Italian infantry helmets. For these men were paratroops, 'Folgore' and their hats were made to withstand a drop from a flying aeroplane. Ruspoli did not mind the lack of smartness. He was no stickler for dress. What did it matter on the battlefield as long as you fought well? But sometimes though, he longed for the old days, the parade grounds, the pomp and the marching bands.

Ruspoli turned to the new boys: 'Any of you sing?'

One of them looked sheepish and coughed and said nothing. But another, lean and grinning pointed at him: 'Of course, Marco is a great singer. He was studying at the conservatoire in Milan when he volunteered. Eh, Marco?'

The sheepish one smiled: '*Si*, Colonel.'

Ruspoli nodded: 'Good. That's very good. What can you sing then? Opera? Verdi, Puccini?'

'*Si*, Colonel. All opera. Puccini best of all.'

'*Bene*. Well then, you must sing for us some time. The general loves opera and since the gramophone got hit by a shell splinter we've missed our music here. Santini, remember that for me. I'll hold you to it.'

Ruspoli brushed three flies off the salami, popped it into his mouth and looked across at Santini, still grinning at the new boys. They think that the spanner story really is a joke, he thought. But he knew that it was true. If the current situation held up then the only way they would be able to defeat the British tanks would be to undo them bolt by bolt. The long-promised guns had still not arrived and with every day Ruspoli could feel the attack building. He sensed it on the wind. He was quite sure that the British and their allies would come soon. Before the winter set in at least. Montgomery and his generals wanted to push them back to Tripoli and according to reports they had enough armour now and the men to do so.

19

And all that he and his men, his paratroops could do was sit and wait. The Germans were their masters. Gave them their orders, told them how to die. And all for what, he wondered. He and his men, like all the Italians in this accursed place, had come here to fight for their Duce, for the dream of the new Italy, and instead they now found themselves at the whim of another country. And who was to command them? Divisional HQ had told him that Rommel had flown home sick. So they were left with his deputy, the redfaced General Stumme.

Ruspoli turned to his second-in-command, Captain Carlo Mautino de Servat, who was seated on an ammo box close behind him, and spoke quietly, ensuring that Santini and the others could not hear. 'Carlo, did I tell you the latest casualty figures? Major D'Esposito told me yesterday, at HQ.'

'No, Colonel.'

'A thousand of our officers and fourteen thousand other ranks dead and wounded in all Divisions since the last push. Funny thing is the Germans have apparently lost roughly the same. So why do you think then that they still moan about us always running away, about us refusing to fight and expecting them, the Germans, to win back our colonies for us?'

Mautino shrugged: 'I heard from a German officer last week, sir. Nice fellow, in the Fifteenth. He told me how well supplied we were. Assured me that we had better provisions than them. Plenty of wine, water, meat and bread.'

'What did you say?'

'I laughed and told him he was wrong. That we lived on a quarter-litre of water a day and that we hadn't seen any fresh meat or fruit or vegetables for a month.'

'What did he say to that?'

'He laughed. He didn't believe me. Asked me to remember him and send back a case of wine.'

Ruspoli shook his head. 'No one believes anyone any more out here, Carlo. Nothing is real. Think about it and you start to see mirages. Like Morgana le Fay.'

He was referring to the wispy figure that appeared in front of you if you stared into the desert for a long time, as many of them did when on guard duty. It seemed to take the form of a woman, wrapped in a long robe and sometimes carrying water pitchers. He'd seen it once or twice. That's when you knew you had been out in the sun too long. He wiped his forehead. Even under the camouflage netting the day was oppressively hot. He called to his orderly.

'Santini. Direct those boys to their companies, will you. You, Marco. I look forward to hearing you sing.' As the replacements were taken away he turned back to Mautino: 'I suppose it's occurred to you that we're an embarrassment to the Germans?'

'No. Not really. How, sir?'

'Well, think about it. The great Colonel Ramcke and his paras teach us how to drop from the sky. How to act like proper Wehrmacht soldiers. We're trained up for Operation Herkules. We're told that we're going to take Malta. Then what? The operation is called off. Cancelled by personal order of Hitler himself. Why? He doesn't want to lose his precious Fallschirmjäger like he did in Crete. Of course he's got other things for them to do. There's Russia for one thing. But what about us? Good Italian troops? Impossible. The Germans can't admit to that any more. We're meant to be cannon fodder. So we're sent here, to the bloody desert. We are paratroops, by God! Paratroops. Airborne. You know what Folgore means, Carlo? Of course you do. Lightning. We go in like a thunderbolt. We're not bloody rats to fight and die in stinking trenches.'

Mautino, the youngest son of a family of Piedmontese

aristocrats, looked down at his boots, concerned that his colonel had lost his temper, an increasing occurrence over the past few weeks. 'I know, sir. I thought that they were going to drop us over the Suez Canal. We all did. That we would be the first into Cairo at the head of the advance. With the Duce on his white horse.'

'Well, we all thought that, Carlo. Until they took our 'chutes away. Then we knew.'

Another voice joined in from behind them: 'It was when they told us to take off our parachute flashes and wings, Colonel. That's when we knew.'

Guido Visconti was smaller than Ruspoli but had the same fine features that marked him out as being descended from a line of aristocratic blue-bloods. He was from a small village near Vicenza and had volunteered for the army aged sixteen back in '33. But that had been a lifetime ago. Now he passed the hours with his head buried in whatever reading matter he could find. Mostly he liked the Italian lyric poets. But when he couldn't get them any popular magazine would do. Particularly *Cinema*, the new movie magazine. Film stars and directors were an especial passion. There was very little about Italian film that Visconti did not know.

Mautino nodded: 'Right, Guido. You're quite right. That was the end of it.'

Ruspoli added: 'You know the reason for that though, don't you? So that the Brits wouldn't know we were here. That was fair enough. We have a reputation, boys. It was tough though for the lads after going through so much to earn them.'

'Now they're just exhausted, sir. Men are being relieved not from wounds but from sheer physical exhaustion.'

Ruspoli was reflective: 'How long have you been here, Carlo?'

'Same time as you, Colonel, since June.'

22

'Since June, and tell me how much action have we seen since then?'

'Enough, Colonel.'

'Certainly enough. Do you remember our first time in action here?'

'Could I forget it? July twenty-second. We'd only been disembarked for a few hours. We lost so many they had to make one battalion out of two. And we've been here ever since, waiting for the British to attack.'

Visconti looked up, tearing his concentration away from the torments of Dante's second circle of hell. 'Oh, I meant to tell you, sir. While you were on sick leave, Captain Camino had a direct hit on his dugout by a mortar bomb. He's fine but was concussed for four days.'

Mautino spoke again: 'Sir, have you noticed anything?'

'What?'

'Well, it's long after 4.15 and the British haven't fired at us.'

He was right. Every day for the past two months at precisely 4.15 a salvo of four huge 88mm shells had arced their way across the sky and crashed into the Italian position.

Ruspoli looked at his watch: 4.45. 'Something's up. Guido, get Benezetti and radio Brigade HQ. Tell them that something's not right. We haven't been fired on. Ask them if they know anything.'

'I read the intelligence reports, sir. Heavy movements of troops again on the Telegraph Track, the Red Track and the Water Track. Point is we're in the centre of the line. We also know who we're facing over there. The British Fiftieth Division. Mainly light infantry with a few Greeks and the Free French.'

Ruspoli stood up and peered down the trench at his men who were slouching, exhausted, against the sides. They may, he thought, be descended from Caesar and

23

Scipio but these men have no resemblance to any ancient warriors. I know they can fight though. It's just making sure their morale holds up. For once, he wondered whether new uniforms might help after all.

He turned to Mautino: 'We're fighting in rags, Carlo. No more than rags. Can't we get on to Division and ask for more uniforms?'

'We've tried, Colonel. But we just keep being told that they're coming.'

Visconti smiled: 'Like everything else in this damned war. It's on its way. On its way. The reinforcements. The new tanks. The gasoline, the rations. It's all on its way. But it just never gets here, sir.'

Ruspoli tried to inject a high note. 'You know that when the Duce was out here in July, he stayed for three weeks longer than he needed to.'

'Yes I know, sir. But he took his white horse with him when he went. We might have had a few nice steaks out of that.'

'Very funny, Guido. But I know what you mean. I'm as loyal as anyone to the Duce but I'm fighting for Italy. We all are. And the men can see what's going on. The Germans are using us as cannon fodder. Even the hardline fascisti are beginning to wonder.' Ruspoli shook his head. 'Look. I command the bravest men in the Italian army. Of that there's no doubt. But how can we send them into battle unclothed and unfed? And seriously, Carlo, how do you think we can fight tanks? What weapons do we have?'

'With the magnet bombs the Germans have given us?'

'That's it. And with Molotov cocktails. The only way to use either of them is to get close enough to a tank to attach the bomb or throw the bottle. What that means is that I'm expected to sacrifice one man for every tank.'

Visconti spoke: 'You have to admit it's a reasonable

ratio. Montgomery's only got five hundred tanks. We've got one and a half thousand men.'

Mautino grimaced: 'Ever the realist, Guido.'

'*Cui exhibetis vos servos ad obediendum, servi estis eius.*'

'What?'

'"When you obey someone like slaves, you become his slaves." It's a quote. Romans. The Bible. That's what's happened here with us and the Germans.'

'Don't exaggerate, Guido.'

Another voice spoke as they were joined by another officer, Captain Maurizio Polini, a tall thin man with a beak of a nose. He brushed sand from his clothes and unwound the scarf from his face then took a swig of precious water from his canteen. 'Sir. Gentlemen. If you ask me you can forget our problems with the Germans. The desert's our real enemy. More dangerous than the Brits even.'

Mautino looked at him: 'Been out again, Maurizio?'

'On patrol just short of the depression. Couldn't see a thing. No sign of the British. But then again they come and go as they please. They're like ghosts.'

Visconti, who had been reading his book looked up: 'It's the heat I can't stand. Forty-three degrees. Non-stop all day. It just saps away your energy. How can we fight like that?'

Mautino spoke: 'Then at night it's freezing. Below zero. It's the devil's own country. Your Dante would know it.'

Caporale Santini had returned now from directing the new intake to their company commanders and joined in with the officers in the informal manner that they had become used to, particularly in the elite band of brothers that was the Folgore; the other ranks treating their superiors with just enough deference, the officers looking on the men as underprivileged younger siblings.

'The water's foul, sir. You must agree. We never have fruit or vegetables. Tinned food and biscuit, that's it. And they might say it's for safety, but you know the real reason the rations come up at night? So we can't see the flies that are already inside them.'

'It's an old joke, Luigi.'

'But seriously, sir. It's no surprise that we all have dysentery or something worse.'

Ruspoli detected that perhaps they might have gone too far. 'Think yourself lucky, boys, that we only have the shits. General Ceriana's got colitis. Did you know that? They say he's very ill.'

'Perhaps another camel will wander into the camp. Beats me how the last one got through our minefield.'

'Didn't you hear, Carlo? You must have been away on attachment. The British had cleared a path through it in the night. Five metres wide. We had to get the mobile sappers out to re-lay the whole damn thing.'

'But you ate the camel?'

'Of course. It made a very tasty ragout. Didn't we save you any?'

Mautino shook his head. 'It wouldn't have kept. But I'm sorry to have missed it. Perhaps another one will come.'

Santini spoke: 'If it does, sir, then we should really worry. The Brits'll be right behind it.'

Ruspoli wondered what his family would make of him eating camel. He supposed that at some point one of his ancestors might have done the same. Perhaps on a crusade. They were princes of Florence, a warrior family. But while one ancestor fought with distinction at Lepanto against the Turks another was a poet. It was often the way with Italian soldiers. Fighting and poetry went hand in hand. They had raised a regiment in 1708 to defend the Pope against the Austrians.

He thought of the family home, high on the hilltop in Umbria. Castello Ruspoli with its acres of olive groves and vineyards. What he would give now for a sip of that heavenly wine or just one of those olives. He supposed that his elder brother Costantino was thinking the same thoughts wherever he now was on this damn battlefield. At fifty-one he must have been one of the oldest men in the fighting. But he was still fit. Ruspoli knew where Costantino's unit was meant to be, but in this war who knew if anything was where they told you it was. As for little brother Carlo, the baby of the family and still in his thirties, well, it was anyone's guess where he might be, flying his fighter across the desert skies, chasing the RAF.

It was amusing he thought, that the family should be able to trace its origins back to the Scots. To Marius Scotus from somewhere called Galloway, after whom he had been named. His mother of course was French. Pauline Talleyrand, great-great-niece of Napoleon's foreign secretary. He knew that across the sand a Scottish division and a regiment of Free French were waiting to attack them. Not least, his own mother-in-law, his darling Virginia's mother, was English. So how could he hate the enemy? So much irony. But then he supposed that was what war was all about. Absurdities, like the camel and Luigi's spanner.

But they were all Italians here. Mostly men from the north and whatever their families' origins, high or humble, he respected them. They were his men, all of them. Men like Aroldo Conticello, the baker's son from Orvieto and Umberto Galati, just nineteen, from Pavia, who liked to wear his hair long. How it infuriated his company commander, thought Ruspoli. Tenente Piccini was forever shouting at Galati to get a haircut but Galati would only ever have a trim.

He would come back and protest: 'It's enough, Tenente.

27

Just enough.' But back he would be sent to the battalion barber only to return too soon and then Piccini would shout again. Ruspoli smiled. Such things were necessary when death stalked a battlefield looking for his next victim. Anything to keep the men amused. Ruspoli was still thinking about them as he walked along the trench. It was eerily quiet. Perhaps there was something in what Mautino had said. This was not right. He'd be happier when that report came through. He heard voices up ahead and stopped. The men were talking. Intrigued, Ruspoli stood and kept silent and listened.

'So tell me this, Lorenzo. Why are the Germans our allies? My father fought against Rommel himself at Monte Matajur, Caporetto, in the last war. He was wounded. Never recovered. Now that German butcher's our commander. Where's the sense in that?'

'Actually, General Frattini is our commander. And Rommel's no butcher, Giovanni. He's an honourable man and a good general.'

'Frattini? In your dreams, Lorenzo. Don't get me wrong. He's one of the good ones, the general. Wasn't he our commander when we formed? But now even he has to take orders from the Germans.'

Another voice cut in: 'And what about the Yanks? Some of the guys have got cousins living in the States. What if they end up fighting against them?'

Ruspoli rounded the angle of the trench. On seeing their CO the men stood up and snapped smartly to attention. Ruspoli waved them down: 'Not here, boys. America hasn't sent any troops here yet. Don't worry, you won't meet an American in this desert let alone fight against one. Besides, do I look worried? You know me. I was born in New York. My brother too. Then we came home to the motherland. How do you think I'd feel killing an American? You might say I am one myself. So shoot me!'

28

They laughed together. But their smiles turned quickly to looks of concern with the arrival of a runner. Twenty-three-year-old Captain Pietro Bonini saw Ruspoli and saluted, then paused to get his breath back. One of the best in his regiment, thought Ruspoli. A shrewd boy who always had a knack of being in the right place at the right time.

'Bonini. You have news?'

'The radio's down, sir. Nothing. So I ran to Division. I had the good luck to encounter Colonel Guiglia.'

'The radio wizard?'

'The very same, Colonel.'

'That man has a nose for radio signals. He can guess their contents long before our deciphering teams get it. Heaven alone knows how he does it. So what's up?'

'There's going to be an attack.'

'We know that, Pietro, but when?'

'Well, Guiglia said, "Mark my words, Capitano. It's a question of hours, not days!"'

Ruspoli said nothing. He looked into the dark, frightened eyes of one of his men and then turned back to Bonini. 'You're quite sure that's what he said, Pietro?'

'Certain, Colonel. He said that the British radio activity had really fallen off. There's something going on in the southern sector. Down here in fact, between Qaret el Homar and Somaket e Gaballa. His men had picked up lots of messages meaning nothing. You know, "X279, I'll call you back". That sort of thing. He seemed certain, sir. And he was sweating.'

Ruspoli nodded. He knew exactly what Guiglia meant. The attack was imminent. And there was no doubt in his mind. They would come tonight.

FOUR

6.00 p.m.
Some way to the rear of
Kidney Ridge
Major Tom Bird

The long day wore on. Tom Bird carefully unfolded the letter he had written to his parents two days before and began to draw a picture. It showed two of the men of his unit, both officers, chatting over a boiling stewpot in the style of Jon's 'Two Types' featuring two popular cartoon characters – officers in the desert, one army the other RAF.

In Bird's picture one of them was wearing a hebron coat, that gloriously non-regulation bit of kit made from cured goatskins, which he himself had not been alone in adopting among the British officers. He was pleased with the drawing. He knew that he had some talent as a draughtsman and had for a while dallied with the idea of art school but architecture was his true métier. He thought that perhaps after the war he might join a good practice or even form his own. A partnership. After the war; that was a good one. Who knew how long it would go on? What Bird knew was that Hitler needed a proper bloody nose. They needed to prove that they weren't frightened of him, that they could give as good as they got and that was what they were here for. His father had been wounded at Gallipoli in 1915 fighting against Germany's then ally, Turkey, and had never spoken of his experiences.

Bird took care when he wrote home. He knew that his father must be aware of what he was going through. The extraordinary, bizarre, once-in-a-lifetime experience of war. But he did not want to cause his parents any undue worry. He had good reason. His brother had been killed at Calais in 1940 and the loss was achingly raw. His brother's death he knew was at least in part why he was here. Not for revenge but from a sense of justice. He felt the need to right a wrong against a foe who must in any case be defeated at all costs. A foe so monstrous that they stood against everything he held dear.

As always, then, he had tried to lighten the tone of the letter, writing with schoolboyish expression about his friends and comrades as if they were all about to take part in some momentous rugby match: 'Hugo Salmon still my second-in-command and Jack Toms is another great standby. I should hate to be without either of them now . . . I may not write again for a little bit. Best of love, Tom.'

That was it. His father he knew would see through the last line and know instantly why he would not be able to write 'for a little bit'. His mother though must suspect nothing. For her to know that her only surviving son was about to be thrown against the might of the German army would kill her or at least drive her mad.

And their enemy was mighty. Of that he had no doubt. Over the past two years they had conquered most of Europe and had run circles around the British army in North Africa. Now though it might just be their turn. The talk in the mess was all about the newly-arrived ordnance. Hundreds of tanks, great war machines that rumbled forward on tracks, unstoppable, able with a

31

single shot to destroy a house. Tanks. That was what this battle, this war, was all about. The Germans had started out with many more, and better. Tanks filled him with dread. He had a secret fear of being crushed beneath a caterpillar track. A fear which he had never told anyone. A fear that had him waking in the night in a cold sweat. Tanks.

Bird wished to God that they had just a few of the new Sherman tanks with them. Instead, they had guns, the new six-pounder guns that they said could take out a tank with ease. He had yet to see it. And now they were under his command. He had been thrilled to get his own company. He had been promoted to major now and had a bar to his MC as well. He'd won that back in July at Gazala. He had been in the south with the Free French in the Bir Hakeim box, fighting the Italian Trieste and Ariete Divisions and the Twenty-First Panzers. He'd taken a column of twenty-five lorries carrying food and ammunition through minefields to reach the beleaguered French in their strong-point. And once there, the commanding officer of the French garrison, General Koenig, had persuaded him to break out. They'd done it and saved 27,000 men from being taken. On top of that he'd captured fourteen Jerry prisoners and not had a single casualty among his own men.

It was more, far more than he had thought he would achieve when he had joined back in '40. He knew that it had much to do with Colonel Turner's opinion of him. People had wondered why he had joined the Rifle Brigade, or the Sixtieth Rifles as the colonel liked to refer to them. For of course they were not a brigade at all but a regiment, one of the finest and proudest in the British army. A regiment that had come out of the colonial war as a response to the American practice of using light infantry skilled with smoothbore rifles. A regiment that had fought with pride against the French in the peninsula.

The colonel was a sound chap. More than that, a father-figure, or as Bird often thought of him, like a kindly housemaster from his old school. The regiment was like that. An extended family. The mess was filled with Etonians and Wykehamists. Sometimes Bird sympathized with the newly-commissioned officers who had to infiltrate this public-school elite. 'Temporary gentlemen' were not always welcome in the mess. He did not mind them himself, but there were others who did. The lads were good enough though. They'd come through a lot in recent weeks. They were Londoners mostly, Eastenders, most of them conscripted into the ranks. But none the worse for that. And then there were the old sweats, the NCOs. They'd taken to the new men, had spent some time on them and it had worked. Bird felt that now he was in command of an efficient fighting unit. In fact they constituted a formidable little brigade; 2nd Battalion had three motorized infantry companies, a carrier platoon, a machine-gun platoon and most importantly his four platoons of six-pounders, sixteen guns in all. Aside from that the colonel had also been given an attached force of another eleven guns from 239 battery of 76 AT regiment RA.

They were all mounted on 'portees', lorries from whose flat-bed top the gun could be slid down and into position. It was not an ideal method of transport, slightly Heath Robinson-ish. But it gave them mobile anti-tank power and that was vital in this war of machines. All day they had been sitting here, keeping watch over the minefields. Static and in support. It was not his way and he was impatient to be in the action. But Bird knew that their time would come and when it did, he knew too that they would acquit themselves with honour, whatever the odds.

33

FIVE

6.00 p.m.
Tactical HQ, Eighth Army
The beach, El Alamein
General Bernard Law Montgomery

It was, anyone could see, a superb defensive position. And he cursed himself for not having been the man who had found it. For this was Auchinleck's position, a defensive line chosen by the General whom he had been brought in to replace. Auchinleck – the man who had failed in all else but this. The chance to define this sublime line which ran for forty-five miles from the Mediterranean in the north, due south across the desert to the impassable vastness of the great Quattara Depression. It was the last line of defence between the enemy and Cairo. The perfect place to make a last stand. Here it was that they had fallen back to in the face of the enemy's last attempt to take the city. Here it was that they had regrouped and rested. And it would be from here, he knew, that they would attack.

He looked at the map spread out before him on the table which stood in the middle of his small command caravan and traced a line along it from north to south. Forty miles of front line, all of it more or less level but

with two passages of high ground: Ruweisat Ridge and
Alam Nayil. Though on the map it looked flat,
Montgomery, like the men who had lived out there in
the desert, some of them for two years, knew that it was
far from that. That it was marked by small hillocks and
dunes, dips that seemed as hard to climb as ravines
and sheer drops that could catch you off your guard and
swallow you up. And it was not just sand, but rock
and everywhere was punctuated by clumps green bushes
of sharp camel-thorn. There were no roads and precious
few houses. In short, it was the perfect terrain for
modern, mechanized warfare. And 'modern' was a word
that he liked very much. The whole essence of modern
warfare could be reduced to three things: concentration, control and simplicity.

In short it was about modernity. It was the only way
to win. Complete change in the British army. Dunkirk
had taught him that. But it had taken till now to bring
it in. Two long years. So many of the old guard had gone
now, he thought, and they were so much the better for
it. There was Ritchie, sacked after the Gazala disaster in
June and his replacement Corbett who everyone knew to
be an idiot. 'A complete fathead' his chief of staff had
called him. So Gott had been brought in. Old 'Strafer'
Gott. And it had been he that Montgomery had replaced.
Though it had been unfortunate that it should have
happened the way it had with Gott being killed in a plane
crash. Montgomery had simply been the next man in line.
In truth he knew that the Chief of the Imperial General
Staff, Sir Alan Brooke, had turned Churchill's ear.

And what great good fortune to have been given
such a chance. Surely God was rewarding him for his
faith over the years and his devotion to the army. The
army had been his life. Was still. Of course his late
wife Betty had been so dear to him and her sudden

and quite unexpected death, exactly five years ago this month had left a dreadful vacuum in his life that could never be filled. But at least he had their son, David, now thirteen. He'd left him at school at Winchester when he'd come out here, in the care of his former headmaster from prep school. David was just a boy, but, he reflected, he was not that much younger than so many of the 'men' he now led.

He turned to see his ADC, John Poston, a twenty-three-year-old captain in the 11th Hussars. Poston was a pleasant Old Harrovian, a good horseman who had been in the desert since 1940 having joined straight from school. He was only ten years older than David, he thought. A fine, handsome young man with a pair of honest and engaging pale grey eyes. He had taken to young Poston instantly on his arrival in the desert, and had asked for him in particular. Well, he had also been poor Gott's former ADC and he clearly knew the ropes. Wouldn't drive him into a minefield as young Spooner, the ADC he had brought with him from England, had done on his first day. Montgomery smiled at the boy's clothes. Like so many of his officers, particularly those in the cavalry and yeomanry, he had adopted his own style of dress: suede desert boots, spotted silk cravat, corduroy trousers. Montgomery indulged it. He knew Poston to be somewhat apart from the class-conscious society of the mess and admired him for his simple professionalism. Hadn't he himself been somewhat unorthodox in his own dress? He followed Wellington's dictum; what mattered was not following the drill book to the letter but the quality and professionalism of the man. Besides, hadn't he re-written the drill book?

'Did you realize, John, that we have the longest supply routes the history of warfare has ever known?'

'I think I overheard you say as much to the Field Marshal, sir.'

36

'What very sharp hearing you have.'

'I'm sorry, sir.'

Montgomery tugged at his right earlobe, a habit of which he was hardly aware but which was often remarked on behind his back. 'No matter, you should know in any case, John. It is true. Although unlike Herr Rommel of course, our lines are not at full stretch. It will be all about materiel, this battle. Rommel needs fuel and he needs ammunition and according to our intelligence, he does not have sufficient supplies of either.'

Intelligence, he thought, was everything, worth fifty thousand men on the battlefield. And they had the finest intelligence in the war – Ultra. The code-breakers at Bletchley Park were now able to break the German Enigma code. Since 1941 they had been receiving intelligence based on radio messages from Fliegerführer Afrika. But he knew too that intelligence alone could not win a battle. It was down to the generals and it was down to the men. In his case men who were itching for victory, the men of Eighth Army. Men who had fought at Gazala and been twice up to Benghazi. The 'Benghazi handicap' they liked to call it. Men who had run from Tobruk to be able to fight again. Well, this was their battle and everything was at stake. Not just the Allies' vital hold on the Middle East and Suez. But also he knew, as Churchill did, the war itself and indeed his own position as leader of the nation.

He looked again at the map. Of course they could have stood at Sidi Birani or Mersa Matruh. But the present line was superb, unassailable. And it exploited the fact that there were only three ways by which Rommel could attack them. In the north in the gap between Ruweisat Ridge and the railway line, in the centre where they were strongest and in the south.

He had to admit, no matter how it galled him and it surely did, that Auchinleck had been right. Of course, he would never have admitted that in public, or indeed in private to anyone. It was all-important that the men should believe that the new man in charge of them had his own plan and his own original methods. He had shown them as much from the moment he had taken over, had made them the fighting force they now most surely were. Fitness was the key. Physical exercise and a sense of purpose. Drill, drill and more drill and battle training. For now they were ready. And now he knew they could win.

He did not intend to defend. Rommel had had his chance, had attacked in June and had failed. Concentration, control and simplicity. The holy trinity of the battlefield had defeated him at Alam Halfa. They had lured him in and destroyed his strength bit by bit. Rommel had overplayed his hand and now it was their own time to attack. Well, of course that had apparently also been Auchinleck's plan. But Churchill had perceived that Auchinleck's heart was not in it, and the men knew it too. They could tell a soldier's true feelings. Auchinleck had made too many plans for the evacuation that he felt must follow their defeat. That was no way to treat an army, to act as if they had been beaten already.

Emerging from his reverie, Montgomery turned back to Poston: 'Do you think the men are really ready for it now, John? The big attack?'

'More ready than ever, sir. They've had enough of fighting a defensive war.' Poston paused and smiled, then went on: 'Do you recall, sir, that joke circulating in Cairo back in August, when you'd just arrived. They said that General Auchinleck's defence plan was to allow Rommel to break through right up to Cairo. But that when the Germans reached the Gezira Club in the capital all the staff at GHQ should instantly turn out with their sidearms and chase him back to Tripoli?'

Montgomery laughed, that strange high-pitched laugh that made his features appear even more birdlike. When he spoke it was with weak 'R's, turning them to 'W's which coming from anyone else might have appeared comic.

'Very good, John. Yes, I do seem to remember that one. I think we can afford to be a little more positive now, don't you?'

'You've worked miracles, sir. Nothing less.'

'We've a different army now, John. And we're going to use it.'

He knew that he had achieved something important. He had got rid of all the belly-aching, and had told his staff quite bluntly on the first day that if any man wanted to continue to invent lame reasons for not doing his job then he could get out of it at once. They were staying here. And if they could not stay and win and remain alive then they would stay here dead.

He had also decided that the plan of battle should be known to everyone from general to private soldier. And so he had attempted to visit them all. Not just the Brits, but the Aussies, the New Zealanders, the Indians and the rest. He had even taken up the offer of an Australian slouch hat which he decorated with regimental badges as he toured the other Divisions.

He knew that his presence had had an effect on the men. Freddie de Guingand, his chief of staff, had told him that the sick rate dropped off dramatically. In fact men were desperate to return from sick leave so as not to miss the big push. He was confident that now every single one of his soldiers felt a part of the plan. All that he had to do was to make sure that it worked.

He looked again at the map and this time traced another line, to the west of his original. Rommel's own position was certainly impressive, but it had a fundamental flaw.

What had Bill Williams called it? An Italian corset strengthened by German whalebones. Yes, he liked that. A bit like Wellington at Waterloo, strengthening his Belgian and Dutch regiments by placing them beside a battalion of seasoned British veterans. But it was not quite the same here.

He wondered where they would be now without Williams. He was the finest intelligence officer that Montgomery had ever encountered: an Oxford Don with a quite brilliant brain, now a major in the King's Dragoon Guards. And Williams had said something further to him. The phrase continued to go around in his mind. If they could separate the German whalebones from the soft Italian corset they would smash through the Italians. It was simple and quite brilliant, and Montgomery had readily adopted it as his own.

So they would attack. Alam Halfa had paved the way. Ultra had revealed the losses. Fifty-one German tanks destroyed and more damaged and over 3000 German and Italian casualties.

Churchill, impatient as ever and keen to please the Allies, had sent Montgomery a peremptory memo telling him that it must be in September. Of course he wasn't having any such nonsense. They would never have been prepared and he told Churchill as much. He would not risk men's lives in a premature offensive. General Alexander, the commander-in-chief, had presented Churchill's case, but Montgomery was having none of it. He would launch the offensive in his own time; four days after the anniversary of Betty's death. The twenty-third of October looked set to be the perfect night. Tonight.

'John, is Freddie back from Alex?'

'Yes, sir, he's in his HQ I believe.'

'His HQ?'

'He's adopted an old Italian pillbox, sir. Made it quite like home apparently. Still smells a little.'

'Very good. Then I think we might pay him a visit, don't you?'

Both men stepped out of the caravan and walked over to the former Italian strongpoint which now acted as the HQ for Freddie de Guingand. It was draped with camouflage netting and around it some armoured cars had been dug in, connected by shallow slit trenches. He was pleased that Freddie should be so close at hand.

They were complete opposites, it occurred to him, and not for the first time. Freddie de Guingand was fourteen years his junior. He had first met him at TA HQ in York in 1923. Montgomery had been teaching soldiering skills and young Freddie, devilishly handsome at twenty-two, a trainee second lieutenant, had impressed him with his perceptive intelligence. Despite their shared love of golf and bridge, how very different they were. Freddie forever living on his nerves, highly strung, a lover of wine and women; an inveterate gambler, an epicure. And he himself, Montgomery. Calm, self-controlled, abstemious. Those at least were the virtues which he liked to claim as his own, the heights to which he aspired.

He had decided to make Freddie his chief of staff almost instantly after having taken up the command of Eighth Army. Chief of staff: his invention. The army did not work on that principle. It believed that the army commander could use his staff officers himself. But Montgomery knew that a good CoS was essential to coordinating any campaign. That was surely what had cost the other generals in the desert their commands. That was why he was here. With Freddie at his side – Berthier to his Napoleon – and Alexander, the overall commander, behind him, he had the framework of an unassailable team. If only he could be sure that he could

41

rely on all his corps commanders: Horrocks, Lumsden and Leese. Brian Horrocks he had known in the Great War and had personally appointed to XIII Corps. As for Leese, he had taught him at Staff College back in 1926 and had appointed him like Horrocks on his own merit. But it had been at Horrocks' suggestion that he had given Lumsden X Corps and he already felt uneasy about it. Lumsden was certainly a game fellow. Lanky, dashing and with a liking for sartorial excess, he had been an amateur jockey before the war. But Montgomery disliked the arrogance that went with it. He might be a tremendous horseman and have a creditable handicap at golf, but he was not sure that the man had enough real 'pep' for such a plan as he had in mind. And therein, he suspected, might lie something of a problem.

Ducking beneath the low lintel of the pillbox, difficult even for his diminutive frame, Montgomery entered with Poston as ever close behind. 'Freddie? Ah, there you are.'

De Guingand stood and saluted then grasped a thick sheaf of papers from his desk. 'Sir. I have the latest sitrep here. I was just coming to find you and hand it over.'

Montgomery stared at him and a brief smile flickered across his face. He shook his head in a fatherly manner. 'Don't be silly, Freddie. You ought to know by now. You know I never read any papers when I can get the person concerned to tell me himself. Put all that bumpf away. See if you can find General Leese and ask him to dine with me. Oh, and why don't you join us? Shall we say seven o' clock? Outside my caravan. Don't be late.'

Their frugal meal began at precisely seven o' clock. But the food was of no great consequence to Montgomery. They sat within a large tent of mosquito netting into which the flies had still managed to gain access and dined as was his habit on bully beef and lemonade. But he was more concerned with the words of his corps commander and chief of staff. Leese went on: 'As I was saying, I toured the positions today, sir. The men are mad keen, especially the Highlanders. They know they've got the Australians and New Zealanders on their flanks. They say they feel safe, sir. That's the extraordinary thing really. They're so remarkably confident. Never seen the like. And they really understand the plan.'

Montgomery smiled and tugged at his earlobe. 'Thank you, Oliver. That's most reassuring.' He turned to de Guingand: 'How d'you find the food, Freddie? Not a patch on what you sampled in Alexandria, I'll bet.'

De Guingand laughed: 'No, sir. I'm afraid you're right. But it's really not bad don't you think?'

'Where were you, the English Speaking Union?'

'Yes, sir, it's always a safe bet.'

'How was it, the town? As confident as Leese's men?'

'More so, sir. It's a different place from two months ago. They really seem to believe that the threat has gone.'

'It has, Freddie. All we've got to do now is prove them right, gentlemen, isn't it?'

The others smiled and Montgomery stood. They followed suit as he placed his hat on his head.

'Now I think I'll turn in. You, Oliver?'

'I rather thought I'd watch the barrage, sir.'

'As you will then. But what you think you'll see I don't know and whatever good do you suppose you'll do?'

'None, sir, of course.'

'Quite. None whatsoever. You know that there is absolutely nothing you can possibly do now which will influence the battle. Your job, Oliver, is to get to bed early so you're fresh in the morning. You must be on top form. This battle is sure to be full of shocks and you will have to take them.'

Leese nodded: 'Yes, sir. Perhaps I should reconsider.'

43

'I think you would be wise to do so. And now I really must get to bed so, gentlemen, if you'll excuse me.'

He turned and walked up the few steps to the caravan. At the top he looked back. 'Remember, Freddie. Any developments, be sure to wake me instantly.'

Montgomery twisted the door handle and entered the small wood-clad room. It was surprisingly cool. He closed the door behind him, removed his hat and ran his hands through his thinning hair. He sat down and stared at the floor. It was good. Leese's report had backed up all that Freddie had told him. Everything was in place, the men were spoiling for a fight. It was all running to plan. But, he wondered, what will the situation be when I have taken 10,000 or 20,000 casualties and have lost a hundred or two hundred tanks?

He dismissed the thought. There was no going back now. Everything was ready. They must attack and force the issue. 'D' Day and 'H' Hour were set. Within half an hour the terrible barrage would begin, heralding perhaps the most important battle of the war to date. And he was its master. If he won he would be lauded and rewarded. But should he fail both the politicians and the people would vilify him. This then was to be the test of all the years. This was to be his chance.

He opened his diary and took up the pen that lay permanently beside it. 'The enemy knows that we intend to attack and has been strengthening his defences. On our side we have the initiative and a great superiority in men, tanks and artillery and other materiel. We also have an army in which the morale is right up on the top line, and every officer and man knows the issues at stake, knows what is wanted, and knows how the battle will be fought and won.'

Every man might know, he thought, but only he had the ultimate responsibility. He might delegate and inform but ultimately the decisions were his alone.

44

He continued to write in the diary and as he did so wondered how posterity would evaluate his words. There would be bloodshed. Much of it. There was no way of avoiding that. And in the end a battle won here would save many more lives and might help to finish the war.

He wrote: 'The battle will be expensive as it will really become a killing match.' And as soon as he saw the words, he thought of their true meaning. How many men would they lose? 10,000 men, 20,000? He wrote again: 'I have estimated 10,000 casualties in this week's fighting . . .'

All that they needed now, he thought, was good weather. That and perhaps just a modicum of good luck.

SIX

7.00 p.m.
Near El Alamein railway siding
Josh Miller

He opened the dusty, dog-eared book and read the passage
again, savouring the beauty of the lines. Xenophon was
such a beautiful writer, he thought, interspersing his information with passages of real poetry. In the two years that
he had been studying the classical historians at Harvard,
Josh Miller had learnt to distinguish between their styles
until he was able to spot them blind. Xenophon's account
of the Battle of Cunaxa between Cyrus's Greek mercenaries
and his brother's Persians had always held him spellbound and here, in this endless desert which he supposed
might with a small stretch of the imagination resemble the
battlefield in Babylon it seemed even more real. He read
on: 'They all wore helmets, except for Cyrus who went into
battle bare-headed. It was now midday and the enemy had
yet to come into sight. But in the early afternoon dust
appeared like a white cloud and after some time a sort of
blackness extending a long way over the plain . . . far from
shouting they came on as silently as they could, calmly, in
a slow, steady march.'
   Imagine that, he thought. Coming on into battle in a
slow, steady march. Having to keep your body from

breaking into a run, or running away, as the arrows and the spears began to rain down upon you. It occurred to him that he was for the first time in his life sitting in what would soon he presumed become another battlefield, surrounded by so many thousands of modern-day warriors. The thought sent a shiver down his spine. He steadied himself, placing a strong, muscular hand palmdown on the rocky ground on which he was sitting.

They had parked the Dodge ambulance at a crossroads of the coastal road that ran into the west and the southern track that had been christened Springbok Road in honour of the South Africans who now held most of its length from their Australian comrades near the sea down here into the desert.

Miller gazed out towards the west, towards the enemy and thought about the men who lay out there in their trenches and foxholes. Men from Germany and men from Italy. Men who knew this desert better than he by far, who had been here for years when this war was in its infancy. He was glad to be here, to be part of this great adventure. He knew that if he had not come he would forever have regretted it. Not for missing the chance to fight. As the son of a Quaker and a pacifist in his own mind, he would not have joined the regular army and would have protested if conscripted. Killing was anathema to him. But helping his fellow man, whatever his nationality, now that was something else. The American Field Service, an independent ambulance unit with a distinguished record in the last war had seemed perfect.

Perhaps, he thought, that was why he had felt the need to learn so much about war. He still believed that there might be another way. While his fellow students ploughed on deep into Plato and Socrates, Miller preferred to stay with Thucydides, Xenophon and Caesar. Now later conflicts interested him. Napoleon in particular fascinated

47

him and in Cairo, after they had finally got there from the depot at El Tahag, while all the talk among his friends had been of pharaohs and pyramids, Miller's mind had been on the image of a small Corsican general standing at the base of the Sphinx less than two hundred years ago. A man bent on world domination whose wars had lasted twenty-five years. He wondered how long this present one would last, fuelled as it was by the megalomania of another European emperor.

He was such a long way from home. Halfway across the world from college, and from the family home in Long Island. And in real terms he might as well have been on the moon.

Aged nineteen and filled with curiosity to see more of the world, he had volunteered without hesitation for the ambulance service. Someone had given him a copy of *Life* magazine and pointed to photographs of AFS volunteers helping the British in North Africa. Ambulances alone in vast expanses of sand; men running with stretchers. He had thought how romantic it all seemed. After he had signed up he learnt how at Tobruk AFS men had died with the British and their allies. Others had been made prisoner. He looked now at the small group who for the last two months had inhabited the ambulance that had made the journey with them five thousand miles across the Atlantic. Thought how they looked for all the world like straight British soldiers with their funny schoolboy shorts and their socks and their boots. They wore the same kit, had the same webbing, even had the same haircuts. It was only when they spoke, as now that you could tell they were Americans.

'Oh Jeeze, Lieutenant. Not again. How come you always get to win?'

'Privilege of rank, Turk. Nothing more. Goes with the territory.'

Charlie Turk, a muscle-bound quarterback with a

navy-cut hairstyle and wearing a T-shirt with his British army-issue shorts, sat on a bunk in the back of the ambulance and paid the lieutenant his winnings. Then he picked up the pack and shuffled before dealing out two new hands on the rough red serge of the British army-issue hospital blanket.

'Double or quits, Lieutenant. What d'you say?'

'It's your funeral, Turk.'

Lieutenant Evan Thomas grinned. This would be the sixth game he had played against Turk. He looked at the wodge of dollar bills at his side and tried to guess how much he had won. Four hundred? He really hated to fleece poor Turk, but if the guy insisted.

They fanned out their hands and took a look at them. Neither man smiled.

At length Turk spoke: 'Card.'

The lieutenant handed him a card. He looked at it and said nothing.

The lieutenant took a card. Turk smiled: 'OK three kings. What you got?'

'Full house. I win.'

'Beats me. You win again. I swear, Loot, you've got the luck of the devil himself.'

'Not the devil, Turk. I sure don't get my luck from him. If anyone's on my side, it's got to be the big guy. Don't you think?'

Miller did not play cards, had not been brought up that way. His family were Quakers. For his part he had not yet decided, but he was pretty certain that there was some deity above them. He only hoped that whatever or whoever it was would be looking out for him in the coming battle. Because they were sure there was going to be a battle. A big one. That's why they had been rushed here from Alexandria so fast. The lieutenant began to count his money. Miller guessed there was a time and place for everything and he had seen more things in this war than he had ever thought he would. And surely, even if God was against gambling, if He could countenance such inhumanity then He would bend the rules a little when it came to a card game. Although it did seem a little unfair that the lieutenant kept winning all the time.

He liked Thomas, who wore his officer's rank lightly. The service was nominally subject to British army law but they had worked it out with the Brits that their own officers could dish out whatever punishments were needed.

Turk was a character too. A football player who had won a sports scholarship to Harvard and come out here to see some action before he was called up to the US army. He figured that it would give him some good battlefield experience and Miller reckoned he would probably be right.

As for himself, he had not really known what to expect. He had joined and volunteered in the fervour that came of adrenalin and then halfway across the Atlantic on the *Aquitania* had almost regretted it when a member of the ship's crew had attempted suicide and the game had become a reality. But by then it had been too late.

One thing he did know. He had not yet seen a dead man, had not even seen a single casualty still on the battlefield. Sure, he had seen enough wounded in the hospitals in Cairo and Alexandria but did they really count? He reckoned not. They were all dressed and bundled up. Even the amputees seemed sanitized. No, Miller had not seen the full horror of war and he was not sure just how he was going to react to it.

Turk's voice cut through his thoughts: 'See this. It's crap, McGinty. Pure crap. The lieutenant wins every time.'

The fourth member of their team, Joe McGinty, an Irishman from New York looked up from his copy of a comic book: 'So why d'ya keep playing, you great lunk?'

'Well I reckon he's got to lose sometime, ain't he? I mean stands to reason that even the lieutenant's luck's got to run out sometime, don't it?'

Miller shook his head and went on reading: '. . . the Persians, even before they were within the range of the arrows, wavered and ran away. Then the Greeks pressed on the pursuit vigorously, but they shouted to each other not to run, but to follow up the enemy without breaking ranks . . .'

He wondered whether it would be like that when the British attacked and conjectured just what 'pressed on the pursuit vigorously' might mean. He envisaged ragged ranks of Greeks hacking in all directions, swords meeting flesh as the Persians fell under the advancing army. Razor-sharp steel slicing through skin and tissue and sinew and bone. 'Pressed on the pursuit vigorously'. It sounded almost modern. Might even feature on one of Monty's orders.

Turk, after his seventh losing game, had dealt an eighth. But no amount of money lost at cards could take his mind off a fear that had got hold of him. He was rattled and he wanted some answers. 'What I don't understand, Loot, is what we're doing here. If we're so strong why aren't we chasing Rommel's men back into the sea?'

Thomas studied his cards as he spoke: 'We're playing a waiting game, Turk. Just waiting. Like when you play cards. We're trying to out-guess the enemy, figure out his next move. The British are waiting for him to make a mistake then they'll pounce.' He played his hand.

'Shee-it! Sorry, Lieutenant. But Jeeze. OK, you win. That's it. I'm done.'

McGinty spoke: 'He's got a point, Lieutenant. How did we end up here?'

From the other side of the ambulance another man emerged. Ed Bigelow was a geology student at Princeton.

His black-rimmed spectacles sat on the bridge of his bird-like nose. In one hand he held a piece of rock, in the other a small magnifying glass. If Bigelow had one failing it was his inability to stifle his penchant for wicked sarcasm. He smiled at McGinty: 'Don't you remember, Joe, you came out on that transporter ship. Across the sea. Big blue watery thing. Took a while to cross. Wow, your memory!'

He hit the side of his head.

McGinty gave him a look that said: *one more comment like that and you're a dead man.*

Thomas saw it too: 'Cool it, McGinty, he's only winding you up. You know how Monty got here. They were pushed back all along the coast. But hey, this is as good a place as I've seen to stand and fight.' He turned to Miller: 'What about you, Josh? You're the student of classical history, you know your battles. Is this a good place to fight?'

Bigelow spoke before Miller could answer: 'Is anywhere a good place to fight?'

McGinty saw his chance: 'Oh, here we go. The philosophy student is here, guys. Say hello to the professor.'

Turk looked at him: 'Aw, give it a rest, Joe. It was a fair comment. Who wants to fight anywhere?'

McGinty shook his head: 'What puzzles me, Charlie, is how you ever got into Harvard.'

'You seen me play? That's how. And if you got anything to say about my brains clever klutz then talk to the fist, big boy. Dumb Mick.'

Thomas stood up, ready to stop the fight. But Miller had seen it too, and knew that they were just tired of waiting and wound up not in fact by each other but merely by the terrible nervous tension which ran through everyone, the sense of the approaching battle and all the uncertainty it brought. He interrupted: 'In point of fact this is a good defensive position. We have the sea on one side and the Quattara Depression on the other. We have no flanks.'

McGinty looked interested: 'So what you're saying is, we're safer here.'

'You could put it that way, yes.'

Thomas sat back down. Turk began to shuffle the cards. Miller looked back at the book: 'Cyrus was pleased when he saw the Greeks winning and driving the enemy back before them . . . but he was not so carried away as to join in the pursuit . . . Seeing that no frontal attack was being made he wheeled right in an outflanking movement . . .'

He wondered whether Rommel or whoever was now commanding the Germans and Italians over there might attempt something similar. Must remember to ask Lieutenant Thomas that one. Thomas was a good guy, in charge of a platoon of Fifteen Company of which they were a section. Each platoon contained five sections three of them with four ambulances, two with five. Each section was manned by one NCO, a spare driver, a mechanic and five drivers, eight men in all for four or five ambulances.

Thomas had been out here since May, taken part in the retreat from Tobruk and had seen a few friends die. Stuka attacks mostly. But there had been one time when the Germans had caught a convoy with machine-gun fire and mortars. Sometimes he spoke about it. Sometimes not. His actual name was Evan Winchall Thomas II and he was heir to a fortune on the east coast. His ambition, he had told Miller one starry evening as they sat drinking beer, was to go into publishing and Miller wondered whether he would ever achieve it.

Since July Thomas's platoon along with four others, with a total availability of twenty-two in all, had been posted to the New Zealanders. That was something else that had struck him in Cairo. The fact that they had come from all over the world to fight this war. Cairo, already a cosmopolitan city, was made all the more exotic by the thousands of battledress-clad men and women who thronged its streets by day and night. Miller had not visited the notorious Birka red-light district, though encouraged to do so by Turk. He had no desire to watch an ugly couple copulating for money. He had luxuriated though in the coffee houses, had drunk mint tea in Al Fashawi's in the bazaar and eaten ice-cream at Groppi's.

Alexandria if anything was better and they had been allowed to use the New Zealanders' YMCA hostel where they could get a clean bed and breakfast for sixty-two cents. Miller looked up. The situation was still tense.

'What's your opinion of Cairo, Professor?'

Bigelow looked up from his rock and twiddled his spectacles: 'Cairo is like a woman. A woman who has let herself go. She is not young, far from it, and is overpainted, overpowdered, overscented and fat. Her vices, while somewhat deplorable can be amusing, but what is really unforgivable is her lack of fastidiousness with regard to her own person. She is though, a lady and something of a wit.'

Turk laughed: 'I never heard such crap, Prof.'

Miller smiled. 'You've excelled yourself, Ed. And I tend to agree with you, on all counts.'

Turk spoke: 'Prof, what I don't get is why you're here out in the desert with us and not back in Cairo in HQ.'

'Because I want to be here. What is the point of observing the action when you can be part of it?'

'Looks like you're about to get your chance.' McGinty pointed to a soldier wearing a tin hat who was running in the direction of the lieutenant. The man presented him with a sheet of paper, saluted and ran off, before Thomas had time to return the gesture.

'I don't think I'll ever get used to this saluting lark.' He unfolded the paper: 'Thank God, orders.' He read carefully then folded the paper and put it in his breast pocket. 'OK, saddle up, guys. We're to drive to the New Zealand field dressing-station.' He pointed: 'It's no more than a mile down that track. Moon Track.'

Half an hour later, as they bumped across the sand, Miller thanked God for the Dodges and their superior suspension. McGinty read his mind: 'This vehicle is the ultimate in comfort.'

'You know, we're lucky to have it. The new guys have had to take what they could, mostly crummy British Humbers and Austins.'

The ambulances had become their homes, infinitely preferable to occupying the trenches and dugouts abandoned by the enemy which were often infested with rats and fleas. Instead the Dodges offered bedroom, dining room and kitchen. An old shell storage box strapped to the front fender made a fine wardrobe, lice and flea-free and the exhaust pipe doubled up as a camp stove. By night they draped blankets across the windows to avoid infringing the blackout while a stretcher slung in the centre made an excellent table.

Miller reflected how quickly they had adapted to the hardships of desert life. The soldiers had been helpful, cautioning them not to put their hand into any holes in rocks; scorpions and vipers liked nothing better than a nice dark hole; always to check their boots before they put them on for the same reason. They had showed them how to 'brew up', that meant make tea, using a sand cooker where you tipped petrol into a tin half-filled with sand then set fire to it before putting your billy-can on the top to boil the water. Sweet and strong, that was how the British soldiers liked their tea, the

New Zealanders too. Miller was beginning to get a taste for it. Well, there was no alternative. Nothing of course could prepare you for the *khamsin*, the desert wind that blew across the sand fifty days of every year. The Bedouin said 'if the *khamsin* blows for three days a man can surely kill his wife. For five days and he has the right to kill his neighbour. Seven days and he may kill himself.'

At length they arrived at the field dressing-station, a New Zealand station just inside the British minefield area. The first thing that struck Miller was the bigger-than-usual lorry parked up beside the surgical tent. Pictured on its side was a vampire bat. A blood truck, refrigerated. No sooner had they pulled up than to their surprise a British voice addressed them, straight from the Home Counties rather than Auckland or Wellington.

'I say, you men there. This way.' A British army officer was standing beside the entrance to the surgical tent. He smiled: 'Captain Anderson, Army Medical Corps. You're the Americans?'

'That's us, sir. All the way from the US of A. Here to help in any way we can, Captain.'

'Well, glad to have you here. I trust that all your men are acquainted with the battle evacuation procedure?'

Thomas nodded: 'Sure, Captain. We've studied it enough. Stretcher-bearers bring the wounded to the regimental aid post where they're seen by the MO then we pick 'em up and take them to an advanced dressing-station for treatment.'

The captain suddenly noticed the door of the Dodge on which was painted the insignia of the AFS, against the background of the red cross on white, an American eagle wearing a top hat.

'What the devil's that?'

'It's the uh . . . unit insignia, sir, officially approved by your top brass. They call it "the chicken".'

'Is it indeed. I mean was it? Do they? Well I never. Mind you if it bonds you all together then we must agree. Where was I?' He paused and stared at the men: 'I say. Don't your men salute an officer?'

'Well, yes in theory they should, sir. But they're not trained soldiers you see, Captain. Perhaps you could cut them a bit of slack?'

The captain stared at Thomas: 'Cut them what? I think it highly improper, Lieutenant, for any man in the King's uniform not to salute an officer. And that includes you. You will rectify the situation and ensure that in future your men salute at the appropriate time. Is that clear?'

'Sir. Very clear, sir.'

'Oh, and incidentally I shall be moving out pretty soon. There's a New Zealand officer taking over here, a Major Coswell. And, Lieutenenant, I suggest that you make sure that you remember what I've told you. He's a bit of a hero from what I hear. He and his team were put in the bag in the big Wavell push. Suffice to say, they escaped. You can stand your men down. I'm sure someone will find you when they need you.'

He walked off into the tent. Thomas turned to the men and removed his peaked cap. 'Well. That told me.'

McGinty spoke: 'Listen, Loot. Way I understand it we're not under military law.'

'We still have to take orders though.'

Turk shook his head: 'But we ain't what was the word? "Amenable to summary punishment".'

Miller spoke: 'In effect we're camp followers.'

'Sorry?'

'In the old days, when an army went to war it took its baggage train and attached to the baggage train were always what they called "camp followers". You know,

57

wives, girlfriends, the guys who provided the food and water and beer. Bakers, blacksmiths. Well in a sense, that's what we are.'

'I ain't no wife or girlfriend. And I ain't no baker.'

'But you are here to help the army. You're part of the army establishment.'

It was true. They were not militarily trained and the British army was nervous of them. They had been given a basic course in the way the army worked and its organ-ization and the idea of saluting by an RASC lieutenant shortly after they had landed. But soldiers they were not and never would be. They were misfits, thought Miller, and not for the first time he worried about how they would fit in in the thick of battle.

Thomas wiped the sweat from his forehead with a spotted handkerchief. 'OK. Now Colonel Blimp's gone I think we can relax for a while, boys. Turk, hows about a game of poker?'

Bigelow took off his glasses and began to polish them as he spoke. 'Have you thought, Lieutenant, that this might not be such a great time to gamble?'

'Say again?'

'Well, sir. You see I reckon that you can only have a certain amount of luck. It's what the Limeys say too. And by the law of averages, it stands to reason, don't you think that if you use all your luck up here, playing cards with Turk, and winning all the time, then when we do get up to the battlefield your luck may just run out?'

Thomas laughed and began to deal: 'OK, Turk and anyone else who wants to make a quick buck. Let's play cards and see if you can win it all back from me before we have to move.'

SEVEN

8.00 p.m.
Behind Bab Al Quattara
Lieutenant Ralf Ringler

It was almost dusk when Lieutenant Ralf Ringler finally reached the area which for the last month had held the small command post of Panzergrenadier Regiment 104. For a moment though he wondered if he hadn't taken a wrong turning somewhere back across the sand. It was easy enough to do in this wretched wasteland. For, instead of the stripped-back, rock-walled and sandbagged strong-point to which he had become accustomed, there stood a huge tent. He stopped and stared at the wall of field-grey canvas and watched as the battalion orderlies went hurriedly in and out carrying boxes of rations and cases of wine. The battalion adjutant, Major Werter, came out puffing on a short cigar and, seeing Ringler's absent-minded look, smiled and went towards him.

'Ah, Ringler. There you are. You did get the invitation?'

'Invitation?'

'To the colonel's party. Well, it would seem you did not. My apologies, but well here you are anyway. How d'you like our new accommodation? It's only temporary I'm afraid. A present from our friends the Italians. They seem to have brought everything with them but the kitchen sink. Even women they say. Though where they might be now the devil knows.'

'Well, sir, they did have a colony here. They seem to own half the houses on the coast road.'

'I know the problems we've had with their damn damage claims. They're meant to be our allies.'

'Kind of them to lend us the tent though, sir.'

'Yes, damn kind. Isn't it splendid? Good target for the RAF too. This party had better be over damn quick. But good to be a bit festive. Well, you know, we had to push the boat out for the colonel's birthday. Come inside and see the old man. He'll be delighted you're here. Be careful though Ralf. His hearing's shot to pieces. Both eardrums perforated. Happened at Alam Halfa. He set up his OP directly beside an 88 battery. You'd think he'd know better at his age. Didn't you know? Best not to mention it. You know how he is, he gets frightfully upset if he suspects that people think he's deaf. Loves music: Beethoven, Wagner that sort of thing. You should hear him sing.'

They entered the tent and Ringler removed his field cap and tried to make his uniform look a little more presentable, bleached as it was by the sun to a sandy tan colour. At twenty-two Ringler was almost the baby of the battalion, but even so he was still a seasoned veteran. He had been fighting out here for the last two years, and the desert was etched into his brain.

Werter continued: 'Now. Help yourself to a drink, Ringler. Witman has brought us some whisky. Courtesy of the British of course, taken on the road from Benghazi. And there's even a case of Münchner Löwenbräu from the Aussies in Tobruk. And the Italians have also given us some wine. Kind of them.'

Ringler nodded his head: 'Thank you, Herr Major.'

The colonel stood with his back to them in the centre of the tent, laughing in the middle of a circle of his battalion officers all of whom, unlike their CO, still wearing his peaked officer's hat, had removed their headgear. Colonel Karl Ens was a hard-bitten veteran whose dark, sun-tanned face was marked with lines that bore witness to both laughter and anxiety. Ringler walked up to the group and was greeted with polite nods of the head. The colonel turned and saw him and not for the first time Ringler noticed the Knight's Cross that hung at his neck.

'Ringler. Good to see you. How are the men of Number Ten company?'

'Fine, sir. We're guarding a lane through the minefield belt.'

'Ah, our Devil's Garden. Our field marshal has done us proud, don't you think, Ringler? What could break through that? Only a fool would try. And look at this. Look what they've all done for me. True comrades, Ringler, eh?'

'Yes, Herr Oberst. It's wonderful.'

The colonel squinted and inclined his head: 'What did you say? Colourful?'

'Yes, sir. Very good.'

The colonel smiled and nodded. 'Very colourful.' He laughed and shook his head. 'Have a drink, Ringler. Take a glass of schnapps with me?'

'I don't think so, sir. I don't often drink schnapps.'

Again the colonel squinted but this time Ringler was not so sure whether it was his deafness or because he was displeased at his apparently discourteous reluctance to drink the schnapps.

'Yes, sir. Of course I shall have a glass of schnapps with you. Happy birthday, Colonel.'

The colonel smiled and drank the glass down in one. Ringler followed suit and managed to stop himself from coughing as the fiery, colourless liquid burned its way

61

down his throat. Now he remembered why he didn't drink the stuff.

The colonel was beaming now. 'Very colourful, Ringler.' He clapped Ringler on the back and turned away laughing.

The adjutant came up: 'Well done, Ralf. The colonel will have his little jokes. You don't care much for schnapps I think?'

'Not as a rule, sir, no.'

'Here, have a glass of beer. It's good stuff and liberated too.'

Ringler took a bottle of the warmish beer and drained it, quenching the burning in his throat.

In a corner of the huge tent, one of the enlisted men, Lance-Corporal Kaspar, a talented musician from Bohemia, began to play on his harmonica. Inevitably the tune was *Lili Marlene*. Nevertheless, however many times Ringler heard it it always brought a lump to his throat. The colonel, hearing the tune despite his deafness, smiled and raised his glass.

'A toast, gentlemen. To the Deutsche Afrika Korps and its unstoppable victory in the desert. On to Cairo and Suez.'

As one the officers echoed the colonel's words: 'On to Cairo and Suez.' They raised their own glasses and drained them before resuming drinking at a more steady pace.

Ringler was standing inside the tent by the entrance next to a fellow lieutenant, Werner Adler, from Number Eight company, a blond, tall Aryan from Potsdam who had been an enthusiastic member of the Hitler Youth before joining the army, leading his local NSDAP boys' group.

Ringler took another swig of beer and turned to Adler: 'D'you really think we'll get there?'

'Where?'

'Cairo of course. D'you think it's really possible?'

'Don't you? You heard Colonel Karl. We'll get there.'

'Werner, how long have you been out here?'

'A year exactly.'

'And what have you seen in that time?'

'Victory in our grasp. We've almost beaten them. We took Tobruk didn't we? Then Alam Halfa. Perhaps this time we'll get them. We just sit here and wait for them to throw themselves at us and then when they're spent we counter-attack with everything we've got.'

Ringler smiled: 'But do you think they'll be spent? And what do we really have?'

'We still have the panzers. Two divisions of them and the Italians too. Some of them aren't half bad. The paras . . .'

Ringler cut in: 'How many tanks do you think we've actually got, Adler? Real tanks I mean, German tanks?'

'I don't know. Four hundred. Maybe more?'

Ringler laughed: 'My dear Werner. I was talking to this boy from Panzerarmee HQ and he told me that the last intelligence was that we had no more than two hundred and forty serviceable panzers. And there's worse. We've no fuel. Well, not enough for more than a few days. Certainly not enough to punch through the Brits and get to Cairo.'

Adler stared at the ground and shrugged his shoulders. 'That's just hearsay, Ringler. I believe we can do it. And you must too. As officers we have a duty to believe in our victory. We owe it to the men, and to ourselves. You know that's defeatist talk. You should be careful what you say to people.'

Ringler walked outside for a moment. His head had suddenly begun to ache and he felt weary. The schnapps, he supposed. An eerie silence hung over the desert. It was a beautiful evening and extraordinarily peaceful. He took another sip of beer and re-entered the tent.

As he did so Monier, the battalion sergeant-major and

also its finest singer, coughed to clear his throat and began to sing. It was a familiar folk song from the Rhine. Soon the battalion officers and their guests were in full voice.

The song finished but just as it did Adler stared at Ringler and smiled. Then he began to sing. A very different song this time and of a more recent vintage, but one with which they were all familiar.

Die Fahne hoch! Die Reihen fest geschlossen!
SA marschiert mit mutig-festem Schritt.
Kam'raden, die Rotfront und Reaktion erschossen,
Marschier'n im Geist in uns'ren Reihen mit.

Raise high the flag! Ranks close tight!
The stormtroopers march with bold, firm step.
Their comrades shot by the Reds and Reactionaries,
They march in spirit within our ranks.

The Horst Wessel song, the marching song of the Nazi party. The song which had carried Hitler to power. In the off beats when in a band cymbals would have crashed out the officers stamped their feet as hard as they could. The colonel for all his deafness had the loudest voice and, thought Ringler, it really wasn't bad. He had never much cared for that song, named after its composer, a Nazi party activist assassinated by a Communist in 1930 and used as an excuse for a massacre.

But he still joined in. It was a symbol of their unity, their determination, their victory. And what was more once you were singing it it did something to the soul. Lifted the spirits from the depths of despair to some higher plane where the Aryan race really was invincible:

Zum letzten Mal wird nun Appell geblasen!
Zum Kampfe steh'n wir alle schon bereit!
Bald flattern Hitlerfahnen über Barrikaden.
Die Knechtschaft dauert nur noch kurze Zeit!

For the last time now the call is sounded!
Already we stand all ready to fight!
Soon the Hitler banners will flutter over the barri-
cades.
Our time in bondage won't last much longer!

Ringler looked at Adler across the tent. He was smiling
now. Full of pride and confident with the certainty imbued
by the music. Ringler too felt the better for it. He left the
tent and found himself in the company of Sergeant-Major
Monier who had come out for a smoke. Ringler liked the
man. He was honest and simple but utterly loyal. He came
from farming stock in the Rhineland and had joined the
Wehrmacht shortly after the annexation of the Sudetenland.
He seemed older than his thirty years and acted as a sort
of uncle to the younger men in the battalion. Somehow he
had always seemed to be at Ringler's side throughout the
African campaign, since the early days of 1941. At Mersa,
when they had pushed the Allies back for the first time.
At Benghazi when they had left it again to be taken by the
British. At Tobruk, when they had gone in through the
warren of stinking caves that the Allies had held for so
long, Monier had been at his side joking about the 'desert
rats'. At Alam Halfa when they had seemed almost at the
gates of Alexandria. And now here, near the little village
of Alamein where they had attacked and failed so recently.
Monier had always been there, offering support and advice.

Yet for all his apparent confidence there had always
been, it seemed to Ringler, a curious air of insecurity
about the man and as they walked back to their trenches
on this chilly night with its bright moon and eerie still-
ness, Monier spoke: 'Cigarette, sir?'

As Ringler accepted and lit up Monier continued: 'Did
I ever tell you, sir, about my home in the Palatinate? You
know that area, sir?'

Ringler, a northerner himself, from Dresden, remembered a family holiday to the lower Rhineland. 'I have visited it once. A very long time ago. I seem to recall it being very pleasant.'

'It's the most beautiful place in the world, sir. If you don't mind my saying so. God's own country really. Have you ever been to Mainz or Koblenz, sir?'

'No, Monier. I'm afraid not. I've never been to Mainz or Koblenz.'

'Then you've missed a real treat, sir. Oh, they're fine big cities, sir. All modern bustle and fuss. But with some fine old buildings too. You'd like them, sir. I can see you there, you'd be in your element. Of course we don't live there. We have a little house outside in the country. Little farm really, sir, just a few cows and some land for crops. But it's enough for us.'

He poked around in his pocket and took out his wallet. Then reaching inside he produced two dog-eared black and white photographs. 'Here they are, sir. Last Christmas that was, on leave. That's Monika there and that's Heidi and the little one is Hans. If I could just see them once more at home, Lieutenant. Once more. That's all I ask.'

'Perhaps you will, later, Monier. After our victory I'm sure that you'll see them and then we'll have all this behind us, eh?'

Monier nodded and smiled: 'Oh yes, sir. That would be a nice thought. And then, sir, if I'm not being too forward, perhaps you'd do us the honour of coming to visit us on our farm. We'd make you feel quite at home.'

Ringler smiled at him: 'The honour would be all mine, Monier. That's a firm date. I look forward to it.'

It had been, he knew, a futile reply and as he shook Monier's hand to wish him a pleasant goodnight, he wondered whether he would ever walk through the doorway of the little farmhouse and meet Monier's smiling children. In truth he did not really believe that any of them had much chance of getting out of this hellhole, let alone getting back to their loved ones. But he thought that at least perhaps with Monier he had behaved creditably. Like a proper officer, the sort of man he aspired to be.

Ringler dropped down into his foxhole and stretched out in its narrow space, placing his head on the bundle of blankets that he reserved for that purpose. The combination of schnapps, Italian wine and two bottles of the hijacked Löwenbräu had addled his mind and induced a welcome sleep. He pressed his head into the soft wool and began to drift off gently into the darkness.

Hardly, it seemed, had he closed his eyes however before his dreams of Germany were cut through with a violence that made him sit up, shaking. An explosion. A huge one and not, it seemed, too far away. Ringler sat, stunned on the floor of the trench. The bang was followed by another equally massive explosion and the world felt as if it was being blown to pieces around him. He looked directly upwards. Above his head and as far as he could see, the sky was lit by the most extraordinary glow. He peered cautiously out of the foxhole towards the Allied lines and saw a flickering line of light. The desert looked as if it was on fire, shuddering with flame along the length of its horizon. Each new explosion now seemed to course right through him.

His limbs began to tremble uncontrollably and then he noticed that the ground itself was shaking. Every bang smashed into his consciousness like a huge battering ram. Thudding, relentless, sudden, awful in its intensity. Looking up again he saw a single huge shell fly above his head, towards the rear of the German lines, whistling as it went, like some terrible iron firebrand. A shiver ran up his spine and it occurred to him that to manage this

67

the British must have countless batteries up there on their position opposite the lines. Countless batteries with which to hurl destruction at him and his comrades.

Monier came hurrying over to him, breathless and pouring sweat. He was wearing his helmet and carrying a slung MP38 machine-pistol. He crouched down at the edge of the trench.

'Lieutenant Ringler, sir. This must be it, don't you think so? The big one. The one we've been waiting for. They're going to attack.'

'I don't know, Monier. Let's not jump to conclusions.'

Quickly, Ringler pulled himself out of the trench and stood up beside Monier.

'But sir, look.'

He pointed and Ringler followed the line of his arm back towards the rear of the German lines. He could see nothing now but a sheet of flame punctuated by fresh explosions, every second it seemed. Sometimes two or three at the same moment.

'Oh, Christ in heaven! Yes, perhaps you're right. Maybe this is it.'

The two men stood transfixed by the sheer enormity of the cataclysmic destruction being wrought to their rear.

Monier spoke first: 'Poor devils, whoever's under that lot.'

'Just thank God it's not us Sar'nt-Major. Where's the signals section?'

Monier pointed to the left: 'Trench over there, sir. I've stood all the men to. As much of the battalion as I can find at least.'

'Well see if you can raise headquarters on the field telephone. Get the colonel. The adjutant. Get anyone. Find out if they have any idea what's going on. Then find the rest of the men. I'm going to find my company.'

*   *   *

68

Five hours later and with his head aching from the endless cacophony of exploding shells, Ringler looked out across the sand from the shelter of a slit trench in the Number Ten company position and noticed that the first light of morning was finally creeping up. The sky hung heavy with thick deposits of sulphur and cordite which cast a nauseous yellow tinge in the air and seemed, he thought, almost tangible, somehow slimy. It was as if some malicious God had wiped an open sore over the beauty of the world. At last the shelling ceased, although in the distance a low rumble indicated that the fighting was continuing and as the day dawned quickly he saw the sky change colour again until it was filled with a black-brown smokescreen that hung at a uniform height across the vast expanse of what overnight had become the battlefield. The smell though remained as it had been before, the unmistakable, sweet and suffocating stench of gunpowder. Acrid and stifling, it penetrated every orifice, reaching into the lungs until you wanted to retch.

At last the sun rose, casting a more healthy light on the smoke-hung horizon. Black plumes curled up from the desert, in particular from the areas containing the Fifteenth and Twenty-First Panzer Divisions and from the heavy artillery batteries. Those he presumed had been the Allies' major targets for their bombardment.

In his trench Ringler's number two, a young second lieutenant named Weber, younger even than he, threw up. Ringler had a quiet word with the boy.

'Hans, it may just be the fumes from the shelling. God knows I feel like puking myself, but we can't be too careful. We don't want more dysentery. Not after the last lot and certainly not at a time like this. Get it cleared up will you and then see if you can find the MO.'

He did not know where Doctor Müller was this morning. He had seen him in the night as he went from foxhole to foxhole, just making sure. It was just as well. Two of the men had become slightly delirious from the shellfire and were unable to move. It wasn't uncommon and Ringler had never seen such a barrage as that they had experienced last night. Rumours had come in all night thick and fast.

He had finally made contact with Battalion HQ at about two in the morning. Word was that this was the big attack they had been expecting and that they should all dig in and prepare themselves for the worst. It seemed bizarre to him that they had so far managed to avoid engaging the enemy. Nor, apart from the two cases of shellshock had they suffered any actual casualties.

For the rest of the night they had struggled to get any further information and Ringler was beginning to despair when he saw Monier coming up to their position. He was covered in dust and his red-rimmed eyes gave away the fact that he had been up all night travelling from company to company with a number of runners.

'Lieutenant, news from HQ. Staff has sent a message. Tommy's broken through in the northern sector. We're counter-attacking.'

'What about the south?'

'According to Staff an English armoured division's been blocked by the Italian paras. The Folgore. They're brave buggers, sir, for Eyeties. Almost good enough to be Germans.'

'Perhaps they've been picking up tips from us.'

Monier smiled: 'And the adjutant says to put plan C into operation, sir.'

'Plan C. He has to be joking. "Extra alertness"? Doesn't he think we might be alert enough after that lot Tommy threw at us last night?'

'There were planes too, sir. Thousands of them.'

'Yes, I heard them. You could hardly fail to.'

70

Weber was sick again. Ringler turned to him: 'Hans, I told you. Find Doctor Müller and for God's sake clean yourself up.' He turned back to Monier: 'Has anyone here had any breakfast yet?'

'There don't appear to be any rations here, sir.'

'No rations? Where the bloody hell are all the rations?'

Monier sneered: 'It seems that some were used at the colonel's party last night. Seems that it was thought that the lorry would replace them this morning. Only the lorry hasn't turned up on account of the British attack.'

'Yes. I see. Though how they expect us to fight Montgomery's army with empty bellies is beyond me. You and I will have to find something for the men to eat, Monier. There's no time to lose. We've no idea of when the British may attack this sector. And see if you can find something extra specially good, while you're about it. It may prove to be the last meal any of us ever have.'

EIGHT

10.40 p.m.
The start line
Samwell

From his position, lying flat on his stomach on the bare rock of the desert at the front of the company, Hugh Samwell had watched the line of white tape for two hours now as it fluttered in the night breeze. It marked the starting point for the attack and he knew that beyond that insignificant marker lay whatever fate had decreed for him. Life, death or something in between that had no name. A lifetime of agony and bitterness. The moon sat high in the sky and lit up the bleak expanse of sand, rock and scrub like daylight.

High above he could hear the hum of the Allied bombers as they flew towards the enemy positions. He was still watching the white tape and thinking about the content of his somewhat disappointing new book, when there was a crash as a single gun spoke and hurled a shell towards the enemy lines. A moment later it seemed to him that the very air itself had been ripped apart as hundreds more took up the refrain. The ground trembled and Samwell hugged himself closer to its heaving mass. Tentatively he raised his head and up in the night sky saw salvo after salvo of shells streaming out from behind the lines towards the enemy. Poor buggers, he thought instinctively. One infantryman thinking of another and thanking God that it was not he who was on the receiving end. Though Samwell knew their turn would come soon enough.

Away in the distance, where the shells and the carpet of bombs had struck home on their targets of minefields, defences and enemy guns, the line was lit up as if by a hundred bonfires. Samwell shuddered at the sight. He could almost feel the searing heat of the explosions and the fire and knew what it must be doing to the men. He knew too that soon they would be sharing the same fate. He did not have long to wait. Ten minutes later it began. He saw the flashes as the forward of the enemy guns opened up and then the shells came crashing in. Crump crump crump crump accompanied by the whizz overhead.

He felt curiously detached, as if he might be at a tattoo at Aldershot watching the performers as they beat out a martial tune, and men depicted in tableaux the Battle of the Alma and the defence of Hougoumont at Waterloo. The impression was amplified as the shells flew high over the infantrymen's heads and landed, he presumed, in the artillery at the rear. He could picture the scenes of havoc, the mangled guns and the wrecked bodies of the gunners; the cries of the wounded, the shouts of stretcher parties and orders barked by officers desperate to keep their batteries firing, mingling in a cacophony. Counter-battery fire was a particularly costly and bloody affair.

He was aware of lulls in the barrage on both sides, as if it were some strange symphony rising in crescendo and dying away again. Then something changed. Another shell passed overhead, but lower now. And then another, and a third so low that instinctively he ducked, although it must have been twenty yards above his head. He watched for the burst and saw it, perhaps two hundred yards in front. He knew what this meant. The guns had switched their targets from the enemy's rear, the enemy batteries, to the forward positions.

He knew what it signified: prepare to advance; a prearranged signal. Suddenly his mouth became quite dry. But curiously the rest of his body was quite cool. Cold as ice in fact. He looked at his watch, flipping back the leather cover which protected it: 9.52. Three minutes to H Hour. He wondered whether the pipers really would play as they advanced. Perhaps the story was just another morale-booster. If they did play though then that would surely be the greatest boost to the mens' morale.

He shifted on his stomach and almost without realizing what he was doing, in a semi-trance, stood up, pushing into the sand with the long ash walking stick which he had intended to leave in the rear at Company HQ. Suddenly the night sky, already made luminous by the brilliant moon, was lit up. Two searchlight beams touched the heavens, intersecting high over his head in the form of a cross; a St Andrew's Cross, thought Samwell, the saltire of Scotland. It was a good omen. He knew that the whole Division, Fifty-First Highland, high up on the right flank of the army, must see them now. Monty had chosen the Scots for a key role. To break through the line and create a corridor for First Armoured. Samwell knew that if they should fail the tanks would be held up and the whole plan would stall.

Now, without thinking, he began to walk forward, trying to gauge the precise pace as prescribed: seventy-five yards a minute. He looked to his right and saw a line of men, stretching out until they vanished into the night. Without knowing exactly where his men were he shouted towards the rear: 'Advance, with me. Forward!'

Then he heard it. Long, low and unmistakable. The sound of the bagpipe. It drifted at him across the night and then rose in crescendo as others joined in. Samwell's heart began to beat faster and he suddenly seemed taller, fitter. He felt a tremendous surge of pride. Pride in the regiment. Proud of the tradition. Proud of what they were doing here and utterly invincible.

He listened to the tune. The regimental march, 'The Campbells are coming'. His stride lengthened and he looked right and left and saw the effect the music was having on the men alongside him. The tune now was 'Hieland Laddie'.

Another man appeared, an officer. Samwell wasn't sure who it was, but he noticed that he had a megaphone and was shouting through it at the men: 'Keep up there! You there on the left. That man. Straighten the line.'

Samwell turned to his left and found his batman, Baynes, who was walking alongside, just as if they might have been out for a morning's constitutional. 'Baynes, run down the line. Tell Sar'nt Dawson to keep his direction by marking from the right. From the right, Baynes. Got it?'

Baynes nodded and sped off. Samwell walked on and as he did, just as he might have when out walking a Highland road, led with the tip of his walking stick. He looked down at it. What the devil was he doing with that in his hand? With a chill he realized that rather than the rifle he had intended to collect from CHQ he was now advancing against the enemy armed only with a .38 revolver and a stout ash stick. He smiled to himself. Then he thought that soon someone was bound to be hit, killed or wounded and he would be able to borrow their rifle. Who would it be he wondered? Which of the men he had come to respect and admire? Perhaps it might even be him. Well, they would know soon enough.

As if in answer, a new sound began which had a higher pitch than the whining of the shells and the explosions. It was a tighter, sharper noise yet still unmistakably that of a gun. A machine-gun; a Spandau, he guessed, or perhaps a Breda. Whatever it was, it was about to make contact with his men. As the thought left him he saw the streams of tracer bullets tearing diagonally towards them through the moonlight.

He turned to the man on his right, the pace-checker whose job it was to count the number of paces forward the company had taken from the start position. The man looked at him, his face lit up by the moonlight, and Samwell saw that he was grinning.

'How many paces, Roberts?'

'Dunno, sir. Lost count we've done that many. Good, innit? Like bleeding Bonfire Night, sir.'

Hardly had the words left his lips when another note was added to the symphony of shells and bullets around them. Crump. Crump crump crump. Mortars! Christ, he thought. They've zeroed in on us. Bastards. Mortars. And as he thought the words the bombs began to land among them, exploding and sending their deadly shards of shrapnel in all directions at anything from head to waist height. There was a loud crash to his left and Samwell heard a moan: 'Oh God.'

He looked across and saw one of the men tumble to the ground. The officer was shouting again through his megaphone. Samwell strained to hear his words above the din and failed. He turned to his front and in the moonlight and flashes of explosions saw a wire ahead of him. It was only a single strand and stretched out at about waist height. Without thinking he rushed towards it and jumped, as he might have once done at Glenalmond, jumping the wire and winning for the house. He rose in the air and sensed that his trailing foot had just cleared the wire. The earth came up to meet him and he managed to his own surprise to land on two feet without breaking anything. He looked behind and saw his sergeant, Perkins, negotiating the obstacle in his own way. The man was built like an ox, all muscle and no room for agility. He looked at the wire and gingerly put one leg over the top. He was just placing his weight down on the leg when Samwell suddenly realized what was going on. This wasn't just barbed wire. A single strand: *Booby trap*.

He opened his mouth to shout to Perkins but at that instant the air was split by a massive explosion as the hem of the sergeant's shorts snagged on the wire. As the explosion caught him, Samwell instinctively turned away and a huge rush of air buffeted him on the back of the neck. In the instant though he was aware briefly of the outline of a man or what at that moment had ceased to be a man, disintegrating as Sergeant Perkins was blown to atoms. As the air cleared, he turned to the men coming on behind him and yelled, all too late. 'Booby Traps!'

He carried on walking and wondered what it had been that had driven him to jump the wire. He had not been thinking of booby traps. He was suddenly aware that all the men around him were running. For an instant he wondered why. He could not remember hearing anyone giving the order. No matter. He quickened his pace and was soon running in time with the men. His body seemed alive with the thrill of the moment, adrenalin pumping. His mind, his whole being, was curiously euphoric. Fear gone, he charged on and was aware that he was screaming at the enemy. He knew that his side would win. He grinned hugely and looked right and left as he ran on. Turning further to his left he was aware of a man, Corporal Sykes he thought it was, running alongside him, and equally caught up in the moment. The man was laughing as he fired a Bren gun from his hip and Samwell could see his mouth was wide open and he was shouting, though no words were audible. Samwell wondered if he were aiming at anything or just 'firing into the brown'.

He looked to his front towards where the Bren rounds were hitting the desert rock and sending lethal shards flying in all directions.

Then as he ran, he saw a head protruding from the ground. For a moment he thought it might have been blown off a body. But then he saw that it wore a hat, a flat peaked cap of the Afrika Korps and that its eyes were wide and blinking. Unable to slow down he ran straight past it and as he passed saw that it was attached to the shoulders of a man crouching in a shallow foxhole. By God, they had reached the enemy without even knowing it! Trying to stop, he turned halfway round and almost collided with the bayonet of the soldier running directly behind him. Samwell raised his revolver and catching sight again of the head, loosed off three rounds towards it. Then he turned back to the front and ran on.

Christ, he thought. Did I hit him? Did I kill him? The worry did not last for long as once again he was caught up in the headlong charge. He noticed that he had drawn level with Baynes once again. Where Corporal Sykes had got to God only knew. His runner, a biddable lad called Brooks had also disappeared. He continued to run and suddenly saw directly ahead a line of men standing in a slit trench. They all had their hands above their heads and were clad in an assortment of ill-fitting desert-coloured uniforms. They were dirty and ill-shaven and would have been on a charge had they been in his company. He laughed and wondered what sort of bizarre training formula had put such a thought into his head at such a moment?

They were yelling at him: 'Mardray! Mardray!'

Samwell wondered what the hell it meant. Mother? What did it matter. He pulled up and waved his pistol at the men in the trench. He could see now that they were Italians. He motioned to the left with his weapon indicating that they should join the group of prisoners being collected by an NCO, Sergeant McCaig of B Company. They scrambled out of the trench but one of them, clearly terrified beyond reason, began to run round in circles with his hands on his head, screaming. Samwell started to yell to a corporal to grab hold of him and then someone, Sergeant Hawkins he thought it was, shouted: 'Watch out!'

There was a sharp blow on the toe of his boot and Samwell was aware of an object bouncing off his foot and to the rear. And then whatever it had been exploded. Dazed, he staggered backwards and instinctively placed a hand across his eyes.

For a moment he began to wobble unsteadily on his feet. Oh God, he thought, I've lost a leg and am being kept up by the shock. Drawing his arm away he looked down and saw nothing unusual. Both legs were still intact and unscathed. He noticed he was shaking. Instantly he wondered who had been hit and looking to where McCaig had been rounding up the Italians saw him stretched out on the ground. A big man, he was lying on his back and groaning. Samwell felt a chill run through him. He had always admired McCaig, a big tough bear of a man with leathery skin and a wide smile. But his voice now betrayed the inner child.

'Mother, Mother. Help me, God. Help me, Mother. Mammy.'

Samwell felt sickened. A grown man reduced to an infant. The cause of his distress was all too evident: where his right leg had been was now a mess of flesh and blood and bone. Samwell knew now what had happened. One of the men in the trench had thrown a grenade as he had pretended to surrender. That had been what had bounced off his boot and on to the unlucky sergeant. He thanked God for his luck and at the same time felt guilty that McCaig should have taken the hit.

Within a second though his regret had been replaced

by anger. A red rage surged over him and he ran across to the edge of the trench. Three of the Italians were still inside and without thinking he levelled his revolver and began to fire into them. Two shots hit home and they screamed and then, when he pressed the trigger again there was an empty click.

'Bugger!' He had forgotten to reload. Throwing his pistol away, he picked up McCaig's rifle which had been blown to the ground, and jumped into the trench. The two men he had hit with the revolver were lying on the floor. One of them was moaning. Two other Italians lay against its sides staring wildly at him. Without thinking Samwell rushed towards them and buried the long bayonet attached to the sergeant's rifle deep in the belly of one. He felt it go in, twisted it and stared into the eyes of the Italian. Saw his anguish and felt nothing but hate. He pulled out the blade and moved to the other man. He was crouching now, in the corner of the trench, his hands in the air. Samwell lunged and as he did so the man muttered something: 'Madre Madre'. The steel shaft slipped upwards through his throat.

Then, as quickly as he had jumped in Samwell climbed out and laying McCaig's weapon on the ground, looked for his pistol. The red mist had subsided now, but a rage still burned in his heart. Stupid to have thrown his gun down, he thought. What the hell would the quartermaster say when he turned up back at Company HQ without it? It occurred to him that he had also lost his walking stick. He cursed. He loved that stick. It reminded him of home. He remembered buying it in Glasgow three years earlier. He had taken it everywhere, even to the picture house in Stirling where he had left it under a seat after he and Klara had been to see a film. *Waterloo Bridge* it had been, with Robert Taylor and Vivien Leigh, a soppy story about a British officer who falls for a dancer. Klara had liked it. The two of them had had to disturb the whole row to get his stick back. She'd been furious then at the embarrassment but had forgiven him later. He thought of her again and wondered what she would be doing at that precise moment. Sleeping perhaps, or tidying the house before going to bed. Then he realized that he had still not yet found the revolver and her face faded from his mind.

He stopped searching and was aware that the advance had halted, for the moment and in this sector at least. Groups of Highland infantry were assembling around him, eager to attach themselves to an officer. He looked about and saw familiar faces and strangers from other companies. It seemed to him that he must be the only officer among perhaps eighty men. He was still looking at them when there was a shout.

'Sir!'

It was followed almost instantly by the crack of a rifle. Samwell turned to follow the direction of the bullet and found himself looking back into the slit trench at the body of an Italian. The man he had wounded had dragged himself to the parapet and judging from his position and the rifle in his hands had been about to shoot him when one of the men had spotted him and taken him out with the single round that had made a neat hole in his forehead and the messy exit wound that was all that was left of what had been the back of his skull.

Banishing the thought Samwell saw that the men were looking at him expectantly and pulled himself back to his remembered orders: 'Consolidate the position for fifteen minutes then move on.'

That was the company order, but where he wondered was Company HQ or for that matter his company commander? They had agreed that he should bring up Company HQ with the reserve platoon with Samwell as second-in-command up front with the others.

'Follow me.' Instinctively, the men trailing behind, he turned and began to retrace his steps in search of the HQ.

Suddenly the night air was rent by a series of explosions. He counted four shells and stood still, then looked down and knew that he hadn't been hurt. He was covered in sand. He brushed himself down and walked on. A shape appeared on the ground and for an instant he raised McCaig's rifle which he had picked up again after his fruitless search for the revolver. But then he recognized the man, Colin Mackay, the highly-strung Company CO, who was sitting on the ground with the wireless receiver pressed to his left ear.

'Hello. Battalion HQ. Can you read me? Say again. Come in Battalion. Copy that.'

Samwell spoke: 'Sir. We've achieved the objective, taken several trenches and a good number of prisoners. Perhaps a couple of dozen. Mostly Eyeties. But we've taken casualties, sir.'

Mackay ignored him: 'Hello. Battalion. Come in. Respond damn you. For Christ's sake, will you come in. Respond, Battalion. Say again.'

Samwell tried again: 'Sir. We've made the objective. We have prisoners, sir.'

At that moment Samwell was surprised to see the Battalion Commanding Officer Colonel Anderson walking towards them: 'Hugh. Good to see you. You've done well. Ah, Colin.'

Instantly the major looked up and like some dog whose master, having ignored it, deigns to cast a glance, leapt up from the sand and moved towards the CO.

'Sir. I was trying to get through to you. Thank God you're here.' At last Mackay saw Samwell: 'Ah, Hugh. Good you're here.' He turned back to the colonel: 'We're doing well, sir. First objective taken and a number of prisoners. Anything to report, Hugh?'

'Just that, sir.' Samwell turned to the colonel: 'Sir, give me the reserve platoon and I'm sure that I can make more ground. I'll detail the right forward platoon to drop into reserve.'

Anderson thought for a moment: 'Very well, Hugh. Take them and see what you can do.' In the moonlit confusion Samwell managed to locate the reserve platoon and called them forward then together they advanced.

They were directly behind the forward platoons now, the men who had taken the brunt of the initial fighting and as Samwell looked on he saw stretcher parties weaving their hazardous way back through the advancing infantry and the wire. He wondered for an instant how he had got there and was aware as he had not been before of his legs working independently. Then he heard a noise. The other company's piper had started to play again and he wondered what had happened to their own, Jock Macpherson.

He turned to the left and found his new runner, a boy from Greenock named White. 'Get back to HQ and see what on earth's happened to our piper, will you?'

The runner sped off without question, happy to be heading back. Again he was conscious of walking forward but as he went, there was a sudden whine and a terrific explosion to his right as a shell came in. Men began to shriek and he called out instinctively: 'Stretcher-bearer!' Another deafening sickly crump and more shells began to fall. Two more of the boys were down, White one of them, his skull bisected by a gigantic piece of shrapnel. The platoon continued to walk forward and as they did so Samwell became aware of a strange sensation. The shells which were falling around them were coming not only from the front, but also from the rear. They were advancing steadily into their own barrage. A shell landed too close for comfort, not thirty yards in front of him.

At that moment the commander of the furthest left platoon of the company deployed on his right came up, a lanky lieutenant named Mitchell who two years before had been full back for Fettes' first XV.

'Samwell. Don't you think we're going too fast? Those are our shells aren't they?'

'You're right. We should stop.'

'Yes. I'll go and warn Major Murray.'

The boy ran off back to the right and Samwell watched as he spoke to the major who shook his head, evidently disapproving of their suggestion. They continued to advance and now their own shells were falling closer still. Samwell walked across to the company commander and looked at him in despair. Samwell spoke above the noise of battle: 'Sir, we really should stop or at least slow down. Those are our shells.'

As he spoke more shells whizzed over their heads and landed not more than ten yards ahead of them. All three men cowered to protect themselves from the blast but it caught them nevertheless. They straightened up and the major nodded: 'Yes, Lieutenant. I think we should stop.'

Samwell hurried back to the left to his own platoon and found Sergeant Dawson. 'We'll halt here. Those are our shells. Pull the men back a few yards and get out of danger.'

The man nodded: 'Sir.'

'And Sar'nt, get word back to Major Mackay will you? Ask him to come up closer. Within the fifty yards.'

Samwell wondered where Company HQ had gone to. It seemed to have lost itself beyond the statutory fifty-yard gap between forward platoons.

Within minutes Dawson reappeared. 'Sir, can't find Major Mackay, sir, or the HQ. Reserve platoon's gone AWOL too, sir.'

Samwell cursed to himself. Had he taken a wrong

turning in this damned desert? His mind was addled and he looked across to the right to C Company only to see that they had begun to advance again and were now some fifty yards ahead. He realized that their own barrage had lifted. The men were disappearing into the night and he wondered why Mackay and the young lieutenant had not troubled to warn him that they were about to restart the advance. Now he and his depleted platoon were left alone out in the 'blue', as the old desert hands called it. Just him and forty men in the middle of nowhere. He turned to Dawson: 'Stay here. I'm going to see what's happening on the left.'

His company had been placed on the farthest left of the Argyll's line of advance and darting between the wire and the bodies, Samwell ran low across to the left where another regiment, Seventh Black Watch, was advancing. But of them there was no sign. Not a man, save the dead and a party of stretcher-bearers. Christ almighty, he thought, we're completely isolated. He ran back to the sergeant: 'We're on our own. The forty-second have buggered off somewhere and C Company's gone ahead.'

'Right, sir. What are your orders?'

For a moment or two he was unable to speak. An unexpected and novel wave of terror swept through him, nauseating and paralysing. He was alone. The company commander and HQ had gone along with the wireless and the 'pilot' officer. Slowly he began to try to calm down. His palms were sweating. Instinct told him that he had simply gone over too far to the left. He realized that they had continued to advance while he had been deliberating and quickly started to swing to the right. 'Sar'nt Dawson. Wheel towards the right.'

Again fear overtook him. Not the fear of being blown to atoms by one of the shells, which were coming in hard now from the enemy guns, but a fear of being left alone

85

here, cut off from the battalion. Ahead of him another strongpoint loomed up in the moonlight, illuminated by the flash of the constant explosions. Samwell yelled across to Dawson: 'Sar'nt, secure that position. Take those men prisoner.'

'They're getting away to the left flank, sir, along the trenches.'

Samwell had to make a decision. Pursue the Italians left along the trench across a battalion front, or continue on to his objective. There was no choice: 'Leave them, Sar'nt. We'll mop up later. Better to get on.'

They began to advance again and Samwell was beginning to wonder if they would ever find the other platoons when there was a shout from his rear: 'Hoi there, Lieutenant!' He turned to see the battalion adjutant, the second-in-command, Jamie Maclachlan. He called again: 'Samwell! Hugh! What the devil are you doing here? Where's C Company? And where are the Black Watch?'

Samwell saw that with Maclachlan were the men of his own Company HQ. A surge of relief replaced the fear. 'Sir. Good to see you. Wondered where you'd all got to.'

'Don't ask. Just after you began to advance your Company HQ took a direct hit. Major Mackay was hit. Quite bad and the signals have copped it. You'd best carry on here. Looks as if you've done well.' And with that he was gone.

Samwell looked around himself. Of the original men who had come with him he could find few. There was Baynes, his batman, and Dawson. And perhaps eight more men from the original platoon in his immediate vicinity. The reserve platoon commander came trotting up, a keen-faced, wide-eyed young lieutenant named McGlashan. 'Samwell. Seems we're still too far to the left. We've been ordered to wheel half-right.'

Samwell found his sergeant: 'Turn the men half-right, we're drifting to the left. Come on.'

Again they set off across the sand and within a few minutes a burst of automatic fire told them they had stumbled upon another enemy position. Dawson pulled the pin from a grenade and threw it into the foxhole. It exploded on target and a few moments later four Italians crawled out of the hole, their hands raised. Two of Samwell's men took them prisoner at bayonet-point, but from the corner of his eye he saw two more Italians running away across the sand towards their left. 'Leave them, Sar'nt. We need to stay together.'

After another three hundred yards he stopped and turned to his opposite number. 'McGlashan, I think we should dig in.'

It was clear that they had taken the enemy's front line of trenches. 'This looks like it must be the objective. Can we raise Battalion on the wireless?'

The men began to entrench and the reserve company signaller gave a shout: 'Mister Samwell, sir. I've got HQ.'

'Tell them we're in position.'

McGlashan went off to reconnoitre and a few minutes later returned. 'Looks like the other forward company's dug in about two hundred yards to our right. This must be the place.'

Samwell felt huge relief, almost elation that his instinct had been correct. He smiled: 'Right, let's get this place secure. Then I think we all deserve a rest, McGlashan, don't you?'

Saturday 24 October

NINE

1.45 a.m.
West of Alamein Station
Miller

The night was a vision of hell. A moonlit wasteland in which every few seconds another explosion would crack the heavens and send an intense light across the low horizon. Ahead of them in the west a continuous line of flame marked the destructive power of the barrage. Dust flew up from their wheels as they attempted to negotiate their way through the columns of Bren carriers and trucks filled with infantry that moved constantly along the track through the minefield. Moon Track, closest of the four arteries in and out of the killing zone to the railway line, was busy tonight. Lieutenant Thomas was driving, riding as the spare for his friend their section sergeant, Brook Cuddy, another Harvard man, a writer, and Miller prayed that God would guide his hand. But right now Thomas was getting jumpy. He moved the wheel hard and shrieked.

'Holy shit! These damn Limey tank drivers need a refresher course. I almost hit that one. Jeeze, Brook.'

Cuddy shook his head: 'I could drive if you'd like, Evan.'

'I volunteered to take a shift and I'll keep my word. And Brook, please try not to call me Evan. Lieutenant or

90

just plain sir would do nicely. Shit, who's driving that thing?'

He swerved again to avoid an erratic Bren carrier packed with riflemen.

'Ok . . . sir. But can I suggest that you keep your eyes on the road and your mind on the job. It would be a pity to kill us all before we have a chance to get those poor guys out.'

They had been called for at 1.30. A section of five Dodge ambulance cars ordered up to the 24th Battalion Regimental Aid Post or in military-speak RAP, as Miller had quickly learned to call it. Everything in the British army it seemed was abbreviated into an acronym. The diner was a NAAFI, high explosive HE, rendezvous was RV and of course killed in action KIA. They were looking for a truck; that was what the RAP would be, a single truck loaded with wounded men. Miller sat in the middle front seat of the Dodge and stared hard into the night, straining for a sign. Thomas sounded the horn and without warning dropped off the road to the left.

Cuddy yelled: 'Christ, Evan! Not down there. That's a damn minefield. We'll all be blown to hell.'

Having circumnavigated a huge Sherman tank Thomas swerved back on to the road and Miller let out a sigh of relief. 'I concur with Sergeant Cuddy, Lieutenant. Please try and get us there in one piece.'

'Shut up, Josh, and keep looking. The damn RAP has to be here somewhere.' As Thomas spoke Miller spotted their target. A Bedford truck with a painted red cross on the side and a tent attached: 'There it is, sir. Just there.'

Thomas brought the Dodge to a dusty halt and the men leaped out. Behind them the four other vehicles detailed for the mission stopped in turn and the platoon spilled out.

Thomas found the MO, a kindly-looking New Zealand

91

major named Coswell. 'Sir, Lieutenant Thomas AFS. We'll take your men now.'

'Thank God you're here, Lieutenant. We're filling up faster than we can get 'em out.'

Together Miller and the others carried the wounded men to the Dodges. Most seemed to have been hit in the limbs; one though had a dreadful stomach wound and another had clearly been shot through the lungs. His gurgling, gasping breath reached into Miller's deepest terrors. He laid the man gently on one of the stretcher-carriers inside the lead vehicle and turned back for the next casualty. Within ten minutes they had the front three ambulances loaded up. Thomas turned to Miller: OK, Josh. Find Sergeant Cuddy, would you. I think we can rest here until more of these poor boys come in. Then we'll all leave together. Safer that way.'

But Miller had not really heard the words. He was too busy looking at the man who was running towards them. He was a New Zealand army officer, clearly a padre by the dog collar on his battledress and the expression on his face spoke volumes. Miller tapped Thomas on the shoulder and pointed.

'With respect, sir, I don't think that's an optio n. Look.'

As Thomas saw him the padre spoke: 'Oh thank heavens. You AFS?'

Thomas nodded. 'That's us, Reverend.'

'D'you have any room in your cars? We've got a lot of wounded men a few hundred yards away to the west. With the Twenty-Fifth Battalion, up on the ridge. They've been shot up real bad. They need your help. There's wounded men all over the place. All over.' Miller could see the distress, heard it in his shaking voice.

Thomas nodded: 'OK, Padre. I hear you. We're with you. Right, Miller, you're the second-best driver I've got. You too, Turk. Get into the two rear wagons. We're going to help.'

Remembering his training at El Tahag with the army ambulance corps, Miller double-declutched and the vehicle sprang forward. A few hundred yards to the west. What did that mean? To the west. Directly into the enemy lines. He wondered how far it really was. For a few terrifying minutes he followed Thomas's car along the track without any problem. McGinty was riding spare and tucked in behind him was Bigelow.

Again the trucks wove their way through the advancing tanks and Bren carriers, although this time there were fewer and as they went on Miller noticed that more and more were destroyed. They passed the burning hulk of a Sherman tank that had clearly taken a direct hit. Something was hanging out of the turret and it was only as they drove past that Miller realized that it was all that was left of the tank commander. It took a moment for the fact to sink in; the fact that this ghastly charred corpse had until recently been a man. Miller turned his head to stare at the cadaver, the first he had seen, then turned back to the road. He felt chilled but curiously not as shocked as he had thought he might. There was something natural about it. It was after all he reasoned what most of the thousands of men in their lines of battle stretching across the desert were here to do. They were killers and this was a place of death.

McGinty looked out of the window at the advancing infantry. 'You've got to admire them, Josh. Thousands of miles away from home and they're walking right into hell up there.'

Bigelow spoke up from the rear: 'Has it occurred to you that we're also thousands of miles away from home and that as we're driving into hell rather than walking there like them, we're highly likely to get there first?'

McGinty glared at him. Miller spoke: 'Look, I'm trying to drive this damn thing without crashing it and it would help if you two jokers would just shut the hell up.'

McGinty spoke: 'Aw, fuck it.'

'What?'

'You see that tape, Josh?'

'Sure I do.'

'Yeah. Like sure you do, now. Well it like marks the edge of a minefield. A British one I'm guessing. And we've just gone through it.'

Miller swerved back towards the road. 'Oh shit.'

He slowed down and pulled at the steering wheel, propelling them back on to the road and directly into the path of an oncoming British tank.

'Christ almighty, Miller!'

He turned the wheel again and ended up at an angle on the shallow bank between the track and the minefield. The tank rumbled past.

Bigelow spoke: 'Nobody said anything about minefields.'

'Weren't you listening at that big briefing meeting? Lieutenant Edwards told us, Prof? We go through British minefields. Then there's a gap where there's no mines. Then we hit the German minefields. Simple.'

'I missed the meeting. I had an appointment with the MO. A running sore on my leg.'

Miller spoke: 'Listen, we just go where we're told. Keep a good lookout, Prof, will you. We're on a marked track but we're still crossing a minefield.'

It was half an hour before they reached the other side of what had been no-man's-land and a few minutes later Miller was aware that once again they were passing slit trenches. There were dark forms in many of them and he knew that they would be the bodies of Italian and German dead. And more than a few Kiwis.

McGinty spoke: 'Where are we now, Josh?'

'German minefield. See the signs?'

McGinty saw them. Stakes with wooden crossboards

94

bearing a black skull and crossbones and the legend *Achtung Minen*.

'As long as I follow the lieutenant's car we'll be fine.'

'And if he gets it?'

'If he gets it I slam on the brakes and pray I'm not too late.'

They were climbing a hill now, and Miller felt the engine labouring slightly. He trusted that they would make it: 'They're on the other side of this minefield. Only a few yards more and we're clear. If they can do it then so can we . . .'

He was cut short by the spectacle which greeted them as the moon revealed the full extent of the task ahead. The ridge before them climbed up steeply. And it was covered in men. The pale waxy white light of the moon lit the scene like some theatrical tableau through the haze of dust. Miller looked around and took in the minutiae of the extraordinary image. He could hear but as yet could not actually see the fighting. What he could see though on his side of the ridge were long lines of the new American-built Sherman tanks crossing the lower slopes of the hill and directly ahead of them, pitifully small in the vastness, dozens of two-man teams of sappers armed with the new mine detectors, patiently clearing a path as if they were out for a Sunday stroll.

McGinty saw them too: 'Now those are really brave guys, Miller. Wouldn't you say? I mean, how brave d'you have to be to do that?'

'Pretty damn brave I guess.'

Bigelow spoke: 'Very difficult I should imagine, burying a mine in this desert. You know the sand is not at all easy. Very unyielding. You'd need to cut through rock to do it.'

'Thanks, Prof. I know geology's your bag. I'm sure that'll be some consolation to the guys out there. How many mines do they reckon Rommel has?'

Miller answered: 'Somewhere about 500,000. But it could be more.'

McGinty whistled: 'Whoo! These guys have got a real job ahead of them. Rather them than me. Let's get through here, Miller. I could do with a . . .'

His words were cut short by a huge explosion and all three men stared in horror at all that was left of one of the sapper teams which had been clearing the minefield.

Miller stood on the brakes, instinctively, and stared towards where the men had been and saw nothing. Then as the smoke cleared his gaze met pools of dark gore and a few body parts which were all that were left of one of the team. The other dead man lay a little way off, but he had been kneeling over the mine with his bayonet when it had gone off and Miller could see that the body was headless. He turned back and shifted gear.

'There's nothing we can do for them now. Let's get up on the ridge. I guess they need us up there.'

Quickly and without waiting to consider the consequences, he drove on through the last few yards of the minefield, acutely aware that at any moment they might be blown to kingdom come. The others said nothing. But within a few minutes they had reached the wire which marked its limits. They were climbing steadily now, passing yet more abandoned gun pits which marked the enemy's original position. Bodies lay slumped in various skewed and unnatural postures across the sandbags. Small-arms fire resounded along the far side of the ridge, punctuated by the distinctive rat-a-tat-tat of German Spandau machine-guns.

McGinty spoke: 'The Krauts are well dug-in over there by the sound of it.'

They had almost reached the crest of the ridge by now. There were British infantrymen everywhere, all of them carrying rifles and in varying states of activity and torpor.

So this is what a battle really looks like, thought Miller. No glory of course. He had not expected any. But neither had he expected the bewilderment he now witnessed. While some men were kneeling, firing into the moonlit darkness, others, clearly overcome by the experience, were merely standing there, directionless or confused. He saw one man with his head on one side staring vacantly at a German corpse.

Miller stopped the Dodge and jumped out. Thomas had halted directly in front of them and looked puzzled. 'Josh. Have you noticed anything? Where the hell are all their officers?'

As if in answer a young captain appeared through the dust. Thomas saluted in his typically relaxed way, awaiting the usual rebuke, but the officer was too tired even to respond. For a moment the young man just stared at them. Thomas tried to make himself heard above the sounds of battle coming from the other side of the ridge.

'Sir. Captain. We're American, AFS. Ambulance drivers, sir. We'd be glad to evacuate as many of your wounded as we can carry in our ambulances.'

The man stared at him for a moment more before finally speaking. 'Ambulances? Ambulances. Ah, yes. Well I'm afraid we haven't had time to collect the wounded yet. You see we've been a bit tied up. Could you see to it? I'm sorry. Captain Horrell, Twenty-Sixth New Zealand Battalion. Would you mind? I can send you over a guide. You'd better hurry up though and get those ambulances away from here. You'll be hit, you know. There's a bit of a battle going on over the ridge.'

Miller stared at his face and saw the classic signs of extreme fatigue. He sounded like a man who had just run a hard race and was desperately trying to reacquaint himself with his surroundings. It was the first time he had seen real battle fatigue and it told its own story.

Thomas turned to Miller: 'OK, let's move it. Come on, Josh, get Turk and the others. Looks like we're going to have to do this ourselves. See if you can find any of the Kiwi stretcher-bearers. Perhaps they could help.'

Miller began to look around the ridge. Every few paces or so he could see a hump on the landscape, no more in fact than a pile of dead or wounded men. Slowly he and Turk began to investigate them, moving from body to body, checking for signs of life.

Amid the dead and wounded two men were sitting on the sand. They were two of the battalion's stretcher-bearers. They sat at opposite ends of their stretcher and stared blankly at the man lying on it. Half a man really. Miller wondered how on earth they had managed to get his mangled body on there in the first place. A piece of shrapnel had cut him from the right shoulder downwards, taking off his arm and penetrating his left side. He was quite dead. Both men were covered in blood, evidently not their own.

Miller spoke gently to one of them: 'Could you give us a hand, Buddy? We're trying to get some of your guys into our trucks.'

Neither man replied. It was as if they hadn't noticed him. Then one of them suddenly seemed to snap out of his trance of exhaustion. 'Sure, mate. C'mon, Jim, you heard the Yank. The lieutenant here's a gonner anyway.'

Miller looked at the corpse and noticed the single pip on its right shoulder. He was no more than a boy, he thought, perhaps the same age as him. In death he wore a fixed smile, as if surprised at what had taken him away. The two stretcher-bearers carefully rolled their stretcher on to its side so that the body fell gracefully on to the sand. One of them laid a tin hat over the boy's face then he picked up the bloody stretcher and followed Miller and the others. Together the four of them went across to one of the lumps. The man was still alive and as he saw them he smiled: 'Oh, thank God, mate. I thought I'd be left here with the others.'

Miller saw that he was a private. He had been shot in the leg. There was a small entry wound and a large gaping exit. He reached into his haversack and pulled out a field dressing. Carefully he straightened the injured limb and wrapped the gauze around it.

'You're gonna be OK now, chum. It's not so bad.'

The man looked at him: 'American?'

Miller nodded.

'Thank God you guys are here.'

'Oh, there's more of us coming. Lots more. An army. That's what we've heard.'

The man laughed: 'Great. But just don't you beat us to Tripoli. Two bloody years we've taken to get there. You're not going to steal our glory now. Did that before, in the last war. My old man told me that. Came in at the end and took all the bloody glory. No offence, mate. You see, once Monty's won this scrap, we'll chase Rommel right up the coast. Take your time, Yank. Just make sure we're first through the gate.'

Miller laughed and finished securing the bandage. Then together he and Turk laid the man on the stretcher. Bending down to take the strain, the two New Zealanders lifted it up and began to walk slowly down the ridge towards the waiting Dodges. Turk spoke: 'One down, how many more d'you reckon we can take?' He paused, then said, 'I tell you something, Josh, this is weird. I've never seen soldiers behaving like that. Not wanting to help out. Ones I've met have always been ready to help their mates.'

Miller nodded: 'Yeah. I was thinking the same thing and I reckon I know what it is. We've come here too soon. They're still in shock. They're fired up. They've just taken their objective and they're all punch-drunk. Bomb-happy. Call it what you like. Look at them.'

It was true. Both men looked around. Everywhere on this side of the ridge men were standing staring or crouching down, or doubled over in sheer exhaustion. Several were in tears.

They were still staring when they heard Thomas's voice yelling: 'Miller, Turk! Move your asses over here and give me a hand.'

They found Thomas leaning over a wounded corporal lying on a stretcher. Another boy, thought Miller. Younger even. The man's left arm had been all but blown off and was hanging by the thinnest strips of flesh. His face was deathly white. Thomas knelt down close to the boy's head: 'Say again, son.'

'We've taken the second objective, sir, haven't we?'

'Yeah, Buddy. You've done well. You took the hill. The Krauts are running. And you don't have to call me sir. I'm a volunteer. A Yank.'

The boy looked confused: 'But your pips, sir. Your hat.'

'I told you, son. I'm just a Yank. Now try to relax while we lift you. OK?' He turned to Turk and Miller: 'OK guys, let's get him in the truck.'

They were about to lift the stretcher when shells began to scream over their heads. Miller looked up: 'Christ, sir. Those are Jerry shells. They're incoming.'

'Get down. Hit the deck.'

Instinctively, they fell over the corporal, conscious that their bodies might shield him. Another salvo flew over-head and then they heard nothing save the crump of the mortars and the rattle of the machine-guns and rifles further down the far side of the ridge.

Miller raised his head and looked down the slope. The Dodges appeared to be intact, but all around them was evidence of shellbursts; craters and plumes of black smoke.

100

Fires had broken out too and bodies were scattered around the foot of the slope.

A New Zealand sergeant appeared through the smoke. 'Who the hell are you?' Then, seeing Thomas: 'Oh sorry, sir, didn't see you. Have you seen anyone from B Company? Captain Horrell wants them to extend to the flank. Seems the Twenty-Sixth haven't crossed the ridge and the flank's left wide open. Jerry could come up any time.'

Thomas shook his head: 'I'm sorry, Sergeant. We're just ambulance men. Yanks. And I've no idea where your B Company is.'

For the first time in his life Miller felt absolutely powerless and sensed an unexpected urge to do something positive. He actually wanted to be able to take some men and defend the exposed flank, to help win this battle against the Germans. For a moment he felt elated, then deeply shamed. This was not at all what he had expected. He had come here because of his sworn intent not to kill anyone. He was a pacifist, he wanted to help save lives. So why then did he now feel the urge to pick up a rifle and help the New Zealanders? It might have something to do with everything that he had seen in the past few hours. It might have something to do too with the young man lying on the stretcher before him, waiting to be put inside the Dodge and driven back to safety. It occurred to him that in order to save lives it might sometimes just be necessary to take lives and the thought sickened him.

TEN

2.30 a.m.
Between Haret-el-Himeimat
and Deir-el-Munassib
Ruspoli

The machine-gun bullets came tearing into the forward trench, ripping their way through wood and canvas and anything else that stood in their way. They found their first human target in a young private from Brescia who had foolishly not remembered his commandante's advice to keep low, and there and then put an end to his family's dreams of their son's promising future career in medicine. Ruspoli saw the young man die and cursed the British as the rounds flew in around him, ignoring the danger he was in.

Mautino put a hand on his shoulder: 'Colonel, please. Please follow your own advice. Take cover. The men can hold them off. We still have the anti-tank battery.'

'Of course, Carlo. I am well aware of that. But how many more good men do we have to lose? We should have been sent more weapons, more ammunition. How many rounds do we have now? Do you know? Does anyone?'

Mautino shrugged: 'Perhaps two thousand rounds

maximum. We keep trying to get through to Division, sir, but the radio's kaput. It's hopeless.'

Ruspoli shook his head and smiled: 'Not hopeless, Carlo. Never hopeless with the Folgore, eh? Where are the 47/32s?'

'Ponticelli has them on the rise a hundred metres over to the west. It's the best position.'

'And the spotters?'

'Two in foxholes directly to their front. Another two either side.'

'Good. That's good. Send a runner. Tell him to wait until he's sure he's in range and likely to score a hit. We can't afford to waste any ammunition.'

Ruspoli wasn't really worried. His gunnery officer, Emilio Ponticelli, was one of the finest in the Division, perhaps in the army, with sixty kills to his personal credit.

Mautino was getting agitated: 'Don't you think it would be more sensible if you were to come back to HQ? There's really nothing you can do up here, sir.'

'Nothing I can do? I can be here, can't I? I am this brigade, Carlo. Raggruppamento Ruspoli. It bears my name, Carlo. I can only be up here with the men. They need to see me. I am the brigade.'

For three hours now they had been under attack and Mautino could tell that it was taking its toll on his colonel's state of mind. It had started with a barrage at 10.45, such a barrage as none of them had ever seen. The shells had been fired at positions to their rear at first and Ruspoli knew that the British were attempting to take out their supporting artillery. But then, within half an hour the barrage had crept closer and soon shells were falling thick and fast over the trenches. It had been at midnight that the enemy infantry first came forward.

Mautino had looked out over no-man's-land, beyond the sprawling silhouette of the wire, lit up by Verey lights, flares and the continuous glow from the guns and the fires they had started. Gradually he had seen their black forms against the skyline. Ruspoli, once told, had wasted no time in going up to the frontline positions. It was plain to see where the British were attacking and that the Seventh would take the brunt of it.

More shellfire to his left and Ruspoli had known that poor Alfonso Salerno's Nineteenth Company in particular must be having a rough time. He had sent out runners to him. There was a time to stand and fight and die and a time to run and save yourself to fight another day, and Ruspoli knew that in the opening stages of this great battle the latter dictum would hold true. They needed every man they could keep alive. Abandon the advanced positions, regroup in the trenches and that was where they had been ever since.

Ruspoli had no real idea as to how many men they had lost in the past two hours. He knew though that it was too many. He turned to Mautino. 'Come on, let's see what's happening out there.'

'Colonel, do you think . . . ?'

'Carlo, I don't think. I *do*. Come on.'

Together the two men entered the small embrasure in the trench and Ruspoli peered through an improvised periscope. Despite the bright night, it was hard to see properly using the two mirrors, but eventually he began to make out a swarm of infantry and with them armoured cars. 'They're coming round the minefield again, through the gap they blew yesterday. Carlo, go and find Gola. We need his mortars.'

Mautino looked puzzled: 'Is he back, sir? I thought . . .'

Ruspoli laughed: 'Didn't you know, he booked himself out of hospital, said the dysentery had gone and the sores too and he came back last night. Couldn't wait to be back with his men and his beloved mortars.'

Mautino shook his head. 'What a man.' He laughed: 'I knew that silver medal wouldn't be enough for him. He always wants more, that one.'

Captain Marco Gola had become a legend in the Folgore. A towering six-foot-six, he had won his silver medal for his work in Albania with the mountain artillery and now he commanded the Parachute Regiment's specialist mortar company. They said that Marco Gola could hit anything . . . blindfold. And if there was ever a time they had needed his expertise it was now.

Mautino came hurrying back, Gola with him: 'Colonel?'

'Mortars, Gola. Now, over there.'

Calmly and unhurriedly, Gola and his men set up the field mortars and equally calmly sent a dozen rounds flying from the trench. The familiar crump resounded and Ruspoli again looked through the periscope. As the smoke cleared he made out the infantry again. But this time the swarm was broken up. Isolated men were taking cover in foxholes and behind dead bodies and bits of debris. Others were pulling back. There were wounded too. Ruspoli saw a young man lying out in the open, his legs severed below the knee. He was shouting or screaming something which the colonel thankfully was unable to hear. He turned to Gola: 'Well done, Gola. Good work. Another two for comfort I think.'

The big man smiled and, moving back along the trench, signalled to his lead platoon. Again the mortars fired, their rounds landing in the midst of the scattered British infantry.

Ruspoli nodded: 'Fine, that should do it for now.' He turned to Mautino: 'They've got to stop sometime. My guess is they'll keep coming till daybreak then try and stick where they are. At least the minefield seems to be holding.'

'Yes, Colonel. I sent Ponzecchi out there to keep an eye open for enemy patrols trying to clear a path.'

'Ponzecchi? Good. Look out for smoke too. That's how they'll try it.' There was a sudden whine from their front. Mautino heard it first: 'Incoming shellfire. Cover! Take cover!'

They all ducked, Ruspoli too, trying to press themselves against the sides of the trench. He knew what had happened The British, pinned down by Gola's men's murderous mortar fire had whistled up artillery support from the batteries to their rear. You paid for every small victory. And he knew that ultimately, man for man, shell for shell this was a battle they could never hope to win. Ruspoli shut his eyes as the rounds came crashing in, perilously close to the trench. If only we could do the same, he thought. Just make a wireless call and bring down the fires of hell upon the British. But there was no artillery to support them. The Germans had taken it to the north. Nor even was there a wireless on which they might make such a call. Again he began to feel horribly isolated. It was as if their brigade, their company, fifty men, was alone in the vastness of the desert against the entire British army.

He yelled above the din: 'Counter-fire please, Captain Mautino. Engage the enemy. If you can see any of them.'

Suddenly, as it had started, the shelling stopped.

Mautino stood up and brushed himself off and shouted to the rear: 'Gola. We need your mortars.' He found a sheltering soldier: 'Bari. Go and fetch Captain Gola.' Then he turned to Ruspoli, smiling: 'Their aim's not so good, sir. Not today.'

Ruspoli too got to his feet, but with a little caution. 'Careful, Carlo. We haven't heard the coda yet.'

Mautino smiled. Ruspoli would have his musical reference. But the colonel was right. The artillery opposite them had recently taken to adding a short final burst to their barrage shortly after it had appeared to come to a halt. Today was no exception. There was another whine. Someone shouted: 'Incoming! Get down!'

The last salvo whistled over above them and landed obliquely, directly on a support trench. They ducked and covered their heads. As it impacted, the ground shook and earth and sand fell from the parapet. As the dust cleared, Gola spoke:

'Holy mother, sir. That was close.' From the direction of the explosions someone shouted: 'Stretcher-bearers. Medic. Here, quickly!'

Ruspoli turned to Mautino: 'Carlo, send someone to find who's been hit. No, go yourself. That fell too close. Gola, better get your lads under cover. Don't respond quite yet. We'll need you again soon and I don't want to risk losing any of you.'

'No danger of that, sir. My boys'll keep their heads down.'

Mautino came running. He had news: 'It's bad, sir. Lieutenant Bartoldi's platoon. Direct hit. Two men blown to pieces, two of the new boys.'

Ruspoli grimaced: 'Not the singer?'

'No, Colonel. He's all right. A bit shaken. He was ten metres away from the impact. Must live a charmed life though, he should be dead by rights. Bartoldi's not so good though, sir. Several shrapnel wounds. I don't think he'll live long.'

Ruspoli threw his hands up in despair. 'Damn. Why Bartoldi? I swore to his mother I'd look out for him. She'll kill me. Is he conscious?'

'Yes, sir. He's still in shock.'

'Show me where.'

Following Mautino, Ruspoli hurried back down the lines and found the ruined support trench. The direct hit had taken away the walls and flattened the entire area into a shallow scooped-out crater. The ground had turned dark red where the two soldiers had been hit. Of their existence that was now the only trace, but five more men of the platoon lay horribly wounded on what had been the trench floor. The medics were doing what they could for them but it was clear that two of them would not make it. Bartoldi was one of them. They had laid him in what was left of an embrasure in the side of the trench, with his head upon a rock. Ruspoli made a quick appraisal. Classic shrapnel wound. The lieutenant had been wounded in the stomach, face and back by three large pieces of redhot metal. One of them was still protruding from the gash in his stomach. His handsome face had been horribly cut from the forehead down through his left eye and into the cheekbone, leaving no more on that side than a mess of blood and bone and tissue. The right side though was unscathed, and the mouth. Ruspoli knelt beside him and calmly took a pad of paper and a small pencil from his own top pocket:

'Ciao, Giovanni. It's Colonel Ruspoli. Listen, I'm sure you're going to be fine. I'm just going to send a letter to your mother to tell her so. Is there anything particular you want to say to her?'

Bartoldi's eyes bored into Ruspoli's with a mixture of growing agony, despair and grief. He opened his mouth. Blood trickled from his lower lip. He tried to speak but at first only air came through.

'Don't force yourself, Giovanni. Take your time.'

Again Bartoldi opened his mouth and managed to raise his head slightly towards Ruspoli's face.

'Tell her. Please tell her that I love her. And Papa. And that I'll see them soon. After school.'

Ruspoli wrote the words in pencil on his pad and nodded. 'Good, Giovanni. Now rest. Then you can go home.'

The lieutenant closed his eyes and smiled and then, as

if startled, opened them again and grasped Ruspoli's arm tightly. The colonel tucked his pencil and pad away in his breast pocket, buttoned it carefully and then cradled Bartoldi's head in his elbow. The lieutenant opened his mouth again: 'Mama.' Then he closed his eyes. His head dropped to one side.

Gently, Ruspoli laid the young man's head down on the ground. 'He's gone. Bury him someone, please.'

He reached down and pulled one of the dog tags from Bartoldi's neck and stuffed it into his pocket.

Mautino spoke: 'Did you hear him, Colonel? He thought he was at school.'

'Yes. And he was going home to see his mama and his papa.' Ruspoli smiled.

'Sir?'

'His father died five years ago.'

He pictured the boy's mother in their pretty baroque villa overlooking Florence in the little hillside village of Fiesole. Donna Bartoldi would receive the telegram within the week, before his letter could reach her. He saw her drop to her knees in the great entrance portico, beneath the trailing vines in the October sunshine which dappled the Tuscan hills. He heard her sobs for her poor boy and shared her despair, imagined her as she asked the old priest in the village's convent how a good God, who had already taken away her husband, her only love, could now take away her only son. And to that question he himself had no answer. He turned back to Mautino: 'Poor sod. It's luck, Carlo. Just luck. Could have been you or I. Or any of us.'

'That's true enough, sir. All we can do is take care and trust in God. Perhaps the Germans will send reinforcements and ammo.'

Ruspoli stared at him: 'Do you really think so?'

Mautino said nothing. There was nothing to be said.

Ruspoli saw his eyes with their look of fear and appre-
hension.

'All I know, Carlo, is that we are Folgore and we will
defend this position until the end. We will never retreat
and we will never surrender. You and I know that, yes?
Make sure that all the men understand that too.'

'Of course, sir. But I don't think I need to make sure.
They're with you all the way, Colonel. This is your brigade.
You made them what they are.'

Ruspoli felt a surge of pride. Mautino was right. They
were his men, his family. As they walked down the trench
back to the front line, he realized that the left sleeve of
his tunic was covered in Bartoldi's blood and drawing
out a linen handkerchief from his pocket began in vain
to try to clean it off. And as he did so he looked at the
men. His men. There was a curious lull in the fighting
and for an instant what seemed like total silence directly
to their front. In the trench though the tension was almost
physical. The men stood and half-lay against the walls,
clutching their rifles and sidearms. Mostly they wore shirts
and helmets but more than a few were stripped to the
waist and some had held on to their tropical topees, the
symbol above all else of Italy's foray into dreams of an
African empire.

So far from home, he thought. All of you. You should
not be here. You, Franco Marozzi, he thought, seeing one
of them, a talented painter from the Veneto. You should
be painting on the Grand Canal in Venice; and you,
Marcantonio, you should be working on the new vintage
in the hills above Siena. You knew them all, even some
of their families. There was Speda, son of the cobbler
from Vicenza and Fratini, one of five brothers from Milan.
They all had other lives they had left behind, peaceful
lives to which he prayed they would return. Even though
he knew that death had already placed his mark on too

110

many of them. How many, he wondered, would know the joys of love, of marriage, of children. How many would be as lucky as he? They were only boys and had seen little of life. Yet for some this would be their last experience.

A whistle blew: 'Here they come again. Take posts.'

Ruspoli edged just the top of his head above the parapet. The British were coming on again, infantry in wide, dispersed formations. At the same time he was aware of a new artillery barrage on their left.

All along the parapet the paratroops were firing on the enemy now as they continued to advance. Occasionally one of the Italians would fall back into the trench, hit by enemy fire and instantly another would take his place while one of the company medics went to see if there was anything that could be done. The field dressing-post was filling up now and the dead were not being put there any more but in a secluded trench to the rear of the front line.

A runner came towards them: 'Colonel Ruspoli. Caporale Ponzecchi sent a message for you. It's smoke, sir, smoke. He says they're firing smoke shells at him.'

Ruspoli turned to Mautino: 'I told you, Carlo. It's as we suspected. The minefield. They're going to come in under smoke and try to clear it. Then we'll all be in the shit. Send out a party. We'll have to meet them out there.' He paused, while he pondered which of his officers might best command it. 'No, wait. I'll lead it myself.'

Mautino stared at him: 'Sir, are you crazy? You're the colonel. We need you here. You can't lead a raiding party. I'm sorry, sir. I can't allow it.'

Ruspoli frowned: 'You can't what? Carlo, you're my second-in-command. I order you to prepare the party. And I shall lead it. You can't stop me.'

'But, sir, Colonel Ruspoli . . .'

Ruspoli smiled and shook his head. 'Don't try. Now who shall I take? All volunteers but you handpick them, Carlo. We'll need a platoon. Good men. Santini for a start. He'll do. You choose the rest.'

Within ten minutes they were ready to go. Ruspoli pulled tighter on the laces of his black jump boots unique to the paratroops. He had strapped on one of the canvas grenade belts, usually worn only by men and junior officers and filled every pouch so that he was carrying six grenades. On top of that he had fastened the old officers' issue green leather belt that had seen him through the last five years, with his Beretta pistol in the holster. More grenades were stuck through the strapping and he had made sure that his combat knife was easily accessible. Finally he picked up a submachine-gun and turned to Mautino.

'Carlo. If I don't come back the brigade is in your hands. Right?'

'Yes, sir. But this is madness.'

'Right?'

'Right, sir.'

'So. Not another word, Captain. See you back here.'

Ruspoli surveyed his assault section. Santini was there, grinning. And Silvio, the short one from Brescia. There was Marcantonio Rosso from the Levanto and with him a score of others whom Ruspoli knew less well. For most of them though he could name their village and all of them he knew by name, some by their forename. He spoke: 'All right, lads. You're all volunteers. You all know what to expect. We've got to take out these mine-detector teams. If we don't they'll clear the field and that will be the end of us. Got it?'

They answered as one: 'Sir.'

'And one more thing. Give no quarter. They won't be expecting any.'

He turned and they climbed slowly up the few steps that had been laid at the side of the trench and crawled out over the parapet and towards the minefield, with Ruspoli leading the way. Perhaps, he thought, this time for once, Mautino was right. This really is madness. But what madness. And what a way to die, if he must. If that was God's will. He was a fighter, from a family of warriors. This was a warrior's death. He was not though as young as he had been. At fifty he felt more aches than the others. But he could still run and he could still fight. And it was vital to show the men too. That was his way, had always been his way. Carefully, he and the small party crawled across the moonlit landscape, taking care not to swear as their knees and hands caught on the jagged rocks. He had asked for volunteers and chosen only veterans. They all knew what to do. How to make the most of the slightest dip in the land. For while the desert might seem flat to the untutored eye, anyone who had fought there knew that it was filled with undulations which could easily hide a man, a section, a whole platoon.

Slowly, they edged forward. So far so good, he thought. The fire from the trenches was keeping the Tommies back and now he could see the smoke cloud where the shells had hit. They had twenty yards to go. Fifteen. Ten. And then they were in it. It was not like gas. Not as choking or as cloying a smoke as you might get from a wood fire. But it was smoke right enough. Ruspoli turned to Santini, motioned to him to stand up and did so himself. He knew that they could not be seen now. Together the men drew up the neckerchiefs which had lain knotted around their necks and pulled them up over their noses and mouths. Then they went forward into the smoke. Ruspoli put down one foot and then the other. Santini was close behind him, watching his every move, both of them acutely aware that at any moment an unfortunate step would result in death or terrible injury from an exploding mine. But there was no other way.

Two more steps. He stopped. He was not sure whether he had heard something up ahead. Another step. And then another. Ruspoli knew that he was testing his luck. The men behind him were marking his path for their return. But here at the front of their little patrol, it was his feet that were mapping the way. He stopped again. He was sure of it now. A noise. A sort of humming. He dropped to his knees and rested on his shins, motioned to Santini to close up. Then he saw it. Not more than three feet away through the smoke, the flat shape of a mine detector. It was emitting a low hum. Ruspoli pointed the submachine-gun directly above it and gently squeezed the trigger. A hail of bullets flew from the barrel and into the engineer holding the machine who let out a scream as he fell. Two of the bullets also hit his mate in the side of the face and the man fell on top of the other, sprawling in agony.

There was commotion through the smoke. Shouting in English and then rifle fire as the teams and their escort opened up in the direction of the Italians. Ruspoli walked to the dead and wounded men. The second man he had hit was lying on his back across his dead comrade, staring upwards. Half his face had been blown away. Ruspoli took out his pistol and fired a single round into the man's forehead.

He called to Santini: 'Luigi. With me. It's safe here. You men, open fire in the direction of the voices. Over there.' He pointed at vague shapes through the smoke, which was beginning to clear. The patrol opened up with submachine-guns and as it did so the rifle rounds hit home. Two fell to the ground. But from the smoke came the sound of men being hit. Then the noise he had been hoping for. A huge explosion rocked the area. One of them has run and triggered a mine, he thought. That's good. Now they'll panic and move back.

Instead though and to his bemusement, the British continued to fire. Santini gave a moan behind him and Ruspoli turned to see him fall. He had been hit in the leg and lay clutching his thigh. 'I'm OK, sir. Don't worry.'

Ruspoli turned back and fired another shot from the Beretta. Then without hesitation he unbuttoned one of the pouches and fished out a grenade. He pulled the pin, counted and threw. A few seconds later he was rewarded by a blast followed by screams. Almost instantly though there was another explosion, louder. A mine, detonated either by shrapnel from his grenade or more likely one of the casualties falling on to it. Surely, he thought, now this was true madness. To stand in the middle of a mine-field and throw grenades into it? All was chaos around him now as his men opened up in the direction of the explosions. Ruspoli shouted: 'No more grenades! We don't want to clear the field ourselves.'

Ahead of them men were dying and as the smoke began to clear he saw the British dead. They lay singly and in pairs where they had fallen. Most, as he had suspected, were mine engineers. A few had not died and were crying out in pain and terror. He looked back to where Santini had fallen. The corporal was smiling at him, although the blood continued to flow from the wound in his leg. His face was quite white. Ruspoli signalled to the rest of the party and yelled: 'Retire. Back to the trench.' The smoke was clearing fast now and he knew that as soon as the remaining British had left the minefield their guns would open up again and he and his men would be sitting ducks out in the open. He turned and bending down picked up Santini, hoisting his huge form onto his shoul-ders as a fireman might carry a woman from a house. He had seen such a thing once, in Florence when a palazzo had caught fire and the brigade had managed to rescue an entire family including a massively overweight mama. He wondered whether she had been as heavy as Santini. The corporal was moaning: 'Colonel. Signore. Thank you, sir. Thank you.'

'Be quiet, Luigi. Save your breath. Let's get you back to the doc.'

The men had done their work well, following in his wake and he was able to retrace the safe path through the field where he had gone before, now marked with small rocks painted red for the purpose that they had carried in their ammo pouches. It had been his idea. He had anticipated just such an eventuality. He supposed that was part of what being a good officer was all about, second-guessing the enemy and imagining what might happen. The worst that could happen. He shifted to take Santini's weight and wondered what that worst could be now. It was something that he had not dared think of. But now it seemed less and less likely that he and his men would survive this fight. As he and the small party reached the parapet the first of the British shells came whining in over their heads. Overshot again, he thought. At least someone was smiling on him today. But he knew that there was always tomorrow and in his heart he acknowledged that the kindly beneficence, his luck, call it what you will, could not last much longer.

ELEVEN

3.00 a.m.
Miteiriya Ridge
Miller

Miller snapped back to reality. Lieutenant Thomas was talking again to the Kiwi sergeant who had accepted a cigarette and was apologizing profusely. 'So you see it was your English battledress, sir. No markings. I thought you were just another bunch of poms who'd got lost. Always getting lost the poms are. Lousy navigators. From the cities most of them I reckon. Either that or you were fifth columnists. You know, Jerry spies. Could have shot you, sir. Oh, sorry, sir. No offence.'

Thomas laughed. 'None taken, Sergeant.'

'Anyway, thanks for what you're doing, sir. I mean all you Yanks over here helping us. Much appreciated.'

As he was turning to leave a New Zealand officer arrived and stopped him. 'Sar'nt Lock, send a runner to Brigade. We've taken a direct hit on Battalion HQ. It's bloody chaos. We've got three men dead. The signal flare's kaput and the aerial's gone on the number eleven set. We're out of touch with HQ. The CO's OK though. Lucky escape.' He saw Thomas and Miller: 'I say. You chaps look like medics. Tell me that I'm right, for God's sake!'

'Kind of. We're AFS actually, Captain. Ambulance drivers. But we'll help if we can. We'll do anything.'

Anything but fight and kill thought Miller cynically, taunting himself more than anyone else.

'Thank Christ for that. Well, Lieutenant, think you can get down the hill to that mess? That's what's left of the Battalion HQ. See what you can do down there. There's a few wounded. Some pretty bad.' The order given, he turned back to the NCO: 'Sar'nt Lock. Keep trying to find B Company. We've got to secure that flank and for Christ's sake get another radio mast.'

'Sir.'

As the sergeant hurried off, quickly, but taking care not to trip over the debris and rocks, and the contorted bodies of Germans killed in the assault that had been left where they fell, Thomas, Turk and Miller made their way to the bottom of the slope, with the two privates carrying the wounded corporal on his stretcher. He was calm enough now and asked for a cigarette, which Turk gave him gladly. Miller was trying not to look, but he could not help but catch sight of one dead German, his canvas-covered helmet still on his head, his finger frozen on the trigger of his machine-pistol in the moment of death. *Was that the last thing you knew?* he thought. *Your last sensation of life was the instinct to bring death?*

At length they reached the bottom of the slope. The captain had been right. The position was a bloody mess. The direct hit by a German 88 had sent equipment flying in all directions and body parts and bloodstains seeping into the sand bore witness to the three men who had died. One of them, minus both of his legs, lay on his back in the slit trench, his dead face turned to the moon.

Thomas spoke quietly: 'Christ, Josh. Let's get that guy covered up quickly.' They loaded the corporal on to one of the Dodges, managing to find a piece of tarpaulin from

118

an abandoned German trench which they stretched out over the dead man. Then Thomas said: 'Now where are the wounded?'

'Thank God, some help.'

The voice came from an older-than-usual officer, a major, who emerged from the rear of the wadi. His Red Cross armband revealed him to be the battalion medical officer. He held out his hand to Thomas: 'Carmichael. I'm MO of the Twenty-Fourth. Those your ambulances down there?'

'Sure are, sir. Tell us how we can help.'

'Well I've set up the RAP in the wadi back there. We've got about eighty wounded. But we need to clean this ruddy mess up and get the blokes out.'

'We've got space for the ten worst cases, sir.'

'OK, I'll go and mark them for evacuation. See what you can do here.' He turned to his left and yelled: 'Sar'nt Bowie.'

A huge New Zealander came running over to them: 'Sir.'

'Help these Yanks, they're with the AFS. Give them a hand to get any wounded back into the RAP. Then make bloody sure they get the hell out of here before Jerry starts shelling again.'

Bowie turned to Thomas: 'All right, sir. Shall we see if we can find anyone alive?'

'Lead the way, Sergeant.'

Miller followed the two men and behind him came Turk and Brook Cuddy who had been working on the lower slopes. McGinty and Bigelow were with them too now. The Professor brought up the rear. They had not gone twenty yards when Sergeant Bowie signalled with his hand: 'Over there, sir. I think that bloke's still breathing.'

Thomas ran across to the body and knelt down. After

a few moments he nodded to the group and Bigelow went to join him. Opening his haversack he pulled out a dressing and applied it to the man's wound, in the upper abdomen. Miller moved on with Bowie and the others.

The sergeant pointed again, to the left this time where a man appeared to be sitting up. But as he did so a stream of tracer bullets hit the dirt around them and scudded past their legs. The sergeant screamed: 'Down, get down!'

As one they hit the ground. Miller tried to keep his head pressed into the dirt but the temptation to spot where the gunfire was coming from was too much and he raised his head slightly. As he did so another stream of tracer cut through the group and he pressed his head down again as far into the sand as he could get it but not before he had caught a glimpse of the flash. He yelled across to Bowie: 'Sergeant, I think there's a Kraut machine-gun up there on the ridge. Two o'clock.'

Bowie yelled back: 'You're right, mate. Let's hope some of the lads take it out. It's done for that poor blighter.'

Turning his head, Miller stared at the man they had been making for. He was not sitting up any more and as he stared, Miller saw that he had been hit by the last burst of machine-gun fire and his upper torso had almost been cut in half. He closed his eyes. Perhaps, he thought, perhaps if I hadn't been so damned keen to spot the Jerry he might not have fired again and that guy would still be alive. Perhaps. But there was no use in wondering. The guy was gone and Miller would never know if it had been his fault. The gun opened up again but miraculously hit none of them.

The sergeant swore: 'Bastard'll get us all soon enough. He's just playing with us. Why don't they get him?' The German fired another short burst and hit the ground right next to Bowie's face. 'Jesus fucking Christ!'

Miller's mind was wandering. Without knowing what

he was doing he began to crawl in the direction of the German machine-gunner. The man opened up again hitting the ground just behind Miller. Suddenly he came back to it, realized where he was. There was a slit trench to his right and he slid into it as another burst kicked up the sand.

The sergeant called over: 'Don't move, mate. You'll just provoke him again. One of our lads is sure to get him.'

The gun rattled out again but this time their luck had run out. McGinty gave a shout: 'Oh holy shit, I'm hit! Turk, Josh, I'm hit. I'm hit, sir.'

Lieutenant Thomas yelled above the noise: 'OK, Joe. Stay down and stay cool. Don't move. Where are you hit?'

'In the leg, sir. Christ it hurts. It hurts bad.'

Again Miller began to act independently, unaware of conscious thought. He did not really know what he was doing. All that he knew was that the bastard had hit Joe. Joe McGinty was wounded. Perhaps he was going to die and the Kraut with the machine-gun had done it. Slowly, he edged to the side of the trench and flipped himself out so that he was lying flat on his back. He gently turned his head towards the enemy gun position. A glint of moonlight on steel showed him where the man was. Tucked in behind a fold of the ridge, the German lay uphill and off to the left and it occurred to Miller that the reason that none of the New Zealanders on the ridge had taken him out was simply because they could not see him. Somehow the machine-gunner had managed to get round to the exposed flank and Miller realized that if he stayed there it would not be just them who suffered. From that angle he would be able to rake the entire area with fire. He heard someone speaking. It was Sergeant Bowie: 'Hey! You there. What's your name?'

'Miller, Sergeant, Josh Miller.'

'OK, Miller. Listen to me. I'm going to throw you three grenades in a minute. You any good at catching?'

'I play baseball for my college.'

'Good. Catch them and hook them on to your webbing. I don't think he saw you leave the trench or you'd be dead by now. So you must be in a blind spot. You're our only chance. Got that?'

Miller said nothing. This wasn't supposed to happen. Could not be happening. And yet it was. Bowie spoke again: 'Got that?'

'Yes, Sarge.'

'Right then. When I signal you, slowly, slowly mind, start to crawl up the hill. Make sure you keep low and in his blind spot. Right?'

'Right?'

'You keep crawling till you're about twenty yards away from the bastard. Then you throw the grenades. Right?'

'Right . . . How?'

'How what?'

'How do I throw them?'

'Oh fuck. Don't you know?'

'No. I'm an ambulance driver.'

'OK. You take the grenade and you gently tug out the pin. Then you put it in your throwing hand and count to four. No more or you'll blow up. Less and they'll throw it back at you. Then you throw it. Got it?'

'I think so.'

'Well let's hope you have, son. Right, here comes the first one.'

Miller rolled onto his side and saw an egg-shaped object fly from the sergeant's hand. Keeping low, he stretched out his hand to catch it. It landed heavily but firmly in his palm, a 36M Mills fragmentation grenade, about two inches in diameter and weighing around two pounds. As Bowie had told him, Miller hooked it on to the webbing strap at his waist. He looked back. The second grenade followed and then the third and soon he had all three secured. That, he thought, was the easy part. The German had not picked up on the movement for there were no more bursts. But just as Miller was preparing himself another round came in and ripped up the sand and rock around them sending up dust and razor-sharp shards.

Bigelow gave a shout: 'Aagh. Oh shit!'

Thomas yelled across: 'Prof, you OK?'

'Yes, I'm fine, sir. I just took a splinter of rock in my ass.'

McGinty howled with laughter: 'Jeeze, if I wasn't so sore I'd cry. The professor of geology gets hit by a damn piece of rock. Damn fuckin' brilliant. Shit, it hurts when I laugh.'

Miller realized that there was no time to waste. The guy had them zeroed and soon he'd turn his attention to the other men in the area. The noise of gunfire from behind the ridge had intensified and as he waited and steeled himself to go, a salvo of German 88s came flying in over their heads, destined for a target to the rear. Their distracting whine was all that he needed. He began to crawl, slowly, as Bowie had told him, up the hill towards the German position. Every foot, every inch was acutely painful as he dragged himself over the jagged, exposed rocks trying to keep himself as close as he could to the ground. He surprised himself at his progress. He made the first ten yards and found shelter in the lee of a dead Kiwi. The man's stomach had been cut open by shrapnel and Miller had to suppress the urge to vomit. But it was cover and it gave him a breather.

After a few moments he ducked round the corpse's feet and started up again. The slope was steeper now, but that also meant that the machine-gunner was less and less likely to see him. He supposed that this was what they taught you at infantry school and it took him back to playing Cowboys and Indians in the woods back of the house at home. Sneaking up and surprising the enemy. Sneaking up and killing the enemy. Suddenly, thirty yards out from the target he realized what he was doing and began to shake. The overpowering urge was to stand up and run away, back down the hill. But logic dictated that if he did that he would die. He heard someone muttering and realized that it was him and stopped lest he be heard by the enemy. The enemy. Not his enemy surely? But yes. This man, this German had in the space of the last half-hour become his enemy. A man he had now been told to kill. Here was that lesson writ as clear as day. If you want to save the lives of five men and probably many more, you have to kill one man. It was simple and brutal and unavoidable. He began to crawl again, the last ten yards, but to his horror found himself unable to move. His legs felt as if they had turned to jelly and there was no strength in his arms. He was sweating and still shaking. This, he thought, is fear, real fear. For a moment he felt as if he might shit himself, but managed to control it. He wiped his face and felt the sweat. Then he began to pray, silently inside his head. Oh God, whatever you are, give me the strength to do this terrible thing that I have vowed never to do. Let me kill this man before he can kill my friends.

He was conscious now that time was passing. That soon the machine-gunner must grow tired of the game and kill them all. He reasoned that the German must also know that eventually he would die himself. There was an inevitability here that somehow lifted the guilt directly from his shoulders. He thanked God for granting him the wisdom at least to see that and tried again to move. Still his body felt like a lead weight. Then there was a sudden flash down the slope below him. He was conscious that Bowie had made some sort of movement, thrown something, he thought. In response the machine-gun rattled out again and bullets hit their position. Miller had to act now. He pushed against the rock with his feet and felt the strength return, then getting into a crouch he ran hunched over the final ten yards. Now, what had Bowie told him? He pulled one of the grenades from the webbing and held it in his hand. Then, gingerly he removed the round pin. Careful to hold down the safety pin, he counted to four and then his arm came up. He thought of Harvard, of baseball. Of all the best pitches he had ever made and then he watched as the metal egg left his fingers and flew towards the gunner. The man saw it coming. Miller could see him clearly now. Not one man in fact but two. He heard the shout as they saw it: '*Achtung! Eine Handgranate!*' Then the bomb landed in their position. Miller watched as they scrabbled to pick it up and then realized that it was too late and still yelling, ducked to find cover. And then the bomb went off.

It was a good throw. The Mills bomb exploded directly in the centre of the gun crew's makeshift position. It blew apart into dozens of pieces of redhot metal. One of them hit the gunner in the face. It entered through the right cheek and passed upwards into his brain, killing him instantly. Five other pieces hit the loader. Two cut into his legs and one hit him in the groin. The fourth ripped open his abdomen and the fifth hit him in the head just behind the right ear which it severed before taking off a section of his skull. By the time Miller got to them both men were dead.

He looked down at their mangled bodies and froze. I did this, he thought. I caused this. He took the two remaining grenades from his webbing and dropped them lightly beside the bodies. His instinct had been to treat their wounds but it didn't take long to see there were no vital signs. As he was looking though he saw the gun, untouched by the explosion, an MG 34. A sleek tube of black metal, hot from firing. Beside it lay spent rounds and four large metal boxes. Miller opened one and saw that it was packed with bands of ammunition. He tried to count how many but gave up. There was certainly he thought more than enough to take out a platoon with ease, perhaps a Company. For all the sickening guilt of killing the two men, he was also hit by a sense of elation. He had stopped them from killing many more. It was true. He'd done it. He turned and began to run back down the hill. The lieutenant and Turk were on their feet now and Bigelow was being helped up. McGinty was leaning on one elbow.

Turk yelled at him, grinning: 'Wow, amazing, Josh. You did it!'

'Sure, I did it. Like anyone could have but it had to be me.'

'You're a hero, goddamit. A goddam hero.'

McGinty spoke: 'Never thought I'd see that. You learn that in those history books of yours, or what?'

Miller smiled at him, shook his head and found Thomas. 'Say, where's the sergeant? Sergeant Bowie. I gotta thank him.'

Thomas stared at him: 'He's over there. He's dead, Josh. Happened just before you went in. That last burst. He threw something over there. Drew their fire. Brave guy.'

Miller said nothing. Merely thought, if he had only had the nerve to go on. If he hadn't waited perhaps Bowie wouldn't have drawn their fire, would still be alive. He turned to Thomas: 'It's my fault, sir.'

'Crap, Josh. The guy was just doing his duty. He drew their fire and let you get in there. It's what soldiers do. It's no one's fault.'

But Miller knew. He'd gone up that hill to avenge McGinty's wound and had come down only to discover that he'd caused another good man's death. And he'd killed two men.

126

He walked over to Bowie's body. He had been killed by a single bullet through the forehead. Clean and instant, thought Miller. A good way to go. He looked across to the place where the object that had caught the gunner's eye had landed and walked over to it. Stooping down, he picked it up off the sand.

It was a crucifix. Silver and on a chain. Bowie must have ripped it off his own neck in desperation at the very moment that he had sat up there, terrified on the hillside. He wrapped his hand tightly around the cross until it cut into the flesh and then put it carefully in his breast pocket.

It just didn't figure. Where was the justice in it all? Of what sort of divine plan was this a part? His head buzzed with a terrible guilt and dozens of unanswered questions, and he had no answers for them. One thing he did know though. He could never be the same again.

TWELVE

7.00 a.m.
HQ Eighth Army
De Guingand

Freddie de Guingand read over the situation report that he had just finished writing. Montgomery preferred his reports to be delivered verbally and Freddie liked to make sure that his were not only succinct but as revealing as possible.

Northern sector: XXX Corps attacked last night under the barrage across a ten-mile front. The Australians on the furthermost north flank managed to reach the objective line 'Oxalic' but met strong resistance.

In the centre Fifty-First Highland Division moved forward in two brigades, each of which advanced with one battalion forward and two in reserve. Unfortunately, by dawn the division had still not breached the main enemy line. It sustained heavy casualties.

To the left of the Highlanders, Second New Zealand Division attacked the western end of Miteiriya Ridge. They have taken heavy casualties. At dawn the first of the tanks from Ninth Armoured Brigade arrived on the ridge but have since been beaten back by anti-tank fire.

To the left of the New Zealanders First South African

Division advanced and managed to penetrate the minefields at the eastern end of Miteiriya Ridge. It has now dug in along the ridge.

Southern sector: General Horrocks' XIII Corps put in its attack with some success and managed to get through the first enemy minefield.

Seventh Armoured Division met with strong resistance and had difficulty penetrating minefields.

In general: The attack appears to have achieved complete surprise. We have created a bridgehead. Most importantly we have a presence on Miteiriya Ridge.

That would please the army commander, he thought. On the whole they had started well. Surprise, he knew, was what Monty had been after at all costs and it had come at a price. The news of heavy casualties would not be welcome.

THIRTEEN

Noon
Near Bab Al Quattara
Ringler

The dreadful night was long past and for that at least he was glad. He had known of course that the Allied attack must come soon but he had not supposed that it would be so ferocious or sustained. But with the day had come new worries, new dangers. Ringler crawled from strongpoint to strongpoint across the parched sand and everywhere the story was the same. Pallid, exhausted faces stared at their officer, harrying him with questions that were impossible to answer. 'How had they managed that terrible bombardment? How many of them were there? Would they continue the barrage again tonight? If so, how could we survive it?'

Ringler had done the best he could, fending off the questions with a mixture of bravado and guesswork. But he knew in his heart that few of them had believed him. They had seen too much in the last twelve hours to ever entirely believe him again. All save a few stalwarts, Monier among them. The worst part of the day had been when he had tried to get the men some food. There was nothing left and after the excesses of the previous night Ringler boiled with the injustice of it all. Sometime in the night a carrier arrived with a canvas container. Ringler yelled to the nearest foxhole: 'Food. They've sent food, boys.'

But when they opened it they found inside not the hoped-for cans of fruit and meat but merely ten hermetically sealed packets of Afrika Bread. Ringler buried his head in his hands. Monier appeared at his side: 'Don't worry, Lieutenant. The men don't mind. Really they don't, sir. It's just that you raised their hopes.'

Was that all he was good for, he thought. To raise hopes only to see them dashed. It was somehow symbolic of all that had befallen them recently. They were, it seemed to him, a forgotten army. And if they couldn't even find the resources to call up food for starving frontline troops then what chance did they have?

He dug deeper into the canvas sack and found some tubes of processed cheese. Twenty tubes for just under a hundred men. There were a few bottles too of cold coffee, the men called it 'negro-sweat' and Ringler thought it was not hard to see why. Still, it was sustenance. He broke out the rations and heard the groans of protest. An eerie calm hung over the battlefield which only a few hours ago had been a vision of hell on earth.

Ringler watched as his men ate the meagre food and looked at their faces. He stood up and found Monier: 'When they've finished Sar'nt-Major, have the men clean their weapons. Full inspection in one hour.'

This produced more groans but Ringler knew that what they needed was for their minds to be utterly distracted from the prospect of impending death. Besides, he reasoned, they might even need those guns in a short while.

He had just concluded his inspection and was congratulating himself on the condition of the machine-gun positions when the runner found him and virtually fell into his foxhole.

In the lowering light, it was not hard to see that the callow youth, a recent arrival in the desert by the look of him, was not over-inclined to smile.

'Lieutenant Ringler. You will proceed to the commander immediately.' The boy left the pit as quickly as he had come and Ringler acted at once. He found the senior company sergeant, a Bavarian named Hoffner.

'Sergeant Hoffner, send the drivers back to the vehicles and get the men ready to move.'

'Sir?'

'We're moving out Hoffner. I'm off to see the CO.'

Ringler moved quickly along the line, to the left where he knew the HQ had been set up. He found it, a large foxhole dug in beneath the chassis of a burnt-out truck and with it the battalion commander, Rittmeister Mitros, a callow unsmiling man with whom he had never felt any particular empathy. Ringler saluted. Mitros spoke, crisply and factually: 'Ah, Ringler. Yes. Ten Company . . . Ten Company is to go through the minefield and occupy point one-one-five in no-man's-land.'

Ringler was not quite sure that he understood. 'Sir?'

'Point one-one-five. Clear? It is to be built up as a strongpoint and held at all costs.'

'Yes, sir. Where exactly is it?'

The captain pointed to the map which lay on the table before him. 'Well you see, here we are three kilometres from the minefield which is about eight kilometres wide. You see? Here is point one-one-five at the exit of the minefield right in front of Tommy. We still hold it. The passageway through the field is well marked as far as we know by the iron poles. Further over there should be one of our forward observation posts with an assault gun. It reported in about an hour ago so everything seems to be all right with them. Any questions?'

He smiled.

Ringler smiled back. Of course there were questions. Thousands of them. Questions like why? Were they to be supported? How many do you think we shall lose? What do we do if we are attacked? May we surrender? What is an unacceptable level of casualties? And simply, like Monier, 'Will I get home again?' But of course he did not ask any of them. The only words that came from his mouth were: 'No, Herr Rittmeister.'

The man replied: 'Do it well, Ringler. Much depends upon holding point one-one-five. Goodbye.'

The captain looked back down to his notes and began to write. Evidently, thought Ringler, their interview was at an end. He saluted and left the tent. Well, he thought, at least it was something to do. He supposed that point one-one-five was of strategic if not just tactical importance and felt honoured at having been chosen for the task. But part of him wished that he had not been.

By the time he had got the company mounted up into the vehicles, half-tracks which coped well with the sand, it was dark. There were fifteen transports in all plus the two 5cm anti-tank guns. It had started to rain which still seemed to Ringler, for all the time he had spent out here in the desert, bizarre.

Monier found him as he was going through the orders for the final time before climbing into the command vehicle. 'Sir.'

'My greatest worry, Monier, is whether I will be able to find the path going through the minefield. Once I've got it I'll be happy. Then we can worry about how we actually get our way through it, eh?'

He had told the drivers to try to keep the maximum distance possible between the vehicles, in case one of them should strike a mine. Under absolutely no circumstances, he had said, should they leave the column. He climbed into the command car, Monier seated himself by his side, and they set off. After they had gone two kilometres Ringler turned to the driver, Obergefreiter Hans Müller: 'You can go a little slower now, Hans.' He scoured the desert landscape for the poles which would mark the safe path through the minefield, then turned to Monier: 'Can you see any poles? Anything?'

'No, sir. Can't say I can.'

They drove on another five hundred metres and then, over on his left against the stark horizon he saw a few shapes which anywhere else might have been shell-shattered tree stumps. 'There they are, Hans.'

The driver turned the car and drove towards them, followed by the remainder of the company.

As they reached them Ringler stopped the vehicle and jumped out on to the track. Behind him the other half-tracks began to pull up but to his annoyance they did not leave the prescribed distance between each other.

He ran to the second vehicle: 'Back up, back up. You're too close,' and repeated the instructions the length of the column until they had opened out. Then he called the drivers over to him. 'Now listen. We've got to find the right lane through the minefield and the only way to do it is on foot. He looked at them. 'Reichler and Barlach. You two, you take the right lane. Sergeant Monier, you come with me. Unteroffizier Schmidt, you're in charge.'

Slowly, he and Monier made their way along the left-hand track. The rain was heavier now and their clothes felt heavy with the weight of the water. After fifteen minutes Ringler saw something in the moonlight. Two tall posts five metres apart. That must be it. He ran across and along and saw two more poles. Sure now that he had found the path, he and Monier returned to the column but the night was dark and it took what seemed like an eternity. The stars had disappeared behind cloud and it occurred to Ringler that annoyingly he hadn't noted their route.

He swore at himself for his stupidity. They remounted the vehicle and started the engine. Then with great care they made their way from post to post of the markers. With every inch Ringler felt that he was going to be blown up. The vital thing now he knew was not to let the trucks be separated from one another. He climbed back up on to the radiator of the vehicle while Monier mounted himself on the gun carriage of the anti-tank gun it was pulling. Curiously he did not actually feel fear, merely a sense of unbearable tension. He kept looking back, checking to see that none of the vehicles was straying off the track and into the minefield. Once or twice he thought he spotted a slight loss of control and waved the driver back on course.

Looking down at the ground he was able to discern the occasional vehicle track but for the most part the drifting sand had covered them. Still, he thought, if there were tracks to follow why not follow them. He could not see any burnt-out hulks on the track itself ahead. As he pondered on this the traces gave out and so did the posts.

'Hans, pull up for a moment. I'm going to go ahead on foot to have a recce and find the next damn post.'

Ringler climbed carefully down and began to walk forward to the right of the vehicle. He had gone a few paces when a shape loomed up before him. Instinctively his hand went to his holster, unbuttoned to allow him access to the Luger within. But as he drew nearer he saw it to be nothing more than the next pole. He turned and walked back to the vehicle and wondered how long it was going to take them to reach their objective. And just as they were setting off there was a dreadful howling noise from their front and a salvo of shells came screaming

135

over and fell directly into the minefield lane. They were quite closely bunched and it occurred to Ringler that they had been spotted. This was target shooting. Another salvo came over and thirty seconds later another.

He turned to Monier: 'Tell the men to keep going. Do not break out. We must carry on and get through this. It won't last for long.'

Again, although he had given the command and sounded self-assured, he was not at all certain of his own words. The salvos were continuing with ghastly regularity every half-minute and he knew that it was a miracle that none of the vehicles had yet been hit.

There was a radio message from Two Platoon's commander, Lieutenant Berndt. 'Do you think that we might be better to disperse? We'd be less of a target.'

Ringler pressed the button on the handset: 'On no account. Stick with me. Stay in absolute formation. Tight as it gets, Ludwig.'

Suddenly the car stopped. Ringler looked at his driver: 'Hans? What's up? Are we kaput?'

Müller looked back at him, his face a mask of fear and misery, tears streaming down his cheeks. 'Sir, I can't go on. I just can't. We're all going to be blown to hell. Christ almighty, we're all going to die.'

Ringler shook his head. First the rain and now this. The rest of the column was still moving. He panicked; what if a single lucky British shot should land on them?

He pushed Müller to the side along the bench seat of the vehicle: 'Get out of the way, man. You'll kill us all.'

Müller sobbed: 'No no no' and, all pride sacrificed to fear, curled up in his seat into a tight ball of sobbing humanity. Ringler grabbed the wheel and came down on the clutch and the gear lever at the same time. The truck roared into life. But it had begun to rain again now and visibility was zero. Another salvo came whining in. Müller

136

sobbed louder. Monier cursed. There was a whoosh and a blinding flash as a shell landed some distance behind them between two of the following vehicles. Ringler pulled up, jumped out of the half-track and still being careful to stick to the marked path, ran back towards the rest of the company.

He saw the damage immediately. A truck was slewed across the road. The driver had left his vehicle and was clutching his right arm which was soaked in blood. Ringler ran towards him: 'Horst, are you all right?'

'Yes, sir. I think so. Lieutenant Berndt's dead though, and Corporal Muntz.'

Ringler ran past him and found the next vehicle behind the damaged half-track. He shouted to the driver and signalled to him to work around the wreckage, still sticking to the marked track. Not waiting for the others he ran back to his truck and climbed into the driver's seat. Müller was still a useless sobbing ball.

Ringler turned to Monier: 'You had better go to the next truck. Make sure the same doesn't happen there.'

Monier nodded, jumped down and climbed aboard the truck towing the gun. Ringler kicked the machine into life and they started off.

It must have been the best part of two hours later and they were still driving through the minefield. English shells were still landing perilously close. Ringler turned to Müller. The man was raving: 'Why? Why, sir? Why do we have to die? Oh God, I don't want to die. I don't, sir, Please don't let me die.' He began to sob.

Ringler shook his head: 'For fuck's sake, Müller.' He gave him a sharp dig in the ribs with his right elbow and the petrified soldier shut up.

Another British shell screamed past the offside of their vehicle, the force of its passage causing it to shake. Müller began to scream like some wounded animal and as he did so there was a terrible shock which threw the vehicle round and ripped Ringler's hands away from their grip on the steering wheel. At first he thought they had been hit, then as the truck came to a standstill and he realized that no one had been wounded, he pushed down hard on the brakes and took stock of the situation and looked out. At the same moment it became clear that although they had been spared a shell had hit the track immediately behind them. A single thought struck him: Monier! Jumping down from the cab he ran back towards where the shell had landed.

The truck towing the anti-tank gun was undamaged and its driver sat unhurt on the ground some metres away. Ringler called to him: 'What happened? Where is Unteroffizier Monier?'

The man stared at him and said nothing, but pointed to his ears whose drums had been perforated by the blast. Ringler looked around and then he caught sight of it. A dark patch on the road near to one of the marker poles. He ran across and found Monier lying in a pool of his own blood. His torso had been almost severed from his legs by the blast. Ringler bent down close to his head and gazed into the man's eyes. He was still alive. But only just. He spoke: 'Sir. I knew it would happen. Today. I knew.'

Ringler smiled at him and held his hand tight. Monier spoke again: 'Please, sir . . . my wife . . .'

Ringler nodded and as he did the grip on his hand slackened and he found himself staring down at Monier's lifeless body. He stood up and began to walk back towards his vehicle. The driver of the stricken truck had stood up and was hitting his head with the palm of his hand trying in vain to restore his hearing. Ringler signalled him to get his vehicle back on the road and keep moving, then climbed back into his cab. He felt curiously detached, as if in a trance. Like an automaton he started up the engine and they rolled off. He looked at Müller who stared back at him with wild eyes, but could not now be bothered to chide him. He turned back to the road ahead and instantly was met by a terrifying sight coming fast towards him out of the half-light. A tank. It was impossible in the dimness to tell whether it might be English or German or Italian. Ringler decided there was only one course of action to be taken. He stopped the truck and jumped down, then ran across to the advancing metal colossus, yelling all the time, 'Naples! Naples! Naples!'

Nothing. The password went unheeded. Oh Christ, he thought. It was British. He stared at the towering metal wall and at the perforated black cylinder of the machine-gun mounted beneath the turret and now pointed directly at his head. In one second, he thought, perhaps he would be . . . He shouted one more time: 'Naples!'

The hatch flipped open and clanked against the top of the tank. 'Vesuvius. Good to see you, Lieutenant. Are you from the 104th?'

Ringler sighed with relief then straightened up and saluted the panzer major who now addressed him: 'Sir. Lieutenant Ringler. Reporting to point one-one-five, I presume, Herr Major.'

'You assume correctly, Lieutenant. Welcome. You met with no misfortune?'

'We lost one vehicle and one man. My company sergeant-major.'

It sounded so prosaic, so matter of fact.

'Ah, too bad. Still, you're here now. Lieutenant Bauer is over there with his team. He'll fill you in as to what's to be done.'

Ringler gave a salute and the tank commander disappeared back down into his armoured cocoon. The oppressive darkness seemed to encroach upon Ringler's soul. He could not get Monier's pleading eyes out of his head. He said nothing more but walked across to where Bauer and his men were sitting at their assault gun.

'We are here right at the end of the minefield. Over there, directly to the east, are the English. There is supposed to be a screen of Italian tanks down there too. But don't rely upon it, old chap.'

Ringler peered through the darkness and saw the vague outline of another strongpoint which appeared to be abandoned.

Bauer was continuing to talk, but Ringler hadn't really been listening. '. . . can't say I shall be unhappy to get out of here, old chap. A few days in the rear they've promised us. Well I'll believe it when I see it. But I suppose it's a few days nearer to old Vienna, eh?'

'You're Viennese?'

'I should say so. Family have always been in the army. Ten generations. Maria Theresa's bodyguard, old chap. Happier on the parade ground really than here, if you understand me. Not that we're not fighters. Warrior caste, that's us. Just never saw myself in desert gear if you know what I mean, old chap. Well, good luck.'

And with that Lieutenant Bauer was off, leaving Ringler alone in the post. He paused for a moment and wondered about Bauer and his family. How they had been swallowed up in the mass of humanity that made up the Third Reich. How the country of Maria Theresa was now a vassal of Prussia yet Bauer was happy to fight for his erstwhile enemy. And he saw quite clearly for once, how all nations had their greatness and their disaster. How war flowed through history bringing a river of misery to Europe's nations as it directed their future. A shout from the rear brought him back to the present. 'Sir, what shall we do now? Shall we unlimber?'

'Yes, Spengler. That's it. At once unlimber the guns.

Four and Five Platoon get up here, start to move the sandbags around and see if you can't scrounge some more and whatever else you can find from that old abandoned position down there. It's Italian. Never know what you might find.' He thought for a moment: 'No, wait. I'll come down with you.'

Gingerly, still nervous of mines, he made his way down the gentle slope for some three hundred metres until he was among a system of foxholes and trenches. Half of them at least seemed to have been filled in and others were now only slight depressions in the ground less than fifty centimetres deep. There were traces of the previous occupants, the occasional Italian helmet and pieces of equipment. The place stank of urine. He looked at his watch; one o'clock and the rain had started to fall again, in torrents. They would need to work fast to make the position on the hill secure. He climbed back up the slope and found the men unlimbering the guns: the two 5cm anti-tank cannon, three heavy machine-guns and a grenade-thrower. That, he contemplated, was his sole armament with which to match the might of the British army. Ringler walked around the men as they worked. He knew that what they did now must be perfect. There would be no chance to improve it during the coming days, or hours, whatever time they had left until they were overrun. For somewhere deep inside he could not believe that he would hold out. All that they could do would be to cause the maximum damage and casualties in the time they had and then hope for the best.

He called over the two platoon commanders and their section leaders: Strauss, Hancke, Wulfenbuttel, Heckel and the others: 'Make sure the position is secure. We won't get a second chance. We need sentries every five yards, dug in. Place your men back from them in zig-zag trenches. Cut more if you have to. The anti-tank guns

141

need to go halfway down the slope, one per platoon. Three hundred yards between platoons. Make sure they're dug into the sand and then pile up the sandbags and whatever else you can find to their front. You all know the drill, I think. I want a machine-gun with each of the cannon at the same level but a hundred yards apart. Platoon command in the centre, with rifle sections on the flanks. The third MG I'll keep with me at HQ, and the grenade-thrower. The medics with me too. Got it?'

The men nodded and went off to supervise their commands. Ringler walked back three hundred yards behind the area he had designated for the forward platoons and found a small slit trench and a foxhole, partly buried in the sand. He signalled to two of the men: 'Here, you two. Get this dug out clean.' That would be his HQ trench. It was not such a bad position, he thought. But he wondered in what state the minefields were directly to his front and whether they would really stop advancing armour. It was already getting light in the east and there was still much to do. The men would have to have their rations and ammunition. They would have to lay what wood they could find over the tops of the trenches and foxholes to protect them against the sun as they lay there waiting for the British.

He felt suddenly utterly exhausted, as if he could have slept for a week. He sat down on a rock, took off his cap and wiped the sweat from his forehead. Tiredness seemed to be crushing his head like a ring of iron. He felt himself falling into unconsciousness.

He had no idea of how long he had been asleep. It must though, he thought, have been only a few minutes as the sun had not yet crawled up and over the horizon. He was rubbing his eyes when with no warning a salvo of shells fell behind the position, thirty, perhaps forty metres away.

Eight explosions rocked the morning and then stopped. He thought it bizarre that they hadn't tried again. If the forward OP had spotted them digging in then why didn't the British gunners simply zero in and blast them all to hell? Were they perhaps merely playing with him and his men? As he was thinking the sun rose over the horizon and the sky became a brilliant blue. A true desert day, majestic and inhuman. And then it began. Another eight shells came crashing in. They had zeroed in now.

'Take cover. Get down.'

Ringler hit the ground and pressed himself into it as far as he could. He raised his binoculars and pointed them towards where the shells were coming from. But the sun was too low and all he saw was glare. That was the worst thing about this type of warfare, he thought. The fact that your enemy was invisible. Yet he had you completely pinned down and could watch your every action, giving him the ability to fire each salvo carefully aimed and corrected. You knew that at some point one of those shells would get you, the one they said had your name on it. Ringler lost his patience. He wriggled over the sand towards Number Two Section. The section leader, Strauss, who was also the anti-tank gun commander was lying comfortably in a large foxhole covered with a tarpaulin. Ringler lifted the side and slipped underneath. Six faces looked at him in the half-light and from their smiles he realized that they were ecstatic to see him. Someone still cared about them.

The gun-layer, Unteroffizier Hancke asked: 'What are we going to do, Lieutenant?'

'Watch out that the British tanks don't come too near to us.'

It sounded pathetic and he half-regretted saying it. But it was the best he could manage. He tried desperately to think of more advice. 'Sleep alternately, but always keep

143

a watch on the perimeter.' Ringler looked around the foxhole. It had been well dug and well fitted-out in a matter of less than an hour. 'Who organized this position?'

Hancke replied: 'I did, sir.'

'Well done, Hancke. It's excellent work.'

Hancke, a taciturn Saxon, looked pleased with himself. Ringler smiled too. Thank God, he thought. I said something right at least. Turning he slipped out of the position and waited for another salvo. As it finished he ran across the sand towards Company HQ before heading for Number Two Section but halfway across he heard yet another shell whistle in. A ninth. He hit the ground running, grazing his knees and cursed. But just as he did the shell struck and a torrent of sand and stones fell on to him. He was still lying in the sand when he heard the shouts.

'They're hit! Over here, quickly. Medic!'

Ringler stood up and brushed the debris from his body. He looked behind and saw the position he had just left. The tarpaulin, so neatly laid by Hancke, was ripped in two and the sand around it had turned a sickening shade of dark red. He ran back towards it. Inside the foxhole four of the section had been badly wounded by flying shrapnel. One of them had a leg almost severed at the calf, another had injuries to the arm and face. Hancke was dead. Ringler stared at his lifeless eyes and at the huge, still smoking shrapnel splinter protruding from his head. The company medic, Unteroffizier Feuerkogel, was with the wounded now. Ringler had not paid him much attention before. Small, squat and dark-haired, he was a quiet, somewhat melancholic Rhinelander who had always seemed to be unobtrusively efficient and did his job without any fuss. Now it was clear to Ringler that Feuerkogel was in fact just the sort of man who appeared when you needed him. The perfect man for the task he now had in hand.

But what, he wondered, could they do, apart from bind up the gashes and lacerations. Mahnke had a terrible wound in his arm and Feuerkogel succeeded in stopping the bleeding with a makeshift tourniquet. Within a few minutes they had re-stretched the tarpaulin over the position. The blood had dried quickly in the early sun but the smell of cordite and burning flesh remained. Hancke they had taken away for burial and Ringler positioned a small casualty collecting point close by the foxhole. Well, he reasoned with a soldier's faith in fate, lightning never struck twice in the same place, did it?

There was another noise above him and a further group of shells exploded close to One Section. Ringler looked from where Feuerkogel was just finishing with the wounded of Two Section and saw two men crawling towards him with blood pouring from arm and leg wounds. He felt a blind fury rising up inside him. It was all very well for them to stand here and be slowly smashed to pieces by this unseen enemy, but he was damned if he was not going to find out where the fire was coming from. That was the least he could do, wasn't it? But how?

The early-morning desert glow of violet-yellow had now passed into the more usual brown-yellow of the day and the sun was starting to burn down with its remorseless heat and Ringler found that he was sweating profusely through the bleached green canvas uniform. He thought over his orders again. *Hold the position*. That was all very well, but how?

They were just being slaughtered in turn. If Tommy went on like this even for a few more hours half his men would be dead and the rest would be nothing more than physical and emotional wrecks. He looked up into the sky and realized that the sun of course had shifted position.

145

Grabbing his binoculars, Ringler looked again into the desert towards the direction of the enemy shelling and saw, behind a sand dune, a flash. That was where they were then. He felt strangely reassured. They were no longer being pulverized just by a noise. Now their enemy could be seen in a flash of flame and a cloud of smoke. There was merely a heartbeat between the shell being fired and it landing among them.

He made his way to Two Platoon where the wooden planks with which they had covered the position were being replaced after the shellburst. Ringler saw that they were spattered with dried blood.

'You'll be pleased to hear that we now know where those bloody guns are. They're just behind that large dune over there. If you look carefully you'll see the blast.'

The men smiled at him. Good, he thought, that improved their state of mind. Morale was all-important at a time like this. He walked across to the number one gun and made the same announcement. Again the men smiled. He dropped down into the shallow command trench, a foxhole no more than half a metre deep which they had lined with sandbags and around which the men had built a parapet. His runner, Burckhardt, was lying in one half, the other being reserved for Feuerkogel. He began to think. If only they could hold on till nightfall then he would send a runner back to Battalion. That could not of course possibly be done in daylight. Any runner would face certain death. But if they could make it till then, surely Battalion could send up more food and drink. And then perhaps they could send the wounded back as well. The transports of course had been driven away with Regimental Sergeant-Major Wiel after the guns had been unlimbered and were waiting for them on the west side of the minefield. At least, that was the theory.

He was still lying there when Feuerkogel crawled up

with a casualty situation report and crouched at the corner of the foxhole. 'Lieutenant. It's not good. A third of the company are casualties. Three of the men have sunstroke and are running high fevers. All the others who haven't been hit are exhausted.'

It was not good. Not good at all. But as Feuerkogel spoke, Ringler looked at his watch. Two minutes between salvoes. That meant that they were due for another . . . True to form the flash came from behind the dunes and feeling the air being sucked away by the shells, Ringler tried to drag Feuerkogel to the floor of the foxhole. There was a short sharp bang directly above them and then dust and rock everywhere. For a moment amidst the stench of cordite and rock dust and the smoke, Ringler froze. No. He was still alive. He crawled out from beneath the pile of rubble that had landed on top of him and found the medic. Through the dust cloud it was hard to see him but he was saying something. 'Lieutenant, I've bought it, Lieutenant.'

'Nonsense, man. Where are you hit?'

But there was no need to ask, for as the dust cloud cleared Ringler caught sight of Feuerkogel. Blood was flowing out of his neck and he was staring helplessly at Ringler. The lieutenant grabbed the medic's bag and rummaged around, desperately looking for a dressing. He found a bandage and unravelling it wrapped it around the wounded man's neck but the blood just continued to seep through the gauze until his hands were sticky with it. Christ, he thought, even the medic's hit and I know nothing of first aid. Perhaps, he hoped against hope, the splinter is not so deep. Maybe the wound isn't fatal after all. He was tying the bandage and realized that Feuerkogel was closing his eyes when he heard another explosion. They had given up on the two minutes' pause. This, he thought, could only mean one thing. He gently laid the medic down on the sand and rushed to the nearest of the anti-tank guns, screaming 'Where is Feldwebel Fiedler?' But Fiedler, the gun-layer was there at the gun, pressed up hard against the gunsight.

'Lieutenant. Thank God. They're coming, sir. I saw movement behind the dunes.'

Ringler looked around: 'Where are your gunners?'

'I've only one left, sir.'

'Right, hurry up, Fiedler, get them in your sights. I'll load and, Knapp, you hand us the ammunition.'

'Here they come, sir.'

Ringler looked over the top of the gunshield and saw them. Perhaps two thousand metres distant. He counted under his breath: two, three, four, five, six, wait, seven, eight tanks. They were deployed in a wedge formation. Ringler wondered how clever the tank commanders had been. Had they worked out the range of the company and the probable range of their guns? They could not possibly know, he reasoned, that one of their guns was out of action because the entire crew was dead or wounded and the gunsight mangled. He turned to Fiedler: 'Let them come on. It's our only chance. We don't open fire until they're four hundred metres away, or less.'

The tanks were a thousand metres away now and the enemy artillery had stopped firing. Ringler felt himself breaking out into a cold sweat of fear. Where, he wondered, where might be the fabled Italian tanks that Lieutenant Bauer had told him of? It suddenly occurred to him that the tanks he was looking at might themselves be the Italians.

He put the binoculars to his eyes and strained in an attempt to identify the tanks. It was damn near impossible in the haze of the midday sun. Fiedler moved the sights to ensure that the enemy were clearly in line of aim and range. How, Ringler wondered, could the man be so sure that they *were* a hostile unit? In an instant he decided that they must be Italian tanks. He was about to say as much to Fiedler when it occurred to him that the gun barrels of the tanks were pointed directly at him and his men and that it didn't really matter now which side they were on. He turned to Fiedler: 'Fire!' The shell flew from the little anti-tank gun and exploded on the lead tank at four hundred metres. A jet of flame shot up from the turret and soon it was flaming. Then, as Ringler watched in horror, shapes began to jump from the tank and crawl and run away from the fire. Those who could began to climb on to the hull of the following tank, the one which Fiedler now had in his sights. 'Fire!' The shell hit the second tank just as the men were reaching the turret. It exploded like the first and the second tank began to burn. The crew of the first jumped down again, some of them engulfed in flames. Those who could were now running over to the third tank leaving their comrades writhing on the ground between. The other six tanks had pulled up and seemed uncertain what to do. One of them fired off an armour-piercing shell which thumped into the ground close to Ringler. 'Fire!' Fiedler's third shot hit the third tank head-on. 'Three out of three, Lieutenant.'

'Well done, Fiedler. Good shooting.'

But inside he was thinking, if they saw us, if they managed to make out our position through the smoke, then we're done for. His thoughts were borne out as a shell came in, fired by the end tank at their gun. Thankfully it missed the position but Ringler was taking no chances now: 'Away from the gun now, Fiedler. Take cover.'

'Shouldn't we use the machine-gun, Lieutenant?'

Ringler looked into the desert and saw what he meant and was shocked. There beside the shattered tanks were several small groups of wounded men, some of them obviously burnt. He thought for a moment then answered: 'No.'

He wondered if he had done right and was still unsure as he thought of Feuerkogel, of Mahnke and of poor Monier. Then he watched the English die in the sand as their tanks pulled back and thought how they could so easily have been him and his men. And it sent a chill down his back, even in the searing heat of the bloody afternoon.

FOURTEEN

Noon
Ruweisat Edge
Miller

The Regimental Aid Post had been secured and a new HQ set up. Miller was still pondering his actions of the previous few hours, unable to comprehend the fact that he had taken lives so easily. They had buried Sergeant Bowie behind the dressing-station with six other dead from the battle. According to the colonel the attack had been a success. The three forward companies of New Zealanders had secured their position shortly after 3.30 a.m. They had dug in mortars and two two-pounders along the ridge and the radio set had finally been repaired. Thomas came over to where Miller was sitting on a rock, staring into the sand. 'That was a brave thing you did out there, Josh.'

'Was it?'

'You damn well know it was. If you hadn't done what you did more of those guys would have died.'

'Maybe. Doesn't seem very brave. Killing your fellow men.'

Thomas put a hand on Miller's shoulder: 'Don't beat yourself up about it. It's war.'

'What now?'

'Now we drive back to the advanced dressing-station.'

'Back through the minefield?'

'There's no other way that I know.'

Three of the ambulances having already returned to the dressing-station they loaded up the remaining two with the wounded, including McGinty whose wound they had dressed and Bigelow who wore his bandage with pride on his scarred buttocks, then started off back the way they had come, Miller and Turk in one of the ambulances, Thomas in the other. There were still more tanks on the track now and several times there was a loud rasping noise as Miller felt his ambulance rake against the side of one of them. The ground was rough and as they bumped along not even the advanced suspension of the Dodge prevented the wounded from groaning. As they bounced over a particularly bad rock, McGinty yelled from the back: 'For Chrissake, Josh, be careful, there's guys in pain back here. Me included.'

By the time they got to 6th ADS it was full daylight. The place was transformed from the way they had left it into a scene of frantic activity. Everywhere there were ambulances and trucks filled with wounded. Stretcher-bearers and medics and drivers were working as fast as they could to get the men unloaded and send the vehicles back to the front to pick up more. Miller stopped the Dodge and got out. The wounded were lying everywhere. The reception tents were full to bursting and there were men up against the sides of the Egyptian mudbrick buildings, in their doorways, in the filthy alleyways between.

Turk shook his head: 'Jesus! Whose in charge here? Looks like the showers after a New York Giants game.'

Thomas appeared from his ambulance: 'Guess we need to find the head guy and get these poor bastards unloaded.'

They picked their way through the stretchers and eventually reached an office. Inside a middle-aged man with a moustache and wearing a peaked cap was seated at a table.

152

A major in the Medical Corps. Thomas approached him and was careful to salute before he spoke: 'Major. Lieutenant Thomas, sir. American Field Service. We've two ambulances full of wounded. Where would you like them?'

The man looked up and Miller could see from his face that he had not slept for some time. Perhaps days. He managed a smile and spoke: 'Ah. Yes, Lieutenant. Well, as you can see, space is at something of a premium. I would suggest that you plonk them down anywhere you can find for now. My chaps'll see to them before long.' He looked back down at his paperwork. Evidently their interview was at an end. Thomas looked at Miller and shrugged. Together they left the office and helped the other drivers to unload the stretchers.

McGinty called over to them: 'Hey you guys, hey Lieutenant. Where am I goin'?'

Turk answered: 'Not home, you dumb Mick. You're not hit that bad, you son of a bitch.'

'Wouldn't you wish it was you, Turkey boy? Could be arranged.'

Thomas waved them down: 'Leave him, Mack. Turk, he'll be back with us soon enough. You're going back to Gharbaniyat, past El Hammam. Remember?'

Miller looked around the dressing-station and did a quick head count. There must be around eight hundred men here, he thought. Away from where the new arrivals lay it seemed better organized, with three rows of seven or eight EPIP tents forming the three wards. The operating theatres seemed to be at the end of the rows in separate tents and electrical generators had been set up outside to supply power.

He turned to McGinty. 'You'll be in good hands here for now, Joe. See you soon. Be sure and get better.' He walked over to the ambulances, which now stood empty, and found Thomas: 'Where to now, sir?'

'Back to the front, I reckon. To the New Zealand RAP. Those are our orders. We'd better see how those Kiwi boys are getting on.'

They were just preparing to set off when an English captain walked up to Thomas. He was wearing an adapted version of officer's battledress with a spotted silk scarf tucked into his shirt collar and a 'fore-and-aft' cavalry forage cap with a blue flash, worn at a rakish angle. 'I say, you chaps American?'

'Sure are, sir. American Field Service ambulance corps.'

'Thing is I'm here trying to find an empty blood wagon.' He put out his hand to Thomas who shook it. 'Sorry, Webster, Captain, Scots Greys. Like a fag?' He produced a silver cigarette case from his inside pocket and flipped it open to reveal a row of oval Turkish cigarettes. All of them took one with a murmur of thanks and after the click of their Zippos the captain took a long puff, blew a cloud of smoke and began again. 'Thing is, we've had a bit of a flap down the line. Several tanks brewed up and we've got casualties lying out in the sun. Don't suppose you could spare one of your trucks and a couple of chaps to give us a hand. Get the men back here?'

Thomas looked at Miller: 'Josh, Turk? What d'you say?'

Miller shrugged: 'It's got to be better than the mine-field, sir.'

Turk nodded. Thomas spoke: 'Why don't you go then? Give the captain here a hand. See if you can help his "chaps". I'll see you back here.' He turned to the captain: 'How far is it, sir?'

'Oh, no more than an hour's drive.'

'Then I'll see you guys back here at three this after-noon. Don't be late, Josh.'

Miller turned to the captain: 'We're all yours, sir. Lead on.'

* * *

154

It took them a little over an hour to reach the place. They had been driving due south and the sun beat down on the ambulance and the captain's open jeep with its usual relentless heat. But Miller was thankful to be away from the minefield. He was conscious that the sounds of battle were on his right yet the captain had taken them away from the front and they had travelled down Sydney Road and then various extensions of it to find their destination. Miller was starting to wonder how much further it might be when they drove around a sand dune and up a ridge. Miller gasped. There in a dip below them were laid out line after line of tanks. There must have been thirty of them, mostly the new Shermans and Grants. American tanks. He pulled up and he and Turk jumped down from the Dodge. Turk whistled.

Captain Webster spoke: 'Impressive isn't it? Shouldn't care to be a Jerry right now. That's only about half of Fourth Armoured Brigade. Should have seen the dummy army that Monty cooked up though. Now that really was impressive. All made of balsa and paper though. Some magician did it all. Damn clever if you ask me and it certainly fooled Jerry. Thought we were in strength in all the wrong places. But this is the real thing. As you can see.'

Miller looked on as the tank crews in their distinctive berets and forage caps busied themselves around the vehicles, fixing on strips of track over their armour plating for extra protection.

'Not much further to go now. It was one of our advance squadrons that stumbled on the Jerry strongpoint. We'll just skirt the brigade and go up that track.' He pointed: 'Not far.'

Miller and Turk climbed back into the cab and followed him slowly down the dune and on to the track. They carried on and passed an all-too-familiar sign: *Achtung*

Minen. Turk cursed: 'Oh wow! Another friggin' mine-field.' They stayed dead in the centre of the track and for once did not encounter any tanks. Suddenly the captain's jeep slowed down and then pulled over off the track.

Miller turned to Turk: 'I sure hope he knows what he's doing and where he's going 'cos I sure as heck don't.' But the jeep did not strike a mine and nor did Miller. The sound of gunfire was closer now and Miller and Turk could both hear the familiar and unsettling crump of mortars. Webster pulled up and Miller stopped behind him. They were in another slight dip, in the lee of a huge sand dune and Miller was suddenly aware that a dozen more tanks, Grants this time, were sharing it with them.

Webster spoke: 'Now the wrecks and the casualties are just around the dune about a thousand yards into no-man's-land. Shouldn't have happened of course. Radio failed. Lack of communication. Usual TABU.' He looked serious: 'I can't pretend that this is going to be a picnic, chaps. You might get fired on.'

Turk smiled and winked at Miller: 'That's OK by me, Captain. I'm kinda getting used to it.'

'Good man. That's the stuff. Now what I propose is that my driver and I go out there before you with a white flag and hope that Jerry understands our intentions. If he doesn't then we're all gone for six. But he knows that we'd do the same for him. Have done before. So in theory it should all be hunky-dory. Ready?'

Miller spoke: 'As ready as we'll ever be I guess, sir.'

The captain, smiling, jumped back into his jeep and grabbed something from the rear seat. A piece of bright white material attached to a stick. He looked at Miller: 'You follow me. And pray.'

Miller and Turk climbed back into the cab. Turk looked puzzled: 'Did you get any of that? What the hell was that guy talking about? Fags I understand now. Cigarettes, right? And gone for six? That's cricket, yeah? And what's Tabu?'

'Total Army Balls Up.'

'Jeeze, Miller. How'd you know all that stuff?'

'I listen. Just listen.'

Together they slowly pulled out from behind the dune. As they did so the captain began to wave his white flag. For a dreadful moment Miller felt utterly exposed. He could see the burnt-out tanks now and the German position, dug into a slope about two thousand yards away from them. He waited for the machine-gun and mortar rounds to come flying towards him, wondering if this would be his last moment and how it felt to die with redhot steel ripping into your body. But nothing came. No shells, no bullets. Instead, when they had got to within 250 yards of the wrecked tanks, he saw a German climb out of the strongpoint and start off towards them. An officer by the look of him, followed by two other men. He was waving what looked like a white shirt on a stick. As they drew closer to the tanks he caught the smell. Burning human flesh. A little like roast pork. It turned his stomach. He could see a number of dark shapes on the sand. Dead presumably.

There were others though who were still alive. They were nearing the tanks now and he could feel their heat through the windshield. He stopped the ambulance directly behind where the captain had pulled up and got out with Turk. Together they walked towards one of the wounded who was moaning in pain. Miller looked up to see what had happened to the German officer and found himself looking into his face. It wore an impassive expression and showed signs of great fatigue. He had powerful blue eyes and Miller stared at him with fascination, trying to determine what if anything made these people so different. Different enough to kill each other? The German saluted and Miller returned the gesture as the captain looked on, his hand hovering over his pistol holster. Then the German officer nodded politely, smiled and turned and he and his men walked back up the slope.

Miller looked after them for a moment and then got back to the wounded. They brought a stretcher from the ambulance and managed to lift the soldier on to it. He thanked them feebly and the captain went over to him and gave him a cigarette. Then they hoisted him into the back of the truck and slotted him into one of the six slings. They repeated the process with three other casualties, in various states of ruination, dressing their wounds as best they could. The worst they left till last. The man was lying on his back near one of the burning tanks. He had been hit in the head by a piece of shrapnel and was also badly burned. It was hard to make out whatever else was wrong, but he was clearly in a very bad way. Miller got out a length of bandage and wound it loosely around the man's disfigured head. With great care Turk and Miller rolled him on to the stretcher. He gave a low moan, barely audible, then sank on to the canvas. They lifted him up and placed him gently inside the truck before closing the doors.

They walked over to the captain who was leaning against the jeep. As they neared him he stood. 'Thank you most awfully for that. Forever in your debt. Will you see they get safely back to the ADS? I'm going to stay here with the squadron. Think we're about to go in. Should be quite a show.'

'Don't you worry, sir,' said Miller. 'We'll get them back. And I'll make sure they get seen to in double-quick time.'

'Thank you. Cheerio. Must crack on.'

And with that he turned and drove off with his driver. Miller and Turk got back in the ambulance and turned over the engine.

The journey back took twice the time of their outward trip and they had known that it would. With five wounded in the back, two of them critical, every rock and bump in the road was important and it took all of Miller's driving skill to keep the Dodge as smooth as she could be. Sobered by what they had seen they did not say much to each other but sat in silence, listening to the engine, the surrounding noise of the increasingly distant battle and most of all the moaning of the wounded.

They finally pulled into the ADS at almost 4 p.m. Miller parked up close to where they had stopped before. There was no sign of Lieutenant Thomas. He turned to Turk: 'You wait here with the guys. I'm going to find a doctor.'

He got out and walked over to one of the wards. Inside the welcoming coolness was countered by the stench of blood, ether and sulfanilamide. Various medical orderlies were busy about their duties and an officer in shirtsleeves, a major, was standing over one of the beds. Miller waited patiently until he had finished and then approached him: 'Sir. Miller, sir. AFS.' The major nodded and looked away. Miller continued: 'I'm sorry, sir, but I've just brought in a wounded man and he needs someone to see him now.'

The doctor looked at him and Miller wondered whether he had gone too far, had perhaps contravened some British army regulation. The major spoke: 'You aren't English, are you? But you're not a Kiwi either. Where are you from?'

'America, sir. But that doesn't matter. This man, sir. He's very badly wounded.'

'America. Good. Well there is a procedure, a process and all that before I see him. He has to be booked in.'

'Sir, I'm not sure you understand me. The guy looks like he's going to croak. I promised one of your captains . . .'

The major looked at him: 'All right, old chap. I'll take

159

a look at him. Bring him in here will you.' He pointed to a makeshift bed by one of the tent walls. 'You can put him down there.'

Miller ran back to the ambulance and he and Turk removed the stretcher and carried the wounded man into the tent, placing him where the major had indicated. The officer walked over to them with another doctor and motioned them away. Miller and Turk walked to the door. For some reason which he could not fathom, Miller felt somehow attached to the wounded man and was desperate to hear the prognosis. As they waited at the tent door, the major looked towards them and then back to the soldier. All the time he was speaking to the other doctor. At last he motioned to Miller to come over. 'He's pretty badly cut about. Would you mind staying with him for a few moments? I just have to consult with another colleague. Sorry, my name's Wilson, Major RAMC. You did well to bring him here. Shan't be a tick.'

Miller stood at the edge of the bed and looked at the man. He was more horribly wounded than he had remembered. Part of his face had been blown away, but he was still alive. He stared at Miller and was trying to speak but only a thin, bloody membrane remained where his mouth had been. Whenever he tried to talk the air from his lungs threw up a thin spray of fluid and blood.

'All right, friend. You'll be OK.'

The man's head moved and Miller knew that he could hear.

Major Wilson came back into the tent accompanied by another officer. They walked across to Miller. Wilson looked down at the man and said nothing. He bent over and began to examine his wounds and then straightened up. Miller looked at him and although he still said nothing it was clear enough what was in his mind. He turned to

160

the captain at his side and nodded. Miller asked: 'Are you going to operate?'

Still Wilson and the captain said nothing to him, but moved away in conversation, so that Miller and the wounded man could not hear. Then they came back and Wilson took Miller aside: 'I'm sorry. It's really of no use. His left arm's gone. Burnt to a cinder. His left leg below his knee is a torn mess. His stomach is full of holes. His lungs must be badly damaged too from the burning. You've seen his face. Rather what was his face. Poor devil. He really should not have lived. God knows how he survived this long. Is he one of your drivers?'

'No, sir, he's one of yours. British tank crew.'

The major shook his head: 'Believe me, if there was one chance in a million that he'd live I'd operate. But he'd never come out. There are scores of others who do have a chance and they need us now. I'm truly sorry.'

Miller looked into the major's eyes. They held a warmth and a sparkle and also now a terrible sadness and he knew instantly the worst part of being a soldier – of being an officer. Having to make decisions about life and death, who to save and who to leave.

Wilson shook his hand and smiled and then, with the captain, turned and walked towards the tent that was used as an operating theatre. Miller turned back to the soldier: 'What are you trying to say to me? Try again.'

Fighting against his natural repugnance, he placed his ear close against the gaping hole in the man's head that had been his mouth. Suddenly the soldier's right hand swung up and grabbed at Miller's tunic. He pulled him ever closer. There was an awful noise. A gulping for air and a heaving deep in the man's body. And then some words.

'Tell, tell Nancy . . .'

'You want me to tell Nancy?'

161

The hand tightened around Miller's jacket. He had been right. Those had been the words.

'Tell me again, soldier. Was it Nancy?'

But no words came now, nor even air and the hand fell away from Miller's jacket as suddenly as it had come. He drew back and looked at the man. The glassy eyes told him all he needed to know. He examined the dog tags around the dead man's neck and took a pad and pencil from his pocket and wrote: '452679 MacTaggart, Scots Greys, KIA El Alamein station, 25 October.'

He whispered to the corpse: 'OK Mac. I'll tell her.' But as he walked back to the doorway and out into the searing sunshine, he knew that if he ever did find Nancy, whoever and wherever she was, he could never truly tell her what had happened to her husband, her lover, her friend. He would give her another version of his death. Of how Trooper MacTaggart had died instantly and with glory, a fine, cavalryman's death. Clean, quick and good, as death never was out here. He would not tell her of the ghastly ruin on that bed of the man who had once been her world. And he thought of how people who had never seen a battle knew little of the reality of war, of its true obscenity and random, merciless inhumanity. He suddenly felt like weeping. Or rather, like shouting out loud for the madness to stop. But just then he caught sight of Turk standing at the doors of the ambulance, waiting for him to help with the four other stretcher cases and he knew that all that would have to wait for another day, another place, another time.

PART TWO

The Dog Fight

Sunday 25 October

FIFTEEN

2.30 a.m.
Burgh-el-Arab, near El Alamein
Montgomery

He awoke; or rather he was awoken. Montgomery looked up, rubbed at his eyes and found himself peering into the gap-toothed, mustachioed face of his chief of staff, Freddie de Guingand. He did not need to ask why he was there. The young man's expression said it all. 'Sorry to wake you, sir. You did say, if there was good reason.'

'I know perfectly well what I said, Freddie. So what exactly is the matter?'

'Well. We've had some "J" reports, sir. The fight at Miteiriya Ridge. I'm afraid it's not at all good, sir. One of our columns has been hit by the Luftwaffe. Eighth Armoured Brigade, Ten Corps, General Gatehouse.'

Montgomery raised himself up. He was clothed in the battledress he habitually wore. He lifted off the single blanket under which he had been sleeping and swung his legs over the edge of the narrow wooden bed that stood against one wall of the wooden caravan that was his headquarters.

'Bad?'

Guingand nodded solemnly.

'Heavy losses?'

Guingand nodded again. 'Pretty much, sir. Near as dammit out of action. Seems that they were just forming up before advancing when the raid came in. Stukas mostly. Took out all the soft-skinned transports, ammunition trucks, petrol too. Worst thing is that apparently the whole shooting match went up like a torch and lit up the entire area and then Jerry really zeroed in with his big guns.'

Montgomery levered himself from the bed and stepped on to the floor of the caravan. Guingand continued as the general laced up his desert boots.

'I've taken the liberty of getting the corps commanders together, sir. They'll be here by three-thirty.'

Montgomery looked up at him: 'Leese and Lumsden? They're coming here at three-thirty? Good. That's good. Well done. I agree with you, Freddie. Quite right. I'll be here, waiting for them. What action's been taken?'

'Well, firstly General Gatehouse ordered Brigadier Custance to disperse the armoured regiments to keep their casualties low. But in fact it sounds as if that only caused more confusion. Point is now they're well behind schedule, sir. Brigadier Custance is advising that the attack be abandoned. That at least is the signal I've received from General Lumsden.'

This, he thought, was the beginning. And also the crisis. He knew it and he thanked God that he had followed his own dictum of withdrawing to bed early. No point in staying up into the night to go over plans with his generals. That was not the business of a commander. Better to conserve your energy for when it was truly needed.

He turned to Guingand: 'Have you slept?'

The chief of staff smiled at his commander: 'Not much, sir. I had a hand or two of chemin de fer with the chaps

167

at Tac HQ. That's where I was when the report came through.'

Montgomery frowned, but said nothing. He liked young Guingand, but he disapproved of gambling almost as much as he did of drink and sex outside wedlock. Still, if the man managed to perform his duties without sleep then why should he criticize him.

The hour passed quickly. Montgomery paced the floor of the caravan, looked again and again at the pictures he had pinned to its walls, chiefly that of the man who was at that moment, according to intelligence reports, still in Germany convalescing from an illness, but who Montgomery guessed would soon, if he had not already, fly back into the desert. Field Marshal Erwin Rommel. Montgomery studied his face and tried once again to gain some advantage by understanding the character of the man. He had read his books on the theory of warfare. What general had not? But they gave little away of this fox of the desert, this man who with quicksilver action could switch a division from one flank to the other and cut off an army. The man who had almost reached Alexandria. He looked too at the three quotations he had pinned up alongside. The first was the Prayer of Sir Francis Drake on the morning of the attack on Cadiz: 'Oh Lord God, when thou givest to Thy servants to endeavour any great matter, grant us also to know that it is not the beginning, but the continuing of the same, until it be thoroughly finished which yieldeth the true glory.'

To the right hung Shakespeare, *Henry V*, Act IV Scene I: 'O God of battles! Steel my soldiers' hearts.'

And to the left he had placed the wise words of the Marquis of Montrose, that great Civil War commander:

'He either fears his fate too much,
Or his deserts are small,
Who dares not put it to the touch,
To win or lose it all.'

That, he thought, was what this battle was all about. A gamble to win or lose it all. Everything hung on this one moment and Montgomery prayed silently that he might be equal to the task that fate and history had set aside for him. He sat down again and lowered his head in prayer. Quietly the familiar words came from his lips:

'Father hear the prayer we offer,
Not for ease that prayer shall be,
But for strength that we may ever
Live our lives courageously.'

At precisely 3.30 a.m. the knock came at the door, just as he had known it would. Montgomery continued to sit in the centre of the small caravan staring fixedly at a map on the wall of the battle area. He spoke without turning.
    'Enter.'
    As the three men came in he turned and flashed a genial smile. Guingand looked serious, he thought, and his two generals, Oliver Leese and Herbert Lumsden had the air of schoolboys called to the headmaster's study.
    He spoke very quietly and calmly: 'Gentlemen. Do come in. Sit down. I gather we have a problem. Now let me hear the full story. You first, Herbert.'
    From outside came the constant staccato fire of the anti-aircraft guns and the distinctive whistle and crump of a bomb landing nearby. Montgomery paid them no attention and waited for Lumsden's report.
    'Well, sir, General Gatehouse has sustained some casualties to his armour. Mostly from mines, sir, and he's reluctant to continue.' He paused. Montgomery stared

169

into space. Lumsden summoned all his courage: 'I have to say, sir, that I'm inclined to agree with him. Should he continue to advance on to the forward slope of Miteiriya Ridge he could be pinned down and suffer dreadfully.'

Montgomery shook his head. Still his voice retained its gentle tone: 'The principle is that the armour must get beyond the infantry. You know that, Lumsden, as well as I do. If that should not happen then the entire attack is compromised. We must provoke the enemy, lure his tanks within range of our anti-tank guns. That is the only way. The armour must move on beyond the infantry.'

'I understand, sir. Perfectly. And I do not intend you to think that I am challenging your order. But, I beg you to speak directly to General Gatehouse personally on the telephone.'

Montgomery said nothing but looked at the other dictum hanging on the wall: 'Are you 100% fit? Are you 100% efficient? Do you have 100% binge?'

The last question was the all-important one; 'Binge'. His own word meaning fighting spirit. That was the key. The men he could inspire. He could ensure they had binge. But as to some of his generals, he was not so sure.

He turned to Guingand: 'Freddie, get me a line to General Gatehouse.'

The room fell silent save for Guingand who was speaking on the field telephone.

Montgomery looked at Lumsden: 'You know that we have overwhelming superiority in tanks and firepower. Of course all our troops are not as highly trained as they might be. If we do anything foolish at this critical time, we could easily lose this battle. There will be no change. Do you understand me, gentlemen? No change from the plan. We must ignore enemy counter-attacks and proceed relentlessly with our own plans. We must

170

keep the initiative. We have it now and we must never lose it. The enemy will dance to our tune.'

The caravan fell silent. Leese and Lumsden looked at de Guingand and then at the floor. Montgomery turned back to the map and pretended to ignore his generals. Warfare was a lonely business. A commander was always alone.

SIXTEEN

2.30 a.m.
Semmering, near Wiener
Neustadt, Austria
Generalfeldmarschall Edwin Rommel

The telephone rang, waking him with a start. Generalfeldmarschall Erwin Rommel was not good at this time of night. Never had been. He rolled over and switched on the light and then lifted the receiver. A familiar voice spoke.

'Feldmarschall Rommel.'

Rommel paused for a moment before replying: 'Mein Führer.'

As he spoke he tumbled from the sheets and sat on the edge of the bed. Hitler continued.

'It has begun, Rommel. Montgomery has begun the big offensive we expected. General Stumme is still missing. He is either dead or captured, we must assume. You must return at once to North Africa and resume command of the Panzerarmee.'

'Yes, of course, mein Führer. At once.'

'Telephone me when you actually take off. I do not want your cure interrupted if this is only a demonstration. Wait until you hear from Feldmarschall Keitel. Yes?'

172

'Yes, mein Führer.'

'And, Rommel, I want a daily report, a *daily* report to my HQ and if there are any developments an immediate report then also. Is that clear?'

'Quite clear, mein Führer.'

'Good, Rommel. Good. You know you are the very finest of our generals. You will defeat General Montgomery. I know it. I know that I can rely on you.'

He had known it would happen, had been waiting for the moment. Keitel had called him and explained everything. Well, as much as was known. The British had been attacking in strength at El Alamein since the previous evening. General Stumme was missing. Later the same evening, just after they had eaten, Hitler himself had telephoned and repeated Keitel's report. He had politely enquired as to whether Rommel felt well enough to return to Africa. Of course he had said yes. What else?

For the best part of a month he had been here clearing up the trouble with his liver and his blood pressure, completely cut off from the outside world, save for the radio, the newspapers and the occasional letter from General Stumme and Colonel Westphal, of course, who was standing in as chief of staff for Bayerlein. But he had been restless.

The papers were full of interesting tales of the Russian front. Little progress was being made at Stalingrad or in the Caucasus. The British were bombing the Fatherland again, this time at night. At least the U-boat campaign against the Atlantic convoys seemed to be succeeding, but he wondered for how long. How long could they keep the Americans out of Europe? The Americans, he knew, were the key to this war and he had taken care to obtain figures detailing their rates of production of arms and materiel. Their manpower too was awesome.

Of course, the war was far from lost. The Wehrmacht was as strong as ever and the will of the people of Germany to win unsurpassable. But he knew that both Stumme and Kesselring were not so sure of that. It all rested on the Americans. He recalled how Göring had responded to his fears expressed at the last conference at the Führer's HQ. Rommel had told the fat chief of the Luftwaffe that the British fighter-bombers were using 40mm shells, American shells to destroy his panzers. Göring had laughed: 'The Americans only know how to make razor blades.'

Rommel had looked at him: 'Well then, we could do with some of those razor blades ourselves, Herr Reichsmarschall.'

It had been madness to declare war on America. Not of course that the Führer was mad. But by doing so they had brought the entire American industrial potential into the service of the Allied war production. It hadn't only been the 40mm shells in Africa that had told him and his men all about the quality of its achievements. During his stay in Europe, he had obtained some figures on American productive capacity. It was many times greater than that of Germany. The battle which was being fought in the Atlantic was deciding whether the Americans would be able to go on carrying their materiel to Europe, Russia and Africa. He knew that there would be little hope left for him and his countrymen if the Americans and British succeeded in eliminating, or reducing to tolerable proportions, the U-boat threat to their convoys. But if we could strangle their sea routes, he thought, then the entire industrial capacity of America would avail the Allies little. If only. It was much to ask and he prayed that it was not too much.

He buttoned his tunic over the shirt in which he had been sleeping and sat down again to pull on his high riding boots. Then he stood up and walking across to the mirror on the dressing table began to brush his sparse fair hair back from the temples. He looked at his face, saw the clear blue eyes of the boy soldier and knew that within that breast there still beat the same youthful heart. If only the body would be strong enough now to support it. He knew that the attack he was about to attempt to stop, the battle to which he was returning, would be one of the most momentous of his entire career.

He wondered in a way why the army was still there. He had in effect ordered them to be ready to abandon the Alamein position before he had left for sick leave in Germany. It was, without doubt, a sound enough position and well defended. The problem was however, that he had nothing substantial with which to hold it. Hitler had promised him Tiger tanks and the new Nebelwerfer multiple rocket-launcher. But neither had appeared. And now that the new American-built tanks were beginning to arrive with the British he knew that it could only be a matter of time before Montgomery launched his big push. Funny that he should think in those terms, for this was surely exactly what Montgomery intended. Just the sort of push that they had all seen in the Great War and had come to abhor. But still the British clung tenaciously to their doctrine.

Rommel worked differently. Not for him the plodding battle of attrition. He was a thinker, a doer. The man with the lightning touch who could turn a panzer division on the circumference of a coin. Rommel the ingenious, Rommel the magician.

He had known that the British would have to try for a break-through. And he had no doubts about the suitability of the British army for such a task. Hadn't its entire training been based on lessons learnt in the battles of materiel of the First War? And, although technical developments had left their mark on this form of warfare, they had brought about no real revolution. Although the tactical consequences of motorization and armour had been pre-eminently demonstrated by British military critics, by Fuller and Liddell Hart, the responsible British leaders had not taken the risk either of using this hitherto untried system as a foundation for peacetime training, or of applying it in war. But this failure, which had told so heavily against the British in the past, would not affect the issue of the approaching battle of position and break-through. His minefields, his 'Devil's Gardens', would rob the British armour of its freedom of movement and operation, and would force it into the role of the infantry support tank.

This would be an infantry battle and he knew that the infantry that faced him along the defensive line at El Alamein, English, Scots, Australian, New Zealand, South African and others from the British Commonwealth, was among the best in the world. And then there were the guns. More than a thousand of them his intelligence had reported.

They had to prevent the British from breaking through the line at all costs. There was simply no way in which he could fight a mobile defensive battle. The Panzerarmee's motorized formations would hardly suffice to cover a withdrawal of the infantry from a front some forty miles long and, in any case, the infantry themselves might by that time have become so involved in the action that disengagement would be unthinkable.

There were, he knew only two inescapable conclusions: the position had to be held at all costs and any penetration would have to be cleaned up by immediate counter-attack to prevent it being extended into a break-through. For if a break-through occurred, the British would throw their whole striking power into the breach. And that, he was in no doubt, would be the end.

He picked up the telephone again, dialled a number and spoke quickly to his aide, General Albert Gause: 'Gause. Call Wiener Neustadt. Order an aircraft for seven a.m. We're going back to Africa.'

SEVENTEEN

11.00 a.m.
Tactical HQ Eighth Army
Montgomery

It was not good. That was quite clear. All morning news had been filtering in from the front line and Montgomery had been becoming increasingly concerned. Now he began to see just what sort of problem Auchinleck had faced. Principally it involved a lack of belief in one's immediate junior commanders. Auchinleck's problem he knew had been with his lack of faith in Ritchie. But it had really been his predecessor's attempts at counter-attacks that had been his downfall. And now Montgomery was able to see just how easily those mistakes could have been made. Of course he had known that desert warfare was never going to be simple but in truth he had never really admitted it. How could he have? Well, now there was no alternative. He cursed all those damn Jock Columns, the defensive boxes and everything else. Everything he had inherited and whose memory he had still not been able to eradicate. His generals simply had to learn to trust him. Gatehouse had proved unreliable and weakhearted and it seemed that every hour now brought news of some other mishap.

Briggs' First Armoured Division was not on course. Kidney Ridge, the small area of high ground that extended as a salient towards the enemy in the north of the position, was held not in force, as he had been told by Lumsden, but rather it seemed by a mere whisker and only at its southern end. In the southern sector it was even worse. The French had signally failed in their attempt to capture the Himeimat Heights. Well, he had never had much faith in them. But Horrocks had been too over-optimistic. Rather than forcing the Twenty-First Panzers to attack he himself had been drawn in too far and been compelled to withdraw with heavy casualties to the Seventh Armoured. Montgomery had been furious. And then Gatehouse had had the audacity to suggest that they retreat behind the minefields and give up everything he had won in the past day. He wanted, he had said, to avoid taking heavy casualties.

Montgomery had scarcely been able to speak. Avoid heavy casualties? He had known at the outset that casualties would be taken. Lumsden of course had agreed with Gatehouse. Montgomery had spoken to the idiot on the field telephone and had gritted his teeth. Particularly when the fool had admitted to being not at the front but ten miles behind his leading tanks. Montgomery's cool had broken then and in a way he now regretted it. But what was the point of a general being so far to the rear? He had ordered him to the front. 'Take charge of your battle, man. Lead from the front.'

And now it was desperate. Anyone could see that. Montgomery pondered for a moment. He stood outside the caravan surrounded at a respectful distance by his nervous staff. Yes, it had definitely been a mistake to have shouted at Gatehouse, no matter how great an oaf the man was. Freddie de Guingand stood closest to his commanding officer, as he always did and John Poston

178

next to him. This, Montgomery realized, was the real crisis of the battle. He had thought it to have been last night when he had called their conference. But this was it. Like Wellington at Waterloo as the French cavalry had flowed against the squares. Like Marlborough at Blenheim, moving the battle from one flank to the other. The great duke had been at his old school, St Paul's and he had learnt John Churchill's tactics from an early age. Well, here was his own great test and he knew that now he must rise to it. It seemed particularly appropriate that it should occur today, on the anniversary of two of Britain's most celebrated military engagements, Agincourt and Balaclava. He prayed that his would be the success of the former and not the notorious disaster of the latter. Time for a visit to the New Zealanders' commander, he decided.

He called to de Guingand: 'Freddie. We should leave now. We need to see General Freyberg at once.'

De Guingand looked over his shoulder and signalled to the driver who had been waiting for the last half-hour expecting just such a summons, and running his engine for the last ten minutes as Montgomery had paced the sand. Slowly he brought the Humber staff car round to the front of the caravan and de Guingand, and Montgomery climbed in, with Poston in attendance. It was a short drive in the course of which Montgomery said nothing. They soon arrived at Freyberg's HQ, a large tent erected in the sand at Burgh-el-Arab. Montgomery opened the door of the car and got out. He walked over to Freyberg at the open entrance to the side of the tent and greeted him warmly.

'Hello, Bernard. We seem to be running into a little trouble with your New Zealand Division.'

Freyberg smiled but Montgomery could see that it was forced. 'Yes, sir. You might say that. Things are getting a bit hot.'

'General Gatehouse has assured me that he only has one regiment out on the Wiska Ridge.'

'No, sir, with respect. There are actually three regiments out there. All of Eight Brigade as well as the infantry. But they've taken some hits, sir.'

'Bad?'

'Pretty bad. The Staffs Yeomanry have been pretty badly cut up. Thirteen out of fifteen Crusaders and fourteen of the twenty-eight heavy tanks.'

Montgomery bristled: 'Why wasn't I told this?'

No one spoke.

'Tell me the worst. The very worst.'

Freyberg led him over to a table in the centre of the tent on which was spread a map of the area marked with the deployment of all units and the enemy. Freyberg pointed to their position: 'He's pulled them all back, sir. General Gatehouse. Pulled them all back.'

'What?'

'The bare fact is, sir, there are no armoured division troops, no tanks, no anti-tank guns, nothing in fact beyond Miteiriya Ridge.'

De Guingand interjected: 'Nothing except the tanks of the Warwicks Yeomanry, sir.'

One of Freyberg's staff, a Major Stewart spoke up: 'What we mean, General, is that there's just no armour to our south at all.'

Montgomery half-closed his eyes: 'You're telling me that the operation that I had so carefully planned in the utmost detail, the "crumbling" plan that your New Zealand troops are currently undertaking, you're telling me now that it's utterly unprotected?'

Freyberg spoke: 'Yes. In effect, sir, I am.'

Montgomery stood and stared at nothingness. It was unthinkable. That early morning conference with the generals had clearly had no effect at all. Montgomery realized that he had gone too far with it. Perhaps he had frightened both Lumsden and Gatehouse, the former into taciturn silence, the latter into outright deception. Well, at least to a shortening of the truth. The word crisis hardly seemed bad enough. This was tantamount to almost losing the battle. It was beyond reasoning. The New Zealand infantry had been left utterly exposed. At any moment Rommel's panzer divisions, even the Italian Littorio could come pouring over the ridge and there would be nothing anyone with the New Zealanders would be able to do about it. They would be annihilated and the Germans would break through in a flanking counter-attack.

'Freddie, get General Leese and General Lumsden here now.'

His fury boiling over, Montgomery walked to a quiet corner of the tent and waited. Within a few minutes Leese and Lumsden arrived. Montgomery walked over to them: 'Thank you for coming, gentlemen. We have a problem. The question is, what are we going to do about it?'

Lumsden spoke: 'Sir. The problem is that Miteiriya Ridge has a greater number and depth of mines than we had previously supposed. We are taking time to move them, sir. Time we had not allowed for and under constant shellfire.'

Freyberg interrupted: 'Sir. If I might speak. It is simply unbelievable. General Gatehouse is holding back while my lads are being blown to pieces.'

De Guingand smiled at him and waved him down politely, but Freyberg was having none of it. 'Sir, please. We must have armoured support. It is impossible to proceed with the plan as directed, the "crumbling" manoeuvres with my infantry. Certainly not for the rest of the day. I'm afraid to say, sir, that I simply cannot believe that General Gatehouse's division will break out through Miteiriya Ridge. I would strongly advise, sir,

181

that we hold off the operation until this evening. Then perhaps we can attack properly and get General Gatehouse's tanks through.'

Lumsden nodded: 'I agree. That seems an excellent idea. Sir?'

Montgomery waited for a few moments and then slowly shook his head. 'No.'

The three generals stared at him. 'Sir?'

You heard me, did you not, gentlemen? I said no and I mean no.' He paused: 'General Freyberg is right. His New Zealand infantry are some of the finest we have. They are not to be squandered. They put up a fine fight in the first day and took heavy casualties. We must do all we can to preserve them, gentlemen. We cannot use them in this way now and thus run the risk of losing them.'

He thought fast, his gut reaction taking over from the much vaunted scientific approach. They must shift the focus of the battle, that was the only answer. Gatehouse was weak, both as a man and in his materiel. His armour had been compromised. What to do now? The answer was clear; he must ignore the weaknesses and think positively, exploit his own strong points. The armoured brigades seemed to have no stomach for the fight. This was turning into an infantry battle. Montgomery knew that his commanders, old desert hands, would protest. Their vision was of wave upon wave of tanks sweeping across the sand. But that was not the way it was to be. This battle would be fought now through close cooperation between all arms.

He knew too that what he must do now was keep his opposite number guessing what he would next attempt. General von Thoma was in charge now. Stumme had been killed apparently, according to intelligence. Rommel it seemed was still on sick leave in Germany. Montgomery prayed that he would stay there. There was no point in going in again along the ridge. That would simply eat up more of the tanks to no effect. No, the answer must lie in moving the attack to a different sector. He looked at Freyberg and smiled gently.

'Bernard. I advise that your men should not attack tonight, brave as it would be. You have performed beyond all that we asked. Perhaps you should rest for a while.'

Freyberg made to protest: 'Sir, we could put in an attack with artillery support and take a position here.' He pointed to a place on the map some 4000 metres beyond the ridge. 'Then General Gatehouse's tanks could occupy that position.'

Montgomery shook his head: 'No, Bernard. That would also take too many lives. We cannot afford to lose the infantry. I need them for the days ahead.'

Freyberg opened his mouth. De Guingand looked at him with a telling gaze and he closed it. Montgomery went on: 'Freddie, have General Gatehouse's brigades, all of Tenth Amoured, withdraw from the battle. Place them in the reserve.'

The assembled group looked at him waiting for the next bombshell.

After a while he spoke: 'Freddie, gentlemen, what we're going to do is this. We're going to throw everything we have over on to the right flank.'

De Guingand looked at him. 'Sir?' Lumsden gave a sharp intake of breath. The others looked down at the map.

'Everything. We turn everything 180 degrees. We change the entire direction of the attack. And in so doing we catch the enemy unawares, gentlemen; XXX Corps will stop as of now. Is that clear, Freddie? Oliver? Effective immediately. They will hold Miteiriya Ridge and will not operate southwest beyond it as they have been doing.

We will push out the First Armoured shield and begin the crumbling again. But this time we aim into the north but towards the sea. First Armoured will fight its way to the west with the object of threatening the enemy's supply routes in the area of the Rahman Track. That is also vital, Freddie. Threaten the enemy's flank. They should establish themselves here.'

He pointed again to the map. 'Kidney Ridge.

As the generals pored over the map, Montgomery stood back from the group. He knew what he had just done was momentous. He had made the decision on which the outcome of the battle would rest and indeed quite possibly given its significance, that of the entire war. It was the turning point. He walked over to the map and pointed to a spot by the coast just to the north of Tel el Eisa. He looked at de Guingand: 'The Australians, Freddie. I know they're spoiling for a fight and we damned well need them now. Ask General Morshead to meet me at my HQ. The Australians, gentlemen. It all lies with them now.'

EIGHTEEN

5.00 p.m.
East of Trig Twenty-nine
Sergeant Bill Kibby

Bill Kibby shovelled another spoonful of cold corned beef into his mouth and when he'd almost finished chewing it turned to the man at his side who was writing something in a notebook. He swallowed the mouthful and spoke: 'Herb, mate. See if you can call the men together. I reckon it's about time I told the lads what's going on.'

Herb Ashby, Kibby's platoon sergeant, looked up from his diary and nodded. Kibby, normally so outspoken, had been unusually quiet since he had returned from the CO's briefing of platoon commanders at midday and Ashby knew something was up.

'Will do, Bill. Do I get any clues?'

'Well it sounds like a big one, mate. We've got our work cut out right enough. I'll clue you in with the others.'

Ashby closed the little notebook and tucked it into his breast pocket and as he ran off to summon the men of their platoon, Kibby contemplated his current position. He was sitting in a captured German trench some five miles from their previous day's start line. And he was about to brief his platoon. Christ, he thought; 'His' platoon.

Since yesterday he had been platoon leader and it still shocked him how quickly his promotion had come and why. He had originally been platoon sergeant to Diver Derrick's Eight Platoon but with a massive shake-up after the last big fight at Alam Halfa and that business in August a new lieutenant, Peter Crompton, had been given command of D Company. He'd moved Bill across to Seventeen Platoon. That had been promotion enough, he'd thought. But fate had more in store.

Bill had led Seventeen into the fight yesterday night, had taken them forward through the wire and the mines and into the German positions. Had watched them fall and then as they'd reached their first objective had seen his officer, Lieutenant Lewin, Tubby as the men called him, fall to the ground – hit in the knee.

He knew from that moment that command had fallen to him. As the bullets had flown around them, Kibby had found Ashby and told him that he was taking over and he was his new sergeant. It stood to reason. Ashby had served with distinction at Alam Halfa and Bill knew he would be a fine leader.

His chance to prove it had come just a few minutes later. Together they had led a charge into the secondary German positions. It had been madness he knew but then again there was no other way. They'd fixed that Jerry strongpoint for sure. Got a few of the blighters and the rest had given up.

Kibby liked to lead from the front, to set the pace. Not just for his own platoon but for its neighbours. Now though he guessed that he and the rest of the company of which his platoon was part were in trouble. They had just advanced too far too fast. D Company were on the north, C and A west and northwest respectively. They had expected an enemy counter-attack at first light on the twenty-fourth. A strong one. The engineers had set a

186

double row of Hawkins mines around their new position. Daft bits of kit he thought, nothing more than tin cans full of explosive placed on the ground. But the sappers assured him that they would do the job. Against what, he wondered? Jerry panzers? He didn't bloody think so.

And sure enough at daybreak there came a terrible squealing and clanking from beyond the sand dunes to their front. The tanks were out there, a hundred yards to their front. Unseen, lurking. Kibby had waited for the first shells to come ploughing in taking men with them. Instead though, planes had come over, British planes. This, he thought, was what Monty meant by working together. They had cheered as the Brylcreem Boys had taken out the panzers.

But now there was a new nightmare. Ashby was back in the trench now, their men following close behind him, thirty of them in all. Kibby called them closer around him so that while he stood in the trench they were crouching around the perimeter.

'All right, fellas. I'm not going to pull any punches. Some clever brass hat at GHQ's dreamed up a real blinder of a plan. Guess what we've got to do?'

Someone, was it Marsh, said: 'Go and capture Rommel, Sarge?'

Kibby smiled: 'Not quite, son. But damn close. No, You see, seems there's a hill up there.' He pointed towards the south. 'Trig Twenty-nine they call it. Well, according to Battalion there's a forward observation post of ours up there that's been spotting for the guns and not been doing a half-bad job of it. It's a high point. You can see everything. The railway line and the whole of XXX Corps too. So the Jerries are a bit narked and want it for themselves.'

There were sniggers from the ranks, cries of, 'Selfish buggers.'

'It's about a mile forward from us. And for the last

187

few hours the Jerries have been plastering it with shell-fire. Well, seems it's getting a bit hairy for the lads up there and they've asked for some proper soldiers to come and sort the Jerries out. And that's where we come in. They want us to secure the hill and the spur around it.'

Another voice piped up. Morrison, a sheepshearer from Canberra: 'What, just us, Sarge?'

'No, you drongo, Morrison. The whole of Twenty-six Brigade. Morshead's whole crew. Us and the rest of the 2/48th and the 2/24th an' all.'

Someone whistled. 'Where exactly do we go, Sarge?'

'Good question, Marsh. Good question. We, boys, are part of an attack against somewhere called the Fig Orchard.'

'Coo, Sarge. Does that mean we get to eat some figs?'

'You can eat all the figs you bloody-well like, Malone. But only after you've taken the bloody place. And after we have taken it then we move out and see if we can't take somewhere called Thompson's Post. All right? All clear?'

There was nodding. 'When do we go, Sarge?'

'Midnight, Marsh. We go at midnight. So everyone try to get some rest before then.'

He had never imagined that this could happen to him. To be not quite forty and to be leading a platoon of his countrymen in this bloody barren wilderness so many thousands of miles from home. Was this what he had been preparing for all his life? Of course he still felt an allegiance to the old country. His family had only emigrated in 1914. He was a Geordie, as his granny told him every time he had seen her. Newcastle was his family home although for the past twenty-five years it had been Adelaide. Maybe when this was all over he'd set up on his own. He reckoned they could be in for some sort of payment for war service and every town needed plasterers. That's what he'd do, start a little business and they could all move to a nice house in Brighton, Glenelg or even Kensington Gardens.

He didn't mind it when the lads called him a 'pom'. He liked it, if the truth be known. He thought about Mabel and their two girls, back in Helmsdale, aged fourteen and twelve now. He wondered what they were doing at this moment, and tried to work out what time it would be down under.

'How're ya doing, Lofty?'

Kibby stared at him and shook his head. 'I've told you, Herb mate. Try to call me Sarge or something. I'm only your bloody platoon commander.'

'Sorry, mate. I mean Sarge. S'pose I should really call you sir.'

'Come on, Herb. The day I make officer you can ship me back to Adelaide. You'll never see a pip on these shoulders.'

Herb Ashby grinned at him. He liked Kibby. They were good mates in fact.

Lofty was the only nickname he could ever have had in the army, Australian army at least. At five-foot-six Kibby was the shortest man in his platoon. But he made up for his lack of height with a formidable strength. Riding, football, cricket, anything outdoors and Bill Kibby was your man. It had been only natural to have joined the Militia six years back. They'd made him an artilleryman, a gunner. He'd liked that. The idea of sending a huge heavy shell through the air appealed to him. But when war had broken out he'd joined the infantry. So here he was, a bloody footslogger, in the Twenty-fourth Australian.

But even as Ashby smiled, Kibby was burning with a need to tell him. Tell anyone. That was why he knew he'd never make an officer. He was too keen to share all he knew with the men, even though now he realized why you didn't want to tell the men everything. Since he'd assumed command of the platoon he'd quickly come to have a different regard for officers. He'd always thought them a bit dim really. It was the sarges that did all the work, everyone knew that. But now, well, now he wasn't so sure. Of course, the NCOs did all the real work but there was something else that went with being an officer. A horrible responsibility.

He yearned to tell the men but dared not, because he knew or thought he had a pretty good idea of just what sort of hell they were headed into.

Lewin had called him and Ashby over before the assault and had shown them Monty's orders to the Ninth Australian Division. They were specific and chilling: draw everything on to yourself. It is vital.

'Draw everything on yourself'; they were going to be used as decoys, a target to get the Jerries away from where Monty wanted the big attack to go in. It was a classic tactic but that didn't make the knot of fear in Kibby's stomach go away.

NINETEEN

5.30 p.m.
Point 115
Ringler

They had been here for near on thirty hours now, had beaten off another British attack with heavy casualties and Ringler wondered whether they would manage another one if, or rather when it came in. In that time though he had witnessed one of the most haunting things he had seen in a war that had brought many bizarre episodes.

During a lull in the fighting earlier this afternoon a British jeep and an ambulance had appeared from behind one of the sand dunes. They had been about to fire on the jeep when he had noticed the red cross marked on the side of the second vehicle, and a curious emblem with a bird painted in its centre. He had shouted to Fiedler to find a white flag and wave it. They had found a dirty shirt. The English had driven in and so he had run down the hill with two of the men and for a moment caught the eye of a young man wearing the uniform of a British soldier but looking somehow different from the infantrymen he had encountered before. The young man had stared at Ringler, long and hard, as if he were trying to understand something about him. He had not spoken but had turned and gone to attend the English wounded. Ringler had wondered who he was. He had a kind face and did not look like a soldier. Perhaps, he thought, he was one of the volunteer ambulance drivers they had heard about. An American. He wondered what it could be that would make a man want to come to this hell on earth and not fight. To come here to be shot at and simply to help his fellow man. He found it hard to comprehend. The desert, this desert, was a place of death, an arena where two sides stood against one another to decide the fate of nations. There was little room for mercy here. Yet in the past few months he had seen his fair share of it. In a sense, he thought, this battle, this tiny part of a much bigger conflict is surely the last war fought by gentlemen, where chivalry and fair play have a hand.

Now they were down to thirty-two men. Mahnke and the rest of the badly wounded had been taken back to the reserve lines. Feuerkogel though, despite the extent of his injuries, had stayed on, making do with his makeshift bandages.

Half an hour the truce had lasted but fifteen minutes after the British ambulance had driven away the shelling had begun again. And so it had been on and off ever since. As he thought about it another salvo came in and hit their position. There were no shouts, no casualties. None at least save the morale and the nerves. It was the incessant nature of it, that and the randomness. Ringler buried his head in his hands. One thing was certain. They could not stand another day like this.

Fiedler came up to him: 'Sir. The men are on their last few drops of water. Is there any chance of getting any more?'

'Not at present, Fiedler, I'm afraid. Be assured that my thirst is as great as anyone's.'

As the despondent sergeant wandered off with the unhappy news, Ringler raised his field glasses and scoured the dunes to their front, as he had done every few minutes for the last few hours. Nothing. Sand and the burnt-out hulks of the tanks and a few other vehicles caught in a previous fight littered the desert landscape. He swept the glasses in front of him in a 180-degree arc. Nothing. Then he froze. Suddenly every fibre of his being was on fire. There, two or maybe three thousand metres away to the northwest: Tanks. Enemy tanks. A great wedge of them approaching their position freely and with no opposition. They looked larger than any he had seen previously. Were these the new much-talked-of Shermans sent from America? How the hell had they got there, he wondered. There must be another way through the minefield. As he watched the tanks continued on their path and cut through the desert on their flank. My God, he thought, they're coming around to attack us in the rear. They would have no chance; unless – he had an idea. There was an observation post sited five hundred yards directly to his rear. Perhaps if he were to make contact with it he might be able to get in touch with Battalion HQ. He looked behind, uphill. It was just up there he knew, a little distance behind the assault gun. Quickly and without more thought, Ringler sprang out of the foxhole and took off up the slope. He ran stooped, trying desperately not to attract the enemy fire. It was in vain. He had been running only a few moments when the sand around him began to sing with incoming bullets. He flung himself to the ground but realized that he must go on. The bullets were flying everywhere around him but he knew that it would be just as bad going back as it was going on. He got up and still stooped ran the rest of the distance up the hill. His chest was pounding as he reached the summit and the perimeter of the OP. With a last desperate effort he leapt into the position and landed in a heap. He looked up and saw Lieutenant Bauer. He smiled.

'Congratulations on your three hits, Ringler.'

'I thought they might be Italians.'

'Rubbish. They were obviously English.'

Despite Bauer's arrogant tone, Ringler felt relieved. Bauer went on: 'If they had come on a bit we would have helped – but I can only shoot if the OP is directly threatened.'

'Thanks for that! Well perhaps now you can let me get in radio contact with the Battalion HQ.'

Bauer shrugged and smiled: 'Well, we can try – perhaps I can get them through Divisional HQ.'

They walked across the floor of the OP to where a private was sitting beside the radio transmitter. Bauer spoke: 'Hans, see if you can raise Division for Lieutenant Ringler.'

The set crackled into life and after a few attempts the operator managed to get a response. Ringler looked at his watch and spoke and the man transmitted the message: 'Situation report at 1800 hours 25 October. About fifteen enemy tanks have broken through approximately 3000 metres to the north. My company is reduced to thirty-two men, one anti-tank gun and one machine-gun still working. We have no food, no water, little ammo, three enemy tanks knocked out by my men. Please send further orders soonest.'

He turned to Bauer: 'Thanks.'

'Yes. We'll see how you get on. I shouldn't build up your hopes. I think things are looking pretty grim right now.'

Ringler smiled and turned. He looked out beyond the OP and saw the advancing wedge of tanks, closer now. He turned back to Bauer: 'Good luck, Bauer. See you back at HQ.'

'Hope so. But if you ask me you're the one who'll need all the luck, Ringler.'

Not bothering to reply, Ringler climbed back over the sandbags and without thinking began to run down the slope. Again the machine-guns from the Allied lines leapt out at him. A word came into his mind, 'Kismet'. An Arab word meaning 'fate'. He repeated it over and over again with every step as he plummeted back towards the position. The rounds thudded into the earth around him and with one last bound he threw himself into the foxhole. Then brushing himself off he settled down to watch. The shells came crashing in, and slowly, the sun went down below the horizon.

TWENTY

7 p.m.
Rommel

The little plane circled again and then regained its course, flying east, away from the setting sun.

Rommel looked out of the window of the little Fieseler Storch down at the Libyan coast which was now passing several thousand feet below him, and knew for certain what he had guessed the moment he had boarded. No, from the moment he had received the phone call from Keitel telling him that Montgomery had attacked. He was flying to his nemesis. He brushed a speck of dust from the pocket of his distinctive olive-green leather overcoat and strained for the first signs of his army. The Panzerarmee Afrika. The Afrika Korps. Some of the best fighting men ever to wage war under German colours. Men of such courage, such audacity. Men who he knew would follow him to death whenever he asked them to, as had the men of all his commands, for the last thirty years. He had the power to inspire. Hitler himself had told him so. But Rommel had known it from the moment of his first commission as an infantry officer.

He turned to his aide, General Albert Gause, who was seated close behind him in the small aircraft. He liked Gause, a clever easy-going Prussian with a notably dry

196

wit. He had earned his spurs in the Great War and taken several wounds. Rommel had been instrumental in obtaining his Knight's Cross the previous December.

'Nothing's changed then, Gause? Eh?'

Gause smiled: 'It would appear not, Herr Feldmarschall.'

'It would appear not, Gause.'

Nothing had changed. But then everything had changed. And in such a short space of time. Only a few months ago, in August, he had felt sure that they could triumph. But now. The truth was, he had not been at all well since August. All that stomach trouble had set in again. He'd called in a specialist, Professor Horster. Then things had got even worse. He had even begun to have fainting fits and dizzy spells. Horster had given his condition numerous names, none of which made it any better. He said it was something to do with the circulation of the blood. Liver and blood pressure.

Rommel had never had blood problems. Aches and pains yes, but in his own opinion he was as fit as ever. It was ironic, he thought, when he recalled the words of his doctor back in February 1941 when the Führer had first appointed him to command of the African theatre. It would be good for his rheumatism. Sunshine it seemed was the best treatment for that old trouble. A holiday in North Africa would sort him out. Holiday? He wished that doctor were with him now. He'd show him what sort of holiday this was.

Instead of a cure, Africa had given him a worse illness than he had had. His every nerve felt strained to the limit. His darling Lucie had been so worried about him. Well, at fifty years old, he thought, he was bound to have health problems. Even someone as fit as he was could not hope to work as he did, without some aspect of their health suffering.

Of course, his marriage had helped to keep him calm.

He and Lucie had been married twenty-five years last year. A quarter of a century of love and happiness and with the added blessing of their son, dear Manfred, who had recently joined the local Hitler Youth troop.

And in all that time, while other officers had had their flings, he had never been unfaithful to her. He loved her as much now, more even, than he had when they had first met and wrote her letters almost every day. Darling Lu. He had told her, of course, about all the admiring letters he himself had received from women and girls at home, some of them more amorous than he could ever have imagined.

He'd wanted Heinz Guderian sent out to replace him. But his old friend was not in the Führer's favour, worse luck, and so Kesselring had taken over. Albert Kesselring. Rommel grimaced. He did not trust the man, he knew for certain that he was plotting to have him replaced. It had been Kesselring who had suggested General Stumme as a replacement when he had flown off for the rest cure. Amiable, robust, fat Georg Stumme, who it now appeared was either dead or a prisoner. He had been missing for twenty-four hours. The Führer had called Rommel personally the previous evening to tell him as much. And so Rommel was back. And Kesselring would be manoeuvring again. He knew it.

The little plane swooped low for a second time, taking its customary avoiding action to evade the Allied fighters. The pilot was a novice. Normally Rommel would have taken over the controls and flown the plane himself, but in truth he was not really feeling up to scratch. He had taught himself to fly back in the years just after the war. He loved the exhilaration of soaring above the clouds, so different from the ground-centred nature of his career. He was an infantryman at heart. He supposed that his love of flying was a natural response for one who had been mired in the trenches of the Western Front although he had been lucky, being posted to the mountains of the Italian front and in fact long before he had decided to become a soldier he had nurtured a love of flight. That had been his first desire. But once again his far-seeing father had predicted that there would be no future in aeroplane design.

He looked up at the underside of the single wing of the plane, examined the aileron and enjoyed the elegant lines. But then the plane turned again and as its wing tip touched the horizon his line of vision was interrupted by the blackened shell of a burned-out tank. An Italian tank. It brought him back to reality.

Alam Halfa had been a mistake. He admitted that now, although he had not said as much to Hitler or Keitel. How could he really have hoped to win with barely 500 tanks, and half of those Italian. As for the fuel that Kesselring had promised him, most had never reached the front. Oh, it had been airlifted in from Italy all right but as it had travelled up the line it had been handed out to all-comers. The tanks had received hardly any. Their advance had been slow, not helped by the soft sand. Speed and surprise were of the essence and his force drowned in that moment.

September had been worse. Six attacks. So many of his own staff killed, seven good friends. And so he had given the order to pull back, and here they had sat ever since. Two months.

Before he had flown he had made sure that the defensive line was in place, 450,000 mines, deep minefields. Of course, these alone would not be enough. But they would delay the British. If only the Führer would send the promised tanks. But they would have no defensive 'cages', and no tanks. So he would use the motorized infantry. Hold the reserves back until the Allies penetrated the line and then rush them forward to defend the gap.

It was so different from the way he was used to fighting a war. He was an attacker. Wasn't his book about all that? *Infantry Attacks* it was called and that was just what he did. It had hurt him almost physically to have to order the retreat to El Agheila last December, his first retreat as a soldier. But it had been the only way. With Tobruk relieved and his fuel running low, he had realized that he could not go on.

So even if he believed they could win the war, in his heart he felt that they would probably lose Africa. Hitler's strategy was basically flawed. Malta was the key. Rommel knew it. They must take Malta first to ensure supplies, ammunition, fuel and men. But Malta was not theirs yet and despite that fact, Hitler insisted that they should still push on to Cairo. But with what? With his name? His reputation?

He was aware of his value, his status. He was Rommel, wasn't he? Rommel the hero. Didn't Goebbels say just that every time they met? He was 'a miracle worker', a 'genius'. Worth 50,000 men in the field. But Rommel was beginning to wonder whether his luck hadn't run out and whether if he failed here, Germany would not fall out of love with the hero.

He wondered what his father would make of him now. He had never wanted his son to join the army. He remembered the day in 1910 when he had left the classroom in his father's school in Heidenheim and walked off to the barracks of the 124th Württemberg infantry regiment to enrol. He recalled quite clearly his father's red-faced rage. Well, who could blame the man. He was a maths teacher. He had already persuaded young Erwin from meddling in aeroplanes. What did his son want with the army?

He cursed at the interminable flight. He had gone first from Munich to Rome. The meeting with General Rintelen had confirmed his worst fear; the British attack was

200

making progress and Stumme had gone missing. Further to that Rintelen had confided that there were only three issues of petrol for the army in Africa. They had tried to send more from Italy in the past few weeks but the British had sunk what ships they had. He had cursed the Italian navy and their lack of available transport. Rommel shook his head, watched by Gause. It was nothing less than a disaster. Didn't the Führer realize that the war in Africa was all about fuel? It was a desert war where he who had the most vehicles was king. Such lack of petrol meant that every vehicle in his army, every tank and truck had a maximum range of 180 miles. How could he resist Montgomery and Alexander? No fuel would mean that his tactical decisions would be impaired.

He had personally ensured that on his departure for Germany there had been eight issues of fuel in hand for the army, precious little in comparison with the thirty there should have been. But three! Good God. He knew that to fight effectively the army would need one issue of petrol for each day of battle. Without that you could only sit where you were like some cripple, allowing the enemy free range. They were in effect not equipped to fight any longer than three days, and so far the battle had been raging for two days. It was nearing dusk now. Rommel peered down again at the ground below and recognized landmarks.

'So, Gause. What first? We land and then what. To the front? Yes? Or have I some other duties? Remind me.'

'I'm sorry, Feldmarschall. We have promised that you would find time to award the German Cross to Colonel Bayerlein. It's protocol, sir.'

'Of course. Protocol. Bayerlein deserves it too. Then what?'

'Then we rejoin the army, sir. Your caravan has been kept locked as you instructed.'

Rommel gazed out of the window: 'How do you like the desert, Gause? Better than Belgium or the Russian front?'

'It must be better than Russia, Herr Feldmarschall. It stands to reason, sir.'

'Yes, Gause. Much better than Russia for sure. Even with the sandstorms, eh?'

He remembered his first experience of the sandstorm, the *ghibli*. That terrible frenzy of dust and debris so dense that its red clouds darkened the sun. He recalled the gasping for breath and the incredible searing heat, like standing before an open furnace.

That of course had been in the glory days. The spring of 1941 when he had gone against orders from Berlin that had told him to halt and carried on, chasing the fleeing British out of Benghazi. He recalled how he had driven himself into the abandoned base at Mechili and, walking through a column of abandoned British vehicles, had reached into one of the cabs and quite by chance found a pair of Perspex sand goggles, with an elastic strap. They were the latest thing and hardly worn. He had attached them to his cap and there they now sat on its peak as they had ever since that day. His trademark. The men liked such individual touches. He remembered turning to his aide, the affable Lieutenant Schmidt: 'They're just booty, Schmidt. What d'you think? Even we great generals are allowed a little booty, eh?'

Charisma. That was what it was about. It was all very well being a good tactician. He had told Schmidt that too: 'If you really want to be a leader of men then charisma is vital.' And Rommel knew that he had charisma. In spades. Even the British respected him. The 'Desert Fox' they called him now, had done since the race to Tobruk. And how quickly his own men had taken it up: 'Der Wüstenfuchs'. It suited him. The little animal was an expert at fast manoeuvre and concealment, and speed was Rommel's trademark, along with the ability to vanish like a ghost. And that was what they had christened his Panzer Division in 1940 when he had charged into France, unseen and invincible. He was proud of his reputation. Well, it had been hard-won. Although he was well aware that there were those in Berlin who despised him for it.

Wilhelm Keitel for instance, the great Field Marshal, who he knew resented his individual style, and Franz Halder, Hitler's ultra-conservative Chief of the General Staff. Rommel knew Halder had poisoned the Führer's mind against him. How could they ever win the war with such idiots in command, content to sit on their own arses and lick the Führer's. It had not done Halder any good. Hadn't he beaten off the British attack at Halfaya Pass? Hitler had promoted him and given him two new limousines.

He had taken to Hitler on their first meeting, late in the summer of 1936 when he had been personally chosen to command the escort party for the Führer at the Nuremberg rally. He had managed to control the crowd of hangers-on with conspicuous determination and Hitler had sent for him afterwards. They took to each other instantly. It hadn't surprised him that he should have been appointed the following year as liaison officer between the War Ministry and the Hitler Youth. But to be the Führer's headquarters commandant during the invasion of Poland had been the greatest honour.

Rommel admired the Führer's hatred of the old Germany's elitist class system. Both of them had come from relatively humble origins. Both of them had done well. And then after Tobruk had fallen in June the ultimate accolade – Field Marshal. Lucie had cried down the telephone when he had told her. She had heard him too speaking on Greater German radio, heard the words which came back to haunt him now: 'Soldiers of the Panzerarmee Afrika. A great battle has been won. The enemy has lost all his armour. Now we will shatter the last remnants of this British Eighth Army.'

Again, of course Halder had forbidden an advance. But with the huge supplies of captured British fuel, Rommel had disobeyed again and knew that he must chase them. He had known they would be in Cairo by June. Everything had felt right. Victory so close, Cairo within his grasp. So what had happened? The answer was simple.

He looked up from the ground below them, realizing that they were about to land. In truth though he had not been looking at anything. He found himself staring into the face of his aide.

'You know the problem, Gause?'

'Sir?'

'The problem. The reason why we may not win this battle.'

'Sir? I'm not quite sure I understand.'

Rommel smiled and put a fatherly hand on the man's shoulder. 'Fuel, Gause. We just need more fuel. Without fuel for the panzers this damned desert is just going to swallow us up. Without more fuel, Gause, we might as well all go home.'

TWENTY-ONE

9.00 p.m.
Point 115
Ringler

After two hours there was still no news from Lieutenant Bauer up on the hill. Ringler was concerned. He had promised to get the answer down to him as soon as it came through. In that time the shellfire from the enemy guns had increased and Ringler was feeling very uncomfortable. At least with the twilight which bathed the desert in a strange violet light, visibility was reduced and so the British gunners were having problems with their aiming. He turned to one of the men with him in the foxhole: 'Lance-Corporal Kater.'

'Sir.'

'Take a run up to the OP and see what's holding up Lieutenant Bauer. We need that reply from HQ.'

Kater leapt the sandbag wall and began to run up the slope. As Ringler had known they would the British machine-guns opened up on him, again kicking up spurts where they hit the sand around him and the lieutenant watched with concern as the man neared the top. But Kater jumped clear and disappeared behind the dune. Ringler breathed a sigh of relief and was equally pleased when the his head and torso appeared above the skyline. Kater was waving his arms excitedly, but in the twilight it was hard to make out what he was trying to indicate.

Within a few minutes though Kater was back with them in the foxhole. He was out of breath: 'Sir, the OP's taken a direct hit.'

'What casualties?'

'Only the driver of the assault gun's left alive.'

'Lieutenant Bauer?'

'Dead. Killed by a piece of shrapnel in the head.'

'The others?'

Kater looked grim: 'Nothing left of them, sir. Just fragments.'

'What about the radio?'

'Kaput, Lieutenant.'

'Did our report get through to Division?'

'The driver thought that it did.'

Ringler said nothing and together they all waited. The evening began to grow darker and Ringler wondered that even if the message had got through, just how quickly HQ might be able to send them fresh supplies. He had an idea: 'All right. I need five men. A recce party. We need to know whether there's anything worth salvaging over there by the burnt-out tanks.'

Slowly one of the men stood up. 'I'll go, sir.'

Then another: 'And me, sir.' Soon he had assembled his five men, led by Fiedler.

'You know the drill – anything worth bringing back. Food, ammo, guns, water, anything.'

They nodded and slowly began to make their way out of the system of foxholes and stumbled through the twilight down the slope towards the wrecked tanks. Ringler lost sight of them and waited. The minutes passed. Ringler gazed out into the darkening evening. Shots. From the direction of the tanks. A few minutes later he heard approaching runners. Seconds later four men tumbled into the foxhole. As three of them lay panting on the floor, Fiedler got up and made his report. 'We were just about to turn around and come back, sir, when we heard a noise. We were being shot at. In the open, sir, with the horizon behind us. We had to get away. Kranzhauber was hit, sir. He's dead. I'm sure. We couldn't bring him back with us or we'd all have had it.'

'Did you fire back?'

'Yes, sir. We must have hit one of them. We heard a scream.' He paused: 'Don't worry. We'll still get Kranzhauber, Lieutenant.'

Ringler said nothing and tried to think but seconds later there was a scream. Faint and shrill and barely audible, it split the evening and came from the site of the wrecked tanks. As they listened the screams became louder. Ringler looked at Fiedler and nodded. Then, with the lieutenant leading, the corporal and the three men who had just returned with him climbed out of the foxhole and began to walk back down the slope. As they neared the wreckage the screams stopped abruptly. Then there was a different sound. A man crying. Ringler listened. It was, he thought, not unlike the noise made by a dying animal. It brought him back to the woods around his home in the lower Rhineland. Hunting country. The noise was more plangent now and he could not help thinking of the first deer he had shot, the wounded animal dying in agony and the huntsman telling him off for missing the heart.

Then he saw them. The bodies, directly in front of them. They were lying quite close together. Kranzhauber was dead. That was obvious. He was lying on his back and his cap had slipped off his head at a comical angle which was now grotesque. What made his pose all the more poignant was that his arms were folded flat behind his head, like a sleeping child. There was another body. The Englishman had crawled towards Kranzhauber. His bloodstained hands

207

were yearningly close to the German's body. Ringler could see the trail of blood left by them as the man had pulled himself closer and closer to Kranzhauber. He was a young man with a shock of red hair. His untouched face seemed peaceful in death. Ringler tried to piece together his last moments and arrived at the conclusion that he had simply wanted to be close to someone at the moment of his death. But instead all that the young Englishman had found was another corpse. How senseless it all was.

He looked at Fiedler: 'We should dig.' And so they dug a grave. Deep and wide. Wide enough for Kranzhauber. They hacked and dug into the rock and sand, oblivious to the fact that at any moment a British machine-gun might mow them all down. A deep, wide grave. Deep enough for Kranzhauber and deep enough for the Englishman. When they had finished they all stood for a moment and rested. Then they lifted the two corpses into the grave. They took care and put Kranshauber's weapon in with him. Then they filled up the space with sand and stones. When the bodies were covered they placed the cap and the helmet on the top of the graves. Two more bereaved mothers, he thought. Two women waiting in vain for news of their sons. Two more families destroyed by this senseless war. Of course he could not say as much to any of the men, nor even to his fellow officers. But at this moment that was exactly what it seemed. And there they were, two men, brought together by the war that had killed them, and buried in a common grave.

Together they moved quickly and silently back up to the position. Ringler was drained, exhausted, burnt out. Fiedler turned to him: 'Sorry, sir. Orders from Battalion. Sent by runner. We're to go back through the minefield at once. Abandon the position.'

Ringler said nothing. Then: 'Fine, Fiedler. Get the men on their feet. Let's go.'

208

Fiedler smiled at him: 'Sir. Have you seen them? Most of them are exhausted and asleep. I don't know how I can rouse them.'

From his side Ringler heard heavy breathing. Kater and Feuerkogel were sleeping deeply, the former's head nestled on the latter's shoulder. How could he wake them? Ringler felt suddenly energized. There was a new objective. He called the section and group leaders together, what was left of them. 'Listen carefully. Our withdrawal must be swift and silent. The English must not realize that we are leaving here, or at least not until it's too late for them to act. We'll go in groups. Crawl over the edge of the dune and then through the minefield. Assemble at the other side.'

He turned to Müller, the one who had broken down under fire. Remarkably, since then the man had been composed. 'Müller. You go with the first group. Take my car to the OP and gather up the dead. We'll carry the wounded and anyone who can't walk on the assault-gun carriage. Fiedler, you and I will go last and spike the gun.'

He turned to one of the sleeping men and prodded him. No response. He tried again and was met with abuse. They were sleeping the sleep of the dead. It took a full fifteen minutes to rouse the survivors. At first Ringler shook them but they made no response and it was only by beating them repeatedly with their fists that he and the four men of the scouting party finally managed to get their comrades on their feet. One by one they began to crawl away from the position back up the hill. In silence Ringler signalled to those men who were most awake and fit that they would have to move the undamaged anti-tank gun from its position in the side of the dunes. Then he, Fiedler and three of the others got their shoulders beneath its chassis. He felt the metal warm against his shirt, took the strain and began to push. It moved by inches. One of the men fell away panting for breath. Ringler signalled for more help and another man appeared in his place. Eventually after another twenty minutes they got it to the crest of the dune and pushed. The gun tumbled down the other side into the soft sand. The men who had been pushing it followed and lay on the ground gasping with the effort. Ringler allowed himself a couple of minutes of rest before getting to his feet again. He had no idea whether the British could make him out against the night sky. There was little moon tonight but the desert was capable of playing treacherous tricks. Slowly, he made his way back down the slope and reached the position. There were only six men left there with the wounded. As he entered the foxhole for the last time there was a whistling above their heads. The world rocked as a shell exploded a few metres away to the right. There had been no time to take cover. Lukas, one of the anti-tank gunners, screamed in agony. Ringler spoke quietly: 'Any more been hit?'

There was a murmuring. He looked across the foxhole and saw that one man, Kater, was not moving. He crawled across the floor and looked down at his face. It was ashen white and beneath his forage cap a pool of dark blood was seeping slowly. Ringler carefully lifted off the cap and saw that a shell splinter had neatly sliced off the back of his head. It was clear though from his eyes that the poor devil was still alive. He moaned and looked at the lieutenant full in the face. Ringler whispered: 'Does it hurt, Kater?'

The man said nothing but shook his head. Thank God thought Ringler. He knows nothing of it and soon he'll be dead. He wondered again whether the British had noticed the activity in the post or whether it had just been a random salvo. If they were to attack now he and his men would be helpless. He wondered whether they should surrender or fight on to the end. Silly to think about that. There was still time to get away, wasn't there? He turned to Fiedler: 'Put an explosive charge down the barrel of that gun, will you? Then with a bit of luck we'll all get away.'

210

TWENTY-TWO

9.30 p.m.
The start line, Kidney Ridge
Samwell

It was nine-thirty and still they had not moved. For the last five hours they had lain in the shellholes listening to the incessant bombardment. The midday briefing had suggested that they would go in at 1600 hours. 'It is clear that our position is precarious as long as our left flank remains open. The reserve company will walk across the gap and take the objective of the unit which should be to your left. The intention is to bottle up any enemy in the gap and try to find that damned unit.'

It had sounded so urgent. Imperative. So why, he wondered, were they still waiting here?

Naturally Samwell had had a rocket for his folly in the first night's assault. How, he wondered, had he not had the sense to send men after the running Italians in those trenches? Apparently they had simply run back after he and his men had passed and shot up the reserve companies and Battalion HQ who were coming behind. He still did not know how many lives, how many wounded his inaction had cost the battalion. Nor did he particularly want to find out.

Certainly the loss of officers had been horrendous. His

two original forward companies now had only two officers between them, himself and a captain who had been transferred from the right reserve company. And Samwell knew that that company had only its CO and one subaltern left. Number Four company had been dispersed to fill holes in the others and the remainder of the company which had been detailed to follow up with the tanks had not been seen for ten hours. In all the total strength of the rifle companies was not more than 150 of all ranks. Sitting in the shellholes they had been amused to see tanks come up in the afternoon and move forward to a rise in the ground. They had lined up as if they were on a review at Aldershot and then had been hit by enemy fire one after the other like ducks in a fairground shooting gallery. It was about as depressing and demoralizing a spectacle as they could have witnessed and he hoped that it had not had too bad an effect upon the men. Thankfully at 9 p.m. some rum came up prior to the attack, and Samwell thought of the first war and the way it had been. Officers had died then too. In droves. His father of course had been spared. But he could not help but think that if this was Montgomery's great new modern plan of attack how exactly did it differ from that employed on the Somme in 1916?

The rum was not enough. The men did not get their regulation tablespoon swig each and they were obviously disgruntled. Naturally the NCOs and officers declined theirs and Samwell wished that his whisky bottle still contained something more than water.

They moved up to the start line. A long trench, but quite shallow. Again he thought of the Western Front, of his father. It occurred to him that it was cruel for two generations to have to undergo this ordeal. The two missing platoons had come up now and the reserves left to rejoin their original company. Samwell did a quick head count. He had thirty-two men left, the company sergeant-major, two corporals and himself.

The moon rose high in the sky. Sergeant-Major Macdonald turned to him and spoke quietly in a lilting, gentle West Highland accent: 'D'you suppose, sir, that the moon might tell Jerry that we're coming to pay him a visit?'

'Yes, Sar'nt-Major. I think you might have a point. And with the new company arriving and the reserves being up at the start line this place sounds like Piccadilly Circus.'

'Wouldn't know, sir. I have never been there, sir. But now if you were talking of Sauchiehall Street on a Saturday night, well I might just take your point.'

'Sauchiehall Street it is, Sar'nt-Major. Perhaps I'll see you there after this lot's over.'

'That would be fine, sir. I'll stand you a pint in the Horseshoe Bar.'

'It's a deal. And I'll get in the chasers. Whisky. Or rum if you prefer it.'

They laughed together. Then a whistle blew and they stopped laughing and looked to their front. Slowly the men began to climb up and over the top of the sandbags. Just like my father's war, thought Samwell again. They stood on the parapet and began to advance and almost instantly the German guns opened up. There was no artillery support, as there had been on the previous attack. The idea this time, he and the other officers had been enthusiastically informed by the CO, was to surprise the enemy. In any case the position they were to assault was held only lightly by frightened Italians who had apparently tried to surrender to the recce officer earlier in the day. He had reported that he had been forced to refuse as he had been alone, but that some of his friends would be along later to gather them up. The men had been heartened by the news. Now they walked on with confidence.

They had gone no more than a few yards when streams of machine-gun tracer bullets began to whistle across their front, intersecting at a point a hundred yards directly ahead. Alarm bells rang in Samwell's head. Again he was a soldier on the Western Front in 1916. The enemy were firing across their front on fixed lines, just as they had twenty-five years ago.

There was a heavy crump and in an instant mortar shells began to land just to their right and rear. Samwell knew that it would only be a matter of seconds before the mortar commander found their range. There was only one way to go now and that was forward. He turned his head and yelled to the men: 'Come on! Into them!'

He could still see the intersecting machine-guns' tracer ahead and it felt bizarre to be walking directly into it, to know that within seconds they would inevitably be among that hail of death. But there was nothing to be done. He stepped into the intersection and felt the bullets skidding past him. There was a cry from his left and he saw one man fall and then another, and another to his right. Then they were through the worst of it. Samwell breathed with relief but then looking to his left realized that the company that had been walking forward there had disappeared. Again the same feeling of isolation returned that he had experienced on the first night and with it the nausea and tightness in his stomach. He could hear noise from that direction. Shouts and rifle and machine-gun fire and realized that the company must have run into some enemy positions and encountered stiff resistance.

He turned to the sergeant-major: 'Looks like they've found some of those "frightened Eyeties" Sar'nt-Major.'

'Aye, sir, and there must be some on the right and all.'

He pointed to their right flank where C Company was supposed to be and again Samwell found himself looking into an empty landscape. His company was utterly alone, ahead of the rest of the advancing infantry and beyond the deadly machine-gun fire.

'Nothing for it, we'll have to go on.'

Together they continued with what was left of the company, soon they came up against barbed wire. Samwell ran at it and jumped, followed by the men. Ahead of them now he could see several sandbagged strongpoints. This was it. He knew that within them men would be sitting, their fingers poised on the triggers of machine-guns and rifles. This though was the moment for which they had all trained. He yelled to the men: 'Scotland forever! Charge!'

From behind him thirty voices joined in a chilling scream, the battle cry that countless drill sergeants had instilled in them during bayonet practice at Camberley, Aldershot and all the other training camps across the British Isles. They held their rifles horizontally the bayonets gleaming in the moonlight and they yelled for Scotland and ran at the enemy through the night, as fast as their weary legs would carry them. As they ran, Samwell saw the tops of distinctive German helmets in the foxholes and cursed the reconnoitring officer for his lies. There was a rattle of fire and fifteen yards half-left of him a machine-gun opened up. From the corner of his eye Samwell saw the tracer bullets coming straight for him and beyond them the heads and shoulders of the three men manning the gun. The next instant he felt a heavy blow to his thigh as if someone had hit him very hard with a hammer. He spun round a full circle and managing to keep his balance, began to walk on towards the enemy. He managed a dozen paces and then to his surprise and annoyance his left leg suddenly gave way and he lurched forward on to the rocky ground.

He was conscious as he fell of seeing the men behind him do the same, although they seemed to be falling on

215

purpose and it occurred to him that they had not realized that he must have been hit; they had mistaken his fall for an attempt to take cover.

There must have been a dozen of them he reasoned, lying no more than twenty yards away from the enemy positions as the bullets whistled over their heads, only just missing their tin hats. Samwell, frustrated, attempted to get up, but found that he could not. He managed to raise himself on one arm and looking behind, yelled at the men: 'Go on! Charge them!'

The men closest to him looked quizzically at him, wondering why he was not getting up himself.

He realized that he could not see the sergeant-major, nor indeed any of the NCOs. He was wondering what to do when a corporal from the reserve section doubled over to him through the hail of tracer bullets. 'Sir, what's happening? What should we do?'

Samwell yelled at him: 'Get in there, for God's sake. Get the buggers in there. Take that bloody position.'

At that moment the company sergeant-major arrived. Samwell was just about to repeat the order to him when he pointed at the German lines: 'Look, sir.'

The enemy were shouting to them and without waiting for a reply, they stood up in their trench and put their hands up. Instantly the men who had been lying behind Samwell jumped to their feet and rushed the position. Using every ounce of his strength he managed to pull himself half-up and dragged himself after them.

He drew level with the machine-gun post, the one that had opened fire on him. He turned towards it just at the moment that three Germans jumped out of it and ran off back towards their lines. Realizing that he was still holding his pistol, he aimed at their backs and fired off four rounds. One of them fell forward on to his face and Samwell felt a frisson of satisfaction tinged with

216

nausea before sinking back down to the ground. There was a shout of triumph and he knew that they had taken the position, and moments later he was being picked up by two of his men. They carried him into the German trench and laid him on a bunk in a dugout. The place was full of British wounded and in the heat the stench of sweat, ordure, blood and broken flesh was already terrible.

He shivered and pulled the blanket on which he was lying closer to him. To his surprise it was warm and he realized that it was the residual heat from the German soldier who until a few minutes before had been sleeping there. A stretcher-bearer bent over him: 'You all right, sir? Look a bit peaky. There's some cold coffee here, left us by Jerry. It's all right, really. Here, you try some of this, Lieutenant.'

Samwell grasped the tin and took a long drink. Cold coffee had never tasted so good. The company sergeant-major came into the dugout: 'We've got the Jerries in the bag, Mister Samwell, sir. There's an officer among them. Right dour sort of bugger. He disna say much.'

'Thank you, Sar'nt-Major. Well done. Sorry for my outburst out there. Had to get them to carry on. Never sworn at the men before.'

'I didna hear a thing, sir. Nothing at all.'

'Can you help me out of here? I think that I should interview that officer, don't you? And we'd better get dug in, in case they counter-attack.'

The CSM grabbed Samwell by the arm and together they hobbled out of the dugout. Samwell knew that he must get as much information as he could from the prisoner. Their position was not good. They were isolated in what had just become no-man's-land. For all he knew the companies on both flanks had been beaten off and he and his men were the only British infantry left out here.

They found the prisoners seated in a corner of the adjoining dugout. Samwell tried to make out their regimental markings but gave up. He spoke to the officer who was surprised to be addressed in German: 'Please tell me your unit name, your strength and your orders.'

'I am only obliged to give my name, rank and serial number.'

Samwell shook his head: 'Do you seriously think that out here in the middle of the desert we can still go by that? You know what I need. If I don't know those things then we could lose a great many men.'

'Name, rank and serial number. I will say nothing else.'

Samwell nodded to the CSM who punched the man hard in the ribs, catching him off guard and winding him.

'Shall we try again, Lieutenant? I haven't got much time. My men are in danger. What is your unit?'

The German stared at him: 'I protest. This is barbaric. These are not the rules of war.'

'I'm sorry. My men will die.' He nodded at the CSM and again the German doubled up. He looked up at Samwell and his expression had changed to one of resignation. He looked overwhelmingly exhausted: 'All right, Lieutenant. You win. I will tell you. We are the 433rd Infantry Regiment, an Austrian unit. But myself and my fellow officers are German. It's often the way now in our army. We came here just after dusk to relieve the Italians who had faced you before.'

So the reconnoitring officer had not been so wrong.

'Thank you, Lieutenant. My apologies for my use of force. You understand.' The German stared at him. Samwell limped away, helped by the CSM. It was useful information that he would pass to Battalion as soon as he could. As soon, that was, as he had the faintest idea where Battalion HQ was. He was about to re-enter the dugout when he caught sight of a group of men, a platoon, moving across the desert outside the position. Among them was the CSM of the missing right-hand company. He yelled across to him. 'Sar'nt-Major! Come here. Over here.'

The man turned and apparently not recognizing Samwell, shouted something back which was lost in the night.

At that moment there was commotion over to the left and A Company, the unit that had started on his left came rushing in. Samwell tried to stop them. 'Where's your CO? I need to hand over.'

A young subaltern appeared: 'Hello. Suppose I'm in charge. What is it you want exactly? Can you be quick? You're rather stopping me from fighting.'

Samwell fought to control his temper. The pain in his leg was beginning to kick in. He replied in a flat voice: 'The fighting's all over here. Can you take over the defence here for the Jerry counter-attack? They're bound to come at any minute.'

The boy, for he was no more than twenty, looked peeved. 'Why the hell can't you do it? I have my own platoon to look after.'

Samwell felt the fury boiling up inside him and was about to reply when he realized that the German officer who had just answered his questions was standing close by. He prayed that he didn't understand colloquial English. 'I order you to take over at once. Can't you see, I'm hit.'

The boy looked suddenly sheepish, and stared at Samwell's bleeding leg: 'Oh!' he said. 'I'm sorry. I didn't realize.'

Samwell lay down again on the German's bunk and tried to relax. But he wasn't happy in the dugout. He felt too enclosed. He was desperate to know what was going on. And if they were going to be counter-attacked he

219

wanted to be able to defend himself. He called to Baynes, who had just dropped into the trench. 'Be a good chap and dig me a shallow trench.' He scanned the perimeter. 'Over there should be fine, on that slight rise.' The man set to work and in a short time reported back. Samwell stumbled across to the trench and found, not the shallow dip he had asked for but a more substantial earthwork. Baynes was smiling broadly: 'Took three of us, sir. Reckon you'll be safe in there.'

'Thank you, Baynes. Much appreciated.' Samwell sent him off to find a weapon and after a few minutes he reappeared with a Bren gun. Samwell smiled: 'Couldn't you find anything smaller, Baynes?'

'No, sir. Sorry, sir. I was to tell you that the company commander of A Company, Captain Macalister, is organizing an all-round defence and that there's no need to worry. But I thought I'd bring you the Bren anyway.'

Samwell crawled into his hole and setting up the Bren, fired a few rounds at the sky to clear the barrel. He was just settling into his new home when Corporal Connolly arrived. 'Sir, they've brought in another prisoner. Thought you might like to talk to him.'

'Yes, bring him here.'

The man did not want to speak. He looked almost bored to be there. He was, he said an Austrian, too old for active fighting. The officers were all Germans. 'We don't get on with them. I should not be here. I'm not well. When is the doctor coming?'

Samwell gazed at him. Was this the calibre of the crack German Afrika Korps? An old man from Austria who did not want to fight? It occurred to Samwell that their original plan had been for Battalion HQ to move forward following on from the attack. 'We should both be safely in hospital before the sun comes up. A British hospital.'

The Austrian smiled: 'Good. Me, I'm glad to be out of it.

I was a machine-gunner you know.' He pointed and Samwell followed his finger to the post from which he had seen the three men running, one of whom he had shot.

Christ, he thought. I shot you. 'Where were you wounded?'

'In the back.'

Samwell couldn't quite believe it. Here he was, talking politely with the man who had first shot him in the leg and whom he had then shot in the back. The Austrian smiled at him again, unknowing and at that moment a great noise broke the silence as German mortar rounds came thumping into the position. The Austrian ducked, instinctively. There was a terrific explosion as one of the rounds hit close by. Samwell pulled himself up and looked out of the trench. Then he heard the screams. A neighbouring trench had taken a direct hit. The mortar rounds were still coming in and one of them exploded close to a foxhole, wounding two of the men sheltering inside. But it was the screams from the first trench to have been hit that were the worst. Abruptly the mortaring stopped and Samwell managed to pull himself out of the trench, leaving the Austrian with a wounded infantryman as a guard and hoping that the lad was not too trigger-happy. Crouching, to make less of a target to any opportunistic enemy sniper, he managed to make it across to the stricken trench. He stopped at the parapet. The trench had been full of light casualties and the bomb had landed directly in the centre. Shrapnel splinters had flown out at high velocity and close range. Two of the men must have been killed instantly and were scarcely recognizable. Another man had a large splinter embedded in his chest and was beyond hope. The fourth was still screaming. A fragment of smoking bomb was protruding from his thigh which it had penetrated and another had torn away part of his groin while a third had embedded itself in his stomach.

221

There was blood everywhere. Samwell gawped for a moment and then took possession of himself. 'Medic! Stretcher-bearers!'

Within a few moments two bearers and the company medical officer were there. He looked at the screaming man and then at Samwell and shook his head. 'All I can do is give him morphine to help the pain. Nothing else.' As the now redundant stretcher-bearers returned to their own trench, the MO climbed down into the bloody trench and pushed an ampule of morphine into the man's good thigh. Then another. Quickly the screaming subsided into sobs. Samwell turned away and hobbled back to his trench where the Austrian and his guard were huddled in one corner. He joined them and they sat there in silence for some time. Samwell felt sleep about to overtake him and was only kept awake by the sound of the Austrian's voice: '*Wann kommt der Arzt?*' The same question. Where was the doctor? 'Oh, don't worry. He'll be here soon.' The man spoke again but Samwell's German was not good enough. Then he realized that he was pointing to his shorts. Samwell looked down and saw that they were soaked with blood. His first thought was that it must be someone else's. But looking down at his wounded leg he discovered that the Austrian's bullet had gone through the fleshy part of his thigh, coming out at the other side. It looked as though when the stretcher-bearer had bandaged him up he had placed the field dressing not on the exit wound where he was bleeding but over the entry wound. The Austrian made a sign to him and said in German: 'I can do it?' Samwell nodded and with some difficulty because of his own wound, the man removed Samwell's bandage and replaced it with his own clean and unused field dressing. Samwell watched him work, feeling all the time guilty for having spoken to him abruptly and even more so for having shot him. The man finished. Samwell spoke in German: 'Thank you. Can I help you now?'

The man nodded and carefully, Samwell examined the wound he had caused. He had hit the man directly between the shoulderblades and it looked as if the bullet was still in there. He could also see that it had stopped bleeding and he knew that was probably not good. There was little he could do. Samwell gave the man his haversack as a pillow and he thanked him to the point of embarrassment.

He tried to restart their conversation and asked in his best German, 'Are you married?' The Austrian fumbled inside his tunic pocket and produced a family photograph. Samwell studied it. His wife, his *Hausfrau* looked typically Austrian with plaited blonde hair, a big smile and an ample bosom. There were three children in the picture, a girl of twelve, a boy of ten dressed in the local costume of lederhosen and a girl of three, perhaps four. Samwell spoke as he handed the photograph back: 'They're lovely. Your wife is beautiful and your children look very well.' He decided to keep their banter going, thinking it would divert both of them from their situation. 'What did you do before the war?'

The man smiled and began to speak very fast in an Austrian dialect that Samwell found hard to understand as the 'ch's became softened and words ran together. Every so often he stopped for breath and as he did so his face contorted showing that he was in some pain. Samwell did his best to make out the words. He was a cotton worker from Linz, aged thirty-seven, he had been called up a year ago for home defence duties. Then a month ago, with no warning he had been sent out to Benghazi with some much younger Austrians. He told Samwell that it had surely been a mistake. Of course, no one would listen to him. He had only come up to the front yesterday

223

and had been with the machine-gunners just since the afternoon. He said that he'd never fired a machine-gun before in his life.

Samwell listened, fascinated and made a mental note to get the information to HQ as soon as they got to a hospital. Elderly Austrian draftees in the front line? That really was news. The thought of hospital filled him with hope and then despair. A wave of panic swept over him that he might so easily be killed here before he was evacuated. He prayed that it would not happen and diverted his mind back to the Austrian.

'Do you ski?'

'Yes. Very well. Since I was a child.'

'Where do you go?'

'Near Salzburg, a place called Oberglau. It's very nice, very remote.'

'I ski in Scotland when I can. I've skied in the French Alps. Before all this.' Samwell desperately sought other topics. 'I've been to Linz. Once. We spent one night there on our honeymoon while we were motoring to Vienna. I thought it a little dull. Do forgive me for saying so.'

The man did not seem to understand and Samwell presumed that his German was not after all that good. He was just trying to think of another subject when he realized that the man had fallen asleep. Thank God, he thought and suddenly felt very tired himself.

His dreams were filled with horror. He was at home but being hit on the thigh by someone unseen. His hands were tied. And then he was in the desert on a route march and he had fallen out to take a piss. He tried to run to catch up with the company but his legs were as heavy as lead. He became terrified of being alone and then a huge scorpion appeared on his thigh, stabbing it with its poisoned tail. He had a raging thirst and an empty water bottle and then he was back in Stirling in the family bathroom and his wife was running a cold bath. He tried to drink but the water fell through his hands. He asked his wife for a cup but she laughed and said they were for the children. And then he woke up.

The sun was beating down and it was deathly quiet. He was covered in sweat and his mouth was so dry that he was unable to move his tongue. He reached for his water bottle and realized it was in his haversack under the Austrian's head. The man appeared to be sleeping, but Samwell had a sudden horror that he might have died. He looked at him closely, at his pale, drawn skin. He felt his pulse. A weak beat. Suddenly the man stirred and spoke in his half-sleep: '*Wann kommt der Arzt?*' Samwell spoke close to his ear: '*Bald, bald,*' and he went back to sleep. Slowly Samwell eased the haversack from beneath the man's head and replaced it with his brown army pullover. He opened the haversack and remembered that he had left his reserve bottle in his dugout. The small issue bottle was only half-full. He opened it and drank slowly, relishing the water and using some to wash out his dry mouth. He was careful to spit it back into the bottle.

The silence was strange and Samwell, curious to know the situation, raised himself to the edge of the trench and looked around. Thirty yards away in another trench he could see the tops of two helmets. They looked British and taking a chance he called out. One of the men got up and doubled over. 'Baynes, thank God. What the devil's going on? Where is everyone? And where's the MO and Battalion HQ?'

'I don't know, sir. We're all split up here. Been sittin' here all night. Haven't seen HQ. I'll try and find the MO. Would you like some water?'

He handed Samwell his water bottle.

'Thanks, Baynes. I left my reserve in the dugout.'

225

'No worries, sir. I'll away and fetch it once I've seen Major Mackay. You take care, sir.'

A few minutes later he was back. He climbed down into the trench and gave Samwell a tin of cold German coffee. 'Here, sir, you drink this. I've got your bottle too. Seems that Major Mackay's trying to get through to the CO. We're cut off, sir, and Jerry's got round behind us. The major's called in an artillery shot to break up Jerry forty yards to the west. But it's going to be damn close shooting. You'd better get your head down, sir.'

There was a sudden crack, a rifle shot, and a bullet pinged off the side of the trench. 'Sniper. Baynes, you'd better make a run for it.'

Baynes jumped from the trench and with bullets singing around him in the sand made it back to his own hole and jumped in. He was not a second too soon, for mortar shells began to fall across the position. Damn, thought Samwell, they've obviously seen that we're here. The next few minutes made it fairly plain that the enemy also believed his trench to be the HQ. Mortar bombs began to rain in. Three times he was covered in sand and then a redhot shard of metal landed on his chest. He brushed it away with his map case before it could do any damage and watched it smoking in a corner of the trench. At that moment the Austrian woke up. Disorientated, he raised his head and hauled himself up to the edge of the trench. Another mortar round came in and Samwell was momentarily dazed by the explosion. At first he thought that the entire trench had been blown in. He raised his head and saw that the bomb had created a huge crater about five yards away. Then he saw the Austrian. He was sitting in the bottom of the trench at the end closest to the crater, staring in disbelief at what remained of his left hand, a mangled, bloody stump of flesh and sinew and bone. Samwell felt his gorge rising. Quickly, he tore at his shirt and made a makeshift bandage with which he bound up the mutilated mess. The Austrian murmured a word of thanks and shut his eyes. He could hardly breathe. Samwell was overcome with a strange, almost irrational concern for this anonymous man, for he realized that he didn't even know his name. But then he thought of all they had spoken of. Of his wife and children, skiing, a love for life and he began to realize how stupid, how simply idiotic this war, any war was. How could it be, he thought, that he should shoot me, then I should shoot him and then we should become friends and then he is maimed by his own people? Why, he wondered, were they at war anyway? What was it all for?

And then he remembered the massacres in Poland, France and Belgium, the innocent civilians mowed down by the Nazis, Hitler's brutal regime and his lust for world domination and he shook his head. Yes, it was a necessary evil. If only war could stop all that, then war must be just.

The man moved: '*Wann kommt der Arzt?*'

'*Bald,*' said Samwell and the man replied, almost with annoyance: '*Oh bald, bald, immer bald.*'

Of course Samwell knew that they were cut off from all help. That there was no MO who was on his way. That his friend would soon be dead and that he too might not survive. His thigh was throbbing and the pain had become much worse. He saw something sticking out of his haversack, a copy of *News Review* sent by his wife. He pulled it out and tried to read an article about Tommy Handley, but could not concentrate. Reaching in again he found the photograph of Klara and the children standing in front of the house. It all seemed like another world. An unreal, magical, heavenly world removed from this place of filth and death. An image came into his mind of his dream; of the bath. God, he felt thirsty. He reached for the water bottle and began to drink and just then the Austrian opened his eyes. '*Wasser, Wasser, bitte.*'

Samwell paused for a moment and pondered. Why should he give this man his precious water? He was dying anyway and that was a waste. Besides, he was an enemy, the man who'd tried to kill him. Nevertheless something made him hold the bottle to the man's mouth and let him drink. A quarter of the bottle? That was enough. A bullet whizzed past his ear. The damn sniper had found them again and then more shells came crashing in. But this time they were fired from the British lines. Samwell put his head down and pushed the Austrian too, down into the safety of the trench. A figure came running across the sand and Samwell recognized him as the subaltern with whom he had argued over the position. He shouted to him and the boy rushed across and peered down into the trench, smiling.

'Samwell, good heavens. How's the leg? Lucky it wasn't further round, eh? I'm off to bring in the carriers. They're lost.' And with that he rushed off. Seconds later Samwell heard a series of grenade explosions from the direction in which he had run and instantly regretted their argument.

Mortar shells continued to fall and then there was a new sound, the sharp crack of tank cannon. Samwell peered out to see a squadron of Shermans advancing directly towards his trench and those around it. From his position they looked as tall as houses. He shouted: 'Stop! Stop!'

But of course it was pointless. A tank rumbled across the far side of his trench and as he watched he saw another push in the sides of a neighbouring foxhole in which half a dozen British and German wounded had been shelter- ing. It buried them completely. Samwell turned away and sank down inside his trench. This was madness. There was the noise of an engine and dragging himself back up he saw an armoured car approaching with a British officer sticking out of the turret. He shouted: 'Over here!' and the man turned and saw him. He leapt from the vehicle and doubled over to the trench. 'I say. What the devil are you doing here? Who are you?'

'Seventh Argylls. We've a lot of wounded. Who are you?'

'Yeomanry. You've landed up in a tank battle, old chap. I should keep your head down if I were you. Tell you what, I'll report your position and try to get you out.' He raced back to the armoured car and within seconds was gone. Samwell wondered whether he would ever see him again, and if he would keep his promise.

He looked across at the Austrian and noticed blood seeping out of his mouth. He glanced at his watch. It was shortly before 6 p.m.

He awoke two hours later to find the trench full of people. There was Major Mackay and an MO, but not their own. Samwell held out his arm and the doctor injected him with an ampule of morphine. Samwell motioned to the Austrian: 'You might like to give some to him.' The doctor complied and the Austrian smiled.

It was long after dark when they came for them. The Austrian was still alive, as far as Samwell could tell. He found himself in the front of a 15cwt truck and as they drove across the bumpy ground he began to wish that he was back in the trench. After a few minutes they stopped and Samwell felt himself being lifted on to a stretcher. He was aware that he was in an ambulance now, wrapped in blankets. A young man leant over him and spoke softly and Samwell was surprised to hear an American accent: 'OK, old chap. You're goin' to be OK now. You're going home.'

TWENTY-THREE

11.00 p.m.
Point 115
Ringler

Ringler watched as Corporal Fiedler gently pushed the explosive charge down the barrel of the gun while the rest of them tied Kater to the outside of the assault gun carriage to move him. He went to look at Lukas's wound but the man was smiling. 'It's only a flesh wound, Lieutenant. Nothing serious.'

Ringler turned to Fiedler: 'All right. Light the fuse. Now with me, all of you, let's go. And don't make a sound.'

It must have been midnight, he thought. Soon, if he wasn't already, Tommy would know they were up to something and would come after them. He looked at his watch. It seemed to have stopped at ten o'clock. He tapped it. Nothing.

They moved off and within ten minutes were at the spot behind the dunes to which he had told his car to return to pick them up. He prayed that it would come soon. The night was split for a moment by the crack of the explosion as the charge left in the gun barrel went off. What did it matter now, he thought, if the British came? They could do nothing. He doubted whether any of the men had the stomach for a fight. He looked around him at the surviving men of the company, thirty of them. Close beside them lay the bodies of the dead they had recovered: Bauer, Hancke and poor Monier. How long ago it now seemed that the two of them had been walking back from the colonel's party talking of his family and Ringler's projected trip to the Rhineland. There was no point in planning such things, anything, at this time. The future meant nothing. All that any of them had was the present and to find the best way to get through the moment. The future, if there was one for any of them, would come soon enough. He began to worry about the car. Where was it? Had they been forgotten? Had it gone over a mine? He heard the noise of an engine and nudged Fiedler awake from semi-consciousness.

'Hear that?'

Fiedler nodded. It was an engine. But whose? Were the British advancing on them? He couldn't tell from which direction it was coming. For a moment he was sure that it was the British. But then he saw his car, driving towards them through the minefield. It stopped a few metres away and Ringler hobbled across to meet it. His driver got out and Ringler saw that he was shaking. 'Klaus? Are you all right?'

'Lieutenant, I can't drive back. Not through that. Through the mines. I just can't do it, sir.'

The man sat down on the edge of the seat and buried his head in his hands. Ringler said nothing. There was little point. He was beyond orders. It was clear that his nerves were shot to pieces. Ringler turned to Fiedler: 'Get the men to carry the corpses and strap them to the back of the car as best you can.' He put his hand on the driver's shoulder. 'All right, Klaus. Move over. I'll take the wheel.'

Ringler climbed into the car as the last body was secured

to the back, its feet protruding from underneath a piece of tarpaulin with which all three had been covered. Ringler looked down at the sand as something caught his eye. It was the shadow of Bauer's feet in the moonlight. Fiedler was sitting beside him now and the driver stood on the running board alongside. He started up the engine and began to drive into the minefield, slowly. For no particular reason, he thought, what difference would it make if they hit a mine fast or slow? Thank God, the moon was out now. In its light he was able to see the fresh tracks in front of him created by the assault gun as it had gone on before them. Slowly, slowly he drove on. Seconds seemed like minutes, the minutes like hours. He panicked, thought that he might have lost the path, then saw the tracks and was able to breathe again. The other two men said nothing. There was a jolt from the back. Ringler stopped and looked round, afraid that one of the corpses might have fallen off. But they were all still there, six feet pointing upwards. He hit a patch of roughed-up sand and the wheels began to sink. Quickly he changed gear and managed to get a grip before driving on. As he did so he began to smell burning oil. The clutch. He prayed that it would hold out and not leave them alone in the minefield.

He was sweating hard now, trying to concentrate on keeping to the path but deflected by the thought of the dead men in the back. Something kept making him turn round to stare at the feet. He thought at one moment that he saw one move. Was he dead? Were they alive? Impossible. The desert seemed as cold as the moon. The smell of the burning oil invaded his senses and the grinding of the wheels began to jar on his brain. How long had he been driving, expecting at any moment to be blown to eternity? He had no idea. He knew that it was only eight kilometres across the minefield. How long could that take? He glimpsed something up ahead. Movement, a vehicle, men.

He turned to Fiedler. 'What's that?'

The sergeant peered into the night: 'I don't know, sir. Can't see. Wait. I see men. Vehicles.'

The driver spoke: 'It's the company, sir. We're through.'

Ringler slammed his foot hard on the brake and his hands dropped from the steering wheel. His forearms felt like lead weights, his head incredibly heavy, his senses clouded. He pulled himself out of the seat and dropped to the ground taking deep breaths, trying to speak. No words came. He tried again and again. Getting up he began to walk around the car. He tried to call to Fiedler but found he couldn't shout. Only a feeble cawing came from his throat. He thumped at his chest, but still no sound. Giving up, Ringler looked around. There was no sign of the assault gun. Merely thirty of his men in various states of exhaustion and with a number of wounds still needing attention. He sat down on the hard, cold sand and looked around. He saw the three covered corpses in the car and Fiedler in the front seat fast asleep. There was the sound of approaching vehicles and out of the early morning light came three jeeps. They pulled up just short of the half-track and he looked on amazed as three smart, clean and rested drivers got out. Three officers. Two of them he did not know, were they replacements? But there was Werner Adler, looking as neat as he had at the colonel's party. He went up to Ringler, smiling and clapped him on the back. 'Well, old boy, you've had a bit of a time of it.'

Ringler said nothing but, exhausted as he was, got back into the car and started up the engine. And then, with Fiedler and the driver beside him, he drove on, past Adler and the others, past the old company HQ and then further on to Battalion. And all the time he kept turning round to look at the three dead men: Hancke, Monier and Bauer. The adjutant was impressed, he said. Ringler had done his duty. He had held off the advance and brought back his dead. The words hung in space as he drew back the tarpaulin and looked at the three bodies. This was as far as they were going to go. They would never feel German soil again but would stay here for ever. And in time they would fall to dust and become as one with the sand of the desert.

TWENTY-FOUR

Midnight
Trig Twenty-nine
Kibby

Bill Kibby stood at a line of white tape that had been carefully stapled into the desert sand. It marked the start line for their attack and he knew that once you had crossed that line there could be no turning back. The knot of fear he had felt earlier that day had gone now, to be replaced by a gnawing emptiness and a craving to be through this ordeal. He stared before him. Trig twenty-nine, their objective for the night, looked like a huge sand dune, a real mountain towering above the flat plain of the desert. The moon had risen high above the horizon now and the dune lay full in its light. Christ, he thought, this is going to be fun. If we can see it all lit up like that, what the hell's Jerry going to make of us. We'll be sitting ducks.

The barrage had begun at 10 p.m. But it had not been for them and Kibby knew it. Away in the south another attack was going in. The Springboks of First South African were making a diversionary attack. The Australians' battle was the real show and he hoped that they would get something similar before they went in. He did not have long to wonder. He was looking at his watch when he heard them. As it hit midnight the drone of bombers came clear on the night, right above their heads and in an instant Trig twenty-nine exploded in a blaze of flame as a squadron of RAF Wellingtons dropped their load straight on target. Bill breathed a sigh of relief. It was hard to think that anyone would be able to live through that lot. He turned to Ashby: 'There they go, Herb. Told you we'd have support. Look at that lot, mate.'

'You're not joking. I even feel sorry for the poor bastards copping that.'

'Save your pity, mate. You'll be up there yourself in a bit. Then we'll see how sorry you are for them.'

A whistle blew and he heard Captain Robbins' voice behind him: 'Forward!'

He took up the cry: 'Forward the Twenty-fourth! Here we go, lads.'

They marched forward as they had done before, at a careful seventy-five paces a minute. Ahead of them in the night sky coloured tracers fired from their rear showed the way. For a few moments it was easy going. Then it began. There was a whoosh and enemy shells came crashing into their advancing line. Kibby looked to his right and saw two men blown to pieces by a direct hit from an 88. 'Christ,' he called to no one in particular, 'how the fuck did Jerry live through all that?'

As he spoke more Spandau bullets thudded into the dust and rock around them. For a few moments Kibby lay prone, expecting at any moment to be hit.

They walked on. Two hundred, three hundred, four hundred yards. And then like a counterpoint to the boom of the artillery came the staccato rattle of the enemy machine-guns. More men began to fall and Kibby yelled: 'Cover! Take cover!'

The company hit the ground and found what cover they could in shellholes and abandoned foxholes. He heard

Captain Robbins shout: 'Jerry machine-gun post dead ahead! Get down.'

As he spoke more bullets thudded into the dust and rock around them. For a few seconds Kibby lay there, prone, expecting at any moment to be hit. He knew that there was only one way to silence that machine-gun, and it was not by lying here. He turned to Ashby who was next to him, pressing himself into the sand. 'You're in charge, Herb. I'll be back in a few minutes.'

Kibby got to his feet and ran madly in the direction of the machine-gun. He reasoned that if the gunners were firing on a fixed point, which they probably were, then they would be reluctant to move their angle of fire even if they saw him coming. He had a slim to average chance of getting through and if it was a chance that would save lives and shorten this bloody war then it was worth taking. He ran on, his tommy gun grasped hard in his sweating hands. The machine-gun was louder now. A Spandau, he was sure of that. So they were Germans up ahead, not Italians. Then he was on them. He saw them at the same time that they caught sight of him, a screaming madman in a bush hat running at them out of the darkness. Desperately they tried to turn the gun, but Kibby was there already, spraying them with his weapon. He caught the loader straight in the face and another man in the chest, killing them both. Two others were hit in the arm. The remaining two men put their hands above their heads and muttered something in German. Kibby kept the gun pointed at them and motioned them out of the trench before herding them back to the company. He saw Robbins: 'Found this lot sitting in a funk hole, sir. Path's clear again.' Robbins smiled at him and nodded. As one of the corporals led the prisoners to the rear, Kibby rejoined his platoon and found Ashby grinning.

'You bloody fool. I thought you'd gone nuts.'

'Well someone had to do it. Come on, we'll be late for the party.'

Together they trudged on towards Trig 29 but after only a few more yards bullets began to fill the air. Again they hit the ground. Kibby looked towards the direction of the fire. He could see the trench quite clearly in the moonlight this time. Three flashes. Three riflemen. A fourth. He knew what to do. He began to inch his way forward as the bullets hit the sand all round him. There was a cry from behind him as one of the men was hit. Kibby kept going until he was about thirty yards from the trench. Then, oblivious to the fire, he reached down to his belt and unhooked a Mills bomb. In a matter of seconds he had pulled out the pin and holding the trigger down counted to five then hurled the grenade. It landed in the trench and for a dreadful instant he watched as the Germans panicked and tried to get out. But it was too late. The explosion killed two of them and wounded the others. Kibby and his platoon got to their feet and rushed forward, firing from the hip. This time there were no prisoners. As they advanced past the trench however, he saw a dozen Germans with their hands on their heads being escorted in by Eighteen Platoon. Kibby called to a rifleman: 'Your mob doin' all right?'

'Bonza, mate. We've taken a few prisoners. But there's loads of men hit. Lieutenant Johnston's bought it too.'

'Bloody shame. He was a real dinkum bloke.'

Kibby meant it too. Johnston had always been one of the finest officers in the company. Fair, easy-going and not averse to putting himself in danger. Presumably now he had done that once too often.

He walked on and found himself at a trench line recently vacated by the Germans. Captain Robbins was directly behind him: 'Good to see you, Kibby. This is the Jerry front line. That's our first objective taken.' He turned to his runner: 'Send the signal back to HQ. Captain Isaakson will want to know that he can bring his carriers through. Oh, and then run and tell them we've taken thirty-eight prisoners. That'll make up for the other news.'

'Other news?'

'Didn't you hear? We lost Johnston and Perry.'

'Both of them, sir?' Kibby shook his head. 'Then you're the only officer left in the company.'

'Yes, doesn't feel too good, that. Platoon sergeants have taken over.'

The runner fired the Verey pistol he kept for the purpose and the flare lit the sky above them, the signal for initial success which would launch stage two of the attack. Kibby knew that this meant Isaakson's Bren carriers, now laden with C Company, dashing hell for leather at the Jerry front line. Moments later the artillery behind their lines started up again, plastering the position with shells. Sure enough within a few minutes he heard the familiar roar of the V8 engines and the Bren carriers roared towards them from the rear, six men to a vehicle moving at fifteen miles an hour. Kibby watched them go and waited. Eight minutes later the summit of Trig 29 resounded with the noises of a fierce firefight. Captain Robbins shouted to the company, 'Forward boys. We're needed up there,' and they began to advance again on the right of the line directly towards Trig 29 with A Company on their left. They had gone a mere five or six yards however when all hell was let loose. Two machine-guns opened up on them and at the same moment Kibby heard the dreaded crump of a field mortar: 'Incoming. Mortars. Get down!'

The company dropped to the sand but the mortar round struck home, killing a corporal and wounding another man. Robbins' runner came crawling up to Kibby. 'Bill, the comms cable's been cut. We're cut off from HQ. D'you have anyone who can fix it?'

239

'I could do it. Used to be a dab hand with electrics.'

'I'll tell the captain. Thanks. It's about twenty metres to the left rear.'

Kibby nudged Ashby: 'Herb. I'm off back to fix the comms cable. You take them on if you can and keep low.'

He turned and crawled back the twenty yards, then finding the broken cable, he knelt and began to strip down the wires. Carefully he spliced the individual wires together and finally joined all of them. Shells were landing all around him now. It was almost as if the German mortar team could see what he was trying to do. He dropped down again and crawled back to where he had left Ashby. The men had crawled on for around twenty yards through the constant fire and two unmoving dark shapes suggested that they had taken casualties. He got up to a squat and ran like that, hunched up, until he caught up with them. A German trench was firing at them from the left. Kibby found two of the men from Seventeen Platoon: 'Morse, Hacket, over there. Give them a few rounds then follow up with grenades if you can.' He found Robbins: 'Sir. Managed to fix the cable.'

'Well done, Kibby. Come on, I'm not waiting around here. Let's get to C Company. We can't let them have all the fun.'

Robbins straightened up and yelled to the men around him: 'Come on, lads. Up that bloody hill. That's C Company up there. Those are Australians.'

As one the rest of the company got to their feet and following Robbins' example broke into a run. Within seconds they were all sprinting as fast as they could towards the German position. Kibby ran close to Robbins and as they reached the slit trenches, began to spray a deadly hail of bullets from the Thompson gun. By the time they reached the third line of trenches the Germans were coming out with their hands up.

It was now 2 a.m. The flashes of explosions on the top of the great dune were closer and more intense. Kibby looked hard and saw figures pouring off the hill, streaming towards the German lines. They might be the enemy, he thought, or they might be ours. But whoever they were they were leaving the hill and that could only mean one thing. C Company had taken Trig 29. From the top of the dune a light flew vertically up in the air and then arced slowly down in an orange glow. A Verey flare – the success signal. He suddenly noticed that the machine-gun and mortar fire which up till now had been constant had stopped. He yelled: 'We've got it, lads! They've taken it,' and as the company began to cheer he joined in, the tears streaming down his face.

He found that he was standing in what looked like an orchard. The ground was littered with small round shapes. He stooped to pick one up and yelled across to Ashby: 'Hey, Herb. Figs. It's the bloody fig garden.'

Together they walked on through the garden, munching on the juicy fruits as they went. Here and there a German corpse lay on the ground, but apart from that and the men of the platoon who came with them there was no sign of life.

Captain Robbins came up: 'All right, Kibby, let's get dug in. And make them deep, men. They're sure to want us out of here, want the bloody figs for themselves.'

The platoon unslung their equipment and unfolding the entrenching tools, began to dig into the rocky soil, Kibby with them. They were still digging when the night was split by an explosion that rocked the very ground. Together they turned in its direction and found themselves looking down the hill towards the rear of the battalion. It looked as if the whole desert was on fire. A wall of yellow flame straddled the track up to the strongpoint and all along it lorries were burning. As Kibby looked on he saw men

241

leaping from the blazing vehicles, men of fire who threw themselves on to the sand and rolled desperately to put out the flames. He finally spoke.

'My God, it's our supply trucks. They've gone up. The poor bastards.'

Eight trucks were on fire. Eight trucks which he knew were crammed full of ammunition supplies intended for the companies on the hill along with a quantity of mines to act as a defensive perimeter. The night was filled with the agonized screams of the burning truck drivers. Kibby watched as men tried to rescue them, only to be themselves engulfed in the inferno. One man emerged from the blaze carrying a comrade on his back only to miss his footing and fall back into the flames. One of Kibby's men began to mutter: 'Oh God. Oh my God. Oh my God.'

'Quiet, Wilson, there's nothing we can do about it. Those poor sods.'

A shell flew down over their heads and fell on the blazing trucks. As if it was not bad enough, the intense light from the blaze had attracted the attention of the German artillery. Ashby spoke: 'Bill, have you thought what else this means? That's our bloody ammo down there, and our bloody mines. I'll tell you what it means, mate. It means we're fucked.'

And Kibby knew that he was right. For so vital was this position to the Germans that Rommel was bound to throw everything he could spare into its recapture. Kibby continued to dig and wondered just how soon the counterattack would begin.

Monday 26 October

TWENTY-FIVE

9.00 a.m.
HQ Eighth Army
Montgomery

'Well, Freddie, what news?'

Montgomery sat, his arms folded, at the little table inside his command caravan waiting for the morning's report. De Guingand began to read.

'In the northern sector First Armoured Division attacked in a northwesterly direction, but were unable to make headway in the face of strong resistance from anti-tank defences. They have however succeeded in beating off an enemy armoured attack but they lost thirty-four tanks.

'During the night Fifty-First Highland Division took more ground towards the first-day objective on the Oxalic line and Ninth Australian Division attacked Point Twenty-nine and succeeded in taking their objective. They are now dug in. Much of the minefields reported penetrated if not entirely cleared, sir.'

Well, so much, thought Montgomery for that part of Rommel's 'devil's garden'.

'Twenty-Sixth Australian Brigade made the assault along with tanks from Fortieth RTR. The RAF flew seventy-nine support missions.'

He paused. Mongomery smiled and de Guingand continued: 'In the southern sector Fiftieth Division has failed in its attempt to penetrate the extensive minefield to its front. Forty-Fourth Division has moved up into ground taken by Seventh Armoured Division. That's it, sir.'

Montgomery thought for a moment. There was no alternative, the tanks must go in. Now was their moment. He looked up at de Guingand: 'Freddie, I think we'll have a conference, corps commanders. Call it for one-thirty at General Morshead's HQ.'

'Very good, sir. Shall I tell them why?'

'No, don't do that. They'll find out soon enough.'

'If I might be permitted to ask, sir, what are your intentions?'

'The tanks, Freddie. We must use the tanks now. Give the infantry a rest. Allow the cavalry their moment of glory.'

He scanned the faces in the small group of his personal staff who stood with him around the map table outside his field caravan, and found John Poston.

'John, would you take this down and issue it to all corps commanders. I want it to reach them shortly before I speak to them.'

His army was being bled dry. He had calculated on 10,000 casualties over his projected twelve-day battle. Yet here they were on the fourth day and already his infantry had suffered 7000 men killed, wounded, missing and taken prisoner. He had to safeguard the infantry. They were the backbone of the army, how could he sacrifice them? And what he wondered would history say if he did. Would he be tarred with the same brush as the generals of the Great War? That could not be allowed to happen. Reputation was everything. Posterity. It could particularly not be allowed to happen again as he had promised so many friends from those dreadful days to avenge their suffering.

The Australians had done well in the night and driven a wedge into the northernmost German defences. Rommel's defences now, for intelligence had briefed him that the Desert Fox had returned yesterday evening to resume command. Now, he thought, I have a proper fight on my hands.

'John, are you ready?'

'Yes, sir, quite ready.'

'XXX Corps will carry out no major offensive operations until further notice. It is to defend the existing bridgehead and reconsolidate ready for the next time it will be called upon. Seventh Armoured Division will henceforth conduct no offensive tasks. X Corps will go on to the offensive. It will make progress to the west and northwest from the Kidney Hill area. This will require one hundred per cent concentration and defence of the bridgehead is no longer an issue. Have you got all that?'

'Yes, sir.'

'Good. Send it to all corps commanders. Freddie, would you ask Brigadier Kirkman to come and see me forthwith. I want to know more about the artillery situation.'

He did not have long to wait for Kirkman, his chief artillery commander. As always his key officers were concentrated around the central hub of the command caravan. Kirkman was as sanguine as ever.

'As far as I can find out we can continue with this battle for ten days at the present rate – but we can't go on indefinitely, sir.'

'Oh it's quite all right, absolutely all right. Don't worry about ammunition. This battle will be over in a week's time. There'll really be no problem.'

'Very good, sir. Oh, there is just one more thing. It may be nothing in particular but I thought that you might want to know that General Lumsden has not been keeping in touch with his corps artillery chief. Can't understand it.'

Montgomery stiffened; Lumsden again. 'Kirkman, will you be so kind the next time you see Herbert Lumsden to point out to him that he must keep his corps artillery officer in the picture.'

As Kirkman left the caravan, Montgomery reached for his diary and started to write in a small, energetic hand. 'I have just discovered that LUMSDEN has been fighting his battle without having his CCRA with him . . . Lumsden is not a really high-class soldier.'

Six hours later the same book lay open at the same page and Montgomery stood looking down at his words. Throughout the day he had been haunted by the significance of Kirkman's parting shot. For most of the day he had managed to keep himself away from the business of the battle in the monk's cell of his caravan. From time to time he had sought inspiration in the Bible. Reports had come in and he had responded where necessary; 329 tanks had been lost or temporarily put out of action; X Corps already had 93 under repair. So his total of tanks fit for action stood at 900.

This had been a time for calm reflection. Now, finally, he thought, was the moment to act. And so, for the second time in that day he decided that something must change. He left the caravan and found Poston outside. 'John, would you ask Generals Leese and Lumsden to join me soonest. Here. Now, if they wouldn't mind.'

Poston muttered a polite 'yes' and as he hurried off mused on the commanding general's state of mind. He seemed uncharacteristically on edge and unusually nervous.

Leese and Lumsden were not long in responding.

Montgomery welcomed them outside the caravan with a smile. He was standing in pullover, scarf and his usual hat beside a table made from sandbags on which rested a corkboard to which was pinned a map. He turned to Leese.

'Oliver, I need you to change the plan. You are to engage the enemy in close combat with XXX Corps. The Highlanders, the Australians, the New Zealanders and the South Africans. Every man who can still fight. I intend to build a reserve. We sidestep. Bring the New Zealanders and Tenth Armoured into the reserve and use the Australians again as planned, "crumbling" northwards from the salient at Trig Twenty-nine towards the sea. That way we write off all the enemy positions in the coastal sector by getting in behind them.'

Leese nodded. Montgomery went on: 'Herbert, I'm putting you in charge of plans for an armoured reserve corps containing the New Zealand division and Ninth Armoured Brigade, Tenth Armoured Division and possibly Seventh Armoured. And use the artillery in support. You will hand over command of First Armoured Division to General Leese.'

Lumsden nodded: 'Sir.'

'And then, gentlemen, we shall have the force that we need to deliver the knockout blow. And then we shall carry the day.'

TWENTY-SIX

4.00 p.m.
Near Camel Pass, the Quattara Depression
Ruspoli

For two days they had been waiting for this moment with dread. He had known that it would come. But the reality of it was more horrible than all his imaginings. Tanks. It seemed like hundreds of them, and for the last hour they had been advancing upon their position. And he and his men had been powerless to stop them. He had known, of course, that their guns, the little 47/32s designed to be light enough to be dropped by plane, would have no effect on armour plate. The most that they could hope for was that a lucky shot might set fire to the tank tracks. He had known all along that their guns were there for the men's morale. The only way for them to fight the tanks was in close combat. It was suicide and they all knew it. Ruspoli had called together a meeting of his platoon and company commanders as soon as they had heard the tanks' engines and felt the earth begin to tremble.

He had spoken bluntly and without pretence, offering them the chance of an honourable surrender, knowing that all would refuse. And then he had shaken each of them by the hand and kissed them on both cheeks. Then they had taken their posts and waited. Shortly after the last engagement they had moved a little to the south into new trenches, recently vacated by the Germans, which had been solidly built, with good walls and substantial sandbagged fore-stations. That at least was comforting. Beyond the main trench line the Germans had put in a dozen equally strong foxhole positions, and in each of these Ruspoli had placed two of his best men. They would be the first line of defence against the tanks and he prayed to the blessed Virgin that they were ready.

The British came on in the way they had expected: tanks and infantry advancing behind a barrage of artillery fire. Now in the final moments before the infantry came into range of their machine-guns and mortars, Ruspoli took one last look at the men directly to his left and right. Santini of course was lying to the rear in a new casualty bay. But the others were there, as it seemed they had always been. Mautino, Bari, newly-promoted corporal, Marozzi, Marcantonio, Speda, Fratini, Silvio, Rosso; Gola was in a mortar pit slightly to the rear, with his men and his beloved mortars.

He tried to judge their distance from the advancing infantry. A thousand yards. Eight hundred. Six hundred. He called to Mautino: 'Carlo, open fire at one hundred metres. Not before.'

They still came on. The artillery barrage was falling on the foxholes now and Ruspoli watched as a direct hit wiped out two of his crack troops, blowing them into eternity. The tanks were firing too now. Seventy-five millimetre shells began to crash into the ground behind the Italian trenches. A few minutes more, thought Ruspoli, and they will zero in on us. We have to take out a few tanks before they overwhelm us. The tanks' turret-mounted machine-guns raked the forward trenches. 'Keep down!' yelled Ruspoli. Mautino took up the command with the NCOs as the bullets hit the parapet, thudding into the sandbags and sending pieces of wood and rock flying off in all directions. How many metres now, he wondered? He decided that they were close enough: 'Fire!' At once every machine-gun in the company opened up on the advancing infantry. Ruspoli watched as they fell in the hail of bullets. He heard the thud of Gola's mortars and saw more of the tin-hatted British go down in a storm of splintering metal. Now, he thought, for the tanks.

One of the foxholes to the left of his command post had been selected for the company's remaining flamethrower, manned by a big man from Milan, Sergeant Nicola Pistilli. They had built the post into as impregnable a state as possible given the materials at their disposal and Pistilli was able to push the nozzle of his flamethrower through an aperture which gave the maximum cover. Now Ruspoli saw the area in front of it begin to smoke. In the next instant a sheet of flame shot out from Pistilli's post and collided with the front armour of one of the leading Shermans. The tank went up in a wall of flame and within seconds an enormous explosion blew it high into the air as the petrol tank and then the ammunition exploded in the intense heat. Ruspoli smiled and the men who had seen it happen gave a ragged cheer. Before the noise had died away he saw Pistilli turn his weapon on a neighbouring tank with similar effect. There was a louder cheer from the men and cries of 'Folgore!' This was all that he had hoped for. Two tanks destroyed and the men in as good a state of morale as he had seen. But he knew too that there was only one Pistilli. Only one flamethrower and that it could not be everywhere. In the centre and the right of the battlefield the British tanks still came on and now there was only one way to hold them back.

He looked on in awe, knowing what was about to happen. One of the Shermans approached the line of advanced foxholes and as it did one of his men leapt from the safety of the pit and for an instant was silhouetted against the tank, David standing against Goliath. This was it, he thought. Flesh and blood pitted against the brute force of mechanized warfare. It was the bravest thing he had ever seen and as he watched he felt the tears course down his cheeks. What chance did the man have against armour? One man, young d'Agostino rose from his foxhole and ran towards a tank but was machine-gunned before he had gone five paces.

Others had a better idea. Ruspoli watched as another man waited for a tank to pass over his foxhole and looked on with pride as he leapt from his hole and ran back towards their lines, to the rear of the machine. Catching up with it he gave a huge leap and sprang on the back, clinging on to the objects slung around the turret, regained his balance and placed a dark object just above the right-hand track and below the turret. Ruspoli knew what it was. A mine, plucked from the sand and carefully placed in position in the foxhole along with half a dozen others like it. He watched as the man (was it Cafolla?) rolled off the tank, being careful to avoid its track and any others coming in its wake. The soldier ran back the few metres and threw himself into the foxhole as the following tank raked the ground around him with its machine-gun. The tank rumbled on and as to whether the crew were aware of their impending fate he never knew. There was an explosion, a huge flash and a heavy thump and the machine stopped dead, its right track slewed off the sprocket wheels. Its turret, at a bizarre angle, had turned a dull black and as Ruspoli watched flames began to lick around its edges. Then the hatch flew open and a man jumped out. He was on fire and his screams could be heard cutting through the cacophony of fire. He threw himself from the stricken tank and rolled on the sand. Another man followed in a similar state and began to writhe next to the first. And that was it. As Ruspoli watched the tank exploded.

Meanwhile over on the left flank Pistilli had turned his flamethrower on a third tank. Soon, thought Ruspoli, his fuel will be gone and then he'll be easy meat for the British. Unless we can get him back. He saw d'Agostini, fresh from his first kill, jump out again from the foxhole clutching a second Teller mine. He tried the same manoeuvre and ran back behind the tank that had just ridden over his position. Ruspoli watched in admiration, as the boy took a huge leap towards the rear of the tank, and then in horror, for the leap froze in mid-air as a stream of bullets fired from the neighbouring tank's machine-gun cut through the boy from shoulder to waist. D'Agostini just seemed to hang in space for a timeless instant and then he fell, like a modern Icarus, thought Ruspoli, and his lifeless body hit the sand, his hands still clasping the mine. Another of the men in an adjacent foxhole saw his fate and threw himself out in a rage, shrieking at the top of his voice: 'Italia! Italia!' He flung his mine at the nearest tank and it hit with full force, exploding on the unarmoured underside of the hull. The metal flew apart and the tank died from the underbelly up, a sheet of flame shooting through the hatch. But the blast came back against the Italian and a huge piece of steel severed his head from his body. Ruspoli shook his head in despair while all the time the Italians' machine-guns rattled out and the British infantry, desperately trying to take cover behind the wrecked tanks, fell by the dozen. On the left Ruspoli saw Pistilli, most of his fuel gone, run from his foxhole for the trench lines. He yelled across to Mautino: 'Carlo! Covering fire. Save Pistilli.'

Mautino shouted a command to the nearest section and six rifles and two Bredas opened up on the infantry closest to the retreating engineer. Pistilli, running for his life, had just reached the parapet of the trench when one of the tanks in the centre traversed its turret and a burst of machine-gun fire hit him in the back, igniting the little fuel that was left in the container. Pistilli screamed and fell into the trench, his back a wall of flame. Ruspoli, unable to watch the agony, turned back to his front and saw that there were now five burning tanks. He could not count the numbers of the British dead and wounded. And then, nothing less than a miracle. The remaining tanks, there must have been twelve of them, stopped and then they began to reverse. Still firing of course, but pulling back. And with them went what was left of the infantry. He could not believe his eyes. They had beaten them off. For now, at least.

The men gave a huge cheer. Ruspoli turned to them and beamed. Those closest to him rushed up to shake his hand. He found Mautino. The captain was jubilant: 'Colonel. Did you see that? We beat them. Just us, with nothing more than machine-guns and small arms. We beat off the tanks.'

Ruspoli hugged him and then stared at him and smiled. 'Yes, you're right. We beat them off. But we had more than machine-guns, Carlo, more even than flamethrowers and mines. We beat them because we're Italians. Because we're Folgore. We beat them with our guts.'

Tuesday 27 October

TWENTY-SEVEN

'Snipe' position, Kidney Ridge
2.00 a.m.
Tom Bird

Lying at the forward lip at the top of the shallow depression which held his command – A Company, Second Rifle Brigade – Tom Bird dug his elbow into the sand-covered rock, looked out across the endless desert through his field glasses and watched the lines of tracer bullets as they criss-crossed in the night sky. And as he did so he reached down further into the deep pocket of his hebron coat and searched again in vain for a cigarette. He was certain that there had been three or four in there when they had set out from the start line. He cursed silently and hummed to himself; he hadn't been able to get the damned tune out of his head for days. 'I Know Why', it was called, by one of the new Yank bands. A fellow officer had kept playing it in the mess on a wind-up just before the push, over and over again until two of the subalterns had spear-tackled him and brought the gramophone down. And now the melody was stuck in Bird's mind. Funny how these things came to you in the strangest of places. 'I know why and so do you.'

Bird was damned if he knew 'why'. Why he was here and not at home in Henley. Why he was lying on the edge of a desert filled with hostile Germans who, if he so much as stuck his head up a few inches more would compete to send him to eternity. He supposed though that he did have an inkling as to why they were all really there. They were on a mission to save Europe, save the world, from the scourge of a tyranny unparalleled in world history. And that, he thought, must surely be worthwhile. Worth all the death that now lay around them. Killing had become second nature to Bird and his men, death a commonplace. Often, as when poor Rifleman Garner had died yesterday afternoon in a shrapnel burst, it seemed so senseless and it was at moments such as this that he had to remind himself of their purpose. That they mattered. And they all mattered. Every one of them. Garner, Corporal Briggs, Colonel Turner, all of them. As long as they all did their own tiny bit then there was just a chance that they might win. The tune came back to haunt him again and again he thought of Moira.

Despite the warmth of the coat, he felt a chill cut through him to the bone and he shivered. At least, he thought, the Jerries hadn't spotted them yet. But he knew that this was the lull before the storm. He fumbled in his pocket for one last time and still having no joy, turned sharply to his right where his batman Briggs was sitting, writing a letter home.

'Briggs, see if you can't conjure up a cup of tea, there's a good chap. I'm sure you could do with one yourself. And see if you can't scrounge a couple of fags from someone. Anyone. I'll pay top dollar. Wills's, Player's, anything.'

'Will do, sir. One nice cup of cha coming up. An' I know that Larbert's got a packet of Woodbines on 'im. Will they do, sir?'

'That'll do splendidly, Briggs. I'll pay, of course.'

257

They had arrived here shortly after midnight, following a deafening half-hour barrage from the thirty big guns to their rear. It had been a major operation, manoeuvring a battalion up and into action against an entrenched enemy position. But Bird was certain now that they had taken a wrong turning, if you could call it that. This damned desert was impossible to navigate. They might as well be at sea.

He knew their orders – only too well. They had been told to take and hold this ground as a key strongpoint in the Allied line. A 'pivot of manoeuvre' for the tanks. They would simply have to hold the positions until first light on the twenty-seventh when the armour would pour in and relieve them. There was only one problem, thought Bird. It was a task that could only be accomplished by infantry. And out there in the desert that he was so desperate to see through the black, shell-lit night, lay German tanks. Panzers, hundreds of them, including the new Mark IVs with their terrible 75mm guns. He shuddered at the thought. Well at least it was better than the minefield duty they had been on throughout the twenty-third and twenty-fourth. Or the bloody tedious traffic control work they had done on the twenty-fifth directing Second Armoured. Bird knew though that his men were exhausted. Yet now they had gone into the offensive. He supposed though that they were no more tired than the rest of the army. One thing you could say for Monty. He had built this army, Eighth Army, into a fit, effective fighting force. There could hardly have been, he thought, a single ounce of excess fat on any one of the thousands of men who that night lay all around him, engaged in actions similar to this. It was reassuring, even if it did not alleviate the worry of the threat from German counter-attack. He yelled back into the depression:

'Corporal. Where's that tea?' A muffled voice from the rear assured him it was coming.

There was a commotion to his rear and Bird turned in anticipation of his tea and cigarettes but saw instead the familiar figure of the colonel jumping into the foxhole accompanied by his runner and radio operator.

'Tom. There you are. Thank God. Well, we're all here then. Your guns in place?'

'Around the perimeter, sir, as per your orders. It has occurred to me though, sir. Where exactly are the enemy?'

Turner smiled: 'Yes, Tom. I had noticed the lack of opposition. We were told by Brigade to attack this place. But as you astutely observe, there's no one here.'

'We are rather late, sir. Perhaps Jerry heard we were coming and made a run for it.'

Turner laughed. 'I'd love to think so, Tom. But I hardly think the Germans intend to leave the field to us without a fight, do you? No. It's the same problem we had getting here. We're not quite on target. Too far south by about half a mile.' He paused, considering the gravity of the situation. 'I'm afraid you lost a few men in that long wait. Stukas?'

'Yes, sir. That was bad, but the MO did what he could for them. We had to leave him there, sir. We've lost some of the trucks too. Fell into their slit trenches.'

'How many do we have left?'

'Twenty guns, sir. And there are six from 239 battery RA back at TAC HQ.'

Turner nodded sagely: 'Well, we're here now, and here we'll damn well stay. Whatever they throw at us.'

There was a cloud of dust as a man scrambled down into their foxhole and hastily saluted. 'Colonel Turner sir? Message from the carrier platoon, sir. Seems we've pitched up between two Kraut tank division laagers.

Leastways one of Germans and a bunch of Eyeties. Krauts are off to the north, sir, 'bout a thousand yards or so. Eyeties to the south.'

Turner's expression remained unchanged. 'Thank you, Rifleman.' The man saluted and Turner having returned the gesture, the soldier scrambled back up and out of the foxhole. Turner turned to Bird: 'That's torn it. Christ almighty, Tom, we're sandwiched between two divisions of tanks.'

Bird managed half a smile: 'Well, it is our job to destroy them, sir. We could be worse off.'

'True. I only hope that we can hold out against them until First Armoured get here. I'm off to find the recce party. I want to know more about these tanks. Good luck, Tom, and good shooting. I suspect you'll need it.'

Their position was more evident now. They occupied a shallow oval depression in the desert measuring some 1000 yards by 400. Whether it was actually the Snipe position was still highly questionable and the officers had no doubt that they were soundly, quite conclusively, lost. Still, it was a good enough hole to be in. The rim of the position was scarcely four feet high, but with its adjacent foliage of camel thorn and tamarisk bushes it became at once altogether more formidable and, thought Bird, offered the only cover in an otherwise wholly unforgiving landscape.

They had taken prisoners as they advanced into the position. Twenty of them. And they were nothing but a hindrance. On the north side the adjutant, Tim Marten, had found the main German dugout and taken it over as Battalion HQ.

Bird supposed that he should check on their welfare. 'Sar'nt Swann.'

'Sir?'

'How are the prisoners?'

260

'Surly bunch if you ask me. All except their officer, sir. He seems a decent chap if you know what I mean. No Nazi, anyways, I'd say. Spoke English to me. All sappers, sir. Don't know if you knew that. Layin' more bleedin' mines, I expect. If you'll pardon my French, sir. Didn't expect to get caught like that, I reckon. Mind you, they could have done worse. Might have been taken by the Aussies. Wouldn't have given tuppence for their chances then. Minelayers. Lucky buggers'll get shipped back to Blighty and land a cushy number in a POW camp. All tea and fruit cake. Cushy. If you know what I mean, sir.'

Bird nodded. Swann continued: 'While you and me, sir, are left out here in this blinkin' desert mopping up their mess.'

Bird laughed: 'You seem very confident that we're going to win this battle, Sar'nt.'

'Course we are, sir. We're going to win the war. Stands to reason, don't it. We've got better men, better tanks and more of both of them. And anyway, General Montgomery told us so 'isself.'

Bird liked Joe Swann. At twenty-eight he was an old sweat already, a veteran who, like others in the battalion, spoke to the men in a curious argot of Cockney mixed with well-chosen words of Urdu and Arabic. And he never seemed to tire. None of them did. How they managed it God only knew. The MO had banned Benzedrine, said that they wouldn't shoot straight. So tea and fags were all that kept them awake; that and the constant knowledge that at any moment they might come under attack.

Swann suddenly jumped into action. 'Blimey, sir. What's all that?'

Away over the dunes to the west they could hear the sound of a huge explosion and machine-gun fire. Corporal

261

Briggs came running up, grinning: 'It's Mister Flower, sir. He's taken the Bren carriers off into the Jerries. Looks like he's blown up some fuel trucks. Bloody marvellous.'

As Flower returned with his prize of sixteen prisoners, they heard another sound from the desert; the ugly rumble of approaching tanks. The moon was rising now and its light silhouetted twenty panzers as they drew up in a half-circle around the brigade's position. Bird knew what had to be done. He yelled: 'Get to the guns! Get on to them. Savill, draw a bead on that big bugger.'

He had spotted a Mark IV, the cream of the Wehrmacht armoury and knew that unless they could take it out they would all be dead or prisoners. It came at them, machine-gun firing and before Savill could lay the gun a bullet sliced through one of his ears. He fell back covered in blood and dazed but his place at the gun was taken by another man, Chard. He crouched behind the gunshield and stared at the huge bulk of the advancing Mark IV. Bird wondered if he was frozen with fear and shouted to him: 'Chard! Fire. Shoot the bastard.'

Chard did nothing. And then by some miracle, he fired. The shell hit the panzer at thirty yards and it stopped dead. Chard reloaded, waiting for the tank's huge gun to blow him to eternity. But instead the hatch opened and one of the black-uniformed tank crew threw himself out and on to the ground. Chard fired for a second time and as Bird looked on incredulously, the tank went up in a sheet of flame. Slowly, the remaining tanks backed away, their leader destroyed and around the perimeter of the depression the men of the Rifle Brigade gave a cheer. Bird joined in with them. But he knew that this was only a foretaste of what was to come and that the Germans' revenge would be swift and deadly.

*   *   *

The remainder of the night had been eerily quiet. At first light however, those of the men who had been able to sleep were awoken by the sound of revving engines.

Joe Swann rubbed at his eyes. 'Blimey. We're right in Rommel's rear. Look, sir.'

He was right.

There were hundreds of German and Italian vehicles of every description all around them, lorries, ambulances and tanks and it looked as if they hadn't noticed the riflemen.

Bird wasted no time: 'Sar'nt, get the guns into operation. Try for the tanks first but fire on anything over there. Take out whatever you can. Leave the ambulances of course. Anything else.'

Right, he thought, this will test the guns. Now we'll see if they're all they're cracked up to be. He wasn't disappointed. Within minutes Bird's thirteen anti-tank guns were firing away. Two tanks went up and there was a cheer. Then another and another. The Germans were sitting ducks. Bird began to lose count. Fourteen tanks were blazing away, along with two self-propelled guns, a handful of trucks, a staff car and one of the dread 88mm guns. But such good fortune could not last long. Within minutes enemy shells were landing around the six-pounders. Their teams struggled to move them and men began to fall. Bird was standing to the rear of a battery commanded by his friend Hugo Salmon when a German shell hit. A massive splinter carved into Salmon's face and sliced it open from forehead to chin. But he was still alive. Bird ran across to help him, took off his spotted silk scarf bought at New & Lingwood on his last leave and wrapped it around the hideous disfigurement.

He yelled out: 'Where's the MO?'

'Still back at the start line, sir. He can't get through the shelling.'

'Well find a bloody medic, can you, and get him over here.'

Salmon was gurgling now. Shock and pain were battling for possession of his tortured body. A medic came up; Bird recognized him, Sid Burnhope. 'Sid, help Mister Salmon can you and then you'd better see to the others. I think you're the only medic we have.'

Bird placed his friend's shattered head gently on the sand and went off to assess the situation. Turner met him. 'Tom. It's looking bad. Seems we're cut off – could be surrounded. Good news is that Twenty-Fourth Armoured are on their way.'

'Hurrah for the cavalry, then. And we've a pretty good position, sir. As good as we could hope for, at least.'

They heard the rumble of tanks and for a moment both men froze. Then they realized the noise was coming from their rear. Turner spoke: 'That should be the Shermans.'

But hardly had he said it than a shell landed too close for comfort. 'Might be Jerries, sir. Perhaps they got round the rear after all. I'll take a recce.'

Bird ran to the eastern edge of the position and saw a line of Sherman tanks with fluttering black and red pennants. It was the cavalry. At that moment two of them opened fire and their shells shot neatly over his head to fall in the vicinity of his own guns. He waved frantically at them: 'Stop! Stop! We're friends. Stop firing.'

But another of the tanks replied with a shell and a burst of machine-gun fire. Bird dived behind the dune. Turner appeared: 'What the devil's going on? Those are our chaps, aren't they?'

'Yes, sir. But I think they must only be able to see the Jerry tanks that we knocked out and some guns beyond. They must think that we're Jerries.'

'For heaven's sake. Where's the sparks? Can we get them on the wireless?'

264

''Fraid not, sir. Different frequency.'

'We must send someone out. Have you seen Jack Wintour?'

Bird knew where the intelligence officer was and went to find him. Turner was becoming agitated as more and more of his men became casualties of fire from their own side. 'Jack, get yourself into a Bren carrier with a white flag and get over to those bloody tanks. Those are our boys out there. That's Twenty-Four Brigade. Ask them if they wouldn't mind awfully not firing on their own side.'

They watched Wintour disappear over a dune and a few moments later one of the Sherman squadrons ceased fire. The other, however, continued with a will. They kept their heads down and Bird presumed that Wintour had made it across to the other tanks because a few minutes later all were silent. Meanwhile it had not escaped Bird's notice that on the German side a number of panzers had come up to the top of the ridge to combat the threat from the Shermans. He ran to his gunnery sergeant: 'Calistan, get those Jerries in your sights and let them have it.'

The sergeant obeyed and had hit two of the tanks before they realized what was happening. Black-coated men leapt from the turrets and ran across the sand, some back into their lines, others towards the British with their hands in the air. What happened next made Bird stare open-mouthed, for the machine-gunners of the Shermans opened up on the running men, cutting them down. They were Yorks and Lancs men Bird had realized, fresh to desert warfare. Didn't they know that there was a code of honour out here? An unwritten chivalry? The German tanks backed away, leaving several ablaze courtesy of Bird's guns, and the Twenty-fourth rolled forward towards the edge of the position. There was a massive

265

whooshing noise above his head as if the air was being sucked away and an 88mm shell smashed into the turret of the leading Sherman, instantly setting it alight. Then another and another. Now it was the British tankers' turn to be picked off. It was just the squalid justice of war, he thought. The crews leapt down from the inferno and Turner's riflemen ran forward to help them in, only to be machine-gunned now in turn by the panzers. The remaining tanks withdrew behind the height of Kidney Ridge.

Bird found Turner: 'So much for the cavalry, sir.'

'Yes, well I never did trust them really. Wellington was right. They just go galloping off at everything. Well, Tom, looks like we're on our own. For the time being at least.'

He had hardly spoken when a shell crashed into the position, wounding three of the riflemen. 'Take cover!' yelled Turner and was rewarded by a near miss from a rifle bullet. 'Snipers, sir. We'd better send out some lads to keep them low.'

'Who's our best shot?'

'I'd say Eddie Blacker, the one they all call "Muscles".'

'Well get him to find some cover and keep those bloody snipers down.'

Bird found Blacker and another South Londoner and sent them out to a makeshift shelter under one of the tanks earlier destroyed by Chard. Bird watched him from down in the depression. The German snipers had come forward and were also making use of the wrecks, but being above the riflemen they had to fire downwards and exposed themselves standing on the tanks. Within a few minutes Bird saw Blacker account for three panzer-grenadiers. Good choice, he thought. He yelled across to him, 'Good shooting, Blacker.'

'Like ducks in a water barrel, sir.'

But the snipers were the least of their worries, for now

the 88s had opened up with a vengeance. More tanks too, German and Italian had moved forward cautiously and were using their cannon to shell the position. But not with impunity. The little six-pounders were still working well, thought Bird, as he crawled with ammunition from one gun to another. Sergeant Swann was doing the same and even the colonel was helping with resupply. But it couldn't prevent the shells from doing their deadly work. Bird counted. There were only thirteen of the battalion's guns left operational. He wondered how much longer they would be able to hold out.

A shell had exploded on the edge of a slit trench and the occupants had been almost buried alive. Bird went across: 'Come on, you're not dead yet.' They managed a half-hearted smile and he chided himself for his lack of tact. He looked at his watch and found that it was approaching 1 p.m. Back home, he thought, they would be having lunch. It was a Tuesday. He did not have to wait long for his mind to be diverted. There was a rumble on the left flank and out from nowhere tanks appeared and began to move at speed towards the position. Bird could see that they were Italian: nine M14/41s and a couple of Semovente self-propelled guns. Christ he thought, there's only one gun over there.

He ran across. The gun was manned by one of the characters of the company, an Anglo-Indian sergeant named Charlie Calistan. He was a popular man. Diminutive and quick, he was a natural featherweight boxer and had won an MM near Bir Hacheim. But all the character and pluck in the world wouldn't save Charlie Calistan from eleven tanks. Bird could see that he was alone with the gun. Two of his men were crawling back with more ammo, under heavy fire while the fourth was just sitting by the gun, his nerves shot to pieces by shellshock. Bird had seen the symptoms before. As he reached the gun he was joined by Colonel Turner and Calistan's platoon commander, Jack Toms MC, an expert fisherman. The officers now became Calistan's gun crew. Turner spoke: 'Hold your fire to six hundred yards.'

They waited and tried to count the tanks in. Eventually when Turner reckoned they were within his prescribed range he yelled: 'Fire!' and Calistan let it go. They watched as the shell flew towards the leader, an M14; it hit and blew the thinly-armoured tank and its crew into oblivion. The casing flew out of the breech to be replaced by another shell and Calistan did it again. And again and again until three Italian tanks lay blazing on the sand while three others lumbered on along the edge of the depression still with their dead and dying crews inside, unable to stop. All the time Calistan's gun had been raked by machine-gun fire and now he had just three shells left. Toms yelled, 'I'll go,' and dashed across the position towards the resupply jeep. It was a hundred yards away but he made it through a hail of bullets. He jumped in and started her up then brought her up to behind the gun. As he was getting out a small German shell flew into the jeep – an incendiary round. The vehicle burst into flames. 'Quick!' shouted Turner and between them they managed to offload all four boxes of ammunition.

As Bird looked on he saw that rather than give up, the three remaining Italian tanks were moving in. So much for all they had been told about the Italians having little stomach for a fight. This was bravery on a scale he had seldom seen. A Semovente shell flew into the position and exploded dangerously close to the gun sending out huge splinters, one of which flew straight at Turner's tin hat, slicing into it and penetrating his skull. The colonel sank to his knees with blood gushing from his head. He muttered: 'Get me up. I need to help.' But Toms and a corporal grabbed hold of him and laid him down in cover behind a piece of scrub. Back at the gun Calistan was still firing. Toms knelt down to reload and at three hundred yards Calistan opened fire on the leading M14. The shell made contact and the tank burst into flames, its crew spilling out of the turret. Toms reloaded, Calistan fired twice more. Two more tanks ignited.

Turner, wiping the blood from his face, had seen it all: 'Hat-trick!' he shouted. Bird smiled but as he bent down to confer with Toms and Flower a shell came in on their left. The explosion sent a piece of redhot shrapnel into Tom's right hand, taking off three fingers and tearing the tendons. Another hit Flower in both legs. A third piece hit Bird squarely in the head and he cursed himself for his bravado at disdaining a tin hat in favour of a soft forage cap. For a moment he lay on the ground, blood pouring out. Then recovering himself he sat up and put his hand to his head. There was blood everywhere but he felt the size of the wound and reckoned it could not be as bad as the colonel's. He tried to stand up and instantly fell over. Sergeant Swann ran over and picked him up: 'Come on, Mister Bird, sir. Let's find you somewhere to lie down.'

They laid him alongside Turner on the rocky floor of the HQ dugout. He was conscious now that the blood was beginning to coagulate, yet he still felt covered in the stuff. Next to him were the battalion signallers and their radios. The adjutant, Tim Marten was there too. But his closest companions were the flies. They seemed determined to swarm across his face and investigate every inch of the blood. Bird tried to brush them away but more landed in their place.

That damned American song was still going round and round in his brain. 'I know why and so do you. Why do robins sing in December?' Stupid lyrics he thought. Better off by far with something safe like 'Room five

269

hundred and four . . . the perfect honeymoon alone with you'. He thought of Moira, of home and began to cry. Not loudly, just a quiet sobbing, and then he realized what he was doing and made himself stop. Beside him Turner had begun to make strange noises and Bird tried to make them out. It was the delirium that often comes with head wounds and fever. 'You there. Aim and fire. Sink that destroyer. They will not pass. They shall not capture this harbour. Fire, fire. Sink all their ships.'

It was 4 p.m. Bird turned to Turner: 'Colonel. There are no ships. They're enemy tanks we have to destroy and we're doing very well, sir.'

The colonel turned to him and stared, smiling and unseeing. Bird gave up. And as he did a salvo of shells crashed into their position sending up showers of sand and rock. Bird sat up and tried to work out where they were coming from and horribly it appeared to be from behind their own lines. He called across to Sergeant Swann: 'Sar'nt. What's happening? Are those our guns?'

'Don't know, sir. I think so. Adjutant's sent someone to find out.'

More rounds came in and this time there were casualties. Swann cursed as two of his men were killed outright by an airburst and over on the other side of the depression another rifleman died. Corporal Cope ran up to Bird: 'Thought you'd like to know, sir, not that it's good news, but the adjutant says those are our guns, 105mils from Second Armoured.'

Christ, thought Bird. Not again. It was typical of this desert war that no one was ever quite certain of what they were firing on, friend or foe. It was hard enough to know where you were yourself. At last the 105s were silent and Bird prayed that dusk would come soon for that seemed to be the only way they would make it through until relief finally arrived.

By night the enemy tanks would be blind and that was his only hope. But it was shattered a few minutes later. Briggs knelt down beside Bird and Turner who had started to rave again. 'Sir, bad news. We've sighted more Jerry tanks. Around seventy of them in two groups. Adjutant thinks they're heading towards the armour in our rear, One Brigade. It's just possible they don't know about us.'

'How many guns have we left?'

'Of our own we've got Sar'nt Swann's and Corporal Cope's, and Sar'nt Binks' and Sar'nt Cullen's. But all the crews are pretty badly shot up. We have got Mister Baer's RA battery too though. There's still four of them left.'

That was good news, thought Bird. Those four six-pounders could inflict a lot of damage on the German armour and Baer, a lively jazz musician from Oxford, was as good a man as any to command them. They heard gunfire: 'That'll be Mister Baer now, sir.' There was a series of explosions, and then cheering. 'Sounds like he's bagged one.'

There was more firing from their left and Bird tried to get up but only succeeded in propping himself on his elbow. Nevertheless by moving position slightly and with some help from Briggs he was able to see one of Baer's six-pounders in action, manned by Sergeant Binks and his crew of three. As he watched it fired, hitting one of the attacking German Mk IIIs which began to burn. Just then however a high explosive shell flew in and scored a hit on Binks' gun. The sergeant was thrown back against the sand and a huge piece of shell casing took the head off one of his gunners while more of the flying shrapnel reduced the other two to objects barely recognizable as human beings. Binks pushed himself to his feet and stared at the ghastly scene then immediately sat back down in a state of shock. Bird too was affected. How quickly in

271

war, he thought, such small victories turn to tragedy. He flopped down on to his haversack and fell asleep to the sound of gunfire.

It was dusk when he awoke and all seemed quiet. Turner was murmuring in his sleep. Briggs was sitting beside him. 'Welcome back, sir. You've had a good rest. Slept right through it.'

'Through what, Briggs?'

'All sorts of fun and games we've had, sir. Let's see. Jim Hine now, he got one of them and then Chard hit another three, or was it four? Then Sar'nt Swann, well he turned an abandoned gun on another one and got it. Captain Wintour couldn't control hisself then. Then Jerry came over and got his wounded. Enough of them there was. I was going to wake you, sir, if you hadn't woken up first. We've been given our marching orders.'

'We're abandoning the position? What time is it?'

'Twenty-two-thirty hours, sir. Seems we've done our bit. First Armoured's coming through here. Major Marten reckons we saved their bacon, sir. I reckon it's a bleedin' miracle. We knocked out that many tanks.'

'How many? Do we know?'

'Not for certain, sir. But Major Marten reckons it must be over thirty tanks and five or six SP guns plus a couple of eighty-eights. That's not counting the ones we damaged.'

Bird listened, amazed. They had held off two entire armoured divisions. Then he asked, 'What about us, Briggs. What are our casualties?'

'Seventy killed and wounded, ten of them officers.'

Bird remembered now, thought about his poor anti-tank company. All those men lost. In his mind he began to draft the letters: 'died gallantly defending a hopeless position against enormous odds.' But how would he

272

end it, he wondered? 'By his action this day he helped to hold off the German tanks and allowed our armour to advance to victory.' He prayed that he would be proved right.

TWENTY-EIGHT

Midnight
HQ Eighth Army
De Guingand

De Guingand looked at his watch. It was midnight. He sat at the small table in his converted dugout command post and began to write up the following morning's report. Second Armoured Division had advanced past the Rifle Corps at Woodcock position but had met with strong and determined resistance from Fifteenth Panzer Division.

Twenty-Fourth Armoured Brigade had put in an attack to the south of the Snipe position and met resistance from Eighth Panzers. Neither of them had achieved success.

He wrote, in a steady, fluid hand: 'During the afternoon of 26 October Twenty-First Panzer Division counter-attacked but were beaten off by our armour. Ninetieth Light Panzers and the Italian Bersaglieri attacked Point Twenty-nine in the late afternoon but were beaten back by Ninth Australian Division.'

There was little real news but at least the report ended on a high note. 'In the last few hours the positions at Snipe and Woodcock held throughout the day by KRRC and Rifle Brigade have been consolidated by Tenth Armoured Division. The front is secure.'

Wednesday 28 October

TWENTY-NINE

11.00 a.m.
Near the Ninetieth Light Division
Rommel

He had committed the panzers, had played his last card. But in truth it had not been his battle. If only he had come back sooner, before the British had lodged themselves on Miteiriya Ridge. They should never have been allowed to get that far. And now all he could do was wait. He could not pretend to himself that Montgomery's move had not come as a surprise and now he found himself no longer in control, but fighting a battle in which he was responding. This was not the way to fight, not his way. He paced the floor of his command vehicle, his *Mammut* which he had used since coming out here. Montgomery, he believed, had a similar command vehicle. He wondered if they were at all similar in other ways. Now he was running around in the shadow of the Allied commander, his men chasing to catch up with the British as they advanced.

He had moved the Twenty-First Panzer Division up from the southern sector, away from the Italians. They would be isolated, but there was nothing to be done. The threat to the north was too great. With them he had brought half of his artillery then committed them and

Ninetieth Light Division in a classic coordinated counter-attack at the salient. It was to be supported by a wave of Stuka dive-bombers. But a few hours ago the news had begun to come in and now Rommel stood surveying the map in his headquarters, stroking his chin and wearing a scowl of concentration. He could not help but wonder where the masterstroke might lie. The battle had been raging for four days, though he had only been in command for barely two of those. There must be, he thought, something I'm missing, some manoeuvre that I haven't yet seen. The salient in the north near the kidney-shaped feature was clearly the focus of attention. But he feared that it was all too late.

His planned air assault on the Australians had been smashed by the RAF. Four squadrons of Hurricanes and two of the new American-built Kittyhawks had seen off the Stukas. He thought back to Poland and France and realized, not for the first time, that the new technology on the Allied side was fast overtaking the supposedly invincible Nazi war machine.

He took his pencil and circled a spot on Kidney Ridge where reports had come in of a defence by anti-tank guns which had brought the Twenty-First Panzers to a temporary halt and cost him dearly in tanks and manpower. And it was not only at the front line of the battle that he was suffering.

Now, after another night of bombing with the RAF taking out his tanks as they were forming up, before they had a chance to manoeuvre, he began for the first time to sense the real possibility of a defeat. And he feared it.

He turned to his chief of staff: 'Bayerlein, what news of the 164th?'

'It seems that they've got through, sir. The 433rd and 382nd are back in communication, with us and with each other.'

'That's good. That's something.'

'We took more casualties overnight, sir. Tanks.'

'The new Shermans?'

'Yes, sir. They sit hull down at over two thousand yards and simply outshoot us. There's nothing we can do.'

If only the Führer had fulfilled his promise of the Tigers. But it was of no use considering that now. 'Have you that list again? May I see it?'

Bayerlein handed him the newly typed-up list of the available tanks: '15th PzDiv–21Mk III and IV, 21st PzDiv–45MkIII and IV, Littorio Div–33M, Ariete ArmdDiv–129M, Trieste Mot–Div34M.'

'Is that it?'

'That's it, sir.'

So that was all he had; 66 German tanks and 196 Italian, but the latter he knew would not survive long against the Grants and Shermans. They were slow, lightly gunned and poorly armoured.

Montgomery seemed to be playing with him. Clearly he was planning a large attack along the coast towards Sidi Abdl el Rahman. But he could not be sure yet if the entire British offensive in the north might not be augmented by an attack in the south. Was it a feint? He picked up from the table a map captured from the British and clearly marked with Montgomery's plan to push northwest from the Australians' salient at Hill 29.

He called to Rolf Munninger, his young personal clerk and a fellow Schwabian. 'I have a new directive for the army. Can you take it down?'

Munninger hurried through from the radio room and began to write as Rommel spoke. 'Any soldier who fails or disobeys is to be court-martialled regardless of his rank. This is a battle for life or death. I demand that every officer and man put forward his utmost effort.' He paused: 'Got that?'

'Yes, sir. Shall I send it to . . . ?'

'To all corps and divisional commanders. At once.'

Life or death, he thought. But now was the time to make provision for the worst. He had to rescue what he could of the Afrika Korps before it was too late, had to gather enough to keep it together as a fighting force.

'Bayerlein, I want every surviving German unit moved up to the northern sector. Every man who can fight, every tank, every gun. Every German. But we must make provision for a fallback position.' He circled the map. 'Here at Fuka. A hundred miles behind the German lines along the coast. If the attack goes against us then we must thin out the front and fight a defence. What have we in reserve apart from the Trieste?'

'Nothing, Herr Generalfeldmarschall.'

'Nothing but one division of Italians. So, we pull back some of the panzers from the front line and create a new reserve. Where's the Twenty-First now?'

'Still engaged with the enemy, sir. Up by the coast road.'

'Pull it back and replace it with the Trieste. The Ninetieth can hold the coast road. And move the Ariete Division south to replace the German units down there. And issue an order to all troops. Munninger, you take this down: "Instead of harassing fire, which involves unnecessary ammunition expenditure, troops are to open fire on the enemy at sight with short, concentrated salvoes".' Munninger went off to the radio room.

Rommel turned to the chief of staff: 'I'm afraid, Bayerlein, that we shall not be able to withstand such attacks as the British are now capable of putting in. We cannot wait for them to make their decisive breakthrough. We must pull out to the west before they do so.'

'But, sir, that will mean losing much of the infantry. Perhaps all of those that are non-motorized.'

Rommel frowned. 'Well then, so be it.' He paused and

279

smiled: 'You know, Bayerlein, I've found again and again that the day will go to the side that is the first to plaster its opponent with unstoppable firepower. Who do you suppose that might be in our case?'

Bayerlein shrugged. 'You shouldn't talk like that, sir. Thinking the worst sometimes makes it happen.'

'I think it may be too late for that sort of wishful thinking, Bayerlein.'

Munninger re-entered and handed a message to Rommel. 'Sir, more bad news I'm afraid. We've just heard that two tankers carrying fuel to us from Italy have gone down in Tobruk harbour.'

Rommel shook his head: 'How much fuel were they carrying?'

'Four thousand tons, and one of them also had fifteen hundred tons of ammunition.'

Rommel said nothing. That was it then. He looked again at the sheet of paper on the table containing the numbers of remaining tanks. The Fifteenth Panzer Division had been decimated from 119 tanks to 21. This was a battle of attrition, a battle that he knew he most probably would lose.

Tired and anxious, he sighed: 'Bayerlein, I am not to be disturbed. I think I need to sit down for a while. I need to think.'

It was the final thing. Fuel, as he had told Gause, was the key to this battle and with the sinking of the two tankers he had just lost irreplaceable supplies. Now, even if he could rally his tanks and make a break through there was no way he could exploit it. The army was virtually immobile. What he feared most was what he already knew. That Montgomery's army was quite the opposite, well supplied, well fuelled and able to cross the desert in fast pursuit of his ragged and wounded forces. A breakthrough anywhere in the line by British armour would almost certainly mean that they would take what was left of Panzerarmee Afrika in the rear. And then it really would all be over.

He sat down at the little table and began to write to his wife.

Dearest Lu,
The battle is raging. Perhaps we will survive in spite of all that goes against us. If we fail it would have grave consequences for the entire course of the war, for in that case North Africa would fall to the British almost without a fight. We are doing our utmost to succeed, but the enemy's superiority is tremendous and our own resources very small.

I haven't much hope left. At night I lie with my eyes open, unable to sleep for the load that lies on my shoulders. If we fail, whether or not I survive the battle will be in God's hands. The lot of the vanquished is hard to bear. I have a clear conscience, as I have done everything to gain a victory and have not spared my own person. Should I remain on the battlefield I would like to thank you and our boy for all the love and joy you have given me in my life. My last thought is of you. After I am gone you must bear the mourning, proudly.
Your own,
Erwin

THIRTY

7.00 p.m.
Near Trig Twenty-nine
Kibby

Kibby sat on an ammo box tucked into the side of an abandoned foxhole and oiled his submachine-gun. He was not a happy man. Captain Robbins had given them the gen and to put it politely it seemed like a pretty complex plan. But then Kibby had never been particularly polite and to put it bluntly, he thought it stank. But if that was what the brass had up their sleeve then who was he to argue with them? The five battalions of Ninth Australian Division were to move north and northeast using Trig 29 as a sort of pivot. Their objective was the railway line and the road; 2/48th were to be held in reserve at first, following on with an eastern attack along the main road to somewhere with the endearing name of 'Ring Contour 25'. But 2/24th would take Thompson's Post. Or die trying to. And it all had to happen before the sun came up.

Kibby whistled and spoke to Ashby without raising his eyes from his task. 'Well, whoever dreamed this one up thought of a real corker. It's going to be like bleedin' Piccadilly Circus out there. More diggers than you could shake a fist at and all done before sun up. What a beaut.'

For what no one had really explained was that for the reserve battalions to get anywhere those in forward positions would have to succeed in the initial attack. If they did not then it would be pure bloody chaos, chiefly because what was meant to happen in the dark might be happening in full daylight and thus in full view of the German defenders.

Kibby carried on oiling the Thompson, checking and double-checking the mechanism. He didn't want it jamming on him. Not if it was going to be as busy out there as it sounded it might. Ashby too had chosen a Thompson for the attack. He was new to the weapon and was copying Kibby's actions while trying to seem as if he knew exactly what he was doing.

'Oh, come on, Bill. Those guys know what they're doing. If they didn't then how would we have got this far?'

'I'll tell you how we got this far, mate. We got this far using our own bloody sense. That's what Aussie soldiers always do. We say "yes sir" to the officers and then go and fight the battle our own way. And you can bet that's what we're going to have to do tonight. If we ever get into action, that is.'

They left at 19.30 hours, moving into lorries which took them closer to Trig 29. For once the platoons were silent. It took an hour to get them into position. Finally, at 22.00 Kibby reckoned they were ready to go. Half an hour later the tanks of the 46th RTR arrived. The plan was that the leading infantry, the boys of the 2/23rd, would be loaded up on the tanks and taken through the minefield. What intrigued Kibby was that the tanks had been specially converted, with flailing steel chains at the front which were intended to explode any mines they might encounter before the tanks ran over them. It was a great theory and had been proven to work, but he was sceptical. From their position he watched the 2/23rd mount up and move off, the blue pennants waving on the turrets of the Grants. Within a few minutes however there was a series of massive explosions. A soldier came running back into the position. 'That's torn it. It's a fuckin' mess out there. Two of the tanks have brewed up on mines and two more have just stopped dead. No one's going anywhere.'

It was the stuff of Kibby's nightmare, a delay that would push them all into daylight. They watched and waited. From their position to the rear of the forward troops they could see the whole tableau being played out and it was not a pretty sight. One after one the tanks were going up and Kibby watched the faces of his men as they looked on. He wondered whether the blokes in command ever considered this. The fact that at the front line it was what you saw that made you a good soldier or a bad one. The simple fact that if you make men wait to fight they will inevitably become not only lacking in edge and adrenalin but also just plain shit-scared.

Kibby found Herb Ashby. 'What d'you reckon then? We going to get shafted or what?'

Ashby laughed. 'Dunno, Bill. But I reckon those poor buggers wish they'd never seen those tanks.'

One of the men began to play a mouth organ. Inevitably the tune was 'Waltzing Matilda'. Almost immediately some of the platoon joined in. Kibby smiled: 'Well, at least its not "Lili Marlene" again, I've got that song on the brain. It's good for morale. Come on, Herb.' And he joined in the song. Another of the men kept time on his billy-can and soon every man in the two platoons was singing. No sooner had they finished than some wag struck up with 'Why are we waiting?'. Of course they all joined in and were in full voice when Captain Robbins walked up. Kibby raised his hand: 'All right, boys. Officer present.'

Robbins smiled. 'You've probably realized that 2/23rd are in a spot of bother. The brass hats can't decide what to do so we're just going to have to sit here and wait. Try to make your men as comfortable as possible. And try to keep them happy.'

'Happy, sir?'

'Well, all right. But you know what I mean, Kibby. Don't let them get too jumpy.'

He walked off.

'And I thought he was one of us.'

'Never can tell with officers, mate.'

'Come on, let's have another song. Give us a tune, Leaney.'

The man with the mouth organ began to play 'Lili Marlene'.

Kibby shook his head: 'Here we go.'

But no amount of singing could divert them from the tragedy being played out before them. Gradually, as things became worse, casualties from the 2/23rd were brought back and the only way was past their lines.

The singing had stopped at midnight. Now it was 4 a.m. Kibby collared a corporal who had taken a flesh wound in the upper arm. 'Hey, mate. How's it going.'

'Not good, mate. Reckon we've taken at least two hundred casualties. There's only a half dozen tanks left and they're moving back.'

Robbins appeared again and took Kibby aside. 'Right, Sergeant. That's it. The show's off. We're pulling back to Tel el Eisa.'

'I can't say I'm disappointed, sir. Never seemed a good idea to me.'

'Ours not to reason why, Kibby, eh?'

'No, sir.'

They reached their bivouac just before dawn and Kibby

settled down in his makeshift sangar. He was just drifting off to sleep when Ashby appeared.

'Blimey, mate. I've just seen Robbins. He was talking about you.'

Kibby sat up. 'What? What did he say? What have I done?'

'It's not what you've done, mate. Least, nothing bad. He told me he wants to recommend you for a bloody DCM. That's all. He told me in case anything happens to him. You know what he's like.'

Kibby said nothing. A DCM? A medal of any sort, let alone a Distinguished Conduct Medal was not something he'd ever thought he could possibly be awarded. He was just a common soldier, a bloke doing his job. Why should he get a medal and none of the others?

'You must have gone doolally, mate. Or he has. A DCM, me? Don't be daft.'

'That's what he said, Bill. He's going to put you up for it. For being an exemplary platoon leader and a tower of strength to the men. Those were his exact words, I swear. Soon as we get back. And I'll tell you something else. The 2/23rd's still dug in up there. They're down to sixty men. The whole battalion. Sixty men left out of five hundred. Still holding on and Robbins reckons Monty's going to need to keep it that way. And that's where we come in.'

'A DCM. Strewth. They'll never bloody believe me.'

Thursday 29 October

THIRTY-ONE

11.50 a.m.
HQ Eighth Army
Montgomery

The Australians had done well. Of that there was no doubt. But they had suffered for it. Their casualties had been high, almost intolerably high and their supporting tanks had been decimated. But they had got stuck in the minefields and they had not reached the railway. Montgomery had decided that he would wait for a day, allow them time to rest and reorganize and then on the thirtieth begin again. Then they would reach the sea.

On the thirty-first they would launch the major offensive: 'Operation Supercharge', he had christened it. He had said as much during that morning's meeting with the commander-in-chief, General Alexander and the minister of state, Casey. And they had seemed to approve.

Freddie de Guingand knocked and entered the caravan. 'Sir. A signal just through from London. We can expect another visit tomorrow from Duncan Sandys MP. And there's a telegram from the prime minister.'

De Guingand handed a paper to Montgomery who read it. 'Re imminent Allied landing in Tunisia. Expect French to assist. Events may therefore move more quickly than had been planned.'

Montgomery put it down on the table. Politics. Always politics interfering with the job of an army commander. So Churchill was telling him to move more quickly. To break through Rommel well before the Tunisian landing date of 8 November. And he was sending his own son-in-law Duncan Sandys out to check up on him. He frowned.

De Guingand spoke: 'Sir. General McCreery, General Richardson and Mister Casey were of the opinion that it might be best to make the attack in the south, where Rommel is obviously weaker. Intelligence confirms . . .'

Montgomery bristled and cut in: 'Nonsense. The Australians have made terrific headway in the north and that is where we should attack. I intend to pull Rommel's panzers into the salient and anywhere else we make gains and meet them on terms hugely in our favour. There is absolutely no question of moving the attack. I won't have it.'

De Guingand left and Montgomery looked at the map. How dare they have the temerity to suggest that he should change his plan. It was a master plan, and only a master could write it.

Of course if de Guingand was right and the intelligence was correct, that was another matter, that might persuade him to change. But not the suggestions of his own commanders. He sat down and wrote in the Army Commander's Directive for Supercharge: 'This operation, if successful, will result in the complete disintegration of the enemy. Determined leadership will be vital; complete faith in the plan will be vital; risks must be accepted freely; there must be no "belly-aching".'

A few moments later de Guingand entered again, carrying another piece of paper. 'Latest intelligence report, sir. Enigma decrypt. Seems that the enemy has moved the Ninetieth Light Division north. Due to the Australians' success, I imagine.'

He waited for Montgomery to respond. The General said nothing at first, and then: 'Yes, no doubt.'

Montgomery thought fast. So Rommel had strengthened the north. Now almost all the German units were massed up there, leaving merely the Italians in the south. This would change everything. Again. And the change would come from him, not from his generals or a politico. Rommel's attacks were failing. The Desert Fox was starting to dance to his tune, just as he had predicted he would.

He had been encouraged by reports coming through from Kidney Ridge. The Rifle Brigade and the Royal Horse Artillery appeared to be managing to keep the enemy away from First Armoured. It was clear to him now that anti-tank guns, whether the German 88s or the Rifle Brigade's little portee-borne guns were the winners in a desert war. Now was the time, he thought, to discreetly move more armour, First Armoured and Twenty-Fourth Armoured Brigade, away from the front line and into Lumsden's armoured reserve. As always seemed to be the case in this long battle, it would have to be the infantry who cleared the way. He would ask the Australians to carry on along the sea road. But now that would not be his direction for the decisive assault. That would now come in the Kidney Ridge area in the north, across the Rahman Track. Freyberg would do the job and through it he would pour his armoured corps and two regiments of armoured cars.

He turned to de Guingand and pointed to the map. 'I've decided to change the plan, Freddie. We're going to punch here.' He circled Kidney Ridge. 'Operation Supercharge. We go on the night of 31 October. We need to have a conference, Freddie. The corps commanders here please, as soon as they can manage it.'

He was convinced now that this would be the decisive stroke. It would be costly of course, but then he had always known that there would come a time in this great battle when he would have to put such dreadful considerations behind him. They had all spoken bluntly of fifty per cent losses. But only he accepted that it might be a hundred per cent. Of course, he had promised himself to spare his men, to minimize casualties. But not if it meant losing the battle. He had more tanks than the enemy, more guns and more infantry. If every one of them were able to take out one of the enemy before being hit themselves then he would win. And winning the battle was what counted. As far as he was concerned, that would be a success.

He stepped outside the caravan to wait for the arrival of Leese, Lumsden and Horrocks and saw that de Guingand and others were standing close by, listening to the loudspeaker which had been tuned to the wireless 'net' which served the forward tanks. Montgomery paused and joined them. The voices crackled over the speaker.

'Look out, Bob, a couple sneaking up on your right flank – you should see them any minute now.'

'King Five, King Five, are you OK? Over.'

'King Five, yes. But I can't see much. We're under fairly heavy fire, there seem to be guns all round this place. Over.'

'King Five, have a look towards the sun. Off.'

The radio fell silent, then crackled again into life. There was a bang and then: 'Get out, sir, we've been hit.'

'King Five, my horse has copped it. Wireless OK but we shan't be able to take any further part in the show. I'll just have a look at the damage and tell you the extent.'

'King Five. That's the second time. You MUST NOT say such things over the air.'

'King Five. Sorry. Bit dizzy. Not feeling too hot. Very hot actually. Over.'

'King Five. Sorry you're dizzy. Try to get out.'

'King Five. Crew gone. All save poor Collins. Not too good, sir. May have to sign off now. Getting a bit hot. Oh God. God no . . .'

The wireless went dead and de Guingand and the others looked down at the ground and said nothing. Montgomery walked quietly back inside the caravan and sat down. Yes, they would take casualties. He was prepared for that. He was prepared for fifty per cent. A hundred per cent. Whatever it took to win. But please, he prayed to God, please don't let them all die like that.

THIRTY-TWO

5.00 p.m.
The road from Alexandria to
El Alamein
Lieutenant Keith Douglas

He drove the two-tonner fast along the dust track, knowing that every yard brought him closer to the front. Unfortunately every yard also threw his two passengers and all their kit violently from side to side and the journey was punctuated with yells and oaths. For the truck had not been designed for the desert and certainly not for battle. It was an old commercial vehicle and the accelerator was far too sensitive. Douglas pressed it again and it roared in response and Douglas swore at it.

His batman, Lockett, a former hunt servant, turned to him and smiled. 'I like you, sir. You've got real style. You're shit or bust, you are.'

Douglas laughed and drove on. He knew that there was every possibility that he might be charged with desertion or at the very least dereliction of duty. For he was not supposed to be here. A bright young lieutenant of twenty-two, he had been posted to the Divisional staff, in a cushy job that thousands would have paid to get, 'Camouflage training officer'. But it was not what he wanted from the army. At Oxford he had revelled in the camaraderie of the OTC. Cavalry of course. Well, he was a superb horseman. But at heart he was a poet and perhaps, he thought, it was this that had made him commandeer the lorry and head for his regiment, the Nottinghamshire Sherwood Yeomanry, part of Eighth Armoured Brigade in General Gatehouse's Tenth Armoured Division. He had tried to go through all the official channels to get to the front. But there was always 'nothing doing, old boy'. How he hated being called 'old boy'. So he had decided to run away. Of course, he had no real battle experience and if found out would, he presumed, be unwanted as well as in breach of King's Regulations. But the devil take that, he thought. He was going to war and no one was going to stop him.

He was driving through other vehicles now, hundreds of lorries which had once been painted khaki or desert yellow and were now the colour of the dusty sand of the tracks and which themselves kicked up dust in clouds although the surfaces of the roads, being so continuously ploughed over by tyres had turned to a white mud. There were weapons too, tanks and armoured cars and quads pulling the RA's twenty-five-pounders rumbling slowly onwards, and in their pits the anti-aircraft guns surrounded by sandbags with their idling crews watching the skies. And everywhere were men as far as the eye could see. He had just been reading Maeterlinck and instantly his thoughts turned to the idea of ants. Thousands of ants. The men, or ants, were doing what soldiers do best when not fighting, making tea on makeshift stoves and squatting and sitting around in groups laughing and chatting. He turned to Lockett: 'Have you any idea where the regiment might be?'

'None at all, sir. Your guess is as good as mine.'

Desperately, Douglas sought out their stencilled insignia but did not find it.

They drove on, Douglas, Lockett and their third passenger,

a gormless fitter from HQ whom he had collared with the instruction to return the truck should he be lucky enough to find the regiment. They had gone about fifteen miles when Lockett yelled: 'Sir! Look.'

Douglas followed his pointing finger and saw the trucks and carriers of their regimental supply column, quite unmistakable on account of the presence of their officer, one Macdonald, a made-up NCO, his towering presence unmissable even at a hundred yards.

Douglas stopped the truck and jumped out. With Big Mac was Bill Owen, the major in charge of supply. Douglas swallowed hard and began to tell his lies.

'Hello, sir. Where's the regiment?'

'Douglas, what are you doing here?'

'The colonel sent a message back to Division, sir. Seems I'm wanted.'

'Ah, so you've come back to us. Good. Good chap. The regiment's a few miles up the road, waiting for the off. Any time now. Good job you're here, Douglas. A Company's lost almost all its officers. They plastered us with everything they had.'

Douglas felt a frisson of danger, smiled incongruously and thanked him, then got back into the truck. They found the regiment with little trouble and the colonel with even less. James Massingham, whom Douglas had christened 'Piccadilly Jim' on account of his habitually perfect St James's turn-out, smiled at him and twirled a moustache that was as perfectly groomed as the rest of him.

'Keith. Most glad to see you. All A Company officers are casualties, except Andrew. I should get him to fix you up with a troop. We're going in tomorrow morning.'

They drove off towards the area where the colonel had indicated Andrew's squadron might be encamped and Douglas found the major sitting on a petrol tin beside one of the tanks scribbling furiously with a chinagraph pencil

295

on a piece of celluloid laid over a map. He was small, with fair hair and a ruddy complexion weather-beaten by the desert into a rich nut-brown. He was dressed in a grey flannel shirt, corduroy trousers and a rakish blue silk neckerchief. Douglas dismounted and saluted:

'Sir.'

'Douglas?'

'Colonel sent me, sir. Replacement. Said that you might have a troop for me.'

'Yes. Very good. You may as well take those two tanks. I'll notify their commander.'

He pointed across to two Crusader tanks and Douglas felt the excitement mount. It was his wish, to command a troop of tanks in battle. However his elation was quickly replaced with terror at his utter lack of training. He had never been inside a tank, let alone guided one into battle. His training in the armoured corps had been confined to theory and rudimentary weapons drill.

'Sir, I'm a little lacking in experience.'

The major looked up from his map: 'Oh, I shouldn't worry about that, old boy.' Douglas winced. The major continued: 'We don't use maps much. No codes and all that. We just talk on the air. It's quite simple really, you'll soon get the hang of it, old boy.'

Douglas, Lockett and the fitter drove across to the tanks just as the newly dismissed troop commander, a corporal, was leaving. He smiled at them. Douglas quickly unloaded his kit and gave most of it to Lockett, who to their mutual regret was not to go into battle with him but to the regimental stores.

Douglas smiled at him: 'See you after the fight.'

'Yes, sir. Take care now. Nothing rash, you know.'

Douglas knew. He smiled again and watched as his batman departed. He supposed that he ought to meet his new tank crews and sought them out. It took him half an hour.

He was not sure about Mudie, the Glaswegian tank driver, whose temperament perfectly suited his name. He seemed profoundly discontent, but then again in Douglas's experience that could be said for at least a third of the soldiers in this polyglot army. The gunner, Evan, was more level-headed, although he was similarly monosyllabic. The other tank crew, of which the commander was a corporal named Browning, was rather more communicative than his own. Browning it seemed had been captured by the Germans early on in the battle and had escaped to rejoin the regiment. He smiled a lot and Douglas could not tell whether it was through relief or nerves.

'Treated me quite well really, they did, sir. Can't say they didn't. Nice bunch of blokes actually, sir. Pity they was Jerries.'

This second crew were in better humour than either Mudie or Evan. Perhaps, he thought, my own crew resent me. Perhaps they would have preferred to have gone into action with their own corporal at the helm. He cursed himself for his ridiculous, schoolboyish behaviour in wanting to join the fight and for thinking that he might arrive at the front and instantly command respect. To them he must surely appear as what he was, a desk wallah with a strange death wish. Well, he wasn't quite sure about the death wish.

Browning had kindly guided him through the controls of the tank. He was to sit on the right of the gun. He had a periscope through which he could see the battlefield as a small square of horizon. The machine-gun bullets were in a belt that ran close to where he sat and behind him was the wireless. He noticed too the various incongruous items: boiled sweets, Penguin paperback books, biscuits. Now he was lying on his bedding thumbing through a magazine, *Lilliput*, that he had found in the tank and listening to the thump of the artillery in the distance. A barrage he presumed for the ongoing attack of which they would soon be a part; 'One hour's notice'. That was what Andrew had told him they were on. One hour then, he thought, till death or glory.

He felt strangely content, if apprehensive. He had after all achieved his goal. The truck was well on its way back to HQ and he was well on his way into the battle. At last he had a sense of purpose and most importantly he had the sense that he should no longer feel ashamed of being out of the fight. He put down the magazine and pulled up his overcoat, a British warm, then looked up at the sky in which the stars above twinkled as bright as diamonds.

He was suddenly overtaken by a wave of mortality. He was going to be killed. Of that he was certain. The only doubts now in his mind were as to where, how and when.

Friday 30 October

THIRTY-THREE

7.00 p.m.
Between Trig 29 and the Fig
Orchard, Thompson's Post
Kibby

The sand was like an ocean, rising and falling in great waves, blinding, suffocating, all-enveloping. It had started shortly after breakfast, just after an unexpected attack by Stukas. But this was something far more deadly, far more to be feared. Kibby pulled his shirt further up over his face and tried to bury his head down into a corner of the trench. The *khamsin* sandstorm was not unknown to most of them but even when you had been through a few of them you still never took them for granted. The wogs said they could drive you mad and Kibby reckoned they were right. It was dusk now and the sand was just beginning to recede. It had raged a full day, burying and uncovering the dead and getting into every orifice. At least, thought Kibby, there was one good thing about it. It kept away the bloody flies.

For a short time all was silent. Kibby lay in the trench and for a while thought about home, about Adelaide and Mabel and the girls and what they would all do after the war.

Captain Robbins arrived. 'All right, Kibby. Here it is.

We're off at nightfall. We're going to take Barrel Hill. Well, actually we expect 2/32nd to take that, we'll follow on close behind. Phase two jump-off is from beyond the railway line and then we're all going towards the sea. We're taking a place called the Clover Leaf.'

'Hope it's lucky, sir,' quipped Kibby.

'Quite. So do I, Bill. Well, that's about it. We leave at eight p.m. for the assembly area a mile north of Trig Twenty-nine. H Hour is 22.30. OK?'

'Fine, sir.'

Kibby briefed the men, gave them a short résumé of what Robbins had told him and ended with his own words of encouragement. 'All right. This is it, the big one. In fact it'll probably be the biggest thing you ever do in any of your lives, boys. So make it count. And we're heading towards the sea, so remember to bring your trunks. You might get a swim.'

As night fell he moved the platoon into the back of a truck and they set off across the mile to the start line. They were skirting the minefield to the northwest so that at least was a blessing. The start area was a mass of Aussies, four battalions of them, waiting for the off. The guns began at 22.00 and shortly afterwards a whistle blew and the 2/32nd stepped over the tape.

Half an hour later it was Kibby's turn. They had gone about fifty yards when rifle fire opened up on both flanks. There was no time to hit the ground now, just the order to carry on and whenever an enemy rifle flashed through the darkness; to respond with a short burst from the Thompson. In this way they reached the railway line within the hour, the rear companies being left to mop up. But Kibby was far from happy.

Running in from the open ground, his platoon came up slap-bang against the rear of 2/32nd. He found a corporal: 'What the hell's going on, mate?'

'It's bloody murder, Sarge. We've been shot up something rotten and we've taken sod-all. Not the hill, not the bleedin' railway and not the blockhouse. Nothing. There's Jerry positions all along a ridge over there.' He pointed northeast. 'Mortars, MGs and tanks hull down. And they're all pointed at the railway line. Got us zeroed good and proper.'

So, thought Kibby, we've lost our start line. Robbins appeared: 'CO's sent out the intelligence section to lay new tape to give us the clear route beyond the railway. But they're getting badly shot up. He wants us to go in as support. You and Ashby to lead the way.'

Kibby nodded and, signalling to his platoon to follow, dashed through the moonlight for the railway line. He was instantly met by a burst of Spandau bullets and hit the sand. He could see the line dead ahead. It was in a cutting perhaps four metres deep which he hoped might afford them some cover. The Spandaus fired again and he counted slowly: one, two, three, four, five, six. Another burst. It was time enough. He yelled to the men: 'Six-second gap between shells. Run for the embankment.' Then he waited after the burst. Three, four, five, six and he was off. Kibby sprinted down the slope and ran for the railway line. As he crossed it the machine-guns began again and he landed panting on the other side. Within a few minutes all the platoon was with him. Further along he could see Ashby and his men. But it wasn't the safe haven he had hoped. A line of Spandau bullets came in and tore into the right eye and forehead of the boy sitting next to him, spinning him round, spouting blood, stone-dead. Kibby yelled down the line: 'We've got to get out of here! Anyone staying here's a dead man. Follow me.'

He moved in a crouching position away from the railway line and immediately saw ahead of him a slit trench with several heads wearing the distinctive flat cap of the Afrika Korps.

He knew that there was only really one good way to take such a position. You ran at it, dropped your grenades right on top of the men as you passed and then turned round and just after the bomb went off ran up and fired your rifle or machine-gun down into the trench. It was effective but messy and was not for the fainthearted.

Kibby yelled at the top of his voice and his cry was taken up by the men. He ran at the trench, saw quite clearly the four flat-capped Germans it contained and their Spandau and their surprised expressions. They opened up on him but their trajectory was too low and Kibby was too quick and before they could traverse, he was over the trench dropping three Mills bombs on the occupants. He ran past and heard their screams of fear and then three explosions rent the night and he turned and ran back, shooting from the hip. Up at the trench lip Kibby almost threw up. The bombs had done their work well.

Two of the men must have been killed at once for there was very little left of them. Both of their torsos were eviscerated and both their heads were a bloody mess. Of the others, one had had his face ripped off by shrapnel fragments and was quite dead. The other though was still moving, even though he was missing both of his legs at the thigh. Kibby fired a short burst of the Thompson gun into him and he didn't move again. All around him men were using similar tactics against other trenches which had been laid out in a pattern of diagonals designed to criss-cross their fire. But the Australians had surprised them and before long the only Germans left alive in the position were prisoners, many of them wounded.

Kibby found a man, Gallagher, an athlete from Melbourne. 'Run back to the CO and tell him we've secured the ground at Barrel Hill. Got that?'

The man nodded and sped off. Ten minutes later he

returned with Robbins. 'Well done, Kibby. Bloody good work. Get your men into that saucer-shaped dip just over the start line. We're going to kick off with another barrage so keep your heads down.'

Kibby found the shallow dip and the men hugged the sides of the crater. Minutes later the British guns opened up. They watched as the enemy positions to the north-west were plastered with high explosive. There were more men sheltering in the saucer now. Sixteen Platoon had crawled in and with Ashby's men as well, it was becoming a little congested. Kibby watched the shells coming over from behind their lines and noticed to his horror that their trajectory appeared to be shortening. He found Gallagher again: 'Run and tell Captain Robbins that unless those gunners lengthen their stride we're going to cop it from our own guns.'

He kept watching and still the distance between the shells and the saucer seemed to lessen by the second. Finally it happened. A twenty-five-pounder shell fell inside the perimeter and burst among Sixteen Platoon. The recently appointed Lieutenant Farrell was hit in the chest by shrapnel. Then a second shell came in, and a third in the centre of Ashby's platoon. All around the crater men were burrowing into the sand. Bob Tremlett was shel-tering next to Kibby as the shells screamed in. 'Jesus, Sarge. I know the poms don't much like us, but this is going a bit far.'

Kibby managed a smile: 'Don't worry, son. They'll stop soon.'

But they didn't, at least not before another five men had been wounded, one mortally. Then the British guns fell silent and the medics muttered as they tended the casualties who had been hit by their own side.

Kibby was stoical. There was no point in getting worked up about it. What could you do? These things happened

304

in war. It was all a chaotic pile of crap whichever way you looked at it. And all you could do was muddle through it the best you could and try not to get yourself killed. Now, with the British artillery temporarily silent before beginning their creeping barrage in advance of the attack he knew that the Germans would be using the time to regroup and recover. He checked his ammo and inserted one of the big circular magazines into the Thompson. The minutes ticked by. He looked at his watch. Fifty-five minutes past midnight. The assault was scheduled for 1a.m.

Then it began again. The heavy guns opened up on the German positions from the rear and a whistle sounded. Kibby urged the men forward and realized almost immediately that they were advancing too far behind the barrage. 'Move forward. Get closer,' he yelled and by example, doubled ahead. The others followed and as they approached the German trenches under cover of the rolling barrage he could see the Jerries getting up and falling back. My God, he thought, we're pushing them back without a shot being fired. They were in the centre of the position now with minefields on either side and their objective, Ring Contour 25, to their left about forty yards away. Then the night exploded with machine-gun fire. It came at them it seemed from all sides and Kibby saw men going down fast: Gallagher the runner, his legs a mangled mess; Morrison, his right arm chopped through by tracer and Morse, shot through the chest and abdomen and screaming in agony. Kibby had a ghastly thought. Of course, in letting the men run from the trenches they had allowed the Jerries to regroup further back and now they were paying the price. They should have killed them all as they advanced.

He hit the ground and tried to work out where principally the fire was coming from. He zeroed in on two

305

small mounds dead ahead of them and as he did the lieutenant of Eighteen Platoon, Treloar, was hit in the leg and
it occurred to him that Robbins was now their only officer.
He heard the captain shout: 'Regroup. With me.' Kibby
and his men crawled towards the voice under constant
machine-gun fire. Robbins walked towards them out of
the darkness and Kibby saw that he was holding his neck.
Blood was pouring down his shirt. He ran forward to
help him but the officer looked helplessly into his eyes
before sinking to his knees and falling lifeless across a
tangle of barbed wire.

Kibby turned to one of the men, Norm Leaney, the
musician. 'Blimey, that's torn it. No bleedin' officers left.'

Ashby spoke: 'Reckon it's down to you, Bill. You're
company commander now.'

It was true, if frankly unbelievable. Kibby turned to
him: 'Herb, get all the men together. Every platoon, over
here. Quick as you can. You're my second-in-command.'

A few minutes later he was addressing his ragged
command. There were perhaps thirty men of the original
eighty that had gone in. 'Right. Here's how it is. We've got
to take those two mounds. Herb, you take a section and
attack the left-hand one. I'll take the other one on my own.
The rest of you stay here as reserve and when you see us
at the top come on in.'

Kibby knew that he worked best on his own and his
logic was, if he could draw all the fire from one gun on
to himself then perhaps Ashby's section would stand a
better chance of getting through.

Ashby started to protest, but Kibby waved him down.
'Let's go.'

He watched as Ashby set off. He would give him a
head-start and then take the Jerries completely by surprise
with a charge against the right-hand mound. He could
see Ashby now at the head of his men, Whaite standing

and firing again and again into the position and Bloffwich with his Bren gun, firing from the hip as he advanced. But as they went forward men were falling fast. It was hard to see through the dust and smoke but Kibby counted them: Diddy the sergeant from Sixteen Platoon was down and now so was Whaite, Martin fell in a hail of Spandau bullets and eventually even Bloffwich collapsed on the sand, his finger still pressing the trigger of the Bren.

Reckoning his time to have come, Kibby jumped up from the sand and charged the right-hand machine-gun post. As he went he plucked a grenade from his belt, pulled the pin with his teeth and threw it at the gunners. Before it had exploded though he was doing the same with another. The first bomb went off, on target and the Germans' screams cut the night. The other made contact too and then he was in the position, the tommy gun doing its deadly work. And then, silence. He jumped down into the trench and kicked at a lifeless body. Then he looked across to Ashby's object-ive and saw the familiar shapes of men in bush hats standing on its summit. Climbing from the trench he walked across towards them. He saw Ashby and was about to congratulate him when the familiar rattle of a machine-gun interrupted him. He saw several tracer bullets hit Ashby but realized with relief they had only torn off his webbing. Kibby smiled and began again to tell him how well he had done, when he felt a terrific whack on the side of his neck. His first thought was of the sheer irrita-tion of not being able to speak for although he opened his mouth the words would not come. A split-second later though Kibby's world exploded in a mist of blood as the bullet that had pierced his jugular vein exited through the back of his head and took with it part of his skull and a portion of his brains. Bill Kibby's lifeless body fell at Ashby's feet and his blood gushed out freely, a spreading crimson flower against the moonlit sand.

Saturday 31 October

THIRTY-FOUR

6.30 a.m.
Kidney Ridge
Douglas

They had moved up in the early morning. He had been duty officer, and had woken the colonel at five o'clock and breakfasted, with pangs of guilt, on whisky. There was no more chocolate. It was the usual tedious grind along the dust track with the crew bunched up in the turret unable to talk above the noise of the engines.

It was growing more fully light now, but a thick mist hung about them and they seemed to be utterly alone. Andrew had told him over the radio that there was now nothing between them and the enemy and it suddenly dawned on Douglas that he appeared to have lost the rest of the squadron. The radio crackled into life. The colonel's voice came on, angrily shouting his call sign: 'Nuts Five, Nuts Five, you're miles behind us. Come on. Come on. Off.'

He yelled to Mudie, 'Give her some speed, will you,' and the tank moved faster through the mist. Ahead of them a German tank loomed up but he quickly realized with some relief that it was a wreck. Now he knew that he was lost. They saw some Crusaders and made for them but they turned out to be from a different regiment, the Staffordshire Yeomanry.

The radio crackled into life again: Nuts Five. Nuts Five. Where the hell are you? Can't see you. Repeat can't see you. Conform. Conform. Speed up. Off.'

He was just beginning to give up all hope when dead ahead he saw several Crusaders and realized that it was the regiment at last.

He swung into line and radioed in a little sheepishly. 'Nuts Five in position. Off.'

Thankfully there was no reply. They stopped the engine and while Evan began to read a cheap crime novel, Mudie spoke: 'Can you pass me a biscuit, sir?'

Douglas found the small packet of hard army-issue biscuits and having given one to the truculent Glaswegian helped himself and cut some cheese for them both from their meagre ration. He had just finished his food and was sitting outside, on the front of the tank looking into the misty dawn when there was a whoosh, followed by a huge explosion and a shell-burst about a hundred yards over to his left.

For two hours the shelling continued. He was constantly surprised by the calmly phlegmatic attitude of his comrades, who acted as though the shells might be as innocuous as a shower of rain. In fact, they kept missing and Douglas presumed the gunners not only were unable to see the tanks clearly but had some problem with their ranging. By eleven o'clock he was becoming bored.

He leant into the turret and pulled out the radio transceiver, clicked it on and spoke. 'Sir. D'you think we'll see any action today.'

Nothing.

He tried again. A fellow troop commander came on. 'I say, Nuts One, what price this? When do we go in?'

There was a crackle and the major's voice came on the

set. 'Nuts Five. Pipe down will you, and don't get over-anxious. We'll be in there soon enough.'

He opened a tin of fruit and the crew brewed some tea. As he was eating a small party of men appeared in the midst of the tanks, an infantry sergeant and three privates with an enemy prisoner, a young German boy. Douglas thought that he could not have been much more than fifteen and hoped that he was wrong.

The sergeant stopped to rest near Douglas and the German sat down on the sand. 'Prisoner, sir. Sniper. Waited for us to pass through and then took pot shots at us. Hit some of my lads. Good men. What do you think we should do with him, sir?'

Douglas looked at the lad. 'Take him back to Brigade, Sar'nt. I should.'

'Shoot the bugger, sir, that's what I say. After what he did.'

One of the privates spoke up. 'Sarge, he's just a nipper. Just give 'im a cup of tea and a fag. We don't need to kill him.'

The sergeant shook his head. 'Well I say shoot the bugger. That's what I say.'

As Douglas watched, they went on their way, still arguing the boy's fate. He wondered what would become of him and just then another infantry patrol appeared. One of the corporals approached him. 'See them Jerry wrecks out there. Them two, sir? There's a machine-gun nest in one of them. Why don't you run over them, sir? Squash 'em flat with that you could.' He pointed to the tank.

Douglas smiled: 'I'll have to ask permission. See what I can do.'

The man left and he radioed the squadron commander. 'Sir, permission to fire on an enemy machine-gun post beneath a derelict tank.'

312

The major thought for a moment, then: 'All right. Give them a few bursts. But don't take any risks.'

Douglas spoke to the gunner: 'See that wreck, Evan. Give them a few bursts of the machine-gun.'

Evan smiled and the gun rattled into life, making the sand jump around the wreck. Then, nothing. Evan cussed: 'Bugger. Bloody thing's jammed, sir.' He cleared the action and re-cocked the gun, then pressed the trigger. The gun sputtered out a few more rounds then stopped again.

'Shit. Done it again. You should have run the belt over the six-pounder, sir, like I told you.'

'Nonsense. It's perfectly free on my side.'

'No, sir. If you'd run it over the gun.'

'Evan, you know that's rubbish.'

'Sorry, sir, but you're talking bollocks.'

'Evan! You can't talk to me like that.'

'But it is, sir. It is total bollocks. Should have run the ammo belt over the gun. Simple.'

Douglas, fuming with rage, turned to Mudie: 'Drive towards the enemy. Slowly.'

Evan, realizing what was happening, wasn't talking now but trying to fix the erratic machine-gun and swearing all the time. Douglas yelled into the i/c microphone: 'Halt.' The tank stopped and he peered through his binoculars.

Evan swore: 'Bugger. Bloody thing.'

Douglas looked hard at the wreck for any sign of enemy activity. If they were still there, he thought, they must be petrified. The radio came to life. It was the major: 'Nuts Five, am going back to the NAAFI for lemonade and buns. Take charge. Off.'

Douglas realized that his troop had been left alone. Evan shouted: 'The only way this bastard's going to fire is if I mount it on the turret and fire it direct.'

They managed to get the gun up through the hatch and lodged it securely in the turret mounting. Douglas yelled at Mudie, 'Advance!' and the tank rumbled forward. Evan opened fire again and hit the wreck. There was a shout from behind them and an infantry subaltern leaped on to the tank and beamed at Douglas. 'Awfully good of you to help us out, old boy.'

The subaltern looked at the wreck, shouted, 'There they go,' and they watched as two Germans climbed from a gun pit to its left. The men advanced towards them, their hands raised. And then an extraordinary thing happened, something which Douglas had simply not expected. From other gun pits all around them, other Germans rose up and began to walk towards them. Evan was the first off the tank but not before he had borrowed Douglas's revolver. Together with the young subaltern they began to walk from pit to pit yelling at the surrendering Germans. 'Come on. Get out of it.' Douglas found a rifle lying in one of the machine-gun pits and pointed it at the men. He tried to think of the German for 'move' and settled on 'Raus, raus', which he began to shout with gusto.

As they collected the prisoners they also picked up their guns and supplies: rifles, machine-guns, Spandaus mainly, and the treasured Luger pistols. Douglas and Evan loaded them on to the back of the tank, tied them in place and then climbed aboard and drove along behind the column of prisoners. There were about forty of them, he reckoned. He clicked on the radio and spoke to the major: 'Nuts Five. Have taken some prisoners.'

'Nuts Five. How many prisoners exactly? Over.'

'About figures four zero. Over.'

'Bloody good show, Nuts Five. Most excellent.'

The colonel came on the line: 'Douglas. We want you to get these chaps straight back to our Brigadier. You deserve to get all the credit for this.'

'Not really, sir. It was my gunner and an infantry lieutenant who did most of it.'

'Nonsense. It's your kill. In at the death. You get the credit. Get it for the regiment, Douglas.'

Evan piped up: 'You're a bloody fool to say that, sir. Reckon you've just thrown away your MC.'

Douglas chose to ignore this last piece of insubordination. 'Well, if that's the case then it was totally undeserved.'

Still wondering what he should do, take the credit or give it to the infantry, Douglas surveyed the turret. It was a mess. The machine-gun ammo belt had coiled itself everywhere and the microphone and headphone wires were a tangled heap into which had melted an upturned tin of Kraft cheese. He managed to find a set of phones and a mike from which he tried to wipe the congealed cheese. It was useless. Nevertheless, he placed the messy but still functioning phones on his head and pressed the on button. 'Nuts Five. Permission to retire.'

'All right, Nuts Five. Retire and reorganize and call in at the CO's tank as you go. Off.'

As he drew alongside Piccadilly Jim's tank a head popped up through the turret and yelled across. But such was the noise from the two engines that he was hardly able to hear a thing. Only the words 'good show', 'recommend' and 'MC' came across. Douglas could hardly believe it. They halted for a quarter of an hour and brewed up in silence before rejoining the regiment. Douglas leant against the tracks of the tank and pulled out a piece of paper from his pocket. Since coming to the front he had been trying to write a new poem, something of how he felt about what they were doing. He had given it a working title, 'The Offensive', and to date had managed two opening lines. 'The stars are dead men in the sky/Who will applaud the way you die.'

It was good, he thought, very good, but he had not been able to think of the following line. He had thought of some deity looking down and watching but could not work out

315

how to express the idea. Something perhaps about the sun. The sun was omnipresent and to the Egyptians the sun had been a deity. Hardly surprising. He tried a line: . . . the way you die: /The perfect sun . . .'

No. Perfect was not right. He needed a word that summed up the mercilessness of the whole thing. Cruel perhaps. Or callous. Or easy. The easy sun. It sounded right. He was about to write it down and it was at that moment that the first of the German tanks began to advance towards them out of the setting sun. Shells came crashing in around the tank and he heard the now familiar whoosh of an 88. Tanks supported by anti-tank guns, a lethal combination that meant business.

He tucked away the poem and saw the major's tank pulling back and spoke to Mudie. 'Retire please. Slowly.'

They moved in reverse and after a few dozen yards came to a halt. The radio crackled. They had picked up one of the other tanks calling up artillery support.

'Smoke. Smoke for God's sake. Give us some smoke, we're being hit from all sides. Smoke. For Christ's . . .' The radio went dead.

He crouched down in the tank turret and waited for the shell that would destroy them. Perhaps, he thought, this is my moment. I've just taken forty prisoners and been recommended in all probability for an MC. Now I get killed. Perfect. He realized that he was absolutely terrified, more than he could remember ever having been in his life. Also that he had no idea whatsoever as to what was going on around him.

There was a shout down the radio. 'Open fire, Nuts Five. Range one zero zero zero. Give those buggers every round you have. Over.'

It was a general squadron order and as they prepared to fire, Douglas heard the other squadron commanders report. 'One OK off, Two OK off, Three OK off.'

Douglas spoke into the intercom. 'Evan. Open fire.'

'I can't see a fuckin' thing.'

'Bugger that man, fire at them. Fire at range one thousand.'

Evan fired the six-pounder and Douglas reloaded it in an instant. Within a few minutes the deflector bag was full of shell cases. Douglas threw out the hot cases with a gloved hand while Evan fired the now mended machine-gun, an entire belt of ammunition passing through it in seconds. The smell inside the turret was vile. Ammo fumes, cordite, smoke and hot metal. They were all coughing now. Douglas could feel the sweat trickling down his back.

Looking out he could see the colours of the tracer criss-crossing the desert. To his left a heavy machine-gun rattled away. Above their heads shells flew towards the enemy, 75s by the sound of them. But the night was drawing in fast and as visibility grew close to nil the firing suddenly ceased. He spoke to Mudie: 'Head for home.'

The tank rattled and creaked back towards the regiment and their leaguer. Douglas felt as if he had been in battle all his life. Every bone, every joint in his body seemed to ache. But there was a sense too of exaltation of a sort he had never felt before. He had been in battle for a day. His first day. It had been a real baptism of fire. Now he knew what it was to be in combat, the reality of all those stories he had fed on as a boy. But there was more than this. Much more. For he had survived.

THIRTY-FIVE

8.00 a.m.
HQ Eighth Army
de Guingand

He looked at the piece of paper that lay on his desk. A note scribbled in haste by John Poston and intended for him to pass on to Montgomery. He thought that instead he would incorporate it in the morning's situation report. He read it again.

'Last night units of Australian 26th Brigade engaged the enemy's 90th Light Division at the railway line. They succeeded in crossing the railway line and reaching the coast but took heavy casualties in the process. Turning east to attack Thompson's Post they removed the 125th Panzergrenadiers from the battle as an effective fighting unit.'

It was the news they had been waiting for. The Australians had broken through and reached the coast at the same time annihilating one of Rommel's crack units. He wrote it out in his own hand and then added a postscript.

'The Australians performed throughout the attack with quite exceptional bravery. They have taken over 5000 casualties.'

PART THREE

Operation Supercharge

Sunday 1 November

THIRTY-SIX

Dusk
Near Kidney Ridge
Miller

He stood by the Dodge and gazed spellbound at the scene before him. It was as if an entire people were on the move, a great horde of humanity busily going in different directions. For two days infantry, tanks and transports had been assembling in the rear echelons of the army. The noise was incredible, a hubbub of tongues and argots combined with a grinding and clanking of the machinery of war and the titanic rumble of the armour. It was only, he supposed what armies had done for countless centuries and he imagined such a scene taking place in Carthage or Rome or here in Egypt. The difference of course was that these men carried weapons beyond the imagining of their ancient forebears and they fought not on horseback but in steel machines.

Miller's world had changed irrevocably over the past few days, but he still could not help but find in the momentous events taking place around him resounding echoes of the past. He had changed. His values had been challenged and he was no longer the utterly self-assured young man who had come out here to help repair the wounds of flawed humanity.

For the last three days there had been a lull and they had spent some days out of the line, being used, it seemed to Miller, to move around everything except that which they had come to move, wounded men. He had transported flour, water, medical supplies and tinned fruit. But not one casualty.

'That's because there ain't been no wounded to pick up,' said Turk, wryly. 'On account of the fact that the Brits are winning. Perhaps the Krauts have just given up and run back to Uncle Adolf.'

Bigelow, now fully recovered from his buttock wound, raised his head from his book and observed, 'No, I don't think so, Turk. I think it's something else. They haven't been firing at us because we haven't been firing at them. And d'you know why that is? Word is that Monty's preparing for a second big push and that this time it's going to be done with tanks.'

Turk looked puzzled. 'What d'you think, Lieutenant?'

Evan Thomas pondered for a moment: 'I think the Prof's right. All I hear at HQ is talk of this big push. It's bound to be a tank battle. The Brits need to give Rommel a real bloody nose and the best way to do that is with their tanks.'

'Our tanks,' Turk reminded him. 'Shermans and Grants.'

'Our tanks. OK Turk, you win.'

'We win, Loot. With babies like these on our side, who's gonna stop us?'

He pointed to a long column of Sherman tanks that was moving up the track and into the divisional holding area. As they came past Miller noticed that on the side of one of the turrets someone had painted, quite deftly, a huge eye. The eye of Horus. It intrigued him. One of the troopers was sitting on the hatch and as the tank drew closer to them, Miller yelled up at him and pointed. 'Hi there. Like the decal. But why the eye of Horus?'

The man, who was actually the tank commander and an old Etonian who had left his classical studies at Oxford to join the cavalry, heard his approval and shouted to him. 'Thanks, Yank. Well spotted. Nearest thing they've got out here to a God of War. Had to have something on there to put the wind up Jerry. I put it on with sump oil and the black off a brew-tin.'

Miller watched him go and prayed that Horus would watch over the fellow classicist, whoever he was. The evening wore on and, without orders, they stood and watched the procession go by. Miller had managed to find some tins of maconochie stew and heated it up over a sand burner. They washed it down with a half-dozen bottles of Egyptian Stella beer, that Turk had bartered in exchange for two packs of Lucky Strikes. And then they stretched out on the bonnet and roof of the Dodge and watched the stars and heard the rumble of the tanks. The sky was alive with lights: starshells and tracers of orange, green, red and blue and bright white.

It was 1 a.m. precisely when the barrage began. A week ago it might have alarmed him, but Miller was used to it now. He heard the thumps, looked up and saw a wall of flame over in the west. So this was it. He knew now that within a matter of minutes the British and their six nations of allies would be advancing, tanks and men moving forward to death or victory. And for the first time he felt a real part of it. That alarmed him. It was not a feeling he had expected to experience. Yet here he was wishing with all his might that this night the British would prevail against their enemies and in simple terms that meant kill them.

No one was sleeping. Thomas, who had disappeared half an hour before, turned up at 2 a.m. with fresh orders. 'OK. Here's the gen. We're a roving unit. We sit tight here and whenever Division gives us the nod, we move out and help whichever guys need us most.'

Turk spoke: 'Like we're the cavalry and we come to the rescue of whoever needs us. Wow.'

'Got it in one, Turk. We're the damn cavalry.'

The first call came through to them at 3 a.m. Thomas got the order over the wireless then hurried around from the makeshift signals hut to the ambulance park. Miller and Turk had been playing cards – brag – with some guys from a New Zealand ambulance unit, and winning well. Around them hundreds of men were hunched up sleeping, or trying to sleep, despite the constant traffic grinding through this terrible place along the single track road. Somewhere, perhaps not too far away some wag was playing a wind-up gramophone – 'Night and Day You are the One'. Intermittently someone shouted at him to turn it off. Thomas coughed and spoke: 'OK, you guys, we're on. There's a British tank regiment about three miles distant due west. The Sherwood Rangers.'

Turk laughed: 'Hey Loot, it's friggin' Robin Hood.'

'Well whoever's driving them, they've taken a pasting and they need our help. Mount up, guys, let's roll.'

It did not take them long to move. Miller reckoned he had got it down to a fine art. Two-point-five minutes from alarm to action.

They drove hard along the track. It was quite a difference, thought Miller, to the first night's fighting, when every turn of the wheel might have brought a one-way ticket to eternity through an encounter with a mine. After a while they entered the battle zone. Shells were crashing around them and the track was lined by an assortment of walking wounded and German and Italian prisoners.

They did not have to look hard to see the tanks. They were not Shermans nor Grants but Crusaders, the more lightly armed and armoured British machine and it was plain to see that they had suffered badly at the hands of the German MkIVs and 88s.

A major approached them. 'Thank God. We were following up the infantry when an 88 opened up on us. Meant to have been taken out. Took three casualties and then a Jerry sniper got a bead on the flank tank. Shot two of the men. Can you deal with the artillery casualties first, chaps?'

'No problem, sir. Just show us the way.'

The major indicated the three closest tanks and Miller and Thomas drove towards them and pulled up close by. The smell of cordite, sump oil, petrol and burning flesh caught the back of the throat and Miller knew it would not go away for some days. He walked over to the first tank which, amazingly, had not caught fire and hauled himself up on to its hull. Why, he did not know. Curiosity perhaps. He leant over the manhole and tried to accustom his eyes to the darkness. A faint sweet smell came up which reminded him of the barbecues his father had organized at their house on Cape Cod every summer he could remember. Gradually the objects in the turret came into view. The tank crew were arranged around the inside. They lay in a clumsy embrace and their faces, pallid in death, were made all the whiter by the light dusting of sand which had already invaded their resting place. One of them had a huge hole in his head. The whole skull had been stoved in behind the remains of an ear. Another man was covered in blood, his own and his comrade's. He was suspended on the machine-gun mechanism, his legs twisted around the tank's levers in a frozen dance of death. A curious silence hung over them which to Miller felt strangely holy and he wondered why such a feeling should have struck him here in particular rather than anywhere else in this country of death. He climbed down. The third member of the crew had already been taken away in a Bren carrier apparently, before they'd arrived.

Thomas came up to him: 'Josh. See that guy over there?'

He pointed to a trooper standing against the side of an apparently damaged Crusader. 'His two mates were shot by a sniper. They're still in the tank. Almost certainly they're dead. He looks a little shaky. Maybe just shock. Can you take a look?'

'Sure, sir.' Miller walked across to where the tank driver was leaning against the side of his vehicle, eating meat and vegetables from a can and drinking tea from a tin mug. At first sight he did not appear shaken. Miller spoke: 'Hi. You the driver?'

'Aye, sir. That's me. As was.'

Miller detected a regional accent but wasn't sure from where. 'Where you from?'

'Barnsley, Yorkshire. You know it?'

'No, sorry, I'm American.'

'I thought so. I said to myself, that bloke there's no Englishman. He's either an Aussie or he's a Yank. Ambulance driver?'

'That's it. Are you hurt?'

'No. I'm fine. Me mates copped it though. Tank commander and operator they were. Bloody shame.'

Now Miller could see the tension and the anger. The man looked as if his face was about to split open and tears rolled down his cheeks.

'D'you want to tell me what happened?'

'Well, I didn't seem to be getting any orders so I had a look at George – Corporal Wood. He were sitting in his seat and at first I thought he were all right. But then I seen that he were dead. Then I had a look at Bert, like, and he were covered wi' blood. Bastard must have plugged one of them when he was up looking out of the turret and the other one when he poked his head up to see what it was. So I came out of the lid, jildi like.'

Miller shook his head: 'I'm sorry.'

The man appeared to be calmer now. He wiped his

327

face and smiled. 'Can't be helped. That's war. That's all. It happens.'

Leaving the poor man to eat his can of food, Miller climbed up the side of the second tank and peered in the hatch, with the desperate thought that George or the radio operator might be alive. But it was soon evident that they were not. The breech of the gun, the wireless, the machine-gun and the shells stacked neatly in the rack were splashed thickly with fresh blood. The machine-gun belt too was covered in it. On the floor the empty cases of bullets lay in an inch deep pool of blood. Miller gawped. His imagination could see the mist of blood as the two men were picked off. He looked at the two corpses. Both had been shot neatly through the neck. The exit wound had splayed open the jugular in both cases, accounting for the quantity of blood.

He climbed down: 'Nothing we can do for them I'm afraid. How about you?'

'I told you, mate. I'm all right. You go and find some bloke who really needs help. I'll be fine.'

But Miller knew from the look in his eyes and his trembling hand that he was far from fine. Nevertheless he walked off towards the third tank. There was still the chance that someone might need his help.

The wounded were sitting in a huddle close to their wrecked vehicle which had brewed up easily. One man, the worst, they had laid on a stretcher. Miller went over and saw that he was very badly burned. The others were not so bad. Two had burnt arms and another burns to his legs. A fourth man looked relatively unscathed but was shivering with shock.

Thomas was with them: 'Josh, all of these guys need to get back to the aid post. I'll take them. You stay on and see if there are any others from that other tank. I think one guy got out alive, but he may be in a bad way.

I'm going to load these guys on now. You take Turk. The Prof can go with me. There's a lieutenant there who'll help you.'

Miller walked slowly across to the fourth tank and on the way his eye was caught by a slit trench on his left. He went over to it and instantly regretted that he had. The bodies of the Italian dead lay there in ghastly attitudes, surrounded by pitiable rubbish: picture postcards of Milan, Rome, Venice, snapshots of wives and children; the wrappings of favourite chocolate bars and hundreds of cheap cardboard cigarette packets. Among the holiday litter lay bayonets and the little tin 'red devil' grenades, little crackers that could blow a man's head off. The helmets of the Bersaglieri lay all around, their proud green and black feathers fluttering in the breeze.

Miller felt sick. He walked a little away from the trenches and threw up. He was mopping the vomit from the corners of his mouth when an English voice spoke.

'Hello, Yank. Pretty sight, isn't it?'

'You mean that?'

The man shook his head. He was well-spoken and Miller guessed not much older than himself, perhaps twenty-two or twenty-three, with a handsome face; a long, aquiline nose, moustache and dark hair. He wore the uniform of a lieutenant in a cavalry regiment. 'Sorry. Just being funny. Matching pathos with pathos if you know what I mean.'

'I do as a matter of fact.'

The lieutenant looked at him for a second, weighing him up then said: 'You're a volunteer, aren't you? Which college?'

'Harvard. You know it?'

'Only by name and reputation. I was at Oxford when war broke out. Douglas, Keith Douglas.'

'Josh Miller. Good to meet you. What were you studying?'

'English literature, mostly. I write poetry, among other

things. You may not believe this but I actually wrote pieces in our magazine, *The Cherwell*, attacking militarism. Look at me now.'

'Yeah, well. War changes things I guess. And people. I swore I'd never hurt anyone and I end up killing two guys. Now I'm real mixed up. How'd that happen?'

Douglas smiled: 'As you say, war changes everything.'

He looked back down into the trench then called to a trooper: 'Get a party over here, Bucknell. Loads of salvage.'

Two men came running and oblivious to the dead, jumped down into the trench and began to recover anything they could. They emerged with rifles, Bredas, Luger pistols, sand glasses, binoculars, British tinned rations and, to Miller's surprise dozens of flat, round German tins of chocolate.

Douglas began to talk: 'You see, as a writer, I felt that the experience of battle was something I must have. Nothing can compare with the excitement of seeing thousands of men, few of whom can have much idea why they are fighting, all enduring hardships, living in an unnatural world, having to kill and be killed. Yet they also feel comradeship with the men whom they kill and who kill them. They all endure the same things you see.'

Miller nodded: 'Yes I know. That's exactly how I feel. It's what I was thinking earlier this morning as we watched the men going up.'

'Yes. All going about their business as they've always done. Happy in their work. And have you noticed how they always whistle?'

Miller laughed: 'No, but now you say that, yes, of course.'

The sound of firing from the west reminded them of their own purpose. Douglas pointed towards the tank. 'A patient for you. Lieutenant, like me, 88mm blast caught him on the tank. Took off most of his foot. Peter Norman. Ever been in a tank?'

'No.'

'Don't bother. They give you a periscope but there's no point in using it. In a battle we, the tank commanders, all sit on the open hatch. Your legs dangle down. It's pretty cramped in there and bloody hot. And when you're moving you can't hear anything else except the engine and explosions.'

They walked across to the wounded man who was lying on his back on the sand, his mangled limb bound in bandages, his head resting on a haversack.

'We managed to give him some morphine. Quite a lot of it actually. And a bit of brandy. Bloody shame about him. He was a show-jumper. Horses, you know. He hunted too.'

'I'm sorry.'

Miller bent over the wounded man who opened his eyes and smiled. 'Hi, Peter. We're here to get you back to hospital.'

The man nodded and smiled again: 'Rotten buggers blew my foot off.'

Then he went to sleep. Together, Turk and Miller laid down the stretcher they had brought and carefully lifted the wounded man on to it. Then they raised it and gently loaded him into the back of the ambulance.

Before they left Douglas went up to Miller and held out a folded piece of paper. 'Here, I'd like you to have this. It's something I've been working on. I think it might have some relevance to you. Read it sometime. Don't worry, I've made a copy. Well, I must go. Have to rejoin the tanks. Good luck.'

Miller took the folded piece of paper and unfolding it scanned it. It was a poem. He re-folded it and put it into his inside pocket: 'Thank you, I will. Good luck.'

331

He climbed up into the cab and turned over the engine. She started first time and Miller put his foot gently down on the accelerator and pulled away. Looking in his mirror he could still see Douglas standing there, beside the ruined tanks, as they crested the small dune that led them on to the road. There were no sounds from the patient, but Miller still drove at a stately pace. The road was quiet for the moment. The prisoners had passed down the line. Suddenly there was a terrific crash from behind and the ambulance lurched towards the left. Turk yelled: 'Shit, we've been hit.'

Miller stopped the vehicle and looked back. There was a gaping hole through one of the sides and one of the rear doors had been blown off.

'Shit.' A shell, a dud or one with a mistimed fuse, had gone into the truck and out again.

Both men threw open the cab doors and ran to the rear. More shells were crashing around them now and they saw the reason. Along the track in the opposite direction, towards the front, a score of Sherman tanks were advancing. The German spotters had somehow zeroed in on them.

Turk yelled: 'Hit the dirt!' and dived under the Dodge.

Miller shouted to him: 'What about the wounded guy?' He peered into the back. The man was either asleep or dead from the shock. He gently shook his shoulder. He murmured something. Miller ducked under the ambulance. 'He's still alive. What do we do?'

'We leave him in there. What else?'

The tanks continued towards them and began to rumble past. One of them had been hit by an 88 and was blazing further away down the track. There was no trace of any survivors. Miller looked at Turk: 'I'm going to see if anyone needs help.'

'Chrissake, Miller. We need the fuckin' help. And you need fuckin' psychiatric help. They're dead, man.'

'Maybe, but I just want to make sure.'

He crawled out from beneath the ambulance and ran along the track past the advancing tanks. The brewed-up Sherman was intensely hot and as he neared it he realized that Turk had of course been right. There was no way anyone could have survived that. He was about to turn round and go back to the Dodge when another salvo of 88s came in. Miller dived to the ground and heard a thump and an explosion. Getting up he turned round and where the ambulance had been he saw a twisted wreck of burning metal. For a moment he froze. Then he ran back but the heat was too fierce to get close. Both Turk and Peter Norman were obviously dead. He sat down on the sand and stared at his boots. Why? How? There were no answers and there was no logic, no fairness any more in this world. Only random death. The tanks went by and then he was alone in the desert with nothing but the blazing Sherman and the burning Dodge for company. And five charred corpses.

He thought of Turk. The first of them to die and wondered how many more of his friends he would leave behind. And then for a moment he realized again that he too might be one of those who did not return. He could see Turk's grinning face in his mind. Thought of him playing cards with Thomas. Cursing himself for losing. Swearing that the lieutenant had the luck of the devil.

He closed his eyes and wept a few brief, silent tears.

He supposed that at some point someone must come down the track and collect him. Take him back to civilization. The sun had not yet come up and the bright moon cast its white radiance on the scene. Miller shivered and wondered what would happen to him over the next few months. The next few years. They said the war would last at least another three years, perhaps much longer. What sort of a world was that to live in? Some of the guys had already left the service and gone home to enlist. He wondered whether he could ever do that. Killing a man to save others in a particular situation was one thing. Being part of a machine that sanctioned mass murder was quite another. Despite all he had seen and done, despite what had just happened to Turk, his conscience was still tearing him apart.

He thought of Douglas, a man of learning, a writer fighting for his country with honour yet able to justify it. How did he manage that? Perhaps, he thought, he might find some clue in the piece of writing he had pressed into his hand. He took it from his pocket and unfolding it, began to read by the light of the burning vehicles.

> Death's logic. Closed in this imperilled earth
> Reflect, the dust and souls of merciful men
> lie still. And not six feet above their rest
> their poor successors go about and waste
> the store of their amassing. Busy then
> and harvest yet among a general dearth.

Miller looked again at the piece of paper and then he turned it over, took out a pencil from his battledress pocket and began to compose his letter of resignation to the AFS. For at last, in that sublime, terrible moment, he knew what he had to do.

Monday 2 November

THIRTY-SEVEN

10.00 a.m.
HQ Eighth Army
Montgomery

Rommel was on his knees. That much was evident and Montgomery allowed himself a small measure of jubilation. He sat alone at the table in the caravan and looked at the map with its red and blue pencil marks showing the current troop positions.

The attack had kicked off at 1 a.m. with a rolling barrage by three hundred and fifty twenty-five pounders. The infantry and armour had gone in on a front of 4000 yards and at a depth of 6000 yards. He had all the statistics in front of him. Fifteen thousand shells fired in four and a half hours. That surely was enough to keep the Germans in their trenches and shatter the remaining minefields. He stared at the map. This time it really did seem to be going according to plan. If they succeeded now he knew it would be the end of Rommel's army. So much, he thought, for those who had doubted the effectiveness of his 'Supercharge' plan. And he knew that among them there were some very powerful voices indeed, both in the army and at Westminster.

Well, let them criticize him now. Within the next few days, the next few hours, he knew that he would be in favour at last. He would have made his name. Like Wellington, he thought, I shall call my victory after the nearest settlement to the rear of the battle. El Alamein. Of course, it was not just one battle, for over the past ten days many battles had been fought, were still being fought.

The Australians in their salient at Point 29 at Thompson's Post had exceeded expectations. He knew too well that had their position been penetrated then his entire plan might have been compromised. But his faith in the Aussies and Morshead had been rewarded. Yes they had taken high casualties, 5000 at the last count. But in doing so they had drawn onto themselves all of the Panzer Corps, most of which they had destroyed with their anti-tank guns. And that perhaps was the point of this great battle. The tank had not proved the king of the desert as so many had predicted. This had been a battle of men and guns.

The armour might yet prove its worth. But to date at least the hard fight had been won by artillery and principally by the infantry. Their losses had been huge and he could not expunge the sense of guilt that he had not really expected. He had thought that to get armour on to the battlefield would smash Rommel but he had not succeeded and he wanted to know why.

Tanks. Perhaps it was Lumsden who was to blame. All along he had thought him a disappointment. He was excitable, highly strung and easily prone to depression. In fact, he was not suitable for the high command at all. He was a good divisional commander but above that, out of his depth. Leese of course was quite the opposite and Freyberg quite superb.

Now all he himself had to do was keep morale up. Part of that was being always visible to the men. Wellington to Rommel's Napoleon. Morale was the key to pressing home the attack. It had been a clever move to put on that Australian bush hat, he knew that he had to create a distinctive persona. But with the Aussies now effectively out of the game it had been time for a change.

So he had braved the minefields in one of the new Grant tanks and had put on the black beret of a tank commander, had even pinned on the general's badge next to that of the RTR. In fact, he had to admit that if the truth were known, which he consoled himself it never would be, donning the black beret had not been his idea but something cooked up by two clever chaps from the press, a man called Charlton who edited *Eighth Army News* and Keating, that fellow who did the filming for the army. Apparently they had told John Poston that his head was unsuited to the bush hat – too big apparently. A beret, they said, would look much better. And what better than a tank corps beret? For, although the two public relations men would never know it, it was among the armour now more than anywhere else that he had had to call for the greatest sacrifice. It was to them ultimately that fell the ghastly dictum of one hundred per cent casualties.

De Guingand had woken him shortly after 7 a.m. 'It's Ninth Armoured, sir. They charged in and I'm afraid they've been shot up rather badly. They've taken heavy casualties. But they are on the feature at Tel-el-Aqqaqir.'

'Splendid. What else?'

'Well, unfortunately, sir, almost thirty of their tanks failed to reach the front line. They, er, took the wrong turning. That slowed up the Warwicks by half an hour. By the time they were into their charge the dawn was coming up. It was only then that they realized they were silhouetted against the horizon and in front of them were some dug-in 88s.'

Montgomery froze: 'What losses exactly?'

'Brigadier Currie lost 75 out of 94 tanks and 230 men out of 400. We could have exploited it, sir, but unfortunately General Fisher's brigade was too slow.'

He had said nothing. Too slow? He loathed excuses. And there was no excuse for a unit to be 'too slow'. But he had let it pass. Now, he thought, would see the breakout. For his masterstroke, while the Germans were pinned down in the north he was throwing two entire regiments of armoured cars at the Italians in the south. The corset had lost its whalebones and was about to be ripped apart.

De Guingand entered, smiling. It was 10.30: 'X Corps armour have broken through, sir. It's become a huge tank battle. They're just blasting each other into oblivion.'

So the tanks were fighting it out and given his superior numbers he knew that they would prevail. But this was not the way he had wanted it to be. Not at all. This was not how armour should be used. It should be integrated, exploited, not allowed to run amok. Although it did occur to him that this had been exactly what he had planned for Operation Lightfoot, the opening moves of the original battle plan, back almost twelve days ago. Although of course he would never admit that now. Everything must look as if it had been meticulously planned by him.

De Guingand was still speaking: 'Looks as though they've encountered fifteenth Panzer Division. We've lost fifty-four tanks. But reports are that we've knocked out one for one.'

This was it. One hundred per cent casualties.

'What of the infantry?'

'Fifty-First Highland are gaining ground. They did it by the book but they've gone even further than we'd hoped. They're actually in the rear laagers of the German tanks. The men have been running up to the panzers and dropping grenades down the turrets. It does look as if the Desert Fox is about to turn tail, sir.'

'Yes, Freddie, it does. But there's only one thing. When he does so, Rommel hasn't enough transport to get all his men out. Who do you suppose he's going to leave?'

'The Italians, I imagine.'

'Quite, and we must ensure that we don't allow him to regroup his Panzerarmee. Get me the air commodore. I want to make sure we've got enough planes in the air tomorrow to slow down any retreating columns. This is our chance, Freddie, and I'm not going to waste it.'

De Guingand hurried off and Montgomery contemplated the growing possibility of total victory and the price at which it had come. The infantry had paid dearly and he hoped they would forgive him. A man's courage, he had realized, was totally dependent upon his loyalty to his commander and it was the duty of any good commander not to abuse that loyalty simply to save shells.

He wrote in his diary: 'There are indications that the enemy is about to withdraw. He has reached breaking point and is trying to get his army away. We have the chance of putting the whole Panzerarmee in the bag and we will do so. He is almost finished.'

Tuesday 3 November

THIRTY-EIGHT

1.00 p.m.
HQ Panzerarmee Afrika, the mosque, Sidi Abdl el Rahman
Rommel

He sipped at the revolting ersatz coffee and managed a slight smile. 'Tell me, Bayerlein, you have no interest in collecting stamps?'

'No, Herr Generalfeldmarschall. Sadly not.'

'Pity. I had hoped we might have common ground there.'

It was true. He had hoped that he might share his interest. Might talk about anything other than the tragedy currently unfolding before him. Anything but defeat.

'I myself have a most magnificent collection. The fruit of thirty years. But you ski, don't you?'

'Yes, sir. Downhill and cross-country. Since I was a boy.'

Rommel brightened: 'Good. Yes, of course and it is the best of sports, is it not?'

There was a knock on the door of the command vehicle.

'Enter.'

It was Müller, Rommel's personal clerk. 'Sir, the reconnaissance reports on the Fuka position.'

'Ah, yes. Come in.'

Müller handed the papers to Bayerlein before leaving. Rommel put down the mug of coffee and moved to the large map spread out on the table before him. It was covered in blue pencil marks, arrows where the Allies had broken through the lines and others showing the possible means of escape for the Afrika Korps.

'So what have we, Bayerlein?'

'It seems, Herr Generalfeldmarschall, that in the southern-most positions the ground is quite impassable by tank. We could hold out there.'

Rommel nodded and ran his forefinger round the position. 'Yes, we'll stand in the position to the east of El Daba.'

He suddenly felt a twinge of pain in his stomach. Probably indigestion from his hurried lunch. But he wondered whether it might not be his recent trouble returned again. He reached for the coffee.

Bayerlein had noticed the spasm.

'Are you feeling all right, sir?'

'Yes, yes. I'll be fine. Just indigestion. This damn coffee. What other news?'

'Nothing good, sir. Twenty-First Panzer is dug in to the north and Fifteenth in the south. The Kampfstaffel have been wiped out and General von Thoma will not be persuaded to leave the front line. It looks like the British tanks are about to overrun Tel el Mampsra. The British armour have taken the Italian right flank. The Italians are fighting well but the British just have bigger and better machines.'

'They're American tanks, Bayerlein. Remember that.' He himself had seen forty of his own tanks knocked out two days ago. He knew the worst.

The army was exhausted. Ten days of endless fighting had worn them down. There was nothing they could do

343

now to stop a breakout. Indeed it had already begun. If he did not move now and fast then they were in danger of encirclement. He knew that an orderly withdrawal of all units was impossible. They simply lacked the necessary motor transport. And so his army would be destroyed, piecemeal. It was the end of a dream.

He looked at Bayerlein who was standing solemnly at the edge of the map, looking at the arrows. 'Do you remember, Bayerlein, how it was when we came to Libya. How we marched through the streets of Tripoli?'

Bayerlein smiled. 'Oh yes, sir. That was a day to remember. A glorious day.'

'You remember what they were singing?'

'"*Heia Safari*". "*Das Deutsches Volk in Afrika*".' He hummed the tune.

Not far away someone else was singing. A different song though no less familiar. A plaintive song of hoping for the impossible, a song more suited to the moment.

> Vor der Kaserne,
> Vor dem groBen Tor,
> Stand eine Laterne
> Und steht sie noch davor,
> So woll'n wir uns da wieder seh'n,
> Bei der Laterne wollen wir steh'n
> Wie einst Lili Marleen. Wie einst Lili Marleen.

Müller appeared again in the doorway. 'Sir, we've had a telegram from Berlin. Just decoded.'

Rommel looked up from the map. 'Yes? Read it to us.'

'Sir, it's from the Führer himself.'

Rommel reached out for the paper and began to read: 'The entire German nation is watching your heroic defensive battle in Egypt, with well-placed confidence in your leadership qualities and in the courage of your German and Italian troops. In your present situation nothing else

344

can be thought of but to hold on, not to yield a step, and to throw every weapon and every fighting man who can still be fed into the battle. Despite his superiority the enemy must also be at the end of his strength. It would not be the first time in history that the stronger will has triumphed over the stronger battalions of the enemy. To your troops therefore you can offer no other road than that leading to Victory or Death.'

Rommel handed the telegram to Bayerlein and shook his head. 'Read that.' Had the Führer gone mad? 'Victory or death'. Here he was trying to save as many of the Afrika Korps as he could and Hitler had sent him an order reading 'victory or death'.

Müller coughed: 'And there's another one, sir. From the Duce, Mussolini.'

Again Rommel read: 'Duce considers it imperative to hold present front at all costs.' Rommel laughed and handed that in turn to the colonel. 'Well, Bayerlein, that one's blunt enough. "At all costs".'

Rommel felt deeply hurt. He did not care one iota about Mussolini's message, had never had time for that man. The arrogant, bombastic fool. But here too was a personal message from a man whom he trusted, whom he valued as a friend and supporter. And that man now appeared to be telling him to die in battle along with every one of his men. He did not understand it. Hitler had promised him Tiger tanks, reinforcements, fuel, supplies, weapons and ammunition. Nothing had come. And now this. This ludicrous order to fight to the death. Perhaps, he thought, Kesselring was behind it. Yes, that in all probability was it. Hitler would never have done such a thing. Yet it was Hitler himself to whom he would now have to reply.

In truth it was too late. With their front broken and the enemy streaming into their rear, superior orders could no longer count. He simply had to save whatever there was to be saved. He would retreat. In fact, a rearguard of artillery and motorized infantry was already on the move and had been for the last fifteen hours.

He knew that the great tide of Allied men and machines was now only being held back by a thin line of armour and artillery. Barely thirty serviceable tanks. One thing was certain. He could not tell the men of the Führer's order. He would tell the commanders, though. Just as well to do so and let them know the scheme of things.

Nevertheless he would authorize the limited withdrawal he had planned. Fifteen kilometres back. But he would order the Ninetieth Light, what was left of them, and the Italians to stand fast and hold on to the last man. They would be his real rearguard. They would be sacrificed.

So, von Thoma was staying with his few remaining tanks. At least that would hold back the British First Armoured Division to prevent it threatening their withdrawal. It was, he knew, as von Thoma must know, a suicide mission. Von Thoma must have seen that the end was in sight. How typical of the man to use his own death as a signal to all at GHQ that there was something very wrong with high command. Von Thoma himself would die. And then perhaps the Führer's anger would be assuaged, thought Rommel. He could not understand it. Such deep resentment from Hitler, that brilliant man, the saviour of Germany.

'Müller, send a reply: "My Führer. I fully appreciate the gravity of the situation and your command. But I beg to point out that an order to stand fast will mean that we lose a proportion of the Panzerarmee that might otherwise be saved . . ."'

It was quite clear to him now that the true scale of the disaster was utterly lost on those in Berlin with their thoughts on the steppes of Russia. He turned to Bayerlein. 'Get me a brandy, could you. Oh, and send Major Berndt to the Führer in Berlin, to explain the state of affairs. He must also ask, no he must demand, complete freedom for the Panzerarmee in Africa to take whatever action is necessary to save what remains of itself.'

He would see Berndt himself later, before he went, and would brief him to explain to Hitler that North Africa was now irrevocably lost. That there really was no more that could be done. That this was the end. The end of the dream. The end of the Afrika Korps.

Wednesday 4 November

THIRTY-NINE

2.00 p.m.
Camel Pass, the Quattara Depression
Ruspoli

This then, he thought, was how it ended. They had little water, food and ammunition, no anaesthetic and no motor transport. Ruspoli knew that soon his brigade would be on the point of disintegration. The order had come through at two in the morning and it had taken Ruspoli completely by surprise. Particularly as only hours before they had received an order direct from the Duce telling them to hold the line at all costs.

They had been ordered to abandon Hill 125, the crucial defensive line between Deir Alinda and Deir-el-Munassib that they had held for the last three days.

Instead, they were to conduct a fighting retreat to Fuka and initially to make their way to new positions between Jebel Kalakh and Qaret el Khadim. That was ten miles to the west. They had moved as quickly as they could and reached the new line just after dawn. Since then though the enemy artillery had been firing everything they had at them. They had not had time to entrench properly and the casualty rate was rising. What chance he thought did the wounded have with no medical supplies?

No morphine? His men were dying all around him and there was nothing he could do. He had already lost two officers that morning: Bonini, whose luck had finally run out, and poor Piccini.

His friends, his comrades, his family. Worse still was that he had only heard yesterday that his brother Costantino had been killed on the twenty-sixth. Ruspoli had been expecting it for some time, just as he expected his own death to come soon.

Visconti came up. 'Sir. We should be at Fuka by now.'

'I know, Guido, I know. But where the hell are we?'

'Somewhere in greater Italy.'

'What?'

'That's what the Duce called it. This is part of Italy.'

Ruspoli laughed. 'Dear Guido. What a wit.'

'It's just what they told us, sir. This is our land. We fight to defend it.'

'We have only one land. Mother Italy. We were sold a lie.'

It was approaching two in the afternoon when three British armoured cars pressed forward. An English voice sounded through a loudspeaker.

'Brave Italians. You have done everything honour and your country demand. You have shown great valour. Surrender now and you will be treated as heroes. Continue to fight and you will be completely annihilated.'

Ruspoli shouted back: 'Folgore!' Then he turned to Mautino: 'Fire the 47/32.'

Mautino shouted to Ponticelli: 'Open fire.'

The small anti-tank gun fired and a shell hit one of the armoured cars square-on, causing it to burst into flames. Its crew jumped from the turret and ran back to hitch a ride on the other two which were now pulling back.

The Italians gave a cheer. Ruspoli spoke quietly to

Mautino. 'We must continue to withdraw. Those are the orders. We've left Fourth Battalion as a rearguard. Only they may have water supplies. For us it's only what we're carrying. Half a litre each. That's all we have. There is no more.'

'We should take the gun, sir.'

'Yes, of course. Come on.'

He walked across to the jubilant gunners and helped them pick up the trail of the little cannon. Mautino ran to stop him. 'Colonel, really. That is not a job for an officer. Especially for you.'

Ruspoli smiled at him and pushed away his hand. 'Oh, Carlo. Don't you see? Officers, men. We're all the same now. Look around you. What do you see? Italians. We must help each other now. Please. If my men do it then so do I.'

He picked up the trail and with six others began to push the gun through the sand. Their initial march had been through the night. By day it was very different, under the desert sun. They moved with painful slowness, every step a new hardship. To his left a man swayed and collapsed to the ground. Ruspoli went across to him. It was Marcantonio, the wine-producer. His skin was dry and wrinkled and his mouth black. He was completely dehydrated. Though it was only the afternoon, the men, utterly exhausted, were falling asleep on their feet. Some of those who fell in the sand did not get back up. Mautino handed out amphetamines to help them stay awake. There was the sound of engines in the sky.

Polini yelled: 'Get down! Planes.'

Three Hurricanes dived low out of the sun and Ruspoli bowed his head as their guns opened up. The shells raked the sand around him and tore through two of the men hauling the cannon. The planes circled and then dived again. This time their fire scudded through a dune where

352

three men were sheltering. There was a scream. Ruspoli ran to see who had been hit. Two of the men were dead, their bodies ripped apart by the cannon shells. The third though was still alive. It was Conticello, the baker's son. Both of his hands were mangled and his left eye had gone. He had obviously put his hands up to shield himself from the gunfire and paid the price. He was staring at his hand and clearly the shock had not yet given way to pain. They managed to make him a makeshift stretcher from a piece of tarpaulin and dragged him along with them.

It was around five in the afternoon that they stopped. Mautino spotted it first. A trench, cut into the desert and built up with sandbags and wooden supports. It was covered with a wooden roof and shreds of tarpaulin and canvas hung off it, giving it the appearance of a street vendor's stall. A signpost in German pointed to Tripoli in one direction and Cairo in the other.

'Must have been a supply depot. Petrol and water by the look of all those empty cans.'

'Pity they're empty,' muttered Visconti.

Ruspoli walked across to the position. 'Better make sure it's not booby-trapped. You know what these Germans are like.'

Galati laughed. Speda volunteered and slowly, inch by inch ran his hands around the perimeter and then inside the trench itself. At last, after a good half-hour, he emerged smiling. 'Clean, Colonel. Nothing. We can use it.'

They dragged Conticello inside the small dugout to the rear of the trench and set up a command post at the front. The gun they placed on the left with as many shells as they had been able to carry. And then they waited.

Ruspoli had not expected the British to catch up with them so quickly. But then he supposed that they must have been travelling very slowly and the enemy were mostly in armoured cars and trucks. Now the armoured cars advanced towards them across the plain of the desert. They could see them quite clearly. Ruspoli raised his field glasses and made out the small triangular pennons that fluttered on the aerials: a red rat on a black background. There was a flash and the first of the shells came towards them, falling far short. Ranging shots.

'Marco. Marco Zianni. Sing me a song, a song from home. Sing for the British. Let them hear how brave Italians fight. We die as we live, to music. Puccini. Verdi, Donizetti. You choose.'

'Now, Colonel?'

'Of course now, Marco. When else? There will be no better time than now. Never. Sing for us now.'

Zianni coughed and cleared his throat. Around him the platoon stood and watched as he began to sing. The flaw-less, perfect tenor voice cut through the noise of battle as the young man summoned every ounce that was left of his strength and courage. Ruspoli smiled. It was a favourite aria of his from *La Bohème*! 'Che Gelida Manina'. The words rang out across the baking desert, evoking thoughts of another place, another time. Another tragedy.

> Your tiny hand is frozen; let me warm it here in mine.
> What's the use in searching? It's far too dark to find it.
> But by our good fortune, it's a night lit by the moon,
> and up here the moon is our closest friend . . .

Ruspoli listened and for an instant was unable to move. For a moment he almost regretted having asked Zianni to sing, and then instantly knew that he had been right to do so. There was no better time than now. It was all that was left them. A memory of Italy. The joy of music and of life. Love, friendship, passion and sorrow. Tears began to course down his face and he looked across at Visconti, saw that he too was unable to control his emotions. Visconti shook his head: 'What for, Colonel? Why do we do this? Tell me why?'

'For Italy, Guido. For our country and our people. For Michelangelo and Giotto. For Verdi and Puccini and for all your film stars too.'

And so Zianni filled his lungs again and opened his mouth and sang of love and loss and life. Sublime music, music, thought Ruspoli, like no other. Divine. Inspired.

The music soared and still the tanks and armoured cars advanced towards them, their rumbling, clanking thunder providing a ghastly bass line to Zianni's tenor. Above the roar and the melody Ruspoli barked an order.

'Folgore, make ready. Take aim. Wait for my command. You Zianni, you keep on singing. Don't stop. Never stop singing. That's an order.'

He turned back to the company, caught sight of Mautino, Bonini, Conticello and Galati, his hair longer than ever. The old faces. The ones who were left. And with the tears chasing each other down his face, he gave the order.

'Now. Fire!'

The entire battalion, what there was of it, barely a half-company opened fire with whatever it had. The bullets flew across the desert and most pinged harmlessly off the armoured cars. A few though found their targets and British soldiers began to fall as the Folgore fought their last battle.

The shots rang out again and now another noise had joined the music and the gunfire. Somewhere across the front one of the enemy was playing the bagpipes. So they were Scots attacking him, thought Ruspoli. Here then was the final irony. To meet his end at the hands of the men of his ancestral homeland. At least they were men he respected, men of honour. A proud race from the mountains, men like him.

They had all fixed bayonets, all who were capable. Even most of the officers had chosen to fight with a rifle and bayonet today, although many also carried sidearms and knives. They all stood alongside Ruspoli now and they all knew what was expected of them. Ruspoli brushed away the tears. Then, as the armoured cars continued to advance, their machine-guns spraying out their hail of death he began to climb out of the trench and the men followed their commander. Ruspoli turned and looked at them, caught their faces in his mind. Then he looked to the front. He called to the bugler: 'Zampetti, sound the charge.' The notes rang out loud and clear above the machine-guns and the tanks. Above Zianni's beautiful tenor voice which still rang out as he had been commanded by his colonel.

Then Ruspoli raised his hand in the air and shouted one word, at the top of his voice: 'Folgore!' And with that he leapt from the trench and up on to the sand. Immediately, he felt himself being pushed back hard as if by a steel hand as the first of the bullets cut through him. But he did not fall. He managed to steady himself and walked forward. He knew that the men were up with him now and could hear the sickening thud as more bullets struck them. They were falling all around him but Ruspoli continued onwards.

He saw Gola, the battle too close now for his beloved mortars, lead a bayonet charge only to be cut down by machine-gun fire. Marozzi, the painter, was standing with a cigarette hanging from his mouth firing round after round into the advancing infantry and died as an armoured car cut him down with its blazing guns. On his right Visconti was leading a charge with flaming petrol bombs

356

against two armoured cars. He saw one explode and then there was a burst of fire and Visconti and his men just seemed to fall over and lie still. He was aware of Marcantonio stumbling back towards him with blood streaming from his head and his hands clawing at empty eye sockets and of Speda, lying somewhere close by, staring at his severed legs.

And then he was hit again. And again. And then he could not really see where his men had gone. He heard Mautino's voice: 'Folgore. Italia,' and he stretched his body as far as he could, reaching his hand to touch the heavens, his thin frame silhouetted against the azure sky. There was no pain, only shock and the realization of death. He had an image in his mind of a saint in a renaissance painting in their private chapel at Castello Ruspoli. A saint, a soldier-saint, painted by Andrea Mantegna. A saint so lacerated by cuts and arrows that he was scarcely recognizable. Yet a man who so transcended mortality by his suffering that he became Everyman. A man whose death atoned for all the sorrows of humanity. Ruspoli felt the bullets tearing at his flesh like arrows. Surely, he thought, this is enough. Surely now the killing must stop? We are beaten. Another rattle of the gun and Ruspoli felt himself falling. For ever it seemed, until his face hit the ground. But he felt no pain. Only sadness and a sense of release. And before he closed his eyes, he looked along the sand and off into the far distance where the land ended and the cloudless sky began. Off into the shimmering haze that hinted that what they said really might be true. That however many empires and tyrants and kings might rise and fall, the desert went on for ever.

FORTY

2.00 p.m.
Kidney Ridge
Douglas

It was as clear to him as it was to the high command that the new offensive had not been a total success. There was talk in the mess that Monty had expected 'one hundred per cent casualties' and Douglas wondered whether he really did and if so quite what he meant by it. The Highland Division and the New Zealanders had gone in. It seemed to Douglas that Monty was always using the same troops, the same divisions, brigades and regiments. They appeared to have taken the casualties but reports from Division were that they had not secured their objectives. Another stand-down, he suspected and then with a logic that he now knew to be typical of the army they were given new tanks.

New tanks? He wondered whose brilliant idea it had been to supply them with new tanks hours before they were due to go back into battle. They had been out of the line for four days. The tanks needed to be resupplied, a complex job which took some hours as the lorries ran from one machine to another handing out essential supplies: water, fuel and ammunition. The last came in a cardboard carton and Douglas helped the others tear it open and prise out the shiny brass shells with their striped black and white nose cones. They ripped the safety flaps off the machine-gun ammo tins and tore the safety clips from the detonators. And when all the machine-guns had been greased and the radio sets tested out they were deemed ready, although Douglas knew that the crews hardly thought them fit for action.

They moved up to the battle line slowly, along the same dust tracks, as characterless as the rest of the desert landscape, with the crews huddled together in the cramped turrets in a fug of cigarette smoke and sweat, snatching sleep where they could, reading when the light permitted. He had left the turret open to make the most of the air and even as night fell was aware of the white dust that blew up from the road and caked his face and hands.

At first light they found themselves at a gap in a minefield marked by metal triangles hung on wooden posts amid the cut barbed wire. They moved slowly towards the west and there on the horizon in front of them he saw vehicles. Enemy tanks. But decently out of range. The regiment began to close on them and as they did Douglas peered over the side of the tank and saw infantrymen in the ground passing below him, lying in trenches. Most of them appeared to be dead but, looking down into one trench he was met by the face of a man who had momentarily lifted his head. His eyes were filled with despair. Douglas yelled to Mudie: 'Stop!'

He jumped down from the turret and grabbed a water can before running across to the trench. Kneeling down he held the man's head and fed him the water before looking to see who he might be: German, Italian or British. In fact he was none of these, but a lieutenant of the New Zealand infantry. When he had managed a few desperate gulps of the rusty water he spoke in a barely audible voice.

'Can you get me out? I'm hit pretty bad. Been here two days, I think.'

He pointed to his leg, which Douglas could see had been lacerated with shrapnel and was caked in dried blood. Flies were swarming across the wound, which the man had tried to cover with towels and canvas. 'Two days. Don't think I can take much more.'

Douglas screwed the top back on the water can. 'You hold on. I'll see what I can do.'

He ran back to the tank, which having waited for him had now fallen back from the advancing squadron and climbing up to the turret, clicked on the set to speak to the major.

'Sir. Nuts Five. Permission to take wounded officer back to RAP. Over.'

The colonel came on: 'Nuts Five. Yes, yes, yes, yes, yes. But do get off the air, old boy, will you. We're engaging the bloody enemy.'

Douglas climbed back down and went across to the wounded man. 'Do you think you could manage it on the back of the tank, with our help?'

'Anything. Just get me out.'

Together the three of them dragged him out of the trench and hoisted him on to the only area of the tank free to take him, the baking hot plates above the engine. It must have been agony, thought Douglas, but the man said nothing and in a few minutes they had retraced their tracks to a small knot of infantrymen standing guard over some prisoners. Here they left the grateful lieutenant and went back to find their regiment. The tanks were grouped in line just behind a ridge beyond which lay a track which could be made out by the tops of its telegraph poles.

Within seconds a whoosh announced the approach of 88 shells, which flew over Douglas's tanks towards some unseen objective in the rear. It appeared from the lack of radio activity that they were to remain put and Douglas decided that it might be best to be out of the tank were it to be hit. He climbed down and was soon joined by Evan. Below their feet in the sand he noticed a magazine. An old copy of *Esquire*. Douglas picked it up. It was stained with oil, damp sand and what looked like blood. He opened it and, with Evan looking over his shoulder, began to turn the pages. It spoke of another world where scantily clad, pouting beauties reclined on velvet cushions and Hollywood stars danced the night away. He was particularly taken with a feature on a white-tuxedoed dandy and his impossibly beautiful girlfriend. He left Evan reading and sat on an upturned ammo box. Then taking a piece of paper from his pocket he looked again at the poem: 'the easy sun won't criticize or carp because . . .' What next he wondered. Then drew out his pencil and wrote: 'after the death of many heroes, evils remain.'

He smiled and was tucking the poem back into his pocket when some British twenty-five-pounders began to reply to the 88s over their heads and the radio set in the turret crackled with the muffled and at that distance slightly comical voice of the major: 'Don't stop. Get into them. Give the buggers hell. Off.'

Douglas and Evan climbed into the tank and began to drive slowly forward. They had hardly gone two hundred yards when the 88s stopped. The radio came alive again: 'Halt. Take a rest. Off.'

There was a grunt from below. Mudie: 'Bloody hell. Make yer bloody mind up.'

Douglas spoke: 'All right. Let's brew up.'

They had just climbed out of the tank and had started a fire in a sand burner when their attention was caught by a noise. A rumble, which could only be an approaching Sherman. But it was only when it came into sight that they stopped what they were doing. For the advancing tank which was heading straight for them appeared to be on fire. Through the driver's aperture the interior was lit by a red glow. A tongue of flame licked up from inside the open manhole of the turret. But still the tank came on.

Evan spoke: 'Bloody hell, sir. Who's driving that?'

Douglas could only think that when the tank had been hit the driver must have fallen on the accelerator. For surely there could be no living being inside it. Then the tank stopped about forty yards from them and to his amazement a figure climbed out of the driver's hatch. Although the man was jet black Douglas recognized him as a brother officer: Lieutenant Nick Davidson of C Squadron. He staggered towards Douglas. 'I say, old boy. Could you give me a hand? Put the fire out, that sort of thing?'

They rushed towards the blackened, swaying officer.

'It's quite all right. I'm quite well really, just a bit hot. Do I smell tea?'

They sat him down and poured him a mug. Douglas stood up. 'Come on, Evan. Mudie, you stay with the lieutenant.'

Followed by the reluctant gunner, Douglas ventured over to the blazing tank armed with their fire extinguisher.

Evan spoke: 'Sir. You do know that there's probably about thirty HE shells in there and a thousand rounds of MG ammo that'll go off any minute like Guy Fawkes night?'

'Yes, I was aware of that fact.'

'Well, don't you think this might be a bit, well, dangerous?'

They continued towards the tank.

'Yes. I take your point.'

Evan shook his head and muttered something that Douglas chose not to hear and together they climbed up

362

on to the tank and poured water from the cans strapped to the fuselage down the turret. It hit the flames with a loud hiss and produced a plume of steam and oily smoke. Evan whistled: 'Well, if Jerry couldn't see us before he will now.'

The fire still burned. Douglas pushed the trigger on the fire extinguisher and the liquid shot out. Within a few minutes the fire had become a smoking ember. They climbed down and walked back to their own tank. A voice came through the commander's earphones that were dangling over the side of the turret: 'Nuts Five. Rendevous on a track six miles in the rear. Off.'

Douglas looked back to the Sherman and saw that a red glow had begun again inside. Evan said: 'Lot of fuckin' good that was.'

They all climbed back into the tank and the lieutenant, scorched though incredibly not badly burned, sat in the aperture. Douglas spoke through the intercom to the driver. 'Mudie. Bring her round. We're off back to join the regiment.'

They raced along as fast as they could go with the lieutenant in the turret and Douglas prayed that he had got the direction right. For miles there was nothing but wrecked machines and groups of corpses, abandoned weapons and other debris of war. And then he saw it, shimmering in the haze. A massive, magnificent spectacle. An entire tank brigade drawn up in column of battle.

Evan was impressed. 'Bugger me, sir. Look at that. Makes you proud.'

Douglas had to agree it did make you proud. He drove into the Brigade, deposited the lieutenant with the MO and at length discovered his regiment among the lines. The sun was going down as they pulled into the squadron leaguer. They had drawn up in three rows of squadrons and that was how they were to attack. In close order formation, three columns, one behind the other. Douglas's troop, now three tanks strong, had been detailed to cover the flank, which they did in echelon, travelling fast – thirty miles an hour – over the flat landscape. They had not gone far when two lorries appeared laden with Italian troops. One of the tanks broke ranks. Douglas saw it was Tom Philips's, a lieutenant in A Squadron. It chased after the Italians. Douglas decided to follow and caught up with Philips just as he was disarming one of the lorries. The Italians did not seem too upset to be 'in the bag' and were handing over their rifles readily. They looked all-in and were dressed in a motley collection of clothing, some of it captured British issue, some of it German. Douglas saw that for all the Italians' evident enthusiasm to become prisoners the other lorry was getting away and Douglas was about to tell Mudie to pursue it when the colonel's voice came over his headphones. 'Nuts Five. You'd better let that one go to ground. We'll find it again.'

'Yes, sir. What are our orders?'

'We're moving on Mersa Matruh to cut off the enemy.'

'Cut them off, sir?'

'Of course bloody cut them off, Nuts Five. They're retreating. We've got them beat. We've been selected to administer the *coup de grace*.'

'And what then, sir?'

'What then?' The major seemed a little nonplussed for a moment, but then he spoke again: 'Why then we go back to Cairo of course and er . . . have a bath. And leave some other buggers to do the chasing for us.'

The line went dead and Douglas looked out into the endless desert and thought of Cairo and of clean clothes and clean sheets and of a soft bed and of life and love. And then, for the first time since the battle had begun, it started to rain.

FORTY-ONE

2.00 p.m.
HQ Eighth Army
Montgomery

The end had come as the battle had begun, in the night. He had sent in two hard punches at the hinges of the breakout area around Kidney Ridge where the enemy was desperately trying to prevent them from widening the breach.

At dawn the armoured-car regiments had poured through the gap, and then the heavier armour had broken into the open desert, First and Seventh Divisions in the lead. There were no minefields here. Nothing to hamper his superiority.

Shortly afterward a report had come through from the Argylls that they had reached their objective of Point Forty-four and found it abandoned. The Germans had pulled out without a fight.

In the south all that the abandoned Italians could do was surrender and now the pursuit could begin. Now he would chase the Desert Fox out of Egypt and out of Africa. And what pleased him most of all was that it had taken exactly twelve days to do it. Just as he had predicted.

There was a knock at the door and de Guingand entered. 'Sir, you have a visitor. We've captured General von

Thoma, at least Tenth Hussars have. In Rommel's absence he commands the Afrika Korps.'

Montgomery smiled. 'Show him in please, Freddie,and extend him every hospitality. We wouldn't want him to think that the British were at all ungenerous in victory.'

De Guingand opened the door and two men entered, one in the uniform of a British tank commander, the other in that of the Afrika Korps with senior officer's insignia, although the jacket and trousers were badly torn and covered in white dust. The latter saluted.

Montgomery stared hard into von Thoma's piercing blue eyes and for a moment was thrown. Here clearly was no fanatical Nazi, but a fellow soldier. A man of war rather than of politics. His reputation as a tank commander was well known. He was a leader of men, a warrior.

At length Montgomery spoke: 'Herr General, I would be honoured if you would dine with me this evening as my personal guest. I'm sure that we have much to discuss.'

The general smiled and nodded: 'With pleasure, General. Thank you.'

Montgomery noticed that von Thoma had sustained some burns about the legs: 'We must have that seen to. Freddie, could you arrange it? We can't have the general in any pain. Besides, I want him at his ease at dinner this evening so that he can advise me what he thinks Rommel might intend next.'

He laughed and von Thoma joined in: 'I'm sorry to disappoint you, General Montgomery. But I can give nothing away. No matter how many glasses of port you might offer me. Although I shall be happy to talk about the battle you have just won and to tell you how you might have won it more quickly.'

Montgomery shook his head: 'You might tell me that, General, but I'm afraid you would be wrong. You see, I planned this battle down to the smallest detail and I knew precisely how long it would take us to win. We simply could not have done it any sooner or with any fewer casualties.' He paused and smiled: 'The fact is though, General, we did it.'

10 November, 1942
Mansion House, London
Churchill

I have never promised anything but blood, tears, toil and sweat. Now, however, we have a new experience. We have victory – a remarkable and definite victory. The bright gleam has caught the helmets of our soldiers, and warmed and cheered all our hearts . . . Rommel's army has been defeated. It has been routed. It has been very largely destroyed as a fighting force . . .

Now this is not the end. It is not even the beginning of the end, but it is, perhaps, the end of the beginning. Henceforth Hitler's Nazis will meet equally well armed, and perhaps better armed troops . . . Here we are, and here we stand, a veritable rock of salvation in this drifting world. There was a time not long ago when for a whole year we stood all alone. Those days, thank God, have gone . . .

I recall to you some lines of Byron, which seem to me to fit the event, the hour, and the theme:

'Millions of tongues record thee, and anew
Their children's lips shall echo them, and say –

"Here, where the sword united nations drew,
Our countrymen were warring on that day!"
And this is much, and all which will not pass
  away.'

Biographical Notes

The Allies

General Harold Alexander, after the Anglo-American forces from Operation Torch and the Eighth Army converge in Tunisia in February 1943, commands 18th Army Group, reporting to Eisenhower. Thus in July under Alexander, Montgomery's Eighth Army and Patton's Seventh Army invade Sicily. During the subsequent advance up Italy Alexander authorizes the bombing of Monte Cassino. In December 1944 he becomes Supreme Commander of the Allied Forces Headquarters. He is promoted field marshal and receives the German surrender in Italy. He is elevated to the peerage in 1946 created Viscount Alexander of Tunis and Errigal. He then becomes governor general of Canada and in 1952 returns to Britain and becomes Earl Alexander of Tunis, Baron Rideau of Ottawa and Castle Derg. He is Minister of Defence until 1954, when he retires from politics. Alexander dies at home on 16 June 1969.

Sergeant Herb Ashby returns to Palestine in December with his unit and refuses the offer of officer training. In January 1943 the battalion moves out to Suez. While there Ashby hears that Bill Kibby has been awarded a posthumous VC. Ashby fights with the Australian army in the Pacific and is invalided out with sickness in May 1945. Recuperating at Mount Gambier he meets a nurse Heather Hancock and they are married in 1946. He starts to farm cattle, expands into sheep and in the 1970s sells up a successful livestock business and settles in Mount Gambier. He also works in veterans' pensions. In 1999 he was awarded the Medal of the Order of Australia. He has five children, eight grandchildren and six great grandchildren.

Major Tom Bird, already the holder of an MC and bar, receives a DSO for his part in the action at Snipe. He becomes one of Wavell's ADCs in Delhi and later while serving in Belgium is badly wounded and invalided out of the army. After the war he sets up an architectural practice in London with Richard Tyler who had been wounded on the same day, losing a leg, while serving with the Royal Engineers and had met Bird in hospital in Cairo. Their practice specialises in country house restoration and housing for disabled ex-servicemen. It is still in business today. In 2004 Bird is awarded the Légion d'Honneur for his part in the Tobruk evacuation. In 2009, a grandfather of seven, aged ninety he pledges to bequeath his medals to the Greenjackets museum in Winchester.

Sergeant Charlie Callistan 2nd KRRB wins the DCM.

Corporal Cope 2nd KRRB is promoted sergeant and wins the Military Medal.

Brigadier Francis 'Freddie' de Guingand collapses from fatigue during the preparations for the battle of El Agheila on 23 November. Monty sends him back to Cairo. He is married to his fiancée Mrs Arlie Stewart and returns to the front. He is promoted major-general after the surrender of the Axis forces in North Africa in May 1943 and serves as Montgomery's chief of staff, from Egypt to the Rhine. Throughout early 1944 he is away on sick leave on several occasions with stress. After the end of hostilities in Europe he is appointed as Director of Military Intelligence at the War Office. But fails to make Vice Chief of the General Staff. In 1946 de Guingand retires from the army to Southern Rhodesia to pursue a successful career in business. He also writes books about his experiences but he is blunt about his relationship with Montgomery and falls out with him. He dies in 1979 at the age of seventy-nine.

Lieutenant Keith Castellain Douglas is wounded on 15 January 1943, in action at Wadi Zem Zem, and sent to Palestine to recover. During the six weeks he spends there, he writes an account of the fighting – *From Alamein to Zem Zem*. Released from hospital, Douglas rejoins his regiment in Egypt and, later, in Tunisia, where he is promoted to captain. In mid-December, he arrives back in England for three weeks' leave. In his absence, he has become a published poet with *Selected Poems*. At the end of his leave, he retrains for D-Day. In February 1944, he receives a contract from Poetry London for a collection of his poetry. He takes part in the D-Day invasion of Normandy on 6 June 1944. The regiment helps liberate Bayeux and on D-Day + 3, 9 June, arrives at the village of St Pierre. Douglas and a comrade leave their tank and head towards the village on foot. A mortar shell explodes directly above his head, killing him instantly without leaving a mark on his body. He is twenty-four. His remains now lie in the Tilly-sur-Seulles War Cemetery.

General Bernard Freyberg is created Knight Commander of the Order of the Bath. He is injured in an aircraft accident in September 1944. After six weeks in hospital he returns to command the New Zealand Division in its final operations in Italy and liberates Venice. He becomes Governor-General of New Zealand in 1946 and holds the post until 1952. Freyberg returns to England and in 1953 becomes Deputy Constable and becomes Lieutenant-Governor of Windsor Castle. He dies at Windsor on 4 July 1963 following the rupture of one of his war wounds. He is seventy-four.

General Alexander Gatehouse is from 1942 to 1944 Chief Administration Officer to the British Military Mission in Washington. After the war he becomes Military Attaché to the Soviet Union and from 1946 to 1948 is Aide-de-Camp to the King. He dies in 1964 aged sixty-nine.

Sergeant Hines 2nd KRRB wins the MM.

General Brian Horrocks takes over command of X Corps, after Lumsden's dismissal. He is then transferred to First Army to take over IX Corps with which he captures Tunis and accepts the surrender of the remnants of Rommel's Army Group Africa. In June 1943, Horrocks is wounded during an air raid at Bizerte. He has five operations and spends fourteen months recovering. In August 1944 he is sent to France to assume command of XXX Corps and drives through Belgium, taking Brussels. In September in Operation Market Garden, XXX Corps under Horrocks leads the ground assault along a corridor held by British and American airborne forces to link up with the British 1st Airborne Division. He becomes a television presenter lecturing on great battles and becomes director of the house-building company Bovis. He is a military consultant for the 1977 film *A Bridge Too Far*, in which he is played by Edward Fox.

He dies in 1985, at the age of eighty-nine.

General Sir Oliver Leese commands XXX Corps for the rest of the campaign and in the invasion of Sicily and is mentioned in dispatches. He is promoted temporary lieutenant-general in September 1943 and in December succeeds Montgomery as Eighth Army commander. He commands Eighth Army at the final Battle of Monte Cassino in May 1944. His rank of lieutenant-general was made permanent in July 1944. In September 1944 he is appointed Commander-in-Chief of Allied Land Forces, South-East Asia. After falling out with General Slim he is himself replaced by him and returns to Britain as GOC-in-C Eastern Command. He retires from the army in January 1947 and became a renowned horticulturist, particularly on cacti. He dies in 1978 aged ninety-four.

General Herbert Lumsden is sacked by Montgomery on 13 December 1942 and replaced by General Brian Horrocks. Liked by Churchill, however, he is given command of VIII Corps in Britain, prior to being sent to the Pacific as Churchill's military representative to MacArthur. He is killed at the age of forty-eight by a *kamikaze* plane on the bridge of USS *New Mexico* observing the bombardment of Lingayen Gulf on 6 January 1945. He is buried at sea.

Lieutenant General Bernard Law Montgomery is knighted and promoted full general. He pursues Rommel into Tunisia. Eighth Army invades Sicily and then in the autumn of 1943 Italy. In December he returns to Britain and takes command of 21st army group and prepares for the invasion of France. He masterminds the D-Day landings of 6 June 1944. However after the successful invasion the British become bogged down and Montgomery falls out with Patton. Eisenhower takes command of Allied ground forces and on 1 September 1944, after the end of the Battle of Normandy, Montgomery is created Field Marshall. Montgomery oversees the British advance to the Rhine and on 4 May 1945, on Lüneburg Heath, accepts the surrender of German forces. He is created 1st Viscount Montgomery of Alamein in 1946 and is Chief of the Imperial General Staff from 1946 until 1948, before becoming Eisenhower's deputy, helping with the creation of NATO's European forces. He retires from the army aged seventy-one, in 1958.

Montgomery's post war views are increasingly controversial and in his memoirs he criticises many of his wartime comrades resulting in a falling out with Eisenhower. He is threatened with legal action by Auchinleck for suggesting that he had meant to retreat from the Alamein position, and has to include a corrective note in future editions and to make a radio broadcast in 1958 explaining that Auchinleck had in fact been instrumental in establishing the front line at Alamein. He dies in 1976 at home in Alton, Hampshire, aged eighty-eight. He is buried at Holy Cross Churchyard, Binsted.

General Leslie Morshead is created a Knight Commander of the Order of the Bath (KCB). He and the Australian 9th Division are recalled to the South West Pacific. In March 1943, he is made commander of II Corps, and in September 1943, moves to the Australian beachhead at New Guinea. A Japanese counter-attack is crushed. In November 1943, he becomes acting commander of New Guinea Force and Second Army and commands forces in New Guinea in the battles of Sattelberg, Jivevaneng, Sio and Shaggy Ridge. Returning to Australia, he commands Second Army and in February 1945, lands on Borneo.

After the war Morshead becomes the Orient Steam Navigation Company's Australian general manager. He dies of cancer in 1959 in Sydney aged seventy.

Captain John William Poston 11th Hussars is killed in action on 21 April 1945, at the age of twenty-five, while carrying out a task for Montgomery who acknowledges the fact in his memoirs.

Major Hugh Peter de Lancey Samwell 7th Argyll and Sutherland Highlanders recuperates in Cairo and, having rejoined his unit, is wounded again in March 1943 having stood on a mine at the end of a patrol. He is awarded the MC for gallantry in action on Mareth Line, North Africa. After hospital in Tripoli he advances through Algeria and takes part in the invasion of Sicily and records his experiences of war in North Africa and Sicily in *An Infantry Officer with the Eighth Army* later published in 1945. In Italy he plays a leading role in defending soldiers of the 50th and 51st divisions, including many Alamein veterans, accused of mutiny in September 1943, as documented in the book *Mutiny at Salerno: An Injustice Exposed* by Saul David (2005). He is killed in action in Belgium in the final phase of the German Ardennes offensive on 12 January 1945, age thirty-three.

Sergeant Joe Swann of S Company 2nd KRRB is awarded the DCM.

Colonel Victor 'Vic' Turner is awarded the VC. His brother had already been awarded a posthumous VC in

WWI. Turner is also made a member of the Royal Victorian Order. After the war he settles with his sister Jane and two brothers on the family estate in Ditchingham Norfolk. He never marries and dies at home in 1972 aged seventy-two.

The Axis

General Albert Gause is made chief of special staff Libya and Tunisia in December 1942. In June 1944 he is moved to France as acting Chief of Staff Panzer Group West. In September he is moved to Germany with SS panzer-armee but in November is relieved of his duties a suspect in the Hitler bomb plot on account of his loyalty to Rommel. But in April 1945 he is made Commander of II Corps. Isolated in Latvia, the corps is captured by the Russians on May 10 1945. It seems probable that Gause was abandoned by General Burgdorf, one of the officers who had given cyanide to Rommel. He is finally released from Soviet prison in 1955 and retires to Karlsruhe. He dies at home in Bonn in September 1967.

Generalleutnant Fritz Bayerlien assumes effective command of the Afrika Korps after the capture of von Thoma. When Rommel leaves Tunisia in March 1943, Bayerlein is appointed German liaison officer under the new commander, Giovanni Messe. He develops rheumatism and hepatitis and is sent to Italy on sick leave before the German troops in Tunisia surrender in May 1943.

He is sent to the Eastern Front in October 1943 to lead the Berlin-Brandenburg 3rd Panzer Division and later command the Panzer Lehr Division in Budapest. After the Normandy Invasion they are sent to France and fight in Caen suffering heavy losses. He then serves under General von Manteuffel in the Ardennes Offensive and commands 53rd corps. In April 1945 he and his men surrender to the U.S. 7th Armored Division in the Ruhr.

He is released from captivity in 1947 and starts to write about military subjects. He is technical advisor to the film *The Guns of Navarone* in 1961. He dies in his hometown of Würzburg in 1970 aged seventy-one.

Generalfeldmarschall Erwin Rommel, despite entreaties from Hitler and Mussolini, does not turn and fight, but withdraws to Tunisia. Here he attacks US II Corps defeating it at the Kasserine Pass in February in 1943.

He then turns against the British forces, occupying the Mareth Line.

In March, he attacks Eighth Army at the Battle of Medenine but after losing fifty-two tanks, calls off the assault. On 9 March he hands over command of *Armeegruppe Afrika* to General von Arnim and leaves Africa on sick leave. He will never return. On 13 May 1943, General Messe surrenders the remnants of *Armeegruppe Afrika* to the Allies.

In August 1943 Rommel moves to Lake Garda as commander of a new Army Group B created to defend northern Italy but after Hitler gives Kesselring sole Italian command, Rommel moves Army Group B to Normandy to defend the French coast against the promised Allied invasion. He speeds up the fortification of the Atlantic coast. He orders millions of mines to be laid and thousands of tank traps and obstacles set up on beaches and throughout the countryside.

On the morning of D Day he is on leave but later he personally oversees the fighting around Caen. On 17 July 1944 Rommel's staff car is strafed and he is hospitalized with major head injuries.

In February he lends his support to the conspiracy to oust Hitler but is against assassination. On 20 July the bomb attack on Hitler fails and many conspirators are arrested. Rommel is implicated after confessions by other officers under torture.

Hitler, realizing that it will cause a scandal if it comes out that Rommel is involved in the plot, offers Rommel the choice of committing suicide or being sent to a People's Court and execution.

He is visited at his home by Wilhelm Burgdorf and Ernst Maisel, two generals from Hitler's headquarters. Burgdorf offers him cyanide. For the sake of his family Rommel chooses suicide and is driven out of the village. Fifteen minutes later he is dead. He is forty-nine. The official story of Rommel's death, is that he has died of wounds from the earlier strafing of his staff car. Hitler orders an official day of mourning and Rommel is buried with full military honours. His coffin, against his wishes, is covered with swastikas. His body lies at Herrlingen, west of Ulm.

Long after his death Rommel's reputation as a general survives undamaged and historians suggest that he might have won the battle or at least ground Montgomery to a stalemate had he not been starved of supplies and the promised new tanks.

Colonel Marescotti Ruspoli is buried in the Italian war memorial at El Alamein, alongside his brother Costantino. He was survived by his wife, a son and a daughter. The third brother to fight in the desert, Carlo, dies in Buenos Aires in 1947. The family villa at Vignanello near Viterbo in the Romagna is now open to the public.

HISTORICAL NOTE

Alamein. The name of a tiny railway siding in the Egyptian desert which for a generation of Britons became somehow magical one autumn day in 1942 as the Second World War was entering its second year and the dark cloud of Nazi tyranny hung low over Europe. Overnight Alamein became a talisman. A beacon of light that showed at last that Hitler could be beaten.

Those born since that time though are less likely to know that once great word and cannot know its significance. To many present day readers it may mean little or nothing. It is part of the purpose of this book to change that.

The task of the historical novelist is to bring the past to life, to allow his readers to see historic events as if they were happening again. We offer a means of experiencing the past. That is our task and it is also, when it comes to an event so momentous as the battle of El Alamein, our duty. For it is appalling to think that such bravery, suffering and depth of spirit should ever be forgotten.

The Battle of El Alamein was a major turning point in the struggle to defeat Hitler. Of that there can be no doubt. It is almost impossible to gauge the magnitude of its effect upon British morale and even more difficult to assess its impact upon that of the Nazis. Both however were huge and without it or its equivalent the war might well have gone a very different way or lasted for very much longer.

Certainly the entry of the Americans into the war with all their industrial might and manpower must have ensured, as Rommel realized only too well, that eventually Hitler would be defeated. But Montgomery and Churchill knew that that would be a waiting game and the already war-weary British people, unaware of such probabilities, desperately needed some sign that the Allies were able to deal a major knock-out blow to their adversaries. That was the real value of El Alamein and that was the reason that Montgomery felt justified in expending so many men and so much material in achieving his victory.

Of course there are those who would argue that it was not entirely his victory and it is certainly clear that, just as he did later, after D-Day, Montgomery attempted to persuade his staff and the higher command that all the decisions he took in the course of the fight had been carefully considered from the start. This was not the case and it is disappointing that he should not have been sufficiently self confident to have admitted that he was in fact a talented opportunist. For that is where I believe his strength as a general lay. He was able to grasp the changing situation, in particular his own mistakes and to adjust accordingly.

It is also true that Montgomery outnumbered the Axis forces two to one in artillery and manpower, and four to one in tanks. But as any general will tell you, it is generally considered that an attacking force should outnumber the defenders by at least three to one to have a fighting chance.

What is certain is that victory at Alamein was never a

certainty. It was a result not only of masterly generalship but at the final reckoning of sheer blood, guts and bavery. Without those the Allies could not have won.

The desert war has been called a war without hate and in truth the dreadful conditions endured in North Africa were partly responsible for producing a code of gentlemanliness which recalls the conflicts of the eighteenth century. The ultimate demonstration of this was surely Montgomery's invitation to the captured General von Thoma to dine with him as the Germans began to retreat. But like the wars of the past it was not without its moments of atrocity, particularly in the use of booby traps and the extensive employment of mines, some of them designed not to kill but merely to demobilize and mutilate and to err too much on the side of a chivalrous ideal would be a mistake.

Also the sheer scale of casualties was dreadful. It was greater than any single battle yet witnessed in the Second World War. The Allies lost almost 14,000 men, the Axis some 20,000. Of the Allied troops it was the Commonwealth soldiers who suffered most. One fifth of all casualties were Australians. The New Zealanders, as my account endeavours to emphasise, lost even more: some 8,000 killed and wounded. The question remains though what was it that made this war fought in such terrible physical hardship so very different in character from the Russo-German conflict of the same era?

There is no easy answer, but I suspect that it might have something to do with the nature of the combatants. As I hope I have made clear in the text, many of the officers in the British tank squadrons were from the yeomanry, made up of the aristocracy and gentry and went into battle using for their call signs phrases normally heard on the hunting field. Their men for the most part treated them with the respect that they would have accorded any gentleman. It was a very different army to that which would fight on the beaches of Normandy two years later and different too to the Australians and New Zealanders with their more relaxed attitude to rank, which produced its own kind of fighting spirit. On the German part, while it is always foolish to make blanket generalizations, Rommel's Afrika Corps was composed of men of the more established units of the Wehrmacht with officers who had perhaps a more traditional frame of mind than many of their SS comrades fighting on the Russian front. While they might have had no less faith in their Führer, they did not believe in the final solution which by this stage had been a year in execution, nor that they were fighting an underclass. They had developed a genuine respect for their desert enemies, more in fact than that they had for their Allies the Italians. The latter, again led by scions of landed families as much as by Mussolini's fascisti, who in fact were often one and the same, were at a low ebb in their morale. They distrusted the Germans and many had begun to wonder what they were doing in Africa. Such a diversity of men and nations had not been seen on a single battlefield for generations and when they came together the result could only be the tumultuous and extraordinary conflict whose spirit I have attempted to capture in these pages.

AUTHOR'S NOTE

It would be true to say that this book began its gestation some forty years ago when as a young boy I would visit the house of my best friend and don the peaked officer's cap and webbing belt that had belonged to his father, Philip Harris, when a captain in the Royal Sussex regiment serving in the desert under Monty. Gradually tales of that campaign entered my mind and my friend's father, now sadly deceased, became a hero in my imagination, leading his men somewhat like the running officer of my Airfix Eighth Army soldiers, pistol in hand across the sand dunes against the devilishly cunning Afrika Korps of the Desert Fox.

Subsequently, I was fortunate enough to become a pupil at Montgomery's old school in London, and not surprisingly reminders of his achievements were a constant presence, embellishing my friend's father's accounts with the bigger picture of his commander.

Two years ago, while researching this book, I visited the battlefield of Alamein and took some time to search out Captain Harris's fallen comrades. There are many of them here, laid out in the British cemetery in long straight lines as if present on parade. The Royal Sussex's men lie together, their Colonel at their head, followed by his officers and finally the men. It was a poignant moment, made all the more so a few minutes later by visiting the towering Italian memorial and finding inside the final resting places of the two Ruspoli brothers, relatives of my late wife, Sarah. Somehow I felt that my presence had united the two sides and that a circle, begun as a boy back in Surrey in the late 1960s, had become complete.

Writing such a work, part fact, part fiction, on a battle of such a recent vintage as El Alamein has been very different to the treatment of the battle of Waterloo which I attempted in *Four Days in June*. Some of the combatants remain alive or are only recently deceased and I am hugely indebted to them and their families for their assistance, and in particular to Dorothy Highland for her help and to Ben Tindall for a memoir of his late father.

A special thanks must go of course to Tom Bird, who I hope will not be offended by my attempt to make his conspicuous gallantry that day live anew on the page.

The principal acknowledgements apart from these are due to the relatives of those men whose memoirs furnished my primary source material, notably Hugh Samwell and Ralf Ringler. The diary of Hugh Samwell was published as *An Infantry Officer with the Eighth Army* (Blackwood, 1945) just a few months after Samwell was himself killed in action on 12 January 1945 in the Ardennes.

The Diary of Ralf Ringler was published in 1970 as *Endstation El Alamein* (Berger, 1970)

The American driver, Josh Miller is of course an invented character. But he stands as a symbol of the bravery of his real comrades of the American Field Service who served and died with such courage at Alamein and throughout the war. Miller's roots lie somewhere in the pages of three books: Andrew Geer's *Mercy in Hell* (McGraw-Hill, 1943), George Rock's *History of the American Field Service 1920–55* (Platen Press, 1956) and most inspiringly Charles Edwards' memoir *An AFS Driver Remembers*, published on the internet.

The best general histories of the battle are Major-General John Strawson's *Desert Victory* (J. M. Dent & Sons, 1981), Niall Barr's *Pendulum of War* (Cape, 2004), Ken Ford's *Turning of the Tide* (Osprey 2005), Philip Warner's *Alamein Recollections of the Heroes* (Kimber, 1979) and John Bierman and Colin Smith's masterly *Alamein, War Without Hate* (Viking, 2002), particularly for its account of 'Snipe'. For more detail on the armies George Forty's works on the Afrika Korps are invaluable (*The Armies of Rommel*, Cassell, 1997).

The memoirs of Field Marshal Montgomery (Collins, 1958) were naturally a key resource as were those of his Chief of Staff, Freddie de Guingand, published separately as *Operation Victory* (Hodder & Stoughton 1947) and *From Brass Hat to Bowler Hat* (Hamish Hamilton, 1979) along with the biography of de Guingand by General Sir Charles Richardson (Kimber, 1987).

For Rommel, his own book *Infantry Attacks* (Greenhill, 1995), along with *The Rommel Papers* edited by Liddel Hart (Collins, 1953), was very useful. In addition there are personal papers in the Imperial War Museum, London. I also benefited from accounts in Heinz Werner Schmidt's *With Rommel in the Desert* (Harrap, 1951) and Kenneth Macksey's well-known seminal work on the Field Marshal, *Rommel: battles and campaigns* (Arms and Armour 1979).

I am indebted to Peter Dornan's book on Herb Ashby's part in the battle, *The Last Man Standing* (Allen and Unwin, 2006) for its account of Ashby's friend Bill Kibby and there is no better Italian account of the battle than Paolo Caccia-Dominioni's moving book *Alamein, an Italian Story* (Allen and Unwin, 1962).

My thanks too must go to Faber and Faber, the publishers of Keith Douglas's memoirs, *Alamein to Zem Zem* and of his *The Complete Poems* (1978). The lines quoted are from 'Do Not Look Up'.

Lastly, I should thank Caitlin Nutten for her invaluable research into the personal histories of those who served, and David Macdowell at Fettes College for a chance to see the relevant passages of his forthcoming work on the college's illustrious military history. And of course I must thank my long-suffering wife, Susie, especially for her invaluable medical expertise with all the 'gory bits'.

THE BLACK JACKALS

is
Iain Gale's new novel,
to be published in February 2011

This had not been what was meant to happen. Not at all. But then Lamb supposed that was what war was all about. The unexpected and the absurd always turning up just when you'd planned for something completely different.

Lamb stared at the bridge and swore beneath his breath. It had not gone according to plan. Certainly, the sappers had come and gone as directed. They had left their packages of high explosive, taped and tied to the bridge, out of sight of anyone who might attempt to cross it. The wire they had carefully concealed in the long grass that grew up the riverbank, snaking it back as covertly as possible to Lamb's command trench where it was connected to a simple plunger.

Lamb gazed at the box and its 'T' shaped handle. When the time came, when the Germans began to show themselves, he would give the command and the little bridge which had stood here at Gastuche for he presumed the last century, would vanish. That at least was the plan. But this was no training exercise. This was war and the Germans had not come along the road obligingly in column like some friendly adversary to be mown down by his carefully prepared ambush and then blown to kingdom come with the bridge. In fact they had not come at all. Instead Lamb had been alarmed to see some hours ago now, a procession of weary Belgian civilians advancing upon the bridge. He had told the men to hold their fire but of course it had hardly been necessary. They were not about to open fire upon a herd of old men, women and children. At first he had watched them with bemusement as they had trickled across the bridge towards safety. But then the thought came to him. If this exodus did not stop then eventually the Germans would be caught up in it and what would he do then? He did not suppose for one minute that his men would fire on civilians but the enemy must not be allowed to take the bridge.

It was quite clear to him that there was no choice. No option. His orders were clear. Nothing for it now but to blow the bridge and he wondered when he gave that command how many of them would have to die.

Peering over the brow of the shallow grassy slope behind which he and his men were sheltering, Lamb looked down towards the river and its little stone bridge and his eyes fixed on the desolate column of humanity moving slowly and sadly along the road towards them; an endless procession of men women and children, driving, pushing and pulling carts and wagons of all shapes and sizes, laden with what few belongings they had managed to gather together before the Germans came.

The River Dyle was a good enough obstacle against tanks and to allow the bridge to fall into enemy hands was out of the question. But it was also highly questionable that they would be able to hold it forever. The German advance through Belgium had been like a whirlwind and he wondered how many of the British, Belgian and French Generals really believed that their armies and the tiny British Expeditionary force would be able to hold back the Panzers. But they might be able to slow them down sufficiently for the French to be able to regroup and mount a counter-attack.

He had sent a runner back to Battalion at the first sight of the refugees but had received no other instruction than that it was had on good authority that anyone carrying a red blanket might be a fifth columnist. As far as Lamb could see, hundreds of these refugees had red blankets. He could not possibly have taken them all prisoner and so he had decided to ignore it. It galled him that he was becoming used to ignoring orders. Only certain ones of course. It was typical of the sort of ridiculous rumours that had been circulating since they had arrived in France. He was surprised though at how readily people accepted them, officers and men alike, and it made him wonder whether he might have been wrong in placing so much faith in the army, and that new and unwelcome doubt filled him with dread. For it was not hard to see that their enemy had no such lack of confidence.

Still looking at the refugees swarming across the bridge, Lamb's eye began to fall naturally on individuals: a woman in a floral dress yelling at her son to come back from the edge of the road, another struggling to keep a curly-haired infant daughter perched on a cart amidst a pile of dark wooden furniture; a father who carried his sleeping baby like a rag doll, his face a picture of worry. He tried to look away. To see these people not as individuals, real people, but as a column, like any other column that might be advancing towards him. Not an enemy of course, merely an obstacle to be negotiated. He began to calculate their numbers.

One thousand, two? More? There seemed to be no end and no beginning. But all the time he kept seeing their little stories unfold. A woman seemed to have lost something, perhaps a pet. An old man who could walk no more and was being helped to sit at the side of the road against the wall of the bridge by a pretty girl.

And then he heard it.

The unmistakeable rumble of approaching vehicles shook the road and sent the civilians into a panic. They quickened their pace. The old man got to his feet and started to walk. Belongings, which a moment ago had seemed so precious, tumbled from the carts and were forgotten in the new urgency to save themselves. Staring hard through his binoculars into the trees in the distance, Lamb began to make out the trucks and men on horses too, with slung rifles. And alongside them now he could see men on foot: men in grey, carrying their weapons at the trail.

He was sweating now, more than he would have normally done even on this hot summer's day. The grey soldiers were mingling with the civilians. He could see their helmets clearly as they moved through the press. Could see them pushing through the refugees, using their rifle butts and shouting commands as they hurried along the dusty road, heaving the carts and belongings into the roadside ditches to clear a way for the trucks. Clearing a way towards the bridge. Towards his position. Advancing into battle. There was no time left. No choice. No option.

Lamb heard his Company commander's words, 'Whatever happens, Peter, blow that bloody bridge. It must not fall into enemy hands. I don't care who's on it. Mr Chamberlain himself. Just blow it.'

The lorries were driving forward now, almost on the bridge, with the infantry running close alongside them. Lamb could see an open topped staff car and in the back seat – two officers. They were laughing as they drove on to the bridge and were almost at the centre now. Three lorries followed close behind forcing the shuffling pedestrians aside. Then one of the men raised his hand and the car and the trucks stopped, although the refugees continued past them. The officer opened the door and got out walked across to the parapet of the old bridge. He leaned against it and scanned the river and the opposite bank forcing Lamb and his men to cower in their slit trenches and then his eye alighted on something, something at the edge of the bridge. He gazed at it for an instant and then turned to the car and shouted something before starting to run back the way they had come.

Lamb muttered to the corporal at his side, 'Blast, he's twigged it.' Then, stifling his conscience, he swallowed dryly and gave a quick nod to the corporal. The man, a recent addition to the ranks, a volunteer named Valentine, looked at him and raised an eyebrow. Lamb nodded again, 'For Christ's sake man, let them have it!'

Valentine shrugged and pushed down hard on the handle and almost simultaneously it seemed the bridge went up with a deafening explosion, sending fragments of brick and stone flying high in the air along with what remained of the officers and their driver and parts of two of the trucks and their occupants and the civilians who had been pushing past them towards salvation.

Lamb shielded his eyes and yelled down the line to the platoon, 'Take cover. Get down all of you. Watch your heads.'

As he spoke small pieces of masonry, wood and nameless debris began to fall among them, clattering off their tin hats. Luckily the larger pieces were confined to the vicinity of the bridge and most fell into the river. And as the smoke began to clear Lamb peered down the grassy bank to survey their handiwork.

He could see the span of the bridge and there in the middle of it a large hole, as if some giant had taken a bite through the side of the wall. Beyond it lay a yawning void. Good, he thought. That should hold them for a while at least. But then as the smoke dispersed he saw around the bridge, across the road and in the river below dozens of bodies and parts of bodies and burnt and shattered fragments of what had been possessions. Lamb stared as his heart filled with guilt and pity and he tried again not to look at people, merely objects. But there was the woman in the floral dress and over there the man and his daughter. What was left of them. He knew that he had timed it as well as he could. Had allowed two German lorries onto the bridge before blowing it. Now he noticed among the civilian corpses a number in field grey and he felt the better for it. But the feeling did not last for long. For amid the patter of the falling fragments, another sound arose. A low moaning, punctuated with terrible screams. He shook his head and Valentine looked at him with pitying eyes.

Lamb spoke, 'Well done, Corporal. That'll slow up the Bosche.'

The man looked at him and Lamb noticed not for the first time, the irritating smirk that seemed to lay permanently around his thin lips and his curiously educated accent, 'Please don't thank me, Sir. Not for doing that.'

'I had no choice, man. You saw. The enemy . . .'

'I saw, Sir. And I promise that I shan't tell anyone what it was that you just did. Why should I want to do that, Sir? They might get the wrong end of the stick.'

Lamb stared at him and was just about to challenge his remark when a voice from his rear shattered the opportunity.

'Sir, look. Over there. In the trees.'

Lamb raised his field glasses and looked through them across the river towards a spinney of poplar trees beside the edge of the road. At first he thought the shapes he could see were more refugees. But then he saw the flash of steel and knew at once that they were the enemy.

'Alright, here they come. No one fire until I give the command.' He turned to his right, 'Parry, set up the mortar over there, zero it in on the centre of the bridge.

They might try and use the wreckage to get across.'

He had hardly spoken when there was a burst of machine gun fire from the opposite bank. 'Take cover.'

Lamb pulled his revolver from the canvas holster on the left side of his webbing belt and yelled at his sergeant, 'Sarn't Bennett, Corporal Briggs. Get that Bren working. Thompson, you and Massey get on the anti-tank rifle. Save it till you see any tanks. The rest of you save your ammunition until you see a good target. Then let them have it.'

He felt an anger now. Anger at what he had just been compelled to do, an act that sickened him and went so much against everything that he believed in. Killing helpless civilians. And here now was the chance to assuage that anger. Against the men who had caused it. He heard the Bren rattle into action and saw the flash from the muzzles of the German rifles as the enemy responded. There were shouts from across the river.

Lamb yelled at the section closest to him, 'Perkins, Dawlish, all of you, keep your heads down and your guns trained on the road. See the first flash of field grey that comes into range and you open fire. Smart get on the blower back to Company HQ. Tell them we have contact. Enemy tanks estimate zero six, infantry four zero plus.'

As his batman spoke into the handset of the .38 radio, the enemy machine gun crackled again and turned over a few sods of earth on the lower part of the riverbank. Smart turned to him, 'Can't raise them Sir. Line's dead. Not a thing.'

'Keep trying.'

Lamb opened the chamber of his revolver, checked that it was full and snapped it shut again. His fellow officers agreed, the Enfield pistol was a sad excuse for a sidearm. They said the enemy had automatics that never jammed and fired like a dream. He couldn't wait to get his hands on one. But that of course would mean either taking one off a dead German or winning one himself in hand to hand fighting. Perhaps, he thought on the next few hours, the next few minutes he would have a chance to see both. But his keenness was quickly turned to disappointment.

Bennett was at his side, 'Pull back, Sir. CO's orders. We're to pull out.'

Lamb shook his head. 'What?'

'We're pulling out Sir. From the CO.'

Lamb shook his head again and laughed, 'No, Sarn't Bennett. This is no time for one of your pranks. There's hundreds of Jerries over there and it's our business to deal with them and see they don't get across this damned river.'

'Sorry, Sir. It came direct from Battalion, it did. Our orders are to withdraw. Clear as day, Sir.'

Lamb frowned. This was no joke. 'You must have got it wrong. We can't be pulling out, Bennett. We've just blown the bloody bridge and we've got the enemy pinned down. And what about those poor bloody civilians down there dead in the river? I'm telling

396

you man, the Jerries won't get across here for hours and then we'll be waiting for them. You can see that. What we need is reinforcements.' He turned to his batman. The poor man was still trying to contact company HQ. 'Anything?'

Smart shook his head.

'Right. Is that runner still here Sarn't?

'Sir.'

'Then get him to take this message back to Company HQ. Need reinforcements soonest. Your order not understood. Please send help. Enemy now in range preparing to engage.'

The Sergeant pursed his lips and nodded. 'I'm sorry, Mister Lamb, Sir. That runner is straight from the CO. It was quite clear, Sir. Pull everyone out he said. Everyone, Sir. And that means us. I'm sorry.'

Lamb stared at him. This was madness. First they tell him to stand his ground and to blow a bridge killing dozens of innocent people and then they tell him to abandon the position.

Lamb shook his head, 'I'm sorry too, Sarn't.' He paused, 'I'm sorry because I just can't do that. Not until we've killed a few more of them, at least. Then perhaps we'll come along. Eh? Why don't you tell the Major that we're . . . I know. Just tell a runner to tell him caught up in a firefight and trying to disengage. Tell him that we'll be with him presently. Just as soon as we can retire without the risk of taking any further casualties.' He was damned if he was going to pull back now. The sergeant looked at him and smiled. He had somehow sensed that Lamb wasn't going to take an order like that without some sort of protest. 'Very good, Sir. If that's your orders, that's your orders.'

'That is an order, Sarn't Bennett. Send one of the men back to the Colonel. Thank you.'

The Sergeant turned and was about to go when he looked back, 'There was one other thing, Sir. Runner said that he'd heard on the wireless at Battalion HQ that Mr Chamberlain's been given the heave-ho. Winston Churchill's the new PM. Fat lot of good that'll do us though, Sir, eh?'

'Thank you, Sarn't.'

Lamb smiled and, as his Sergeant turned and trotted off at a running crouch to send word to Battalion HQ that they would not be obeying orders, he turned back to his front. It was strangely

397

quiet again now, save for the occasional groan from one of the wounded. So Chamberlain the great appeaser had finally gone and Churchill was in. He wondered what his father would have made of that. Had never had a good word to say for Churchill after the Dardanelles. Lamb frowned.

The man was damned old too. Didn't the country need new blood now? A young man at the helm? The news did nothing to raise his downcast spirits. He peered across the river and began to make out small grey clad figures darting through the trees. They were moving up in some strength. Within minutes he knew they would be dug in. Focusing his field glasses he froze as he noticed that at the edge of the road across the bridge, where the charge had blown a hole, a party of men were climbing down into section that remained above the river bed, passing down planking and metal sheets. A bridging party.

Without thinking he shouted to Valentine who was in the neighbouring trench.

'Corporal, how many grenades do you have in that hole?'

'Dunno, Sir. I've still got mine and White has the same. Then there's Perkins and Butterworth.'

'Right. Get them all over here to me and yell across to Mays to do the same with his lot. Double quick. And bring a sandbag.'

'A sandbag, Sir?'

'You heard me. A sandbag. Empty.'

He was staring at the enemy now intently as the Germans began to dig themselves into holes around the places where the debris of the bridge had already raked the earth into shallow holes:

Mays came running up to the trench, clutching four hand grenades against his tunic, 'Here you are, Sir. Corporal Valentine's on his way.'

'Thank you, Mays. Get back and keep up a steady sniping fire against those men. Tell Sarn't Bennett to get the Bren firing at them too. Long range I know. Just try to stop them digging in.'

Mays went off just as Valentine slipped into the slit trench next to Smart and Lamb, 'Grenades, Sir. As many as we could find.'

'How many?'

'I've got four, Sir. And a sandbag.' He lingered over the word as if to emphasise its apparent absurdity and held out the limp piece of canvas sacking.

'Right, with Smart's that makes nine. Thank you, Corporal. Pile them on the floor. There.'

Valentine placed the grenades gingerly in a roughly geometric pile with those that Mays had left and stood back to admire his handiwork.

Lamb, who had still been staring at the Germans through his field glasses, saw him. 'Right. Now get back and help Mays to keep those Jerries heads down.'

He opened the sack and gave it to Smart, 'Right. You hold it, I'll fill.'

Taking the grenades from the pile on the floor of the trench one by one, he placed each of them carefully inside the sandbag conscious all the while that time was running out, 'Well, man, aren't you going to wish me luck?'

Smart stared at him but before his batman could say anything Lamb was up and over the top of the trench and running hell for leather down the grassy embankment towards the German lines, the heavy back of grenades clutched tightly to his chest.

He slipped and slithered down the muddy slope, praying with every step that he wouldn't fall and hearing his heart pounding in his chest, all the while keeping his eye on the Germans ahead of him. Over to his right he was aware of a flash and then the deep rattle of a machine gun. The earth around his running feet began to fly in all directions as bullets tore into the grass and mud. From his rear he heard the familiar answering cough of the Bren gun and the enemy machine gun stopped. But then as soon as the Bren itself had paused to reload and change barrels, it opened up again.

As he ran further to the left, away from the gun, he was aware that it must now be traversing, following him, but always just a fraction behind. He had reached the river now and almost stopped as he felt a bullet whiz past his face. Rifle fire now, from the opposite parapet. The Bren was in action again and he could hear the intermittent crack of the bolt action Enfield rifles. Bennett, Mays and Valentine were doing well. Lamb kept on running, jumped the headless bodies of two civilians and saw dead ahead of him the helmeted heads and field-grey torsos of the Germans digging into the earth to the right of the bridge, preparing a fire pit for mortars and machine guns. That was his first objective and then he'd find the bridging unit. Suddenly nothing else mattered but to reach them and to do what he had set out to do. Any other thoughts of home were now gone from his mind. Nothing there now but the urge to do whatever it took to make sure that the men digging those holes and spanning that chasm would never finish their job.

He was within thirty-five yards of them now and still the air around him seemed to be thick with bullets. As if he were standing in a swarm of bees. He did not think that he had been hit, but then in the past few minutes he had really ceased to care and had begun to feel almost invulnerable. A sudden sense of euphoria swept over him and in the lee of the upper span of the ruined bridge he stopped and used the remains of a civilian cart and its dead horse for cover. German bullets thwacked into the horse's cadaver sending sprays of blood in all directions. Lamb kept his head down and taking two grenades from the bag, primed both. Then, holding one in each hand he half raised himself for a moment and judging his target, threw them quickly, one after the other, conscious that his left arm would not be as strong or as able as his right. Ducking down he watched them arc and saw them land. Then he covered his head. The blast rocked the bridge for an instant and was followed by screams. Lamb took two more bombs from the bag and pulled their pins, careful to hold them down. Then he rose again and again threw them in swift succession. Two more explosions and a rattle of machine gun fire told him that they had done their job. There was shouting in the German lines now along with the screaming of the wounded. One of the bombs had burst off target, against the side of the bridge sending a welcome column of brick dust into the air and obscuring Lamb from the enemy gunners.

But as he prepared the next two grenades there was a burst of automatic fire and bullets smacked into the horse, one of them bursting through its withers touched him on the arm and tore open his tunic. He looked down and saw blood but was aware that it had merely grazed him. He stood now, hoping to get a better aim and hurled the two bombs towards the Germans. From behind him a welcome salvo from the Bren and twenty rifles told him that his men were still giving covering fire. Three grenades left. He was unsure what effect he had had thus far, but judging from the commotion he had connected with something. His heart was beating faster now, the sweat pouring off him. Half blinded by the dust, he primed

400

two more grenades. The blood from his arm had trickled down his sleeve and was slimy in his fingers, almost making him drop one of the Mills bombs. He looked up and through the smoke saw the figure of a tall German officer signalling to two men carrying a machine gun and pointing directly to him. Not hesitating, Lamb threw the first grenade at the group and then turned and slung the other towards the half-dug in gunners. He knew that he had hit them and that the immediate threat had gone but they would lose no time now in pouring all their fire on to him and there was only one way back. He pulled the last grenade from the bag and drew the pin, still holding the lever. Then turning he began to run. After five paces he turned back and found himself looking at the levelled rifles of a score of the enemy. He threw the grenade and, not waiting to see the result, turned and ran. Uphill now. Harder but he knew that the explosion would cover him for a moment. Again the grass flew high as the bullets struck home. He felt a sharp pain in his heel and presumed he had been hit but kept running. Now was not the time to stop and look at any damage. He was aware too of a growing pain in his arm where the bullet had grazed it and hoped that that was all that it was. He was nearing the trenches now and the German rifle fire had lessened although the machine gun on his left was still firing. Where the devil was the Bren? Reaching the last few yards before his trench he could hear the men cheering him on and then he was home, slithering down the side and thumping on the muddy floor. He could hear his breathing, almost as if it were another man's and a steady thumping which he realised was his heart.

Fred Smart just stared at him, 'Bloody hell, Sir. That was fuckin' incredible – if you'll pardon my French, Sir. Sorry, Sir.'

Lamb grinned, happy and surprised to be alive and wiping the sweat from his eyes with his bloody right hand, gasped for breath, 'Thank you, Smart. How did I do?'

'Pretty well, Sir, I'll say. You blew that lot in the bridge to blazes and that machine gun that was setting up with them an' all.'

'Did I stop them digging?'

'You stopped them, Sir. They won't be doing any more digging where they've gone.'

He looked out over the top of the trench and surveyed his handiwork. In the centre of the bridge lay the bridging party, six of them, all dead. Beyond, where the Germans had been entrenching positions, were more dead and he could see wounded being carried back by enemy medics. Across to the right a crew lay about its mangled machine gun. He had killed perhaps twenty men, all told. More importantly though he had stopped the enemy digging in positions and crossing the river. For the present.

Smart looked at him, 'Hadn't you better get that wound dressed, Mister Lamb? Get Thompson to have a look at it, Sir.'

Private Thompson, aside from being in charge of the Boys anti-tank rifle, was also the platoon medic and while every man carried a field dressing he had charge of the medical supplies.

'No, Smart. It's nothing. Just a graze.' Although he wasn't so sure. And he felt the twinge in his foot and looked down to see that the back of his boot had been shot off. Fearing the worst he quickly bent to see what damage had been done and was relieved to see that although covered in blood his heel had only been nicked. Looking back at his arm though he could see that what he had thought a mere graze might well be something worse.

He unbuttoned the cuff of his tunic and rolled up the sleeve then did the same for his shirt. In his forearm just below the elbow was a neat gash where the bullet had torn through the cloth and into the flesh and muscle. It had not gone deep, but enough to cause him discomfort and to restrict his use of the muscles.

'Damn.'

Smart held back the tunic and began to swab at the wound with some gauze.

'Looks clean enough, Sir. I'll get Thompson though and we'll get you fixed up back at Company.'

Lamb shook his head. 'I have no plans to move to the rear just yet, Smart. We've got unfinished business here.'

Smart stopped swabbing and listened: 'They've ceased firing, Sir.'

Lamb listened. It was true. Since he had regained the position the Germans had ceased fire. He wondered why. He saw Bennett running across to him, careful to crouch down as he did so.

Valentine came close behind him, 'My God, Sir. That was the most heroic thing I think I've ever seen. Well done, Sir.'

Lamb smiled: 'Well done you, Bennett, with that covering fire. And you, Valentine. All of you. Where's Corporal Mays?'

402

'Bren's jammed, Sir. He's trying to fix it now. Perhaps you should 'ave a look, Sir.'

The men were well aware that in civilian life Lamb had been in charge of a motor garage and respected his expertise with engines, which on more than one occasion had proved useful in camp.

'Yes, perhaps I should.'

He started as Smart's final swabbing touched a particularly sensitive area of the wound in his arm. Bennett saw it, 'You're hit, Sir. Not bad is it?'

'No, Sarn't. Not that bad. I'll live.'

Valentine, who was squatting at the edge of the trench looking with interest at Smart's handiwork spoke, 'Have you noticed they've stopped firing, Sir?'

'Yes, and we were wondering why.'

Valentine smiled. 'Perhaps they're just frightened in case we're all as mad as our Lieutenant .'

Bennett glared at him but said nothing.

Smart, winding a bandage around Lamb's arm, piped up, 'That's it. I reckon you've terrified them good and proper, Sir. They didn't know what they were up against. Perhaps they're packing up now to go back to Germany like good little Huns, Sir.'

They laughed. But Lamb did not smile. He was looking back down towards the bridge, 'No. I think they're just waiting.'

So they waited. For two hours they sat in the afternoon sunshine, drinking strong sweet tea thick with powdered milk. Lamb listened to them chatting. The conversations ranged over football, their girls and about some film with George Formby that had them laughing in the aisles, and it seemed almost as if for them the war had ended here. Some of them he rightly guessed would be praying that by some miracle it had. One of them, Butterworth, the platoon wit, even suggested that Mr Churchill had been on the telephone to Herr Hitler and told him that he might as well go home to Berlin because their Mister Lamb wasn't going to give up his bridge.

Lamb laughed with them at that and was even beginning to think that he might take some rest when he heard it. A low rumble which quickly grew in intensity until the ground seemed to shake. Christ. They were bringing up their tanks.

Instantly he shouted down along the line and back towards the woods, 'Sarn't Bennett. Enemy tanks to our front. Bring up the anti-tank rifle.'

He thought that they would try a crossing now. While they had surprise on their side and they think we're shaken. But if we can stand our ground we might just hold off the first wave. We can't really destroy tanks. No hope of that with what we've got to hand. But if we can take out as many of the infantry as we can before we pull back then at least we'll have done something to atone for the deaths of those poor blighters in the river.

He yelled towards the rear and saw the Boys anti-tank rifle gunner and his mate sitting in a nearby slit trench lining up the slim-barrelled weapon on a make believe target on the opposite bank. 'Thompson, hold your fire with the Boys, until you can get a clear shot. Five hundred yards. No more.'

There was an answering 'Sir'. Lamb cast a pitying look at Thompson. The recoil from the anti-tank rifle was well-known. He took out his binoculars from their canvas case on the right of his belt and scanned the road again and the trees on either side. And then he saw them. There were two in the lead. Panzer Mark IVs by the look of them, with small triangular pennons flying and the squat angular turret and a short-barrelled cannon that he recognised from the silhouettes on the recognition charts at the officer training school. His stomach felt suddenly hollow and he could feel himself sweating. More tanks were following on behind.

A whole squadron. Perhaps more. And he knew that save for the single anti-tank weapon, the less than reliable Boys anti tank rifle, they were powerless against such armour. Not that the Boys was that much good itself. Certainly, when it had first been introduced four years ago, it had been able to penetrate the armour of any tank. But tanks had come a long way in four years and Lamb knew that against the machines facing them, the best the Reich could muster, it would be almost useless. Even their grenades, the egg-shaped Mills bombs developed in the last war, would merely bounce off the hulls. All they would be able to do would be to rake the ground around the advancing vehicles with small arms fire as the infantry crept forward in the lee of the tanks and try to keep their heads down as the shells crashed in.

He yelled again, 'Wait for it, lads. It's the infantry we're after. Wait for the . . .' He had not finished his sentence when there was a whoosh from the opposite bank and a shell flew towards them hitting the bank just to their front, its explosion sending up a cloud of earth and foliage. 'Keep down. Keep your eyes on the road.'

Another shell flew in, closer now and there was a yell as a shard of shrapnel hit one of the platoon. Lamb kept looking at the road. The tanks had pulled up now and were just sitting there, lobbing their shells across the bank. Of course he thought, there's no need for them to move forward. They think they can just blast us out and they probably can. They must know we've no heavy weapons.

Two more shells came crashing into the position and one hit home. Lamb looked at where it had landed and was aware of a jumble of bloody bodies and the noise of men in agony. He wondered whether he had been foolish to stay here. Perhaps they should have pulled back as battalion had ordered. Perhaps the Colonel knew best after all. Lamb began to doubt himself and then banished the thought.

Something inside him said that they had to make this count. They had to take out some of the enemy to atone for killing the civilians. Except now he had been responsible for the death of his men. Perhaps he thought it's too late. They have us pinned down. How can we retire now? If only their infantry would come forward.

As the thought crossed his mind he saw the small grey figures moving in the wake of the tanks which began to rumble forward towards the river bank. He put his field glasses to his eyes and picked up the figure of an officer in a peaked cap, shouting at the infantrymen, urging them on with his hand. Against all probability they were advancing to attack. Lamb smiled. Someone somewhere in the enemy higher command had obviously decreed that this crossing had to be taken and taken by a certain time. That was the German way and nothing in the field manual could stop that order. Lamb knew that it would be the death warrant for some of the men out there behind the tanks. As many as he could kill he thought. 'Sarn't Bennett. Here they come.'

He turned to the men in his immediate vicinity, 'Open fire. Make them all count.'

At once the slit trenches became a frenzy of action as the men fired at their chosen targets, loosing off round after round against the German infantry. Lamb could see figures falling now as the men in grey tried to tuck themselves in behind the tanks. But still some were left exposed to be picked off by the keen-eyed British riflemen. And even as the infantry fell the German tanks continued to fire as they advanced and the shells crashed in. Now their machine guns had opened up from the tanks and there was sub machine gun fire too coming in from a handful of infantry that had found some cover on the opposite bank.

Corporal Mays came running at a crouch up to Lamb's slit trench, enemy bullets raking the ground around his feet and threw himself flat on the earth. 'Sir, Austin's copped it. Jerry machine gun, Sir. We've got to get out of here, Mister Lamb.'

Lamb nodded. Yes, that was enough, he thought. Enough for the poor devils who had died on the bridge. Now they could go. 'Yes, Corporal. Find Sarn't Bennett. Tell the men to pull back. Keep as low as possible don't look back and run as fast as you can to the woods. We'll form up on the other side of them, behind cover and get back to Battalion.'

'Sir.'

The man took off and Lamb turned back to the enemy. The lead tanks had lined themselves up and were pouring shellfire into their positions. There was a cry from along the line and Lamb was aware of a man tossed into the air like a puppet amid a cloud of earth and debris. He saw Bennett to his left.

Bennett shouted over the noise, 'Runner from Company, Sir. Battalion says to disengage and get back. There's a barrage coming down to cover our withdrawal and CO says that unless we want to be under it we'd better move. We've to fall back through the Guards, Sir.'

Lamb managed a smile. He knew that he had done all that he could.

He waved the men back out of the trenches and saw them follow Bennett into the woods. Then he took a last look at the great grey monsters as they loosed off another barrage and then at last turned towards the rear. The shells were crashing around him now, hitting trees and ripping off their branches. Lamb began to lengthen his pace, but he had not gone two yards before something hit him hard on the back like a hammer blow, knocking the breath from him and he was briefly aware of being shoved forward, face down in the mud. And then his world went black.

406